## Praise for *Love You Madly*

*"A novel that is* [illegible] *d heart. Nostalgic and immediate, a he.* [illegible] *eties."* Anna Hug



*"The characters* [illegible] *d myself laughing with them (often) and* [illegible] *I had to turn that last page."*
Maire Fisher

*"The prose is funny, heartbreaking and luminous. It gives you fizzing in the veins and makes you want to be in love. I devoured the book in almost one sitting. A friend was visiting and kept saying: 'You can put that down now.' I couldn't."*
Vanessa Hilton-Barber

*"You have written a truly wonderful novel."* Jeremy Boraine

*"I had such a good read. It's a very intelligent book, really high-quality writing, and an awesome story … funny, emotional, human."* Bieke van Aggelen

*"The book surfaces a lot of personal things. These last three days, I have been 20 again. I could picture absolutely everything. The whole time I was reading, I was watching the remaining pages getting fewer and wishing they weren't."* Jenny Wade

*"It highlights the human struggle. We are all battling something, and our struggles are all very real."*
Trudy Mofutsanyana

*"So light but true. Brilliant!"* Emma van der Vliet

*"I love this novel hugely. It is such a parable of the times."* Richard Aitken

*"You guys can both write like bombshells."* Jeremy Daniel

*"An engrossing read – flowing and funny and tender, chatty and lyrical. It casts a very shrewd eye on young love, social foibles, and getting through a certain time of life. It brought back a million memories."* Henrietta Rose-Innes

# love you madly

DAISY JONES AND
LUCINDA HOOLEY

THE
LANGUAGE
LAUNDRY

First published in South Africa in 2021 by The Language Laundry



All characters in this novel are fictitious.

Cataloguing and Publication Data is available from the National Library of South Africa

ISBN 978-0-620-97319-9

ISBN (ebook) 978-0-620-97320-5

Cover design by Angela Tuck of Hands-On design studio

Images used courtesy of www.unsplash.com (Virginia Vinassa, Afsane Bz) and www.pngwing.com

Typeset in Adobe Garamond Pro by Boutique Books

Printed and bound in South Africa by Castle Graphics

The Language Laundry
5 Lock Road
Kalk Bay
7925

www.thelanguagelaundry.co.za

*You have to leave the city of your comfort and go into the wilderness of your intuition. What you'll discover will be wonderful. What you'll discover is yourself.*

***Alan Alda***

# PART ONE

# CHAPTER 1

*Saturday 23 December 1995*

Marigold Ashford is walking backwards up Kloof Nek Road. She doesn't want the view.

Table Mountain is imperious. It just sits there, looking down on everyone, with its square top like a forbidding brow. The cliffs are its scarred chin, the slopes its green jowls.

Marigold – or Mare, as people other than her parents and institutions of similarly long standing refer to her – prefers to look at the City Bowl. She's aware that central Cape Town doesn't throb like those cities in the movies. Still, there's movement down there: pedestrians, taxis, traffic lights. Her eyes follow them along the streets like a finger tracing patterns on a quilt.

Beyond that, there's the sea: flat, wide, open. It changes colour. It shifts. It's moody. And there's the sky.

*Blue is the sky and birds can fly. Deep is the sea and so am I.* She squints.

Mare is wearing flip-flops. The temperature's rising by the minute, and she can feel the heat on her feet, the sting on her neck and cheeks. The sun is trying to reach her skin through her faded black T-shirt. It's trying to get its fingers through her pulled-back hair, under her ponytail elastic.

She wasn't thinking when she left the house. Not about the weather – that's why she's wearing black, and jeans – or about the crowds. Of course it's mad out here, the weekend before Christmas. Gridlock. The sun catches windscreens, mirrors and sunglasses. In cars on both sides of the road, people in bikini tops, kikois and shorts have windows down, elbows out. They're crawling up to the traffic circle, where they might turn left for the cableway or right for Lion's Head. If they keep driving, they'll sweep down towards Camps Bay or Clifton, to the beaches. A lime-green VW Beetle putters past. She catches a snatch of Savuka through a bakkie window. Today, it's all mirage and suntan lotion and fumey buses, trundling up the hill like elephants.

On good days, Mare is fond of the buses – has a desire to hop onto one – but most days, definitely today, she resents the noisy gear changes, the heat of them, the smell.

Mare has walked up and down this road since she was a toddler. Right though primary and high school, and for most of her four years at art school, where she drew figures in charcoal and painted self-portraits in oils. She knows this feeling, being boiling hot and thirsty. She also knows about being freezing cold, and blown to bits.

The stupid mountain. It blocks coastal breezes, traps air and limits the sky. It's also responsible for the climb: every sweaty footstep is the mountain's fault. So no, Mare has never gazed at it like some sappy tourist.

All these people have somewhere to go, but not her. She's already here, right where she started.

Amelia Ashford is at home. She ascends the stairs at Eland House, taking care not to catch the hem of her floral skirt with her toes.

She's carrying a tray. On it, she has placed a pot of tea, a small milk jug, a saucer and two Marie biscuits, plus a sprig of mountain fynbos in a cut-glass vase.

"Dad, you awake?" she says at her parents' bedroom door.

"Amelia, darling," Philip Ashford smiles as she enters.

She places the tray on the smooth side – her mother's side – of the bed. She lifts his back off the pillows and straightens his pyjama top; plumps both pillows and eases him into a half-seated position. "There. Comfortable?"

"I am," he says. "And I was comfortable before. I'm not a complete invalid, you know."

"How you feeling today?"

"So much the better for seeing you," he says. "How was the audition?"

*The Taming of the Shrew.* In her mind, Amelia relives the fight scene from earlier that day. She's still mildly shaken by the force with which her feet had hit the boards, and her voice – deep and scornful. What the hell happened? At what point had the words started rushing out of her mouth like rope through a pulley? Why had her voice broken? God, had she spat in that other actor's face – or had she just imagined it?

"It went fine thanks, Dad," she says.

In all her years of acting, Amelia – Mielie, to her friends – has never given a performance on stage that wasn't controlled, or "predictably crafted", as Mare had observed. For one thing, Mielie knew, although she wasn't particularly gifted at music, she had a very good grip on rhythm. Shakespeare's iambic pentameter. Mamet's staccato. O'Neill's lilt. It wasn't just an intellectual thing. It was a technique. And it was this technical and cerebral talent, Mielie suspects, more than her emotional range or ability to "let go", that had earned her top honours in Acting class.

"Oh, and I stopped to pick you this on the way home." Mielie places the vase of fynbos on the windowsill.

"Exquisite," says her father. "From above De Waal Drive?"

"Yes, I walked up a bit. I don't think I've ever seen scarlett crassulas so late in the year."

"Oh, people say things like that," Philip says. "The rain is early or the fruit is late. Nothing's predictable. Things happen in their own time."

Mielie leans forward on the bed, then, peering into his face.

"Don't look so horrified," he says. "I'm not about to drop off the tree."

"Daaad–"

"Now, Christmas," he interrupts. "There's something predictable. Have you done your wish list?"

"I haven't written anything down," she frowns.

"Then lie down next to me and tell me now," he says.

Mielie releases her hair from its scrunchy. It's long, thick and wild. She flicks it out at the back, impatiently, with one hand.

"I want to know what you want," he says. "Just you."

Mielie hesitates.

"If you can't tell me," her father says, "tell the ceiling."

Mielie closes her eyes. It's what she does when she needs to answer a difficult question. Why is this role so important? And what part of her chose to use her gut, and not her skill, to get it?

"I really want to play Kate, you know, Dad. At Maynardville."

"Just that?"

"No, I want it all. But I want the part in a different way to wanting other things."

"You realise that Kate is the older sister, like you, except she's the wild one."

"Yes." Mielie doesn't think she wants to be wild, if that's what her father was implying. She closes her eyes again. *Stretched*, that's the word that comes to mind. She wants to be pushed, she wants someone to push her, to do something unimaginable: to be herself and the opposite of herself at the same time. She wants to exist in the taut space between the two, acting. Really acting.

"I just think, Dad, that it would be like flying. I think it might make me feel weightless."

Mielie turns to her father. His eyes are closed and he is smiling.

"Awrk!" says Mare, tripping on a sharp bit of pavement. She stops walking and gazes instead at her glinting ocean.

If she'd thought, she might have got on her bike and gone down to the proper shops for Christmas presents and wrapping paper. She still has that to do. And the Christmas list that Dad's asked her to write. He's never asked for one before – so why now? Why not the usual: books, tapes, art materials?

"I don't know, Dad," she'd said, when he explained that he wanted to know what she *really* wanted. "If I could make you better, I would … Don't look at me like that. Relax your eyebrows. Come on. I know what you want me to say, but it's weird telling you."

Yes, she wants a boyfriend. Yes. Desperately. She wants it more than anything. She thinks about it all the time. She writes about it. She longs and longs and longs but she's too weird, too outspoken, too isolated.

He said there would be many boyfriends, but there was only one her. He thought that one day she might be famous. "As a what?" Mare wanted to know.

"I don't know. An artist, a writer, something," he said, as if it had already happened and he was merely relating an interesting nugget of history, uncertain of the secondary facts.

Mare can't imagine it, what she will be. It's like trying to remember a proper noun during a quiz show. It's there, somewhere, but it won't show itself.

Now, looking out beyond the harbour, and cheered by the idea of being *somebody*, she narrates a dramatic camera pan: "Below us, Robben Island," Mare whispers. "Famed for being the prison of Nelson Mandela, Oliver Tambo and Robert Sobukwe in apartheid's darkest days."

She continues to walk backwards, resisting the urge to hoist an imaginary video camera to her eye. She imagines it sweeping in and hovering, momentarily, over the fields of Cape Town High. "And after the harbour and the CBD, we have the high school where Marigold Ashford – Cape Town's most beloved daughter – began her creative life."

She turns around and walks faster now, breathing heavily. Sweat runs down her back. To distract herself, she counts the trunks of the trees on the other side of the road, then turns into her street and slows right down. She swings her arms, partly from relief and partly to dry the sweat patches under her arms.

"We are now approaching Eland House," she says under her breath. "Pronounced *Ee-land*, an Anglicisation, not *Ear-lunt*, the correct Afrikaans pronunciation of the name of Africa's largest antelope ... where Ashford spent her formative years. It's a place – no, a time – about which she has written absolutely nothing."

Leaving her father resting, Mielie takes the tea tray downstairs again, empties the washing machine and carries the laundry out to the line. Two loads of it. The family's. Behind her is the permanent and ever-changing backdrop that is Table Mountain, her favourite place on earth to ever be.

She does this washing-hanging thing every day, and likes the routine of it. Laundry, anywhere, always looks like hope to her, somehow – it suggests continuity, stability, confidence in the fact that there'll be another day.

She reaches into the tub and pulls out one of Tess's bras. Tess, whose school uniforms don't fit anymore. Somewhere in the attic, reeking of mothballs, Mielie knows she's stashed her own old uniforms. She needs to haul out the ladder and get up there, someday soon. Mare chucked all of hers, of course.

Mielie pauses to stare at the big tree in the middle of the garden. She read once that not everything in nature is ruined by human intervention. Certainly, this tree is improved by the swing that hangs from its biggest branch – straight, symmetrical, at the right height. It links the tree to the house, and the humans in it.

When Mielie hears the gate start to open, her calm vanishes.

Mare. She notices the sweat on the back of her sister's neck, and the box of cigarettes in the back pocket of her jeans. Mare's cheeks are mottled red. Her bra is ill-fitting: there are pouches of flesh visible through her worn-out T-shirt. Her jeans have paint stains on the thighs. Her toenails need trimming.

Her sister, who will not make ticks on a list. Who's always late. Who will not follow a roster. Who is self-absorbed and reckless, forcing Mielie to clean up after her constantly – in every possible sense.

"Mare!"

Mare is almost at the steps to the front door when she hears Mielie calling from the garden.

"What?' Mare shouts.

She wants a glass of water, and to get out of the sun. Instead, she strides across the grass towards the washing line. "Where have you been?" Mielie demands, hands on hips.

Mare sees how neatly the washing has been hung. She notices her statuesque sister's white viscose blouse – unmarked, smooth as milk – and how Mielie's skirt fits perfectly across her hips before dropping – dramatically, evenly draped – almost to the ground. Typical. As a child, Mielie would show her the insides of seashells, run satin ballet-slipper ribbons through her fingers. Her sister adores finely beaded handbags, and her room is "off-white" everything: pillowslips, walls, rug, curtains.

Right now, it makes Mare furious. A brief glimpse of a famous life of artistic expression and freedom, and now back to this.

"None of your business," Mare says.

"You," Mielie says, "need to please stop shaving your legs in the sink." Mare makes a move to leave. "Or rinse the sink!' Mielie yells after her.

"*My* hair?" Mare says, turning. "You need to get *your* hair out of the plughole!"

"I beg your pardon?"

"Yes, your hair. The whole plughole is clogged with long curly strands that actually *rise* into the bath when you pull the plug. It's disgusting."

"Girls!"

Philip Ashford has appeared in the kitchen doorway, white-faced and clammy.

Mare and Mielie turn as one. "Dad!" they say together.

# CHAPTER 2

*Tuesday 26 December*

Mitchell Palmer is standing naked in his lounge. He's on the phone to Mare. It's nightfall on Boxing Day.

"He's fast asleep," Mitchell says, his eyes starting to make out shapes in the gloom beyond his balcony doors.

"Sorry," says Mare. Her voice is full of snot. "It's just–. I'm–. You know …"

"I'll get him to ring you first thing in the morning," Mitchell says.

He can see the water towers on Yeoville Ridge quite clearly now, and a small group of people standing on the roof of Helvetia Court, at the top of Cavendish Street.

"I'm very sorry for your loss," Mitchell says, after a pause. "Your father taught me History in first year. He was an excellent lecturer. And a very nice man."

"I know. Okay. Well."

"I'll be sure to tell Johnny," Mitchell says.

He wonders briefly whether the people on the roof have an unobstructed, dark-framed view of him. A lit box like a diorama: *Naked Gay Man in Tasteful Apartment*, Johannesburg, 1995.

"Get some rest, okay, Mare?" Mitchell says. "It won't be a Happy New Year."

*

*Friday 29 December*

Philip Ashford's family is waiting to leave for the church.

Pauline, the widow, is in her best, tightest, paisley wrap dress. Every curve is on display – even those above and below the bra strap. Her cleavage, clearly visible, is as long as a ruler.

Amelia, as the eldest, has positioned herself at her mother's right. Mielie is, as ever, appropriately dressed. Today she's in a demurely patterned frock, complete with demure waist tie behind. Black ballet shoes, size eight. Even though her mother is in wedge heels for the occasion, Mielie stands taller.

Mielie and Pauline have the same auburn curls, worn long. Pauline's hair is washed and she's flicking it off her face, over her shoulders, like an unaccustomed wig.

The younger sisters have shorter hair. Marigold cut hers first, but she'd be a fool to think Tess had opted for the same length by way of imitation. The truth is, Tess had started having a go at her split ends with the nail scissors and her hair was shoulder length before it was even. She and Mare both have their father's hair: dark, inconsistently, inconveniently wavy, not very thick. Mare calls it "English hair".

Tess has run off, now, into the garden, where she's been on and off the swing all day. She is wearing an extraordinary outfit, even for her. It includes a boy's striped blazer.

The group is gathered on the driveway of their home, Eland House. Its wide Victorian façade and generous sash windows give it a benevolent look. The entrance is framed by chubby bay windows and a deep upstairs balcony. The sash windows, despite the dust, reflect the midsummer sun.

It's the last Friday of December. The Ashford women mill around each other, like a pile of grass cuttings shifted by the breeze.

The widow and her second child – on her left – are holding hands. Neither seems to notice that their arms are touching all the way to the shoulder. Mare, with the familiarity of a conjoined twin, is adrift on her own sea of emotion.

Mare is wearing jeans and hiking boots. She's donned one of Philip's waistcoats. Buttoned up, it covers the album cover on her T-shirt. Appropriately enough, it's *The Times They Are A-Changin'*.

That, then, is the front pew.

In the church, Mielie stands and welcomes the congregation. Clear and concise.

Pauline reads the eulogy, her chest rising and falling, her legs trembling under the stretchy print dress. Her glasses slip, her hair falls across her eyes. She loses several words to sobs. She apologises before leaving the lectern. Her mascara has run all the way to her jaw.

Mare reads: "Rage, Rage, against the Dying of the Light" – softly at first, then more vehemently. Her cheeks are wet throughout. Her voice breaks dramatically on the line: "And you, my father, there on the sad height". Upon completion she stares, wet-eyed, at the congregation.

At the end, Mielie announces the wake at Eland. The pews respond positively to her, with nods and sad smiles. Pauline and Mare had spoken mostly over bowed heads.

After the service, mother and daughters stand bewildered on the grass, like saplings, each one leaning at a different angle.

The reading of the will reveals that Philip was talked into a dodgy property investment. He has written all the details in a letter, attached to the will. Everything in the letter is news to both his widow and his girls. Also present at the will reading is Peter, Philip's son from a previous marriage. He is a stranger to his half-sisters.

"What's a dodgy investment?" Tess wants to know.

Mare swings her head towards Pauline, and Pauline looks at her hands. Mielie stares out of the window.

"Actually it was a very astute investment," Peter says, rather too quickly. "There was no reason to suspect it would go south."

"What's 'go south'?" Tess almost shouts. "And how come you know so much about it, *Peeeter*?"

"I only know what's in the letter," Peter says. "It's all there," he pauses to remember her name. "… Tess, you see, your father borrowed half of what Eland is worth and bought some empty land in Bergvliet …."

"Without telling anyone," Mare mutters.

"Yes, well, he would have told some people, like the bank," Peter retorts.

"But no-one in his family," Mare says. "Not even his wife."

"The letter you all have in front of you," Peter sighs, "explains that the land was earmarked for development as student housing. Your father stood to gain a good income from student rentals, annually."

"Except that Council failed to approve the land for building," Mielie says, her finger marking the relevant sentence in the letter. "And," Mielie reads while moving her finger down the paragraph, "my father was forced to sell the land at a huge loss".

Peter opens his mouth to speak.

"Which means," Mielie continues, "that Dad died owing the bank. In the form of basically half the bond on Eland. It's a lot, Tess. And now the debt is ours."

Philip's widow and his children sit silent at the dining table. Pauline lifts her head to speak but Mare leaps from her seat before her mother is able to say anything.

"I can't believe this is what we're talking about! Today! At Dad's wake," she says.

"Mare–" Mielie starts.

"No! I'm not doing this!" Mare shouts at Mielie. Soon afterwards the family hear her pounding upstairs.

*

*Fridge note, Mielie to Mare*
*Saturday 30 December*

Morning Mare
Hope you slept okay.
Tried to wake you. Bad idea.
Guess what?
1. Milk and loo paper finished.
2. Milk and loo paper available at most nearby retail outlets.
– M

*

*Letter, Mare to Johnny*
*Saturday 30 December*

My room

Dear Johnny

You're right, she isn't a bitch. You've told me before, and everyone agrees. She's the furthest thing from it. My sister is not a bitch. This is the central truth of our family, the motor on which we run: the non-bitchness of Mielie.

I, however, am a bitch. I am selfish and a narcissist. This is according to our latest fight, the one that happened in this very room, yesterday, while our father's will was being discussed in the dining room.

I had left to be alone, but there she was, hot on my heels, viscose dress swishing down the passage.

"I'm sorry, but you know what, Mare?" is how she started – not politely.

I guarantee she was not sorry about anything, but who am I to call my perfect older sister a liar?

"I'm sorry," she said, "but you're embarrassing."

Although I wasn't just embarrassing, was I, because I was also selfish and over-reacting.

She doesn't understand, but when I walked out of the room, it wasn't because I wanted to make a scene. I just literally couldn't stand to be part of it anymore. It was so wrong, all that talk about money. I had to leave.

Only, once I'd left, my emotions broke through the bottom of my heart. I felt like I was falling through darkness, with nothing to grasp at. There was nowhere for me to stand, Johnny. Nothing to stand on, nothing to say. No one to say it to, either.

Mielie is supposed to be my sister, but she's the last person in the world I can lean on.

I wish you still lived here, I would have come to find you. I know what you would've said, too. You would've said this is terrible for me. You would've hugged me, and made me laugh. And then reminded me it's also shit for everyone else. Mielie said that too. But you have a way of trusting me to do the right thing, and guiding me there, that is SO DIFFERENT to how my sister treats me. She is SO JUDGEMENTAL!

I'm just so, so sad about Dad dying. It makes me scared of losing the past … It's like the landscape's disappeared, does that make sense? I don't feel strong enough, expansive enough, to create a whole new one.

Excuse me.

Okay, I'm back. I had to go to the loo. Had to have a cry. Blah blah. It's like that now. It's fucking horrible.

Actually, I'll go and make myself some toast. I might even get out of my pyjamas.

Then again, I might not.

X Mare

PS: Thanks to you and Mitchell for the card. Did I ever tell you how much I admire you, moving for love? So romantic. What's that? I did tell you? Was a hundred times enough?

Johnny, seriously, you need to send me a letter. What's it liiiike in Joburg?? I'm on tenterhooks, come on. What's the flat like? How's work? Did you get a car? For heaven's sake stop snogging and pick up a pen!

Bye Johnny, love you.

*

*Letter, Mielie to Toni*
*Saturday 30 December*

Dear Toni

Thank you so much for sending flowers. Dad loved arum lilies. He'd always stop for them when we walked on the mountain, just the two of us, and usually in the wind and rain. "Amelia," he'd say. "Oh darling. Would you just look at that?"

I put your arums on the dining-room table, in Mum's pewter jug, for the not un-dramatic reading of Dad's will. It felt right to have them there – a pure and natural point of connection to wherever he was, while in real life things fell apart.

Mum cries a lot. Silent, leaky, sliding pain. Waiting for the toast to pop. Opening the post.

I haven't cried much, until this morning. I was packing Dad's clothes out of his side of their cupboard. I didn't expect his scent to still be quite so strong, lingering in his folded handkerchiefs and beneath the worn-out collars of his shirts. And then, in a draw-string bag behind his socks and his pyjamas, I found three Krugerrands.

When I found Mum, she was crouched in a corner of the garden – barefoot, in her dressing gown, clasping a cold cup of tea. Her chin was on her knees.

I asked her if she was okay. She looked at me as if I was a stranger.

I sat down then, too. Ground level felt like a good place to be.

Then Mum saw the bag I was holding. "Oh, those silly things," she said.

Apparently Dad bought us each one, "in case of an emergency". He was convinced they'd leap in value every year. Mum doubts they have. Anyway, we were never told about them. Something to do with growing up in the war. Dad was only five when it broke out, but Mum said he often spoke to her about "shoring up" … because who knew what might happen, and what would be needed when it did.

I thought about that, Toni. Dad's shoring up, and how quickly his tide went out, in the end. I thought about the Krugerrands in his cupboard. It's true that if we all sold our Krugerrands we could buy air tickets back to England, but what would we do when we got there? It's not our home, and we don't know our family there. I thought about all of it and cried.

Meanwhile, Mare – sorry, Abject Misery – has plunged headlong into a pit of grief and taken to bed. So once again it's all about her. She's not thinking about the family at all. I wish she'd just get over herself and grow up.

Tess is feigning normal, but is frozen, or reeling, or both. She's in Standard 7 this coming year, can you believe?

I guess nothing will ever be as it was, and there's no point wishing it could be, although of course I do. And I guess however each of us is dealing with that – ranging from badly to terribly to worse – we're still carrying on, because we must, and also because we don't have a choice. We don't have a choice. Not really.

I miss you, my friend. Can't believe it's been a year since you left the digs in Balfour Road. How are things in London? Please let me know, when you have time.

Love always,
Mielie

PS: My father was my lighthouse, Toni. Steady beams on even rotation, slicing through the dark.

# CHAPTER 3

*Monday 1 January 1996*

On the morning of New Year's Day, a large silver BMW appears at the gates of Eland House.

Pauline opens the front door. Her daughters leave the kitchen table and join her in the dark hallway to peer out, unseen, as a pale and paunchy man in a lemon-yellow polo shirt and tan chinos exits the vehicle, unlatches the gates and drives through. The gates he leaves ajar, apparently confident of there being little inside worth stealing.

"Fuckwit," Tess observes.

"Tess!" Mielie says. Tess's language has been foul since her father's death. Inappropriate for years, this week it's been eye-wateringly bad.

"What?" Tess hisses back.

"Language!" says Pauline.

"Well, what are they doing here?" Tess demands.

"God knows," Mare says.

"Peter told us to expect them in the new year," Mielie says, as the car crunches towards the front door. "Don't you remember?"

Mielie is not the least bit surprised that her realtor half-brother has arrived less than twelve hours since the stroke of midnight. On Sunday, she'd listened to his message on the answering machine: "Hi, yes, Pauline? Peter here. Ah, get-together in the new year? Shall we say brunch? Tomorrow?" She'd mentioned it to her mother, but Pauline was struggling to absorb even basic information at present.

Peter, his wife Fiona and their child – introduced on the day of his grandfather's funeral only as "Booboo" – are unknown at Eland. It was only once the three latecomers to the funeral had been seated that the penny dropped for Mare: The ponce in the patterned tie – he of the apologetic hand gestures – was Dad's son from his first marriage.

Peter had never made an effort with their father. He'd lived with his posh mother in England for most of his life, turning his nose up at his poor, distant relations. When he and his South African wife, Fiona, moved from London to Newlands with their newborn, Philip encouraged contact. But Peter and Fiona begged off visits to Eland, despite living just fifteen minutes' drive away in their "original Village semi". Why were they so interested in Mare's family now?

They watch as Peter tiptoes theatrically around to the passenger door. "My dear," he says, opening it with a subservient flourish, like a footman in a fairytale. His wife emerges.

Fiona Ashford is blow-dried and in riding boots. She rises to her full and considerable height, draws back her athletic shoulders and points her profile at Eland's facade.

Peter, meanwhile, is bottom-out, fiddling with Booboo's car seat. The child extracted, Peter positions the boy on his hip and pulls alongside Fiona. She moves her head to tut briefly at her son and his encrusted nostrils.

As Pauline and her daughters watch, Madam and Sir look the house up and down.

"Wonderful bones," Peter can be heard to remark. The couple exchange whispers and then they're both on tiptoes, straining to see the sea view over the foliage at the bottom of the garden.

Having watched the couple murmur inaudibly for longer than would normally be polite, Pauline is woken from her reverie and bellows: "Hello there!"

Peter jumps and Fiona raises a pair of shaped eyebrows. Peter starts moving towards the house immediately, smiling and calling out: "Hello there! Sorry!"

In the kitchen, Pauline fusses over turmeric, lemon and honey tea, brewed in her extra-large enamelware teapot. During Philip's sickness she'd been religious about turmeric, inexhaustible on the subject of its health benefits, until one morning Tess bellowed: "Fucksakes, Mom! We get it! It's from India!"

Fiona is seated at the head of the kitchen table, picking amongst the teacups, apparently unable to find one from which she might be willing to drink. The toddler, Mare notices, is holding one of Eland's mismatched china teacups. Pauline likes to scour second-hand shops and auction rooms for such gems. Peter is opening bubbly. *Was it in the baby bag?* Mare wonders, and then, in a louder internal voice: *Who brings Champagne when their father's just died?*

"Peter," she says.

"Mare?" Peter inquires. He gives her a head-cocked pause, a sympathetic frown. Then he tuts.

Mare replays the tut in her mind, to make sure it happened. She intends to tell people about this later.

"Anyone for champers?" Peter says.

Mare does one of her special stares-with-nostrils-flared, but she can't think of anything to say.

Peter proceeds to hold forth. He and Fiona, he explains, had discussed Philip's will the previous evening – "New Year's Eve, couldn't waste the restaurant reservation" – while drinking in the sunset over the Atlantic.

The will is a sensitive subject, and one that has not been raised at Eland since the wake.

When all is said and done, Peter and Fiona have agreed, the best way forward for everyone would be to make "market sensitive" improvements to Eland and sell it at a "deliciously" high price. This would not only cover the debt, but also provide Philip's widow and daughters with lump sums to set up their own, separate homes.

Booboo interrupts to demand pink yoggy and Mielie seizes the moment to ask: "What do you mean, 'sell Eland'?"

Peter seems to resent the interruption mildly. He has more to say. "The idea is to hammer the debt dow—"

"Sorry?" Mielie interrupts again.

"Look, this place is too much for Pauline to manage, and Fee needs—"

This time it's Mare who interrupts. "What does 'Fee need'?"

Peter turns to Fiona, ignoring Mare: "What I meant to say, darling, is did you bring Booboo's yoggy?"

With the Ashfords distracted by the sight of Fiona unzipping the enormous baby bag and revealing some of its contents – wipes, sippy cups, mini Tupperwares and, yes, a six-pack of pink yoggies – Peter continues.

It's not like Eland's the family's only fixed asset, he says. Philip and Pauline, when they'd moved from England to Cape Town back in the mid-seventies, had indeed been very wise in buying not one property but two: this handsome but frankly run-down early-1900s home, and the smaller Victorian in Balfour Road, Woodstock – which, he understands, they've been renting out as a student digs ever since, and which is now standing empty until the start of the academic year.

What a perfect opportunity, he goes on, as one family is downsizing and the other growing! And with Woodstock in the midst of a gentrification drive, properties doubling in value year on year.

"I don't—" Pauline frowns.

Mare glares at Mielie, annoyed not only by her sister's listening face but also her listening pose: right forearm laid on the tabletop at 45 degrees, hand seeming to clasp an invisible pen, head inclined to the left. The role seems to be: part court stenographer, part divine medium. Mare could bite her.

"The thing is, now," Peter continues, "to act as soon as possible."

In the hush that follows, Mielie brings the invisible pen to her lips. Then directly and calmly she says to Peter, without a hint of aggression: "So, as I understand it – as things stand at the moment – you would like to renovate and sell Eland House and you would like our family to move into the Woodstock student digs?"

Peter pulls an I'm-reluctant-to-have-to-agree-with-you face. Then, smiling at his wife, he adds: "We're offering to put in the capital to renovate, Mielie. No bank loans. And I would sell the house for a reduced agent fee—"

"But this is our home," Pauline interrupts.

"Yes, but Philip's debt is also yours," Fiona says, face downturned, as she pushes the foil lid of Booboo's yoghurt into the half-empty tub.

"Pauline," Peter says rather quickly, "This is a way to make my father's debt disappear. The burden of this old house – the maintenance, the rates, the lack of security – would be lifted from you. And in a few months' time you would get a great deal of money. Perhaps you'd like to buy something more modern? A sunny lock-up-and-go?"

"And where are we supposed to live?" Mare asks.

"Well Mare, surely you and Mielie are thinking of leaving home soon? Both of you are in your twenties now, and Tess—"

"I'm thirteen. Fucker,"

"Tess!" Pauline shrieks. "You must control yourself!"

"Except, Peter," Mielie intervenes, "moving out would make us very vulnerable. Eland would be standing empty. Heaven only knows how much your renovation would cost, and if you could recoup the money. Balfour Road is not valuable, and no amount of gentrification will make it equal to what we have here."

"Why don't we just sell Balfour?" Mare asks.

The kitchen goes quiet.

"I mean, couldn't we pay the debt that way?"

"She's right," Pauline beams. "The university is going to give me a modest monthly pension and that would surely—"

"But as you said yourself, Mielie," Peter interrupts. "Balfour Road is not valuable and no amount of gentrification … Also, how much is that pension likely to be, in honesty …?"

There is a pause. Peter looks around the table, appealing for sense. Fiona, who has been see-sawing a teaspoon, lifts her head rather abruptly.

"Your father's debt will not go away," she says. "And it's rising all the time."

Mielie stares at her.

"We'll leave it with you, then, shall we?" Peter says. "To consider overnight."

*

*Fridge note, Mielie to Mare*
*Monday 8 January*

Mare: moving on.
Auditioning again this morning. Final round.
Fiona wants her brother to look after Balfour Road while it's empty.
He just moved to Cape Town or something.
Mum can't find the spare keys – so please get more cut.
Keys on the rack. Cash in the teapot.
Too much to ask? Hoping not.
Shot.
– M

*Letter, Johnny to Mare*
*Tuesday 9 January*

Westminster Mansions
Bellevue

Sweed-art, first things first. In the words of Stimela: "We are all tributaries of that great river of pain."

You knew I would remind you of this. Everyone in your family is in a state of grief. I can only imagine how Mielie is dealing with it. In my 'umble o-pin-ee-on (French) she should yell and weep more in real life, not just on stage.

Secondly, the part we've all been waiting for, let's talk about you. I've been thinking since we spoke on the phone and then receiving your letter.

I did not skim-read the bit about falling through darkness. I read it several times, you nigh broke my heart. The part about landscape? I understand.

Now, allow me to surprise you.

Mare: Leave.

Do not just move out of the family nest, get out of Cape Town.

You are at a crossroads. If you stay, you will wallow. Your tendency to decline is endearing but unhelpful.

I know you were planning to teach Art or English to spotty youths in the suburbs, but there's a newspaper internship here I think you could get. Or you could waitress, if push came to shovel (as a colleague observed but yesterday).

If there is a silver lining to this cloud – this mushroom cloud – it is this: 1996 has "new beginning" written all over it. Close a door and open a window, all that. You can't keep on as you were – change is upon you – so take the leap into your future.

Who will catch you? Why, that would be me. There I am, spotlit in the Big Ring, my hands chalked at the ready. I'm fairly bursting out of my spangly lycra tights. My bare chest is intimidatingly hard. Thankfully my silhouette is softened by lustrous furring of the pecs and abs. My trapeze tights have ski-pant loops.

Quick, Mare, jump! The limelight is hurting my eyes!

Love,
Johnny

PS: Repeat after me: "Down. Not out."

*

*Letter, Toni to Mielie*
*Wednesday 10 January*

18h00
The Balham Squat, London

Babe

So, then. 1996 is upon us, and we're all going to Hell In A Handbasket: (HIAH – new one, just for you.)

No one has any money, no one has a lover, no one has a job.

Oh wait, Johnny has a professional appointment. And a boyfriend of sophisticated tastes.

Who also just happens to be my very own Brother Mitchell.

And I have Damian the Australian. But not for long.

Our days are numbered, believe you me.

So Johnny tells me he's trying to convince Mare to bugger off to Joburg.

If she does, she is completely deranged, so please convey to her only this:

"Have you lost what is left of your mind, Marigold?"

(Has she lost it entirely, in her grief?)

I, for one, am 100% sane of mind, all while Living In A Squat.

This means, among other things, observing the need to wear flip-flops in the shower.

I am no stranger to wearing rubber gloves in the kitchen. I advocate the concept, as you know.

But flip-flops in the shower, as a hygiene imperative, merely indicates Just How Bad Things Really Are.

Am I a zombie? Did I in fact rise from a grave? I'm that cold, I must have. And now I spend my life staggering around in the half-light with thousands of other zombies.

We go to work in the middle of the night. We come home in the night.

Every day. It's just wrong.

Oh and did I mention that by definition a squat here is a place from which one cannot be evicted. Despite having forced one's way in, and not owning an actual key.

In return for paying zero rent, I get to break into my own place of residence every time I enter.

This entails hooking my arm around a broken pane of glass in the window beside the door, in order to unlatch it from the INside, carefully avoiding deadly lacerations while doing so.

On each such occasion imagine my joy.

Yup, I'm in hell already.

The room next door to mine sleeps eight.

There are four beds. So they sleep in shifts.

Are the sheets changed ever?

My theory is: Not.

The likely cause of my death, therefore, will be scabies before malnutrition.

Oh yes, there's every good reason to worry about my health.

Every good reason indeed.

If I see one more pair of Barely Washed men's socks steaming on a radiator or, worse, be forced to stoop to peel a Completely Unwashed pair of underpants, like Velcro – VELCRO – off the carpet, I shall kill myself.

Wait, there's a pair. If not Damian's, for once, someone else is going to die.

They're not my socks. Not my fatal mistake.

And if I have to au pair for one more snivelling brat in one more over-heated triple-storey mansion on The Thames, I shall similarly have no choice but to do myself in.

Did I study child-care?
Was the laundering of countless bibs and babygrows my major?
Stop the clock. It was Journalism.
And I could-slash-should have come first in my class.
Lest we forget.

Hang in there, sweet-cheeks.
Slaps
Toni

PS: In the immediate term, would one of you Ashford girls please hotfoot it to London and rescue me from this fucking piece-of-shit squat? I need a decent housemate and a proper job. In that order.

*

*Letter, Mare to Johnny*
*Tuesday 16 January*

Eland House
My bedroom

Unbelievable.

Sorry. Dear Johnny, how are you, etc. And thank you for your letter.

But, UNBELIEVABLE.

In two weeks' time I'll be living in Woodstock. Can you effing believe it?

Peter rang last week to say that he and "the family" (i.e. Fifi – yes, my new name for Fiona: Fifi, like a Pomeranian – and their hideous toddler, Booboo) will be ready to "take occupation", sooner rather than later. On oh-one Feb, to be exact. That's in less or fewer than 14 days. I'm saying it both ways so I'll only be 50 percent wrong.

When Mum told us, Tess's mouth dropped open so wide I thought something would actually fly into it. And Mielie was speechless. She would be, wouldn't she, at the exact moment I needed her to say something useful? But no. All she said was: "Honestly?" (Would this not have been a good moment, Johnny, to air her concern – shared with Tess, not me – that Peter's promise of "a great deal of money" in "a few months' time" has not been committed in writing? What guarantee do we have, really, that our family home has not been earmarked by Fifi as HER future family home? And if that's the case, our home is your former home. Yes, Balfour. Forever, potentially.)

Anyway, no sooner does Mum agree to move than Fifi starts on the renovs. This involves consultants and designers traipsing through all the rooms. She's pure class, my half-sister-in-law, I tell you. She's going to change EVERYTHING. It's hell.

In the morning, when she swoops in downstairs, it's like tipping a large cat into an aviary of budgies. Mum, Mielie, Tess and I flap our wings and shoot up into the top reaches of the cage. We retreat to our bedrooms, leaving the lounge, the kitchen, the dining room, the family room, the hall, the stoep – all of them unoccupied.

Downstairs becomes Fifi's domain – the floor of the cage. She prowls from one "reception room" to the next, her heels clacking on the floorboards. She has meetings on the stoep – inexplicably: why speak outside when every word she says travels up to our bedroom windows? Eventually it makes sense to us. She doesn't want us to miss a single opinion – on Mum's "pedestrian" taps, her "sagging" curtains, the "greasy" blinds, and the "horrific" lounge suite. Everything has to go, we hear her tell the architect. Everything. Including us, of course.

I'm back. Just went to get a biscuit.

Let's talk about your letter.

It is a thought: You and me in Joburg.

Do you mean the Independent Newspapers internship? The one at The Star?

I'll think about it. I am thinking about it. I'm seriously thinking about it.

What about application forms? Should I write directly to the company? Do you have any idea about the procedure, and the due date? Never mind, I'll phone and find out myself.

Hey, I wonder who'll get Toni's room in the digs? It wasn't called The Princess Suite for nothing. A dressing room and a separate entrance off the stoep … Will it be Mother or Mielie? The latter, probably. Should be the most senior member of the family. Ha ha, not laughing.

I'm going to make a play for the room in the backyard. It's the closest I'll ever get to a Parisian writer's garret.

One last thing about Fifi.

The other morning I caught her seated at our kitchen table. She was looking at the swing. When she sensed my presence, she straightened the fall of her already smooth, highlighted hair. One manicured hand was curved around one of our coffee cups. Her back was straight, lipliner perfect.

"Why would anyone keep that?" she wondered lightly, as if to herself. She almost frowned at the sight of it, swaying, just slightly, on the lawn – its green rope frayed in places, its seat silvered by the sun. Remember how when you get going, your feet go up, over the peaks into the sky, and your back touches the leaves on the way back up? Dad hung it the week we arrived.

"It's so ugly," she sighed. "It's all so ugly."

This is our life now, Johnny.
Send a chopper.
XX Mare

PS: Okay, I'm GOING TO APPLY! Aargh! I guess it's like dropping coins into a fountain and wishing for love. You never know!!

PPS: It'll never happen. I'm going to be a teacher with no financial management skills, just like my parents.
The loser sister.
Spot the self-pity.

*Letter, Johnny to Mare*
*Monday 22 January*

Westminster Mansions

Dear Mare,

Thank you for your letter, only just now folded and replaced in its envelope after a double read.

Fifi is a total fright, and seemingly the originator of Operation Eland-snatch. The Latin term for this particular form of intra-family theft is "inberundum", making Fifi an "inberuda" – a rough translation: "morally vacant she-witch". An older translation is "inveterate slut for cash". I've no doubt she would cut off Mielie's hair while she slept, if she thought it would fetch a price.

It would also appear that this very same Fifi has done nothing to encourage her husband to be honourable. As Mitchell himself points out: "Peter is well aware that neither Eland's owner nor any of her three daughters has a stable job. One is at high school, and neither of the older two has demonstrated any appetite for earning, having pursued degrees in THE ARTS …"

Mielie has indeed insisted on taking up acting as a profession.

And Mare … the writer's garret – er, room in the yard – in Woodstock? The symbolism kills me. You'd truly be in the back of beyond. In some cultures they call it "failure to launch".

Just put your shit in dustbin bags and LEAVE.

Love,
Johnny

PS: The cracked tile in the Balfour Road shower is my fault. I wish I could say it happened during vigorous love-making. Alas, it cracked under the weight of my heel.

*Fridge note, Mielie to Mare*
*Monday 22 January*

Mare, could you get over yourself already please?
Can't do this on my own, you know.
– M

PS: I got the part.

# CHAPTER 4

*Thursday 25 January*

At twilight, in Cape Town, in the summer, with the turquoise sky so wide open above you, it can sometimes feel like anything is possible.

That's how it is when Mielie meets Edward.

The sun is already behind the mountain when she finds parking in Balfour Road. *It's as if someone dimmed the lights*, she thinks – *the pavements breathing, all lavender-grey, and even the rubbish not seeming to smell quite so bad.*

That she is there to start with is Mare's fault. The previous night when Mielie got home from rehearsals, her sister was all wound up about how the Eland curtains would transfer to the Woodstock house. While the measuring of windows and the execution of curtain alterations wasn't the last thing on Mielie's list, it also wasn't the first. It was only to appease the urgency of her sister's concern that she agreed to go to Woodstock with her measuring tape the following day.

Mielie pauses at the garden gate, looking up and down her new street. It's tree-lined, even if the trees are short and shabby.

Balfour itself is like a smaller, bleaker version of Eland. A tiled roof; shallow steps leading up to a curved stoep with a single pillar. A bay window on one side of the wooden front door, a single sash window on the other.

And now here she is on the stoep – inwardly in free-fall, outwardly composed.

And here's Edward, too. He's opened the door. He is softly spoken and intensely still. That's how he is, in the doorway.

He's looking straight at her, into her eyes, and she straight into his.

What happens next is a chemical thing that takes them both by surprise. There's a fusion, immediate and terrifying. Mielie's heart is already telling her there's no going back.

"I'm Mielie," she says, in almost a whisper. "Ashford. Your sister is Fiona, Mare said ..."

"Yes," he replies. "It's a pleasure to meet you. I'm Edward, by the way."

"Yes," she says. "Edward."

He's looking at her, listening.

"Anyway-so: you know we're moving here soon, and I just need to measure the windows, quickly, if now's not inconvenient … Perhaps I should have called? … I most probably should've phoned first …"

"I'm so sorry about your father," Edward says. "I can only imagine—"

"Yes," she says quickly, nodding. "We're all very sad."

He shakes his head.

"I mean we knew he was sick and everything," she continues. "But still … It's not something you can prepare for, I don't think. You've just got to, you know, you've just got to carry on …"

"I know. I mean, I saw," he says. "When I met your family yesterday. I saw them. Carrying on."

She's shaking now; she might start to cry.

"Mielie …" he says, extending his hand.

"Thank you," she says. "Very much." She's tossing her head back now, laughing. "Anyway … Would you mind if I came in? I won't stay long, I promise."

Edward steps backwards and holds the door open.

Then he holds the chair steady for her while Mielie measures the windows. He writes the relevant numbers down on the back of a cereal box.

Then she thanks him and says she has to go.

He sees her out, walking slowly behind her down the concrete garden path.

Mielie will later discover that Edward does everything in slow motion. It will become one of the things she loves – and misses – about him most.

In the various high-ceilinged terraces where she works, once she's distracted her charges with cartoons on TV, Toni Palmer has no qualms about putting her feet up and phoning home.

On this occasion, she's been connected to Eland for a full episode of "Garfield and Friends" before Mielie says:

"Hey guess what Toni? I've met someone."

"Nnnnnno!"

"Seriously. Yip. Of all the times."

Mielie is seated at the phone desk in the hallway, its green leather surface worn from years of elbows, hands and pens.

First, Toni demands a full physical description.

"What? Oh, quite tall," Mielie says. "My height … What? Blonde … Yesss, surfer blonde."

"Christ Almighty."

"I know. I'll never learn … But anyway, he's different somehow. And get this, he's Fiona's brother!"

"Faaark!"

"I know. I know," Mielie says. "Defies belief. I know! So anyway … He's a junior architect. And he really likes cats …"

"Save it, Mielie! Scene of encounter?"

"The Ruby! I went upstairs to get beers, and he was standing at the window …"

"… with wires criss-crossing the sky behind him …"

"Yes!" Mielie's nodding, smiling, twirling the phone cord around her finger. "Exactly! He was holding a pool cue and talking to someone. And our eyes connected the moment I walked in the room."

"Electrifying!"

"Ja! I'd actually met him the night before, at the digs, so I went over to say hello. And I asked if he was playing next, and he said: 'No, I'd rather be talking to you'."

"Recovering from dead faint."

"I know! And then afterwards, in the road, he put his hand on the door of my car …"

"Stop it!"

"Yes, and he touched me – ever so lightly – on the top of my arm, and said: 'Thank you for a lovely time'… So of course I couldn't think of anything else the whole time after that, and then the next night – Saturday – I saw him there again, when I was with some of the cast, and he just walked in and sat at the table behind me … Chair backs touching, Toni! He has beautiful hands …"

Now Toni whispers into the receiver, so that the children won't hear her next question.

"I'm not telling you that!" Mielie says. "… Okay, it was great, it was beautiful, it was totally beyond. What else do you want me to say?"

Toni repeats the question.

"Toni! … His *name*, not that you asked, is Edward."

*

*Thursday 1 February*

The day of the Ashfords' departure from Eland is overcast. As though echoing the mood of the day, the sky threatens to split several times, its surface wrinkled with clouds.

Throughout it all, the family are close to tears, especially Mare and Pauline. Mielie is downcast but efficient, and Tess is unpredictable – one minute loudly demanding the miniature nail clippers she'd got in a Christmas stocking years before, the next bent over her book on the swing.

It is evening by the time the removal men have finished loading the boxes.

In the dark, crossing the distance between their old and new homes – short, by any standards, yet longer than anyone in the car can bear to say out loud – Pauline's driving is worse than usual.

They mount a pavement at one point, and she drives through a red light.

Mielie and Tess stare out of the windows.

Mare cries.

That night – unseasonably – it pours with rain.

*Letter, Mare to Johnny*
*Monday 5 February*

Balfour Road
Kitchen

Johnny,

GOOD GOD ALMIGHTY I'M IN.

No exclamation mark. I'm not ecstatic. I haven't been jumping round the room like an instant millionaire on live radio. I'm frozen, like an alien abductee.

The lady from the newspaper just phoned.

I was drawing in my room and I heard the phone ringing, but I thought it was next door, so I ignored it. But it kept on ringing. And then I thought that's-our-phone-there's-no-one-home-it-might-be-an-emergency and went pounding down the passage, and by the time I answered I was convinced someone had died … and so it took a while for the penny to drop.

But I got in.

I'm glad I applied when I did.

Don't tell anyone it was "all at my urging, darling". I know how you like to use the word "urging".

So I'm coming.

It starts on the $19^{th}$ of February.

I'll have to leave soon.

I have no money, nowhere to live.

I'm guessing the pay will be terrible.

But I'm leaving.

It's starting to sink in.

I just tried to phone you but Mitchell said you were at gym. Sexy voice, so curt. Just devastating.

I'm going to sit here until you get back. Here, in the kitchen at Balfour Road.

The tile in the shower is still broken, I'm pleased to report. It's like a fossil footprint, evidence of the period when you and Toni and them inhabited the place: a drinking, smoking, staying-up-late gang of bandits, slopping cider on every surface, dropping ash on every floorboard.

I just got up to find an envelope. Mielie's flyers for the play are on the kitchen table. They won't need flyers, anyway. She's going to be so nauseatingly good, people will choke on their Rosé and pâté. She'll be playing to packed lawns every night.

When I read her that part in your last letter – thank you for your last letter – about neither of us having any appetite for earning, she just smiled and said: "Some actresses are paid rather well." Note: calm display of obsessive ambition.

You can't believe how happy she is. Nothing to do with being in the play, either. That she takes in her stride. It's Edward.

Oh God have I even TOLD you?

In between the move and everything?

You will never bloody guess in a million years who turned up at Eland before we left? You won't guess. You've never met him. But it's still shriekworthy.

Fifi's brother, that's who. SHRIEEEEKK!! Edward is his name. He just graduated in architecture at Wits, he just started a job at an architecture firm, and he is charming and delightful (EYE-DOT-EE-DOT couldn't be more unlike his sister).

He was wearing a pair of no-name jeans, nondescript white takkies and a white T-shirt, sleeves too wide and too long. Worst of all: it was tucked in. I'm not sure if a belt would have made the ensemble better or worse. There was no belt.

He hung around all day. Mielie was at rehearsals, but the rest of us got to like him rather quickly. First, I made him tea (he waited to be asked to sit down). While drinking it, he noticed the swing in the tree, and then when Tess got home from school, she showed it to him close-up, and he showed her a way up the tree. It's been attempted many times, you might remember. Chairs carried out, ladders propped, pulley systems designed and abandoned. I'm the only one who's ever made it all the way up on my own.

Big news, anyway: Mielie likes him A LOT. She's snogging him somewhere right now, for sure. They'll be married by the end of the year – or the next year, whatever she decides. She's found the perfect man. His eyes follow her around the room. It's perfect. Their whole world is a stage and she's the only one on it.

Okay. Call me when you're ready. I'm still here waiting for you to do that.

No big rush or anything. Just … er … just on the off chance, would you, you know, keep an ear to the ground for accommodation … It shouldn't be too hard. I need something with soaring ceilings, light and airy, centrally located (the closer to you the better), preferably in an Art Nouveau block, for a rent of, erm … next to nothing?

Obviously I'm going to end up in the scullery of a digs in Hillbrow.

Love
Mare XXXXXXX

PS: Who said: "I'll let you be in my dream if I can be in yours"?
Bob Dylan, Johnny. Come on.

*

*Monday 5 February*

That evening in the Balfour Road kitchen, Mare washes while Mielie dries.

"It's not about you leaving us," Mielie says. "We'll be fine. And stop trying to change the subject, Mare. You always do that!"

Mare plunges cutlery in the sink.

"Like I was saying … wait, Mare, please … Do you have any idea how dangerous Joburg is?" She takes dry glasses to the cupboard. "Have you even read about the crime?"

"Nope," says Mare, starting in on the cutlery, and taking too long with it on purpose. "For God's sake, Mielie, I'll be fine," she says. "I'm going to earn money. Not waitressing money. Actual professional money. And I'll have Johnny, you know. It was his idea in the first place."

"Yes, it was, but he's also got Mitchell in his life now, remember," Mielie says. "They're lovers and they live together now."

"True, true," Mare says, taking the dish towel from her sister and wiping each knife blade individually.

Mielie leans against the fridge and gives her sister a look.

When the phone rings, Mare is more than happy to run to pick it up.

"Waydago, Paula, WAY-da-GO!" Johnny shouts.

"An Officer and a Gentleman!" she shouts back.

"Correct. Like Mitchell and me."

"I didn't think I'd get in!"

"Of course you got in! So listen. There's a lot to organise. We'll have you sorted in no time." Mare hears another voice. Mitchell?

"Hold on – what?" It's Johnny again. "… Oh! Well, that was quick. Mitchell just heard from his very good friend Tom Walker that you have a flat …"

Mare shrieks. "Johnny!"

"No, please don't gush! … Oh, it's nothing. Just a rare-as-hen's-teeth one-bedroom in an Art Deco block, upper reaches of Yeoville …"

"Eh?"

"What? Oh, it's just a fancy way of saying 'towards the ridge'. But 'upper reaches' pleases Mitchell. And it's safer. And you won't hear the din of Rockey Street, the screeching tyres and live music … Hang on … Yes, Mitchell, 'which is which?' Ha ha. No but seriously, Mare, it's not even Yeoville, it's officially Bellevue …"

"Sounds like something out of a Daphne du Maurier novel!"

"Yes! Very Daphne. So … parquet floors throughout … bathtub for a rugby team … balcony at eye level with the jacaranda blossoms … and your own garage."

"Johnny—"

"No really, it's nothing … And just eight hundred South African rahndt a month, not a cent more … Yes, I thought that would please you. Just a sec …"

Mare hears a clatter as the phone is passed from hand to hand.

"Mare, Mitchell here."

"Oh, hi—"

"Listen, I want you to memorise the following: 630 000 violent crimes reported last year. Of those, 50 000 were murders, mostly gun deaths. A woman is raped every 30 seconds in South Africa. Hijackings and muggings are the crimes showing the sharpest increases at the moment. And Joburg is the crime centre of the country."

"Oh. Right."

"Marigold. You are going to take proper care. Understood?"

# CHAPTER 5

*Monday 12 February*

Mitchell Palmer has been organising the kitchen and now it's late and Johnny is asleep. He is less excited than Johnny about Mare's imminent arrival. He knows it's selfish, but Mare – the ingénue – will most certainly disrupt the social dynamic.

The week between Christmas and New Year – the first that he and Johnny had both been off work at the same time – was bliss. Thank God Johnny hadn't shot off to Cape Town for Prof Ashford's funeral. They'd spent it at coffee shops, in the pool here at Westminster Mansions, and in bed.

Mitchell slips under the covers next to Johnny and stares at the ceiling.

It was in the silly season that they'd met, more than a year ago in Cape Town. Mitchell had been visiting his family, staying in his parent's house on the grounds of their Sea Point hotel. Johnny was in his final year at varsity.

Mitchell did not lack experience. Clubs and the Long Street Baths had seen to that. He'd never been in love, though.

Home from a night of carousing, he walked through the dark onto the lawn. He was some distance across before he noticed four bodies sprawled on the grass, over by the trees. They were lying at crazy angles, with their heads gathered at the centre. Cigarettes were on the go, moving from hand to hand like glow-worms. The moon illuminated triangles of flesh. An exposed midriff here, a bare thigh there. Cider bottles, cigarette boxes and lighters scattered about. The bodies looked like they'd been dropped from a plane. They were laughing like geese.

Mitchell suspected that one of the bodies belonged to his sister, Toni. Two of the others he supposed to belong to her friends, the artsy Ashford sisters, of whom he had heard many a mention.

As Mitchell drew closer he noticed that just three of the bodies were laughing: the ones with bare legs and feet, the girls. There was a fourth body – trousered and socked – providing a bass line to the laughter, a hum-drum-dum that set the girls off in fresh fits of cackling every time they tried to draw breath.

He kept walking. The rumbling bass – the joke-maker, the tickler – Mitchell had never met. He stood over them.

"Good evening," Mitchell said.

The boy muttered something. Predictably, the three girls sent up shrieks of laughter. Eventually, barely recovered, Mitchell's sister greeted him.

"Mitchell, this is our hilarious friend Johnny," she said. "He's my housemate in Woodstock."

"Ah," Mitchell said. "Well, I'm going in. Are the parents asleep?"

The elder of the sisters, the one with all the hair, sat bolt upright. "Oh, God!" she said. "What time is it? Never mind. We have to go. We definitely have to go." She found a bag and started shoving things into it. "Mare! Come on!" she said. "Oh, God, I have to be at rehearsals at nine."

The sister leapt up. Toni got up to say goodbye. The mystery boy remained horizontal. He accepted kisses on the forehead and cheek.

In a flash the three had shot across the lawn to the gate. Mitchell lay down on the lawn, parallel to the boy.

"Mitchell," he said.

"I know. I'm Johnny, we were introduced."

"Yes we were, but I didn't see your face. I can't see it now, as a matter of fact."

"Suits me," he said.

"How mysterious of you," Mitchell said.

"Just insecure," Johnny said.

Mitchell didn't know what to say. It was so unlike anything he'd heard a man say. It certainly wasn't something anyone would say in the clubs he'd been frequenting.

Toni returned. She stood over them with her knees pressed together. She "needed to pee", apparently.

"Do you know anything about stars?" Johnny asked when she was gone.

"Not much," Mitchell said. "I know the Southern Cross, the pointers, Orion's Belt, the usual."

"I don't even know that much."

Mitchell pointed out Orion's Belt. He pointed out the sword hanging from the belt. Both men managed to resist innuendo. That was also something new for Mitchell, when there clearly was a spark between them, in spite of the age difference.

When Toni got back, Johnny sat up, gathered his things and made to leave. Mitchell sat up too.

"Toni, if you put the kettle on I'll walk your friend to the gate," he said.

"It's all right," she said.

"No, really," Mitchell said. "You've just done a gate trip. Please. Make me a rooibos."

"Whatever," she said. "Bye, Johnny. I'll phone you tomorrow."

At the gate, the boy dropped a slip of paper into Mitchell's jacket pocket. Mitchell patted the pocket, then took out the paper.

"I know your name," he said.

"Well, yes," Johnny said.

"And your phone number is Toni's number."

Johnny was embarrassed.

"Also, did you consider that it wouldn't make you look terribly good, the fact that you carry around a slip of paper with your name and phone number written on it?"

"Okay," Johnny said. He held out his palm for the paper. Mitchell didn't give it back to him.

"Obviously I was going to phone you," Mitchell said. "I've no idea if I'll like your face, but I like your voice very much."

"So just the phone call then?" Johnny said.

"We'll see," Mitchell said, and shut the gate on him.

That week, the two went places in Cape Town that Mitchell had never been before: ordinary, daytime places like beaches and rivers. They kept their outings a secret. They didn't want to discuss their seeing each other with anyone, not even each other. They wanted to keep it safe. It was fragile. It was like playing with a glass ball.

When Mitchell was back in Joburg he wrote, and phoned. Still no one knew a thing. It was very intimate, but not just because of the secrecy.

Now Mitchell turns over in bed to spoon Johnny.

*It's the way we relate to each other*, he thinks. *It's the way we are disarmed.*

*Letter, Mare to Toni*
*Monday 12 February*

Trans Karoo
Second Class Women's Carriage (Sharing)

Well Toni,

Here I am on the top bunk. Got it, thank God.

Twenty-seven hours with five other women in a cabin the size of a cupboard.

Below me, on the two stick-to-your-thighs leatherette seats, there's a woman with an enormous Tupperware of samosas and drumsticks on her lap. She's accompanied by a pair of young women who look like they're trying to wriggle out of their bodies every time she speaks. Opposite them is a middle-aged lady in a crimplene dress and a stiff hairdo, alongside an almost identical lady in a crimplene dress and a stiff hairdo, plus-minus 25 years older.

We've just had a visit from the guy with the Cokes-chips-and-cigarettes trolley. No member of my family handed me anything at the start of this adventure, no parcel of sandwiches and Scotch Eggs and orangeade – or whatever the Famous Five would have had in a cave while dodging smugglers. So I bought a Tab and packet of Big Korn Bites.

The farewell on the platform was hideous. The less said the better. But I love the train/trein. Did you know the staff translate everything? "Tee/Koffie?/Tea/Coffee?" They're neat as pins in white shirts, even in this 30-degree heat. They knock smartly before popping their heads round the door. Johnny's told me there's a certain decorum to the way things are done on the Trans Karoo. I should have waited for "Bedding/Beddegoed?" before dropping a bunk.

There's the oven-air coming in through the metal-framed window; the lino passages sticky with heat and the old South African Railways insignia on everything from the sheets to the margarine wrappers.

We'll be in the Karoo by dusk. You know how I like a big sky and scrubby vistas at Magic Hour. We'll be woken up in the middle of the night in De Aar, epicentre of the Groot Karoo. Then, after what I'm told will be an undercooked breakfast and a watery coffee, we shall ascend to the Highveld.

Right, approximately twelve hundred kilometres to go.

Dinner in four hours.

Wish me luck with the pork chop.

Love
Your (Night) Mare

PS: How are you and how's the effing squat? Any news on the job front?
PPS: Guess the song: "Big Wheel Keep on Turnin'"
(upside down:) Proud Mary

*

*Tuesday 13 February*

Life in Woodstock is not what Pauline Ashford had imagined. Although also on the lower slopes of Table Mountain, the suburb feels foreign to her, with its dog faeces and broken glass in the street. It's often eerily quiet in the house, without her lovely girls.

In the mornings, after Tess has left for school, she does the housework – hanging up towels, placing keys on hooks, and trying out a Consol jar of dried flowers on different surfaces in the lounge. It seems like a waste of time.

Sometimes, strangers lurch down the garden path between the dusty, overgrown lavender hedges. They ring on the doorbell, lean against the table on the stoep. She speaks to them through the security gate. Some of them are outpatients from the nearby mental home. Some are in pyjamas.

A few months before, she could never have foreseen being alone by mid-morning, looking out of the kitchen window at a yard of cracked concrete, boiling enough water for a single cup of tea.

Philip had not been old enough to go when he did, nor had she been ready to let him. She feels vulnerable these days – a condition exacerbated by the radio talk shows, usually about crime.

She imagines Mare, alone in Joburg, riding around on her motorbike, about to start work in the inner city. On the platform, saying goodbye, a can of pepper spray had been the last thing that passed between them. It seemed inadequate, even then.

Marigold, she knew, was too young to have left.

# PART TWO

# CHAPTER 6

*Tuesday 13 February*

Mare's arrival in one of Africa's largest cities isn't the smooth disembark she's been hoping for. She does not alight with wartime poise, all steam and heels. Instead, it's a seventies technicolour moment, lit by Highveld sun.

From the window of the carriage, she'd caught a glimpse of Johnny on the platform in his red Shweshwe shirt. He's always been her constant.

On their first day at high school, Johnny held her gaze. His smile held too. Even then, he had a way of waiting for her that would make her love him for eternity. Outside her classrooms he stood statue-still in the corridor, blazers and backpacks forced to go round him. Unhurried and available, he was her rock in a stream.

Now, spat out onto the heaving, grease-stained platform, she loses sight of him and stops to crane her neck.

Next thing, a hand on her bag: "Let's not leave luggage unattended in a crowd."

It's him.

After a hug he holds her at arm's length and looks her up and down, taking in the split togbags and cardboard suitcase, the fading T-shirt, and the worn knees of her jeans.

"Karen," he says in his Bror-from-*Out of Africa* accent. "Tell me you brought the Limoge."

They push their way through Park Station, luggage heaped on a trolley, and emerge into the baking, windless day.

Johnny introduces Mare to his first car, a teeny maroon Ford Laser: "Bottom of the range, cheapest on the road. Can't move at speed, but luckily she's ugly, and will crumple on impact."

He assures Mare that driving her, he feels like a leather-skirted Roman in a speeding chariot, whip in hand, locks swept back by the wind.

"Blown-back locks?" Mare snorts. His hair is as short as his stubble on the sides, and artfully mussed on top – as always.

"My budget didn't run to air conditioning," he says. "Windows open at all times."

"And the whip?" she asks.

"I'm considering a sjambok, to protect myself at the lights."

Mare raises her eyebrows.

"Well it's either that or a ceremonial Zulu horsehair whisk." He heads towards the boot. "Where's your bike?"

"It's on the train," Mare says.

"Hm?"

"Oh, GOD!"

Johnny fixes Mare with a mock glare, then puts her bags in the boot. "Right!" he says, turning to her. "Let's go back in."

When they reach the deserted platform they break into an unattractive fast walk. At the very, very end, Mare's motorbike is standing in the sun. It is the only thing on the platform and there's just one guard in view.

Mare fears the worst: she's too late to do the paperwork; she'll have to come back the next day; the bike's going to be impounded. But, no. The man is the right man. She has to show her ticket, sign a few things on his clipboard, and that's that.

The flat is all air and run-down elegance. They deposit Mare's worldly possessions on a few square feet of parquet in the hall, where it looks like holiday luggage – *hardly enough for a life,* she thinks.

Johnny suggests they head down to the heart of Yeoville – Rockey Street.

They start with beers at Elaine's, a curry place where every dish is topped with coriander. At the window, elbows on plastic tablecloths, they people-watch: there's a group of Rastas smoking on the opposite pavement; two girls float past a window, all tie dye and leather fringe bags. Mare feels at home when she spots a trio of screen-printed T-shirts. They might be from Greenmarket Square. She has less experience with Goths – always odd in daylight, particularly odd on a weekday afternoon mid-summer, with glints of metal from various parts of the face. All manner of clubbers are about, even some in neon lycra.

Next, they have several tequilas at House of Tandoor, much further down. There's a pool table on the roof and a stage for live music downstairs.

"So, what, is *everyone* gay?" Mare says, her eyes still screwed up from the lemon that came with her tequila shot.

"What? No."

"Oh, right. And you really don't feel left out? You know, with Mitchell's … friends."

"Mare." Johnny holds eye contact over his beer chaser. "Mitchell happens to have a very dear friend from Cape Town days. Name of Marius Fouché. Dr Marius Fouché, no less. And he, my dear, is the greatest gossip known to gaykind."

"Bingo!" Mare rubs her hands together. She finds her matches and smokes, quizzing Johnny in detail about all the new friends.

They stop at Coffee Society on the way home. It's full of artsy types writing in notebooks and dropping candle wax on their thumbs. Once, Johnny was served a Don Pedro with a frozen potato chip in it, he relates.

"A frozen ship?"

"'Strue. I'm guessing they keep the chips and the ice cream in the same freezer."

Her head is swimming. "Was Mishell with you?"

"He was."

"Aargh."

"I know. He called it 'lack of basic management'."

Mare, laughing uproariously, slops her red wine on the grease-spotted tablecloth. They "cheers" each other messily.

"Hm." There is a rather long pause. Johnny seems to be searching in his pocket for his keys.

"What else?" she shouts.

Johnny focuses on her with slow eyes. He tries to look severe, despite rocking ever-so slightly from side to side.

"No. Mare. Now ish time for us to go."

The poets have been giving them sour looks.

The bill is paid. As dusk falls, they trudge back up Cavendish Street, liquids sloshing in their bellies. Johnny points out Crest Garage, and the laundry next door.

"Tha-s where you must take your washing."

The lift of Helvetia Court has a heavy wooden door and a long curved handle. Johnny, wobbling, holds it open for Mare. They make faces at each other in the foxed mirror.

On the roof, where the washing lines are, Johnny walks Mare over to a half moon at the end. If you join the dots – "plinky-plinky" – from the metal water tower, over the reservoir, to the concrete water tower – "plink!" – that's his block across the road: Westminster Mansions. Beyond that: the famous Ponte Tower. Johnny swings his arm to point out the Hillbrow and Brixton towers too.

They laugh. Their bodies sway a bit. They listen to the traffic, watch the lights of the city come on.

"Mare, sweed-art, sho glad you're here," Johnny says, his elbow touching hers.

"I know. Me too! Hive missed you! An you must have been lonely."

"Mnh?"

"On your own here." Mare indicates the skyline with her head.

"Whayamean?'

"Without me."

"Bu – Dere Mitchell. An all his friends."

"Er-ja. But I mean. I'm here now too Johnny. We can make it hh-home."

*

*Wednesday 14 February*

At the time, Pauline thinks Fiona's visit might have something to do with Valentine's Day. There's something about the way she slammed the car door and strides up the garden path, barely pausing at the gate. Pauline reads excitement in the rushing. Generously, she imagines that Fiona is going to extend an invitation to her and the girls – to a Valentine's dinner, perhaps – to make up for, oh, Philip's death and the sudden loss of their home, and the loss of Mare … Fiona has occupation of Eland, after all, so she can afford to be generous.

Pauline opens the front door smiling, before Fiona has a chance to knock. "Hello and Happy Valentine's Day, Fiona!"

Fiona – in hard-heeled loafers, beige capri pants, and a push-up bra beneath a white T – stands rigid on the stoep. "It is not," she says.

"Isn't it?" Pauline says, turning slightly to grasp the door frame. "I thought today was—"

"It is not a happy day," Fiona spits. She holds two fingers at her temple, resting on the logo of her Prada sunglasses, seemingly undecided about whether to take them off.

"Would you like to come in?"

"I would not," Fiona says, glancing past Pauline into the dark passage. She raises her chin. "I have come here to tell you that your daughter intends to spend this evening with my brother."

"Edward?"

"Obviously." Fiona stares at Pauline.

"My dear, I am not a person," Pauline says, "for whom the penny drops easily. Please tell me why you are so cross."

"We have plans for Edward," Fiona says. "Surely you know that."

"Plans? For tonight? For him to spend Valentine's with … Sorry, Fiona, me and pennies …" Pauline lifts her bell-sleeved arms and raises her palms, ringed fingers clicking together lightly.

"Oh, for Christ's sake. We have plans for Edward's *life*."

"Do you?"

"Obviously. Yes."

"What sort of plans, dear? As I say, pen—"

"For God's sake, Pauline!" Fiona lifts her right foot but resists the temptation to stamp it. She takes a short breath. "He has a promising *career* ahead of him. He is *gifted*. He is an *architect*."

"Yes, he—"

"My mother and I—"

"You and Geraldine—"

"Yes, Geraldine! I only have one mother. Ger—"

"Of course. I'm terribly sorr—"

"Listen to me, Pauline," Fiona says. "Listen carefully." Fiona removes her Pradas. She lifts her right loafer again and takes a small step towards the doorway. She leans her face towards Pauline's. A shadow falls across her features. "Edward is very *important* to us. We—"

"Well, of course," Pauline says.

"Do I have to spell it out?"

"Would you, please?"

"I am here," Fiona says, before drawing a sharp breath through her nose. "I am here to say that given Edward's *trajectory*, it wouldn't be right for anyone to overstep the mark."

Pauline straightens her spine.

"What I mean is," Fiona turns a strained smile on Pauline. "There are boundaries. Your daughter needs to … take her shoes out from under Edward's bed."

"I beg your pardon?" Pauline says. Her tone is frosty.

"Amelia does not have a hope. This will not last. She needs to step away. She is not *good enough*."

Pauline takes a step forward. Fiona takes a step back.

"Is that clear?" Fiona says. And with that, she turns on her expensive heel and strides back across the stoep.

Pauline opens her mouth to say something, then shuts it. But as Fiona reaches the gate, she changes her mind and shouts: "Fuck you, Fiona! FUCK you!"

It is at this moment that Tess comes strolling down Balfour Road. She sees Fiona unlock her car, slam the door and start the engine with a roar. Tess stands in the fumes and laughs. Her mother is standing on the edge of the stoep, both fists on her hips.

"Go Mum!" Tess calls. Pauline is red.

On the stoep, she pulls Tess into a very tight hug.

*

*Letter, Mare to Tess*
*Wednesday 14 February*

Hi Tess,

This is not for Mum's eyes, but I thought you'd enjoy it. It's a story of a scrape. That's what they call them in the Katy books.

So Johnny got me at the station yesterday. The plan was I'd drive behind him on my bike to Yeoville. We set off. It's the middle of the

CBD. I'm terrified. Then I turn a corner and sparks start flying under the bike.

Johnny can't see cos he's ahead. I'm thinking it's about to blow up with me on it. I'm thinking it fell over in the train and now there's a fire, internally. Or something. I'm shouting to Johnny but he doesn't hear. Pedestrians think I'm insane.

We turn another corner. No sparks.

Next corner. SPARKS!

Tess, I'm seeing myself now dead or dying, leaking ribbons of blood on the tarmac, with no transport or luggage in the middle of The Most Dangerous City On Earth and I don't even KNOW WHERE I AM!

I swerve, brake next to Johnny's Ford Laser at the lights.

"There's something wrong with my bike!"

He can't hear me, even though his window is open and his forearm with all its bangles is leaning casually on the frame. I push my visor up and shout again: "There's something wrong with my bike!"

He glances out. "Your stand's down."

The lights change. I flick the stand.

That's me, from the first moment, SETTING THIS CITY ON FIRE.

I'll write a dutiful, to-the-family letter soon.

Don't be good.
XX Mare

*

*Letter, Tess to Mare*
*Thursday 15 February*

Hi Mare

I'm in your room. My new room. Yeahhhhh … I'm guessing you arrived safely. No-one tells me anything. Thanks. Everyone is going batshit out of their minds because Fifi rocked up here yesterday (VALENTINEZ) and basically said Mielie isn't allowed to go out with Edward anymore. Mom told her to f*** off. Afterwards I said "Ja, Fifi must fuck right off." Mom told me I'm not allowed to swear because she did, hypocrite. Nobody knows where Fifi gets off. She said something like Edward's expected to do better things. Better than Mielie? Durr. Not saying he's "doing" Mielie (though he is), just saying.

Mom will skin me if she finds this letter. She's giving private art classes at home. As of soon. You can picture it. Easels, canvas, sketch books, pencil shavings and paint oozing everywhere plus bottles of brushes round all the basins and sinks.

At least it'll be more fun than school. School is Es Aitch One Tea. Not swearing, Ma.

Edward's fixed my Walkman and the hi-fi system. He ran out of house stuff to fix. Reasons why Ed is awesome:

Number one: He makes Mielie happy.

Number two: Fifi hates them being together.

Number three: Edward makes Mom happy.

Number four: Edward is happy.

How come dad studied history? How come we never talked about Peter?

Send me a letter please, thanks Mare.

From

T. aka Tess Ashford (signed)

*

*Friday 16 February*

Helvetia Court is the primary setting in Pauline's middle daughter's own private movie. Mare loves it. It inspires her.

In its glory days, she imagines, girls would have stood on the tiled entrance porch at dusk. Handbag over arm crook, they would have stopped at the top of the three shallow steps, waiting for a long car to curve up the circular driveway. At the steps the car would pause, its heavy door opening on the passenger side, its plump leather seats the colour of caramel or liquorice.

In her dreams, in this heyday, Mare steps out of the brass-framed lift in co-ordinated outfits, like a photograph come to life … She hears her heels clacking across the foyer, waits as the heavy wood and glass door is pulled open onto the evening, the brass half-moon handle gripped by a male hand. She is somebody's daughter, somebody's sweetheart … She steals a last glance in the giant mirror …

The reality is she doesn't use the front entrance. She'd be mad to leave her motorbike outside. Instead, she rides around the back astride her second-hand MT5 – helmetted, sometimes wet, never ladylike.

The bike fails to alert the block to her arrival. Instead, when she revs, it sounds like a startled sewing machine.

Once she's stopped and kicked out the stand, Mare has to fiddle with a giant, rusty padlock, hoist a heavy garage door, park inside, close the door, lock, and then tramp across broken bricks to the back security gate: unlock. Security gate to foyer: unlock. The foyer lights blink and the mirror has watermarks. The postboxes – original – have pigeon holes with a solid little wooden door covering each one. And a keyhole, because of course you need a key.

Each day, she opens the little door slowly, imagining there might be an actual pigeon in there, that there's one behind every postbox door, a whole family of them. A letter from Balfour Road would be one of these pigeons – intelligent, capable. And with a brief clatter it would fly through the down-at-heel foyer and take her with it, straight home.

*

*Letter, Mare to Mielie, Pauline and Tess*
*Sunday 18 February*

Helvetia Court
Sunday morning, bed

Hello Mum, Tess and Mielie,

Work starts tomorrow. I'm … er. Eurgh, I don't know what I am. Restless. Jumpy. A little blue. So come into my flat. I wish you could.

As you all know, I own no furniture. Luckily, I've been able to intercept some of Mitchell's stuff that was destined for the tip. He redecorated when Johnny moved in. The final chuck-outs were in their basement garage. I now have a double bed – he upgraded to queen – and an overlong pair of gold curtains. Another friend of theirs, Fouché, heard I was scavenging and sent over two fake Louis XIV (or is it XVI?) chairs with maroon seats and backs. One has a broken leg and the other has a cigarette burn on the seat.

In addition, Mitchell has given me a hideous couch. I can't imagine it was ever in his home. Maybe he picked it up AT the tip. It's a horrible shape and is covered in the kind of worn-down, synthetic fur you see on soft toys in charity shops. I've done a slipcover effect.

Johnny has given me his old portable TV and I have my ancient radio-tape machine. The curved wooden wall unit at the end of the lounge is a handsome home for my books and music. I'm keeping the design clean, with a generous use of negative space.

I've made some effort on the walls. I've painted the hallway pink with gold trim (the curtains, remember?) The kitchen is yellow, with my East African cloth at the window. And the lounge walls? I took a sponge to them. The colour, it is aa-pree-caht.

I've hung a stern self-portrait opposite the front door. My four final-year portrait studies are in the lounge. There are paintings from life class in the bathroom, postcards on the fridge – all my favourites. Bob Dylan is up there. There's that black-and-white landscape and that cover of What Katy Did At School – the one Johnny gave me after that thing I did at school (not another word, please).

Next to the bed, to protect me when I sleep, I've posted two sentries. One photo, one painted self-portrait. I'm scowling in both.

So there's the way things are. In case you're wondering.

XX Your (Night) Mare

PS: Guess the song, Mielie:
"Your scarf, it was apricot." (pronounced "aa-pree-caht")
...
Carly Simon: You're So Vain

Later, Crackers Deli

Hello again,

Sorry I sounded like such a misery earlier. I was just nervous! And half-asleep. You know what I'm like when I've just got up. I'm now at the deli on Rockey Street, where I am about to indulge in Urban Sunday Brunch. Alone. How very metropolitan of me.

It's a boiling hot day. Johnny's taking me for a swim at the Ellis Park pool later. That's my excuse for ordering eggs.

Oh. Coffee. Wonderful.

So as I was saying, it's boiling hot on the Highveld. The streets suck up the heat. They send up cartoon shimmers, like sketched steam above a coffee cup. The light is so bright and the sky is so wide and there's no water here, that's a weird thing to get used to. No sea, no river to calm the angry smell of exhaust fumes and commuter sweat.

The heavenly miracle of the Highveld is the thunderstorms. I've only been here a few days, and we've already had two.

A storm cleans everything, cools down the evenings, restores calm. It's like having a good cry. Or a good shout. Or a good cry and a good shout and a good sweat all at the same time.

It starts with fat, even drops. Then there are crackles of lightning and growls of thunder. Soon the rain is pouring down, so heavy it clatters. The skies shudder and roar. The air sparks furiously, and is drenched, repeatedly, by the rain.

It's why dust doesn't build up, why the fumes don't become intolerable, why we can smell the frangipani flowers at dusk. It's why, I think, the people don't all go completely mad here in summer.

Here's my breakfast. Pause to unwrap cutlery.

After my eggs I'm going to buy all the Sunday newspapers. I'll try and get on top of it all by tomorrow. I give awkwardness and nerves a week. By then, I'm hoping, the details of existence will have been managed and all will be calm. Then it will just be gentle mind-shifting change and stimulation – like kelp shifting underwater, like light.

What are the odds?

Hold thumbs. Please write.

XXXX Mare

In the days that have passed since Mare left, Mielie has not missed her sister much, nor made the time to write to her.

She wonders if it's her happiness with Edward, or her breakthrough acting part, or the move that's made her neglect her duty.

*It could be anger*, she thinks. *Am I that angry with Mare? From the fight we had after the funeral, and then for just upping and leaving? But why would I be? I don't need my sister for anything. Even so, she could have picked up a pen.*

Mielie thinks all this as she lies next to a sleeping Edward in his Observatory digs room, where the Sunday morning light makes a mockery of his thin curtains.

The night before, in the same bed, he'd unsettled her.

It started with him saying how happy he was.

"God, Mielie," he sighed, putting his hands behind his head and giving her a close-up view of his underarm hair.

"What?" She was still flushed, and smiling.

Edward turned to face her, the moon on his jaw and shoulder. "I have never been this happy."

"I know," she said. "Me too."

"Really?" he said. "Why?"

"You, of course. And—"

"And?"

"Well, the play. I feel bad saying that."

"Why?"

Mielie sighed. "Timing."

"Oh. Your dad," Edward said.

"Yes. The timing is terrible. I've loved acting all my life. It's been the thing I've loved the most and—"

Edward interrupted her, smiling. "What do you love about it?"

Mielie leaned back. Edward almost never interrupted her.

"I'm very good at it."

"Yes."

"And I love the language. Shakespeare. Mamet." Mielie shifted closer to face Edward. He shifted onto his side to face her too. "I love it because when I'm acting I—"

"You?"

"I don't have to do anything."

"Oh?" Edward ran a finger over her cheek.

"I mean it. I don't have to remember to do anything. Or plan anything. Or think anything through."

"Don't tell your director that," he smiled.

"What I mean is," Mielie dropped onto her back. "When I'm being someone else, it lifts me out of my life. It's honestly like—"

"Levitating?"

"Yes. Actually, no. More like gliding. Fast gliding."

"Sounds exciting."

"It is."

She could sense him watching her face in the dark.

"I think you're exciting," he whispered.

Now, lying naked in bed with her ankles crossed, Mielie realises that her conversation with Edward has left her wondering two things.

One: why did she characterise her every waking moment – with the exception of acting – as "remembering things, planning things and thinking things through"?

Two: why had she chosen a job that, in her own words, "lifted her out of her life"? How could these two things be true if she was, as she'd just told Edward, happier than she'd ever been?

*

*Monday 19 February*

On Day One of the internship programme, Mare takes the bus from outside Helvetia Court to the CBD – more specifically, to the busy corner of Pritchard and Sauer Streets.

Her feet hurt. Despite the heat, she is wearing a pair of imported biker boots: black, mid-calf, three buckles. They are a size too small.

She bought them at the Yeoville second-hand shop. She shouldn't have bought them. In addition to being too small, they were overpriced. But Mare felt – and continues to feel – that they were the ideal purchase for this moment of her life. She needed to butch up, she knew, and these boots would get her into the right frame of mind. Besides: no pain, no gain. She would wear them in as the city wore her in. With the amount of walking she'd be doing this year, she hoped they'd be stretched in no time.

Early for once, she enters the Independent Newspapers building through tall glass doors, passing into a bright, double-volume lobby. There are uniformed security guards and cameras.

Paperwork completed at reception and new access card around her neck, Mare walks round the block to have a look at the printing works, to pass the time. There are huge noisy rollers down there, and newspapers on conveyer belts that look like folded meats and cheeses at a breakfast buffet. She watches the papers leave in vans with mastheads painted on their sides.

When she finally – now late, of course – walks into the carpeted room where Cadet School happens, her first thought is that she's in the wrong place. There's a U-shaped arrangement of tables, and a small teacher's table at the front, but also in the room are young men in suits and women in blouses and blazers. There are briefcases on the floor.

Her heart is beating fast when she sits down. What had she been thinking? That this would be just another UCT tutorial group of art students, lefties and literature nerds? Why had she worn jeans? Why wasn't she wearing lipstick? This, clearly, was a place of business, and she'd just taken a seat in a high-rise building in the commercial heart of the country – or the continent, even.

Johnny had warned her about being unprepared, the night before, when he treated her to an early supper at Scandalos, a Greek place on Rockey Street, after swimming. Feeling the very height of sophistication, they ordered a carafe of Tassies and a meze platter to share.

Mitchell – apparently unable to cope with the cuisine and level of service – had declined to join.

"What can't he cope with? Exotic cuisine?" Mare asked.

"God, no," Johnny said. "He loves exotica. When he says 'cuisine and level of service' he means grime."

Then he wiped his mouth with his napkin. "So. State of the Nation. You've read up on the negotiations phase and the rainbow phase?"

"Hm?"

"You know, Codesa and then the whole melting pot thing? Mitchell says it was nice while it lasted."

"We're still the rainbow nation, aren't we?" Mare felt slightly bereft.

"Nope. We're into nation building now. Restructuring. And then the Truth Commission, for healing."

"Right."

Mare drained her glass and stared at the theatre posters on the windows, wishing Johnny would stop talking about current affairs.

"It's a pretty interesting time to be a journalist, anyway," he continued. "And you'll be joining a savvy group."

Now Mare tries to calm down. What had the lady on the phone said, when she'd called to say she'd got in? Was it two thousand people who'd applied for the twelve prestigious internships? Or two hundred?

She looks around the room again. The cause of her panic reveals itself to her. "You're the only white face here," it tells her. "And you've no idea how to behave."

During the opening session, each member of the group introduces themselves. Mare is horrified to discover that several of her classmates are already working reporters for the company. They are here to "consolidate their skills" and "broaden their writing experience". Others in the group are university graduates, with degrees in journalism.

Mare is the last to speak. She says she did "Art, English, and that's all".

"Even though you're English," someone mutters.

The group laughs and Mare feels like her classmates are playing piggy-in-the-middle, over her head.

# CHAPTER 7

*Card*
*Thursday 22 February*

Dear Mielie
Wishing you all the best for your opening night tonight.
I am sure you will receive all the acclaim you deserve.
Whatever happens, I am your one-man standing ovation.
Kind regards
Edward

*

*Letter, Mare to Mielie*
*Friday 23 February*

Helvetia Court

Hello.

How was my first week at Cadet School? Intense, thanks for asking.

Everyone calls it Cadet School, so I shall too, even though the name reminds me of schoolboys dressed up as soldiers, marching on fields. Remember that double period, Youth Preparedness? We all called it Y.P. Like it was fun. Good old Christian National Education. Jesus.

So I heard about Fifi and the double fucks. Not from you. Hey, when Edward's finished mending household objects maybe he can organise for his sister to give our house back?

Anyway. Shorthand class starts, as advertised, at 7.30am. As you know it's not my favourite time of day. After class, those of us who skipped breakfast go up in the lifts to the cafeteria on the 11th floor. Beware the breakfast mince. Up there, we don't mingle with the newsroom staff. At 8.30, they're still in bed, hungover. Or downing Cal-C-Vitas. Or listening for radio scoops in their cars. We breakfast with people in overalls: the night cleaners, the printing staff.

We have a kind-of waiting area in the school where we go during breaks. We are encouraged to call it the lounge. We drink our coffee from the canteen, smoke, and at lunchtime eat King Pies from across the road. I'm usually the only one who doesn't get the joke. I only speak two languages, remember.

The main thing is, I need to keep up. My current affairs knowledge is hopeless. My debating skills are pathetic. I find I possess no opinions about the news. Not about the future for apartheid-era human rights abusers, federalism vs. socialism, or the theoretical basis for a new economy.

We're marked all the time.

We're going to have current affairs quizzes once a week. We had one yesterday. I failed to shine.

When they announced a spelling test today I thought: "Oh, thank God! Bring it on! This I can do! First language, a lifetime of privileged education and – er, herm – a certain natural ability with words." I predicted a full-marks scenario. I would have smiled apologetically, of course, but victory would have been mine. Spelling! If nothing else, then at least … Spelling!

I came fourth. They got me on bussing. They got me on embarrassed. They got me on judgment and – ironically – privilege. They got me on benefitted.

It's almost a poem.

So, the good news is that my classmates are terrifying. We're working in groups to create a Knock and Drop. That's one of those free, suburban newspapers, to you and me. I love "Knock and Drop" though. It sounds like the sort of thing Postman Pat would carry around in his little red van. We have to do real research and produce real stories. I'm hoping that my past experience making Royal Wedding scrapbooks will serve me well for our Big Project.

Until then, I push through the turnstiles with everyone else. To be honest, Mielie, it makes me proud to wear an Independent Newspapers ID card around my neck, proud to queue with columnists and editors for lunch.

Anyway, I wish I could show it all to you.

XXXXX Mare

PS: I had a haircut, at great expense, at lunchtime the other day. I now have a perfectly neat, perfectly schoolgirl, perfectly office-acceptable, shiny brown, dreaded B.O.B. My wardrobe is also expanding to include shiny shoes, tights without runs and jeans without paint on them.

PPS: Do you know the answers to any of these?
Which famous couple's divorce will be finalised this week?
My answer: Charles and Diana
Correct answer: Winnie and Nelson Mandela
Who was elected leader of the Labour Party in the UK last year?
My answer: John Major
Correct answer: Tony Blair
Which team lost to South Africa in the African Cup of Nations?
My answer: New Zealand
Correct answer: Tunisia
Who is the head of the TRC's investigative unit and witness-protection programme?
My answer: Jacques Paauw
Correct answer: Dumisa Ntsebeza
When was the Constitution of South Africa signed into law?
My answer: February 1995
Correct answer: It has not yet been signed into law. The current document is the Interim Constitution (1993)

*

*Newspaper clipping*
*The Argus, Friday section, 23 February*

**SHREW-FIRE WINNER**

By Andre Steenkamp

It is a dream part for any young actress: Kate, the title role in "The Taming of the Shrew", is passionate and sharp-witted. It is a physical part, with some of The Bard's greatest lines.

Amelia Ashford, currently playing Kate at Maynardville's Open Air Theatre, rises to greet me from a table at the Baxter Theatre Restaurant. She is remarkably tall.

I order a coffee. Ashford asks for a refill. She smiles at the waitress. I cannot be sure if she's acknowledging recognition, or if Ashford is sympathetic to service staff.

Has she waited tables herself? She grins.

"Hell, yes. I basically worked every second night while I was a student, and most nights in the holidays."

Did her looks ensure good tips?

She dismisses the compliment: "I was sent home by a restaurant manager once, for looking frumpy."

Our coffees arrive. I ask what has been the best part about playing wild, outspoken Kate?

Ashford stirs her coffee.

"She's vivacious, principled – and furious. I love the joshing tone of the play, especially the rapport between Kate and Petruchio, who is her match in every way."

Her coffee is finished now. The leading lady drinks fast.

"Kate is almost impossibly complex. That's all credit to Shakespeare. It's been a fantastic challenge to study her motives."

Is Ashford unlike Kate?

"I'm terribly serious, she's plain reckless."

Would she prefer to be more like Kate?

"No. 'The Taming of the Shrew', it's not a happy story, not to me. When I think of Kate I think of compromise."

Kate and Ashford have this in common, though: both have younger sisters. In Shrew, Kate's younger sister is forbidden to wed until her sister is married.

Has Ashford been forced to sacrifice for her own sister, as Kate is "compromised" – to use her word – in Shrew?

Ashford chuckles. "No, that's not the way it is. We're very close, though."

"In age?"

"Yes."

"Temperament?"

"No."

"No?"

"My sister's the wild one. If anything I hold her back."

I wonder aloud whether eldest children are wont to play down their own needs.

"Hardly," she smiles her enormous smile. "I'm on stage, doing what I love, full tilt, every night. How's that holding back?"

*At 23, Ashford already has a Vita Best Actress Award.*
*The Taming of the Shrew opened at Maynardville yesterday and runs until March 23.*

*

*Letter, Mare to Tess*
*Saturday 24 February*

Dearest Tess,

Our letters crossed in the air. I wrote you a long one on Sunday, then I got your letter about the Fifi incident. Thank you for that, it's exactly the kind of gossip I require. You're right, we didn't talk much about Peter. But first questions first: How come Dad studied History? Happy to oblige.

BTW, Dad is capitalised if it stands alone as a name; History is capitalised because you are referring to the subject, not the concept … Did I trick you into thinking this was a letter from Mielie? Ha ha.

Right, so, Dad's horrible cardboard parents wanted him to study law. He was their only child and they were broke, even though they lived in a huge house. Dad hated law. He didn't want to regulate the world. He liked stories, like I do. Does Mielie want to regulate the world? I wonder. Anyway, it makes sense. Dad didn't like his world very much, at that time. He enjoyed escaping into stories of the past, and there were things he wanted to understand.

While he was still on track to becoming a woolly wig-wearing wanker (thought you'd like that) – and reading history books in his spare time – he was pursued by a certain Cicely. She was not just posh, but wealthy too. Dad and Cicely met through school chums. They were a good match, these chums said. She was pretty and rich, Dad was clever and well-bred. According to Dad, who was never one for speaking ill of anyone, she wasn't much more than pretty and rich.

Sorry Tess, I can see you rolling your eyes, but there is no way on God's earth I can make a long story short, you know that about me. Heaven help me, writing for newspapers. I should be writing family epics like The Thornbirds.

So. Scandal. Cicely got pregnant while Dad was still at university. Whether it was an honest mistake, or whether she'd decided to speed things up, we shall never know. Dad was too much of a gentleman to say. (I did ask.)

There was a wedding, Peter was born. But by the time he graduated, Dad had decided he couldn't stick the law or his marriage.

Dad and Cicely divorced fairly amicably. Cicely stayed in Cambridge. Dad switched from law to teaching and moved home to Haywards Heath. Cicely swiftly replaced Dad with another clever, rich chap. Dad was single for his first years as a teacher. He travelled up to visit Peter when he could. These visits were not encouraged. Peter had little memory of our dad and considered Husband Number Two his father. This attitude was encouraged by Cicely.

Back to your history question.

Okay, so there's Dad, in the mid-1960s, with all his hair, teaching at Haywards Heath Comprehensive. In 1967, Pauline Foster wafts in. She is the new, not-posh art teacher, freshly graduated from uni. She looks and dresses like the girl in The Raggle Taggle Gypsies, you know the one in Treasury of Poetry. She's all skirts and tresses. She is missing only the "rings on her fingers and bells on her toes" – though it's not impossible she owned such items and wore them at weekends. Pauline is new to West Sussex. The countryside appeals to her. She grew up and studied in London. Pauline is excited to make a new start, inspired by the green of the landscape and the rainbow of her paintbox. Dad, eight years her senior, is smitten. They marry the following year. His parents disapprove, it goes without saying. Peter is at boarding school at the time. They try to keep up contact with him but both our parents are working and Peter is seldom home.

The sixties end and the seventies begin. Philip and Pauline are broke but madly in love. In their little newlywed house, you can be sure that Mum spoke of "passions". I'd put money on it that she persuaded Dad to enrol for the correspondence Masters in History. He graduated in the early seventies. Mum has a copy of the thesis, definitely – about the Anglo-French war in the late 1700s, if you must know.

In 1972, Pauline announces she's pregnant. Mielie is born. Later the same year Dad's mother dies. Soon after that Mum falls pregnant with me and soon after that our Grandpa Ashford dies. So now, instead of just a little house and each other, Mum and Dad have two baby girls and an inherited beast of a country house. Philip and Pauline have their heads down teaching and parenting for the next three years.

Then, emigration. I have it in my mind that Dad was going through a South African history phase when he had the idea of moving to Cape Town. It would make sense, wouldn't it? Otherwise, why here?

One cold night, in front of an inadequate fire, Philip has the idea to sell the beast-house and move to South Africa. The National Trust buys the house. It's architecturally significant. Arts and Crafts something or other. Mielie is two and I'm still a baby when we move to Cape Town in 1975. Apparently Peter didn't seem in the least bothered when Dad told him we were leaving.

We emigrated on a boat, you knew that didn't you? It was called the Windsor Castle. Within two weeks we were on Cape Town's docks. And in the blink of an eye we were settled. Dad had a job as an associate history professor at UCT and Mum got a job teaching art part-time.

In Cape Town, Mum and Dad used the money from the Arts and Crafts house to buy, as you know, not one property but two. It meant they could supplement teaching income with rental income. They must have felt like they'd won the jackpot. They acquired the handsome but run-down Eland House, a road back from Kloof Nek Road, too high up the mountain at that time to be fashionable, and a smaller Victorian in scruffy Woodstock. Once tenants were found for the Balfour Road house, and after you were born two years later, Mum left work altogether and Dad made it known he had no intention of rising above associate professor.

Mielie and I – and later you and Mielie and I – were as happy as crickets, exploring the nooks of Eland, climbing trees, swimming in the cracked pool, burning our noses in the sun.

Mum started festooning Eland with bargains the moment she stepped through the door – and never stopped. Daddy read and read – his favourite thing – and gave little thought to the future. There was no saving. The houses became more run-down. It didn't seem to matter. Our parents were happy, we were happy, and so we all remained – until the will was read. (I think when Dad made the "dodgy investment" he must have imagined multiplying his rental income from Balfour. Shame, he probably knew he was sick when he bought the land. He must have thought it would be the perfect way to keep enough money coming in when he was gone.)

But you asked why Dad studied history, and how Peter fits in. Sorry the Dad and history part wasn't in a nutshell. I know why you asked, though. You have to make subject choices this year and you love history too. Tess, block one ear, I know you hate compliments. But you have a gift for it. You've always wanted to know what happened before. Dad had the same thing. It really was, to use another of Mum's words, his "calling".

Right, let's talk about Peter. I'd rather not, but unfortunately he is rather key to all this – what's going on now.

Peter finished school and went to university in England. One night, at a wine bar in London, he met Fiona Taylor, a Capetonian. Fiona – oh God, hateful Fifi – had a job at the time, doing something horsey. She might have answered the phone at a stables for racehorses, something like that. Suffice to say, she was running with the horsey set, a swishy-haired, bossy boots who could have had her pick of untitled toffs. Instead, she chose Peter. Peter, with his ever-so slack jaw and slightly too-large lower lip. Peter, who was so intensely grateful then, and who has been intensely grateful ever since. Peter, whose religion is: Fee can do no wrong.

They were a fair match. Fiona's family was rich. Peter, still Cicely's only child, stood to inherit from both Cicely and our dad – not to mention whatever his stepfather decided to leave him. Even without any of these advantages he would have been a catch. He was doing rather well at the time, in real estate.

They married. They got pregnant. They were giddily rolling in it. And then they decided to move to Cape Town, for whatever reason pregnant couples decide to move.

An historic Newlands village semi was purchased. Fiona renovated and made it into the mags. Once Booboo was walking, the two-bedroom presumably became too small, hence the interest in Eland.

When I think of Peter arriving at Eland after the funeral, I see his thinning hair blown to the side, at right angles to his head, his shirt pressed against his belly. I think how I would like to blow him, hard, out of our lives, would like to blow his chino-clad legs out from under him and send him bum-bumping off the face of the earth.

You don't have to be Matlock to suspect it was Peter who persuaded Dad to make the dodgy investment. He's a realtor and he's greedy. But I believe he wanted Dad to gain. He couldn't predict what happened. Our half-brother is a chop, no question – but he's not a villain. He's weak and silly. It's only in combination with Fifi – who is lethal – that he becomes dangerous.

Anyway, lesson over.

Thanks for your letter. Keep 'em coming.

Love,
XX Mare

PS: Mum says you have a full schedule of extra-murals this term. I hope you're back on the swimming squad. Your backstroke shows real promise. You might beat me if you train. Mrs Plummer is a good coach, despite the damp takkies.

PPS: Almost every bit of information above I have from Mum. You were sensible to ask me and not her. It's taken me twenty years of listening to her while we wait for the kettle to boil to gather this set of facts. (There's an argument for me having potential as a journalist! If Pauline Ashford can be worked as a "source", anyone can.)

*Letter, Mielie to Mare*
*Thursday 29 February*

Hello Wary Mary, warrior girl

Please forgive my silence. I lost my words for a spell, but right now they're coming in swarms, like the birds did at Eland at sunset.

Remember how Dad would wave his arms around, pretending to try to catch them, whoosh-after-whoosh? He'd be standing at the top of the lawn, waving and waving, and they'd part above him and then regroup. Remember how we'd laugh then, Mare? Do you remember? I do.

Anyway, just so you can picture it, exactly – I know how you like to picture things, exactly – I'm sitting at the table in the Balfour Road kitchen, beneath the window, with the late afternoon light pouring through.

I'm pressing on the back of my plastic flip-file, with your charcoal drawing in the front sleeve – the whimsical, tortured one of you at an easel, in Standard 9, looking over your shoulder as if someone had interrupted you. I've always loved it. Which is why I wouldn't give it back when you were packing, by the way.

We all miss you. A lot. Cadet School sounds intense. God, Joburg sounds intense, the way you describe it. It's like a different country.

Edward's just got back from work and he's weaving the jasmine along a trellis he's installed, against the wall in the yard. I can see him from where I'm sitting.

It's the real deal, Mare. I'm loving Maynardville, of course. Loving performing in a park. Loving the fairy-lit pathways to the dressing rooms, etc. And, more than anything, I'm loving being with Edward afterwards, every night. He waits for me in the yard at the back of his Obs digs, and then we lie on our backs on the paving in the streetlight, blowing dandelions and looking for stars.

He sent roses to my dressing room on opening night, with a handwritten card, signed off: "Kind regards". "Kind regards"! Have you ever?

He also sent a fax to the stage door, wishing the whole cast well. I thought that rather gallant and astute, really, seeing as he lives and breathes in a completely different world.

I must tell you, I saw a picture of his mum. Fiona hung one in the hall at Eland. I saw it when I was babysitting Booboo the other day. (It would seem that Fiona is entirely prepared to overcome her evident dislike of me in favour of shopping at the Waterfront several times a week, leaving her child in my care … I've not had the pleasure of watching her stagger up the driveway, clutching her latest designer-shop haul, because of course they have staff to carry the purchases, boot-to-boudoir. Displaced Zimbabweans, with tertiary qualifications, whom they pay the barest minimum. "Job creation, what can I say?" I think is how Fiona put it.)

So. Geraldine Taylor. There she was in all her lack of glory, presiding over the hallway as if she were The Queen. Think Fifi plus ten years, and just about as charming. Obviously she didn't have Fifi when she was ten, but it looks like she must have. Her hair is coiffed, her face expressionless, her eyebrows thin as fishing gut. Scarier, though, are her eyes – dark blue, and dead as glass.

I like being back at Eland for those times. You don't need to own a place to belong in it, I've realised. Well, technically we still own it, but we don't live there anymore …

Mum's okay, by the way. She's going to post you some knitted gloves, for your winter on the bike. And Tess is staying out of trouble at school (mostly). We're working on getting the detentions down to below three a month, plus she's joined the debating society.

The day you left, she went into hiding up the tree at Eland. She caught the bus, and was up there for ages before Edward and I drove there and found her. He announced we were going to the beach, to get her to come down. And down she came, foothold by handhold, in dead silence, with him at a distance, whistling away and pretending to pull out weeds.

In the late afternoon, we went swimming in the sea. And afterwards, driving slowly home along the cliff road in the twilight, with Tess fast asleep in the back, Edward looked across at me and brushed some salt off my cheek.

I know about blood being thicker than water, but I believe what Edward and I have is stronger and more powerful than family ties.

Mare! I must run or I'll miss my half-hour call! I was actually writing to say that I'm sorry I gave you such a hard time about going. I've thought about it properly and I really do know that you left for the challenge, and the once-in-a-lifetime opportunity. You weren't running away. I know that now.

Hold on tight, please, and look after yourself.

I believe in you.

Mad love always
Mielie

PS: One night after the show – it wasn't opening night, it was just a night – Edward came backstage. He must have come to see the show again.

Maybe he knocked, but I didn't hear him.

I was washing my face at the basin, in my spencer and broeks … light-bulbs round the mirror, cards and flowers and make-up stuff all unpacked and scattered.

He was just kind of hanging out, with his arms crossed, in the doorway, and I think my back was to him when I heard him say: "What do you think you should do, Mielie, when you think you're falling in love?"

Oh Mare.

I watched the water disappearing … well, I couldn't stop it, in the absence of a plug.

Then I dried my face, took a deep breath, looked him in the eyes, and just said: "Fall."

# CHAPTER 8

*Friday 1 March*

Thomas Walker is standing on the balcony of his old friend Mitchell Palmer's flat when he hears the sound of a 50cc entering the parking lot below. He's had a tough week at the office and the Pretoria-Joburg highway was a nightmare, coming home. Now he's resting a can of Castle lager on the ledge, smoking and taking in the view.

He doesn't notice Johnny scooting past him down the passage to the foyer to open the lift door.

"Ooh, hair product!" says a voice he's never heard before.

"Ooh, base," Johnny counters immediately.

Walker smiles. Who's this? She should know not to try to out-queen Johnny. He turns his head as they approach.

She's carrying her helmet. Her skin is very light and her hair is very dark. To Mitchell's friend, her appearance is like a gust of wind that makes the eyes water.

"Walker," Johnny says. "And Mare."

The girl greets him off-handedly, then the two of them go inside.

*Of course,* Walker thinks as he takes a last drag. *She's the one doing the internship, and staying at Helvetia Court.* He should have put two and two together.

At dinner, Walker finds that he is distracted.

The main meal is steak tartare – a shallow dish of raw mince and raw egg yolk, with olives, capers and Parmesan on the side.

At some point Marius Fouché brings conversation to a halt: "You must tell us your surname, darling. So we can look out for your byline."

"Ashford," the girl manages, through a mouthful of focaccia. "It's Mare Ashford."

Fouché lifts his wine glass by the stem, and tilts it musingly: "Good." But, he booms across the table, she *must* start calling herself Marigold – not Mare. "You need a grown-up name in a grown-up town."

*The girl clearly has no idea how to respond. She's not even in the game, this dinner party ping-pong,* Walker thinks.

"Well what about your sister, Mitchell? 'Toni' seems to work fine for her, although she's Antonia." She's blushing slightly now, rolling the corner of her napkin between her fingers. "Actually she's my sister's best friend."

"School's out, darling," Fouché shoots back. "We don't have 'best friends' anymore." He pauses for laughter that doesn't come. Then he launches into a diatribe about how everyone "at this table" knows each other's histories and secrets, and how "this makes us a community, darling … the misfits and the marginals – where else do we belong?"

Walker watches the girl, in the candlelight.

She doesn't answer, so Fouché continues: "So tell us, Marigold, what's your history? Did you leave broken hearts behind in Slaapstad?"

*She'd break my heart most certainly,* Walker thinks.

"Or …" Fouché is on a roll now, "is the broken heart actually yours?"

The girl grips her chest.

Walker looks at his lap. From way back in the early days, in the End Conscription Campaign, Fouché has been like a brother to him. Most of the time, Walker loves him for being irrepressible. But honestly now he wishes his friend would give the girl a break.

Naturally Fouché doesn't. "No but seriously now. What type do you go for, Marigold?"

Mare pauses, then smiles. "Oh, I don't go for anyone," she says, and takes a sip of wine. "I don't need to," she lies. "I draw them like flies."

The table does laugh at that.

*Oh, darling,* Walker sighs inwardly.

"But if I did," she continues, "and I don't. But if I did, my type is boyish, like a young Robert Redford. Or Steve McQueen."

*Perfect,* thinks Walker. *Absolutely fucking perfect.*

*Letter, Mare to Toni*
*Sunday 3 March*

Helvetia Court
Bed

Dear Toni,

You haven't written back. No matter. I know you will. One day.

So I am here to report that your ridiculously over-achieving brother's flat is outrageous. I was round there for supper on Friday. It's a Herbert Baker building, of which he and Johnny occupy the entire top right corner. It's like something out of a décor magazine: balconies front and back, with 180-degree views from Kensington to Killarney and the city between.

I made an effort. Obviously I had to. I arrived wearing red lipstick. In the lift I couldn't decide if it was chic or if it just made my lips look thin.

What's that? Was the lipstick a hand-me-down? Funny you should ask. Yes, it was. It made my lips dry too. It smelt a little of whale blubber. It may actually be from the 1940s. I wouldn't know, all the writing's worn off. There's a reason these things are handed down.

I walk in – middle-aged professionals everywhere. Your brother greets me warmly but is much engrossed at an oversized chopping board. Johnny shuffles me into the main living area where we survey the knots of guests talking animatedly about past glories.

One of them is wearing a veil-thin Indian shirt. It's a conceal-reveal situation, like a Harold Pinter screenplay. He makes a beeline for your brother, puts an arm around his neck, and presses his body along his back, pretending to study the chopping board: "Mitchell, it's insane!"

He comes over to me and Johnny soon afterwards, a bottle of icy Absolut in one hand, three shot glasses dangling off the fingers of the other: "Vodka, darlings," he tells us.

Johnny introduces me and I say I'm Mare for short. Fouché shakes my hand theatrically: "Marius Fouché." You've probably met him. You could've warned me, Toni. Like, "Mare, keep 'em peeled for see-through clothes and Victorian formality."

The pouring of the vodka is a performance. Everyone drinks Absolut, apparently. It must live in the freezer. This we care about. The vodka's party trick is that it doesn't freeze.

Fouché dribbles the liquor into shot glasses shaped, disconcertingly, like test tubes. When he is about to hand me one, a voice cries "Wait!" Mitchell sweeps over and drops a slice of fresh red chilli in the bottom of each glass, then returns to his chopping board as quickly as he left it.

I take a test tube and nod at Fouché. "Bottoms up," I say.

We both drink. My chilli sticks, thankfully, to the inside of the tube.

"Oh my God!" Fouché says, squeezing his eyes together. "'Bottoms up!' Love you already!"

Later
Bed

It's an epic, okay? I live alone, what else do I have to do?

I thought I might make it through dinner without incident. Then Fouché started quizzing me and I ended up saying I attracted men like flies. It was only when I got home I realised I'd meant to say bees. No wonder people laughed. And there I thought I'd done a Dorothy Parker. Gaw.

Plus I'd meant to sting, a little, to be honest. It was all so irritating and pretentious. People going on and on about NGOs, ANC, ECC, PAC, etc. Apparently they've all been flies on the wall everywhere important.

Oh, and there was another guy, too. Walker. Have you met him? Tall. Curly hair. He's like some kind of guru to Mitchell & co. Whenever he says anything (which is very seldom) it's like running a charge through a circuit-board. They all ignite like fairy lights.

The morning after was okay. I slept over after the party. It's not safe to go home alone at night, apparently. Not ever. It was slightly gloomy, we were all hungover. I drove home at noon and seized on my moisturiser like a camel in a desert.

I'm so lazy, all Saturday I avoid taking my clothes to the Crest Garage laundry. I have to heave them in black plastic bags, one over each shoulder, two blocks down.

Bringing it all home is worse. Wet washing, uphill. And so then I put off taking everything down off the line until Sunday evening, when my jeans are stiff and at least one pair of panties has been blown into the gutter.

Which is now.

Toni, hold on.

*

*Sunday 3 March*

It's nearly twilight on Sunday and Tom Walker is in a state. He's spent the whole weekend berating himself.

Why didn't he just talk to the girl on Friday? He might be wrong, she might not have despised him on sight. She might just be shy. And he could have approached her, over the whiskies in Mitchell's lounge when most of the others had left. But at the time he was mortified by what he'd said at the dinner table.

"Boyish?" he'd said. "You have good taste. Don't waste your time on old farts like us."

Had he sounded hurt? God, probably.

"Speak for yourself!" Fouché chimed.

"I didn't mean that," said the girl.

Of course then the table seized on the topic of youth vs. experience. Someone said something about that time when Mandela suggested dropping the voting age – "first and only political misstep" (Mitchell); "nod to the Youth League" (Fouché).

Then Walker surprised everyone – including himself – by saying: "I didn't disagree with him then – I still don't."

Mitchell put down the plates he was stacking.

"Youth is passion," Walker said then. "There's a clarity in that, a unique purpose."

"But fourteen!" a woman burst forth. Half her head was shaved.

"All I'm saying is we need new impetus," Walker responded. "You think people voting for the same old parties is enough? It's not. Affiliation won't reshape the landscape. We need new ideas – new, er, passion."

"No man," Mitchell said. "South African teenagers are clueless."

The table gasped. The shaved woman looked ready to mouth the words "nineteen-seventy-six".

Mitchell held up his hand: "I'm not disputing that young people – children, even – have been politically active, that they've made sacrifices, and an enormous contribution. But democracy is distinct from revolution. It's a different mindset."

There was a murmur of agreement, a collective sigh of relief. Conflict averted.

But Fouché took a different tack. "Walker," he purred, the scent of his lonely friend's attraction strong in his nostrils. "My sense is that you like a young mind."

"I don't deny it," Walker said, looking down.

The table waited. Walker said nothing, but glanced at Mare. Mitchell picked up the plates. Arms reached for wine. A hum of conversation resumed.

"I'm not sure Walker was talking about Mandela just now," Fouché muttered to the girl, one eyebrow raised.

She pushed her chair back and went to the loo, and Walker felt a fool – sure that he'd blown it completely, if he'd ever had a chance.

Now Walker ascends the stairs of Mare's building, cursing himself as he goes. He's rung the owner's bell and been let in, on the premise of taking a photo of the sunset. The plan is to go straight to Mare's flat, ring her bell and invite her for a bowl of soup at Mamma's. He wants to say something to her, though he doesn't know quite what. He just hasn't felt like this for so many years, and he can't bear to let the moment pass.

Instead, he proceeds to the roof. And there she is.

He strides towards her on numb legs.

"Hello," she says. She's holding a peg, and a piece of washing.

"Uh," he looks into the sky. It is dark grey-blue and lumpy with cloud.

Mare looks up too. She's waiting for him to say something.

"I was just going to take a picture."

"Oh," she says. "Who let you in?"

"My friend—"

"God, that's right, you know the owner." Mare looks genuinely regretful. "Shit, Walker, sorry, I just realised. I never thanked you for organising me this flat."

"It's nothing," he says. "Really, Mitchell asked …" He flounders. "It all just worked out."

"No, seriously. It's perfect," she goes on. "I don't know what I would've done without it."

If he asks her out now she'll think he's calling in a favour. Oh God, oh God.

"So, I've missed the moment, anyway," he says, looking up at the darkening sky once more. "I just – I was on my way to soccer."

Soccer. In fact it could be true. Soccer starts at six thirty.

There's a pause.

"Soccer, really?" she says.

"Ja, I play …" He waves his hand in a westerly direction.

"Oh."

"I play on Sunday nights," he says.

"Wow," she says. "Cool."

He smiles. She smiles back at him. She has a beautiful smile. In the half-light. No words will come. He has barely any breath.

"Well, I should let you go," she says.

"Okay." He doesn't move. "Woul—?"

"Wha—?"

"No. Nothing." He can't do it now. Another time. He can ask another time. He rams his hands in his pockets.

"Okay then," she says.

"Right."

"See you around, then," she says. "And thanks again, Walker. Really."

He nods, and then he's off, cutting a brisk diagonal across the dull-silver floor.

*Letter (continues), Mare to Toni*
*Sunday 3 March*

Back again.

I just ran into Walker on the roof. Odd.

There I was, having just rescued my Barely Theres from the gutter, thinking that the roof of Helvetia Court is what I would call, if I were American, "a trip". There's never anyone else up there. I like it actually. Even though I know it's dangerous. There's only one way up and down. You can easily be cornered.

I was thinking about that when suddenly Walker appeared, walking fast across the silver floor. He saw me as soon as he was on the roof but he kept his head down. I stood still, knickers in one hand, peg in the other. He didn't shout hello, or lift an arm, and neither did I. It gave me a chance to look at him. He looks a lot taller when he's not sitting down. Ha ha, I'm hilarious.

Anyway, he was on his way to soccer.

So I finished getting all my dry washing into the basket and walked over to the scoop of the Hillbrow-facing Deco-curve.

The skyline is prickly. Like me.

How you, Toni?

Love
X Mare

*

*Letter, Mare to Mielie*
*Sunday 10 March*

Helvetia Court, table

Dear Mielie

I only just got your letter! I swear I haven't been sulking. I only JUST got it on Friday. Thank you. I can't tell you how it made my heart soar – my heart sore, too – when I swung open the postbox door and saw it there, all neatly addressed and creased at the corners.

Thank you for writing. I'd been feeling like toilet paper dropped in the bath – disgusting image, sorry – all fragile and floaty. I thought it was the move. But it was us, being apart. I'm back on the roll now. Dry, clean sheets, ready for action. Okay, I strung the loo roll metaphor out to annoy you.

Here on the Highveld, summer is resisting autumn. It's so hot, I go most evenings to the Ellis Park pool. Cadet School is over by 4pm. I'm up to a kay and a half.

Sometimes, on an endorphin high afterwards, I allow myself to believe that I have journalistic ability that could extend to hard news, and I should at some point get round to testing that theory.

That's the glamour gig. Best of all? Your name under the masthead: top fold, the front page lead. If you really want your name in lights, double gold is the front page lead scoop. This is a very hard thing. This means getting the story of the day, and no-one else has it. This is the hardest thing in hard news. This is the thing that Pulitzers are made of.

I'm in the deep end here, Mielie. It's exciting and terrifying in equal measure. I know I'm curious and that counts for something. It means I ask more questions. Also, I like the unexpected. I believe in taking risks. And I can write fast, and a lot.

Or maybe I just enjoy immersion. I do like swimming.

But apart from all that, did I mention how much I crave hearing about your life?

Since Cadet School started, mine has settled into surprising predictability.

During the week it looks like this:

Hear alarm.

Go back to sleep.

Wake in panic. Bright sun.

Leap out of bed, put kettle on, get under shower.

Get dressed. Something white, something black, something denim. Failing that, something clean.

Make tea. Eat cornflakes and drink tea while drying hair.

Bus to town. Do homework on bus.

Shorthand.

Coffee with toasted cheese and tomato from canteen.

Class.

Smoke break.

Class.

Venture into searing midday heat for King Pie and Diet Coke. Eat lunch in carpeted, air-conditioned lounge. Try and rise to challenge of interesting conversation.

Class.

Bus.

Home.

Toast with cheese, Hellmans and sliced tomato, eaten while I get into my costume.

Bike.

Pool. Sixty lengths now. 1.5 km, as I said.

Bike. Sometimes in a thunderstorm.

Home.

Instant noodles with frozen peas.

Whisky.

Bed.

Newspapers.

Sleep.

The weekends are different.

Yesterday, when Johnny and I got back from Ellis Park, Mitchell and Fouché were occupying – in princely fashion – the 70s metal loungers at the Westminster Mansions pool.

I call it kidney-shaped. Fouché, I discovered, calls it The Scrotum. He and Mitchell refer to their pool soirées as Resort Time.

Mitchell was drinking Absolut and tonic. Fouché was "on call" for whatever it is that he does. Then Mitchell announced that we were all going to have a Mozambiquan braai. God, the palaver.

I was at the sink in my swimming costume, a T-shirt and nothing else, elbow-deep in squid innards, when this guy called Walker arrived. I don't think I've told you about him, but let's just say he's revered by the self-appointed Westminster Mansions Morality Squad.

When my job was done, I left Mitchell to de-vein the prawns and shot to the spare-room to make myself decent. When I got back there were even more of Mitchell's ancient friends swarming around while Fouché opened bottles of bubbly. I think they all need it to keep themselves awake. I wish they'd just talk about what they did instead of constantly alluding to things. They don't have to be hush-hush anymore.

So there we were, sucking on our prawn heads and marvelling at the succulence of the calamari and the kick of the piri piri, when Mitchell asked me what we were working on at Cadet School and I told him we were putting together the Knock and Drop.

I got quite animated about my column, Browbeat. My favourite bit is called Drive-By Hootings, it's about being whistled and hooted at while walking down the street. And then I got verbal diarrhoea, and told him about my Parktown Prawn story – "Curse of the Middle Class?" – and my story about anti-semitism in the Yeoville Neighbourhood Watch. I knew all the pieces backwards because I'd just written them up, plus we'd been encouraged to use colour so I had metaphors up my sleeve. I admit I went on somewhat, as I am SO prone to do.

At breakfast this morning Fouché suggested I might like to lead his friend Walker astray. Mielie, I have NO DESIRE to do that. And Mitchell said Walker had watched me like a movie.

I thought he was stoned, frankly. Those Struggle heroes often are, in my experience.

More soon!

XX Mare

PS: Listen, Johnny says 34 isn't old. This guy isn't 34, he's more like 74. Did I mention he told us he takes a lunchbox to work? And always orders the same takeaways on the same night every week? And he wears work shirts out at night?

I shudder to think what he wears around the home.

A dressing gown? Slippers?

Is there a covered hot-water bottle?

Postcard, Mielie to Mare<br>Monday 11 March

Newsflash: Mum posed nude for her figure drawing class today.

The model didn't turn up. It's the second time. Can you imagine? It was in the lounge, curtains open to maximise natural light. Mum was under strict orders from Tess never to strip off in front of strangers again. But she did.

Regarding not just the stripping, but the naked draping across one of our kitchen chairs – seen by Tess when she burst into the house after school – our mother is, naturally, unrepentant.

# CHAPTER 9

*Monday 11 March*

Damian is an Australian in London. He fits every contemporary Antipodean stereotype – so much so, you might think he'd mistaken "stereotype" for "instructions".

Here he is, Damian the Australian: short hair, short sleeves whatever the season, short sentences. He's tall and strong, tanned, with good teeth. His hair is blonde. His voice is sometimes embarrassingly loud; he makes no attempt to hide his accent. Damian works, of course, on construction sites. His hobby, it goes almost without saying, is drinking beer. He has many male friends, most of whom look and sound a lot like he does.

Interestingly, Damian has encountered no stereotype for White Australian Male Lover. Perhaps the stereotype-makers assume that men like Damian don't have much sex – that they'd rather pass out on the bed cover every night, bare legs splayed, beer froth in the corners of their mouths. (Which, most unfortunately, is exactly how Toni will find him, any moment now, in their room in the Balham squat, as she returns from yet another day of mindless child-minding in Central London.)

But whatever the reason, Damian has been given no model for his bedroom persona; he's had to make it up. Quite innocently then, he's relied on his instincts. Damian loves women. He adores being naked with them and revels in devoting hours of highly enthusiastic and highly athletic attention to them. In short, Damian is – having had nothing to dissuade him from being so – a sexual genius.

In Damian's mind, the gifts he bestows upon Toni – and her wide-eyed gratitude – are surely nothing out of the ordinary. It makes sense to Damian that men should work hard, and happily, in bed.

Toni, of course, has sense enough not to say things like: "Wow, you're not like the other guys." She knows if she says that, Damian will say, "How come?" and if she replies "Oh, they just bang away at me and then fall asleep," he'll proceed to shorten his lovemaking routine by several hours, and begin to omit the very, very many things that make her endure his dirty fingernails, his faded red briefs, and his hangovers. For Bedroom Damian, Toni has even been willing to live in Balham, and in a squat.

However, in Toni's life, there are times when, as suddenly and effortlessly as a shoal of fish, she changes course. This is about to be one of those occasions.

"Babe!" she calls from the rickety outdoor wooden staircase that ascends to the front door. "Babe, you there?"

The dead silence within the squat suggests that he is not. So in she breaks, again avoiding deadly lacerations from the smashed pane of glass beside the door latch.

In the kitchen, she surveys the dirty dishes. In the sitting room, the overflowing ashtrays and flickering TV. In the bathroom, the laundry sprawled across the peeling plastic floor. And finally, in the bedroom, her boyfriend, lying inert on their bed.

The moment of epiphany comes when he doesn't manage to lift his head off the pillow, or even a simple "Howzit, babe".

*This isn't a life, this is a tip,* she thinks. *And that steaming one-trick pony is my boyfriend …*

She packs her bags and leaves forthwith, in a taxi, in the pouring rain.

Of course the pouring rain.

*

*Postcard, Toni to Mielie*

15-03-1996

Mielie come to London already STOP I have a job STOP Think no further STOP Oysters And Pearls STOP Wimbledon Macbeth auditions imminent STOP Come ON, Lady STOP (blue in face)

*Letter, Toni to Mare and Johnny*
*Monday 18 March*

13h05
Dean Street Post-production
Soho, London

Greetings, twats

One size cannot fit all. Of this I am acutely aware.

I am nevertheless writing to you both simultaneously, as clearly I cannot be expected to spend three hours a day on public transport, plus nine hours working – inhuman – AND write separately to two individuals, living in the same city, on identical topics of note.

Topic 1:

Forgive the office notepaper. By implication: I got a job.

Proper one.

Please alert the in-all-ways-superior Mitchell to this superbly astonishing fact.

Then witness his candid disbelief.

When he enquires further – unable to contain his natural curiosity, having never believed in me ever, all along – do tell him:

Top-drawer post-production house in Soho, darling.

I'll be doing their Traffic.

Topic 2:

London is fine. Laugh a minute. Seriously.

And then of course there's the filth. People don't wash.

Not themselves, not their floors, not one single surface on this incredibly tiny yet equally incredibly densely populated ISLAND that we're all expected to share.

It defies belief.

Oh how incredibly unlike me to do the unattractive bitching thing.

PMA (Positive Mental Attitude) is everything, I know.

So I'm channelling Princess Di, I.E. all we have by way of grace & glamour, and as such without whom life would be devoid of any meaning whatsoever.

Topic 3:

I've broken up with Damian. The one who said he didn't love me and never could, but subsequently recanted.

I am now staying with friends in South Wimbledon and looking for a place of my own. I'd need to share. Anyone interested – I ask with full knowledge of wasting my breath?

WHY the two of you insist on spending the best years of your lives in Joburg is beyond me. They won't last long.

Feel free to disagree, for old times' sake, but I hasten to remind you:

I am always right.

Nevertheless, your choices remain your own.

Topic 4:

Mielie needs to bring Edward to me for closer inspection. The sooner the better, in the best interests of us all.

You see this is exactly what happens when continents divide people – people once close, mind you – over considerably extended periods of time.

They forget key facts.

So let me be absolutely clear on my position:

Mielie might lead by example in many of life's complicated facets, but in the romance department I cannot trust her judgement any further than I could spit.

If I ever spat. Which I often want to but never do.

For obvious reasons.

Look after yourselves in that madhouse and tell Mitchell I say Yo.

With newfound purpose,
Antonia Palmer
(Madam, to you)

"Edward," says Mielie, lying on her back in the mountain grass, both arms above her head, and watching the mist moving fast above them. "Can I ask you something?"

It's early autumn. This high up, on the slopes of Devil's Peak, the clouds can close in any time. It's called the Tablecloth. People can get lost in it.

"You're asking me if you can ask me something? That's funny," Edward says.

"You're funny, you know that?" Mielie says, leaning on one elbow and pushing away the hair that's blowing across her face.

"Funny how?" he says. "Haha or peculiar?"

"Both," she says. "You make me so happy, though."

His hand is underneath the waistband of her jeans, spread across the skin at the base of her spine. He knows it's her favourite place for him to be, afterwards.

They'd known no-one would see them – that the chances of anyone else hiking so high up, on a weekday afternoon, were minimal. Edward, having taken the day off specially, also didn't even care. No one hiking on Table Mountain would know anything about who he was. He barely knew himself. All he knew was that Amelia Ashford had chosen him, and he was powerless to change that, in the present.

"So go on then, ask," he says, in between the kisses Mielie's planting on his eyelids and his lips.

She stops all the kissing then, and looks at him intently.

"What do you think of London?"

"London?" he says. "I don't think of it at all. Except for when you talk about Toni. I try to imagine it then."

There's a pause.

"It seems like quite a harsh place to be."

Mielie sits up now, her arms across her knees. She's looking out over the suburbs, with the massive curve of False Bay in the distance.

"You know she's my best friend, Edward," she says. "And she knows that we're together."

"Are we?" he says, still lying flat on the grass.

"Oh don't be mental," Mielie says. Then she turns to him and peers into his face: "'Don't be comPLETEly mental,' is what Toni would say."

Then: "She wants me to go there and try to act."

"And?" says Edward, after another pause.

"And … I'm thinking about it." Mielie says.

"Okay."

"Is it?" Mielie says. "Okay, I mean? … I mean, I'm not asking you to give me 'the okay'. I mean: how would you feel about going there?"

Again, Edward is quiet. So Mielie continues, chewing on a piece of grass. "See, from when my dad died, it's felt like I've been doing breast-stroke underwater. Just measured and purposeful and intense …"

More wind and silence. The force that is Philip Ashford, dead or alive, is there.

"But now, with the play ending tomorrow and everything, it feels like I'm popping out onto the surface. I'm breathing again, bobbing around. And it all feels deathly calm."

The clouds keep moving swiftly above them. The wind is a classic south-easter.

"Just imagine, Edward," Mielie says. "We'd be free. And away from everyone … The more I think about it, the more I know that's what I really want … And I'm thinking it might not be a bad idea to give it a chance … If you'd come with me. If you wanted to, I mean, and if you could."

"Okay," Edward says. "And I really want what you want, for you."

Mielie turns to look at him again. Her hair's all over the place but she doesn't seem to notice anymore.

'What I want?" she asks. "What about what you want, Edward. Don't you have a dream?"

He sits up. They're shoulder-to-shoulder now. The False Bay view has disappeared. "You're in a ballroom, with ceiling-to-floor French doors, and crystal chandeliers …" he says. "In a red dress – with a very low back – and a glass of champagne in your hand."

"I don't know what you mean," she says.

"There are people all around you," he continues. "You're the flame, they're the moths."

She's looking at him, saying nothing.

"Sorry for the cliché. But it's true," he continues. "You can't help it, Mielie. It's just the way you are."

"Me?" she says. "Are you actually talking about me? Because sorry but I'm not those things …"

"And the music is low-key and sophisticated …"

She looks at him in disbelief.

"And I'll just be standing there. Fool that I am."

Somewhere, waves are crashing, light is falling. But they're up there in the clouds, and there's no sound except their voices and the wind. The light isn't changing.

"We need to get going," Edward says. He's assembling abandoned clothes and day packs. "You're meant for big things, Mielie," he says.

Mielie stays where she is.

"Oh, would your family approve of me, then?"

*

*Saturday 23 March*

Peter Ashford could not be more delighted with himself. He has, without being nagged – without even consulting Fiona! – finalised the transfer of ownership of the Balfour Road house from Philip's estate to his stepmother, Pauline.

It's a lovely, sunny morning. Peter enjoys the drive from town to Woodstock. Turning onto Roodebloem Road off the highway, he takes in the unusually clear view of the bay all the way across to Blouberg.

Fee was right. Woodstock has it all. Pauline loves the mountain. She has it here. It's practically her back garden! She loved the view from Eland. Nothing wrong with the sea view here! Pauline loves a Victorian. She has one here! And of a more manageable size! Peter smiles inside his silent, leather-covered interior.

He parks alongside the cracked pavement, swinging his tyres carefully to avoid a smashed beer bottle.

Inside the house, Peter presents the paper file with a flourish. Pauline doesn't pick it up. She leaves it on the corner of the kitchen table.

"I need to go now," is what she says to Peter. "I have to work."

*Letter, Mare to Mielie*
*Monday 25 March*

Helvetia Court, table

Dear Mielie,

It's Monday evening in Yeoville. There's a sunset sky, cars are zooting around, lots of people are on the streets winding down. I've got my balcony doors open, I'm sitting in the lounge, at a table – another hand-me-down from Mitchell. It's one of my favourite spots in the flat, and outside it's beautiful.

Inside, I've been panicking about money. A proper, free-fall, clawing-at-the-walls panic. I've been at Cadet School for just over a month, see. Today I got my first full pay cheque. It's nothing. No, I don't mean "it's nothing". I mean it's NOTHING. Nearly a third of my salary goes to tax, UIF and goodness knows what. After deductions and rent there isn't enough. Serious, Mielie, there just isn't enough.

But the good news is the phone. I took the advice of my classmates and told Telkom I'm a journalist for Independent Newspapers and need to be contactable at all hours. I've been phoning home and chatting to Mum – rather a lot, as you probably know.

How rude of me. I didn't even excuse myself. But THE PHONE RANG. It's so Pavlovian. The split-second it rings I stiffen, charge and lunge with the eagerness of a drowning person for a lifeline. I'm getting an answering machine as soon as I can, if only as a psycho-social experiment. I think a flashing red light when I come home might actually make me drool.

Anyway, it was a wrong number. And then I got distracted by the TV and a bottle of Three Ships.

The reason I was writing in the first place is that I wanted to tell you about Friday night.

Johnny took us all to his favourite neighbourhood eatery. He's devoted to it. "Trattoria", it's called. A trattoria it is not. I'd call it "A Cafeteria Without the Trays". I suspect that neither the categorisation nor the name matter to Johnny. I suspect his devotion stems from the restaurant's motto, writ large upon the wall: Our Food (new line) Our Prices (new line) To Die For.

The tablecloths are stained, the staff are surly, and it's in a dark bit of Jeppe Street.

Mitchell drinks a tremendous amount but remains languidly drunk, like Sebastian in Brideshead Revisited. He requested a bottle of Alto Rouge. He got a carafe of box wine. Then he cast his eye over the menu. "Oh look," he said. "Our old friend Chicken a la King." He asked for a risotto – "It does call itself an Italian restaurant." He got a pale salad that was the culinary equivalent of a hard stare.

Mitchell despairs of me and Johnny and what he calls our nursery tastes. I suspect his taste has been shaped by the family hotel buffets. He can't abide anything that might have been in a bain-marie.

Johnny taunts him by drinking Black Label from the neck of a quart bottle. He drinks Wimpy coffee and prefers his fillet medium – "You mean ruined."

After dinner, Mitchell informed me that I'm going to Walker's on Easter Monday for a picnic. "He asked me to invite you, specifically."

Naturally this set off Fouché, Mitchell's camp, gossipy friend. Every time I see him he says something nudge-nudge to me about Walker. "Did you know Walker lives on a huge property in Parktown?" (Nudge, nudge.) "Did you know Walker was one of the first conscientious objectors?" (Nudge, nudge.) "Did you know he speaks Xhosa? ... Did you know blah blah blah?"

Hey Fouché, did I want to know any of that? No.

Anyway, he said he found it "suspicious" that Walker mentioned me by name.

I've just seen the time so should probably stop now. Shorthand tomorrow and all that.

Miss you
XX Mare

PS: Guess: "Don't go changin'."
Billy Joel, as if you didn't know.

PPS: My theory on Walker inviting me to the picnic: He's in the closet. He's in love with Mitchell, has been since the 80s, will do anything to stay close to him. He's trying to curry favour with Johnny – and me, by extension.

# CHAPTER 10

*Saturday 30 March*

Just over a week after agreeing to attend Tom Walker's picnic, Marigold Ashford falls in love.

She falls off her bike first.

It's raining – probably the last Highveld thunderstorm of the year. From his vintage black Mercedes, a young man sees her flicking to turn into Helvetia Court. He sees her startled by a hooter, sees her wobble as she turns into the driveway, sees the bike slip beneath her, and then the girl – and the bike – skidding across tar.

She doesn't see him until he's standing over her. The rain is bucketing down. There's the sound of that, the engine still running and petrol sloshing in the tank.

"I can't get it off me," she tells him.

He says nothing. Instead, he switches off the engine, pockets the keys, lifts the bike and puts it on its stand. Then he drops to his haunches, his face over hers. In that moment, he looks a bit like George Michael.

She gets up on her elbows, reluctant to look at her knee. "Bad day for tights-not-jeans," she says.

"Can you stand up?" he asks.

She gets into a seated position and tries to, but can't. "Hang on," she says, all shaky. Next, she rotates her right leg inwards, to examine a large hole in the stocking on the outside of her knee. It reminds her of the one in her school tights when she rode into a stationary minibus taxi on the way to an exam. Inside the hole is what Tess would call "a classic roastie".

"Ow," he says.

His leather jacket is zipped against the rain, but his Levi's – stretched over his thighs – are sopping.

"It's not that bad," she says. "Hooray for biker boots, hey?"

In fact, when Mare had put on her too-small boots that morning, she'd given no thought to protecting the outside of her ankle bone from sliding on tar with the full weight of a motorbike on top of it. She only thought they'd look nice with her empire-line dress and black opaques.

His hands reach out to her chin. She sees rain in his eyelashes, drops of water running down his neck.

"It's okay," he says, unfastening her helmet and easing it off gently. He's smiling, brushing raindrops from his lips with his hand. "There," he says, blinking and touching her hair. "Now let's get you out of the rain."

He picks Mare up and carries her to Helvetia Court's security gate in his arms. The keys are still in his jacket pocket – she pushes her hand into his belly area and then fishes through the bunch to find the right one.

In the lift, he inclines his head towards the buttons. "Could you?" Harry Casual.

She doesn't want to look in the mirror – doesn't want to be caught looking – but she does anyway. And he does catch her.

At the door of the flat, she turns the key, her other arm gripped tightly around his neck to stop herself from slipping.

He carries her across the threshold. "Just married," he laughs. "What's your name, by the way?"

"Oh," she says. "It's Marigold."

"Marigold? Pronounced Marry-gold? God! Marry me, Marry-gold!" He kicks the door shut. "But let me put you down first."

Once inside Mare's flat, and with the Yale click-locked, he fishes around in the bathroom cabinet for some Panado. She intrigues him. She lives alone, it seems. She made the minimum of fuss about her injury, yet she's trusting and open. It's a nice combo. In his experience, tough girls are stand-offish and the sweet ones usually prone to neediness.

He looks at himself in the cabinet mirror, flicks the towel off the rail and rubs his head. Then he arranges his hair carefully, takes off his jacket and checks his teeth.

In the hallway, he encounters her in a dry T-shirt and tracksuit pants.

"Oh, hello. She walks," he says. "I was on my way to look for some whisky."

"Excellent," she says. "Because I have some in the kitchen. Meet you in the lounge."

*Lord, he's handsome,* she thinks. *Olive skin, full mouth, dark eyes, sandy hair.*

In the lounge, he hands her a glass of whisky and two Panados. "Marigold, would you mind terribly if I smoked?"

"Course you can. I'll have one too, if you'll pass my bag … Thank you. And thank you, you know. For helping me."

He lights her cigarette.

"I'm sorry, this is awkward, but I don't know your name," she says.

He looks up from the table where he's rolling himself a cigarette. "It's Wilkinson. Nick Wilkinson, same as my dad," he twinkles. "But no-one calls me that. No-one calls you by your first name at school, so it turns out I'm just Will."

Whiskies finished, Will fetches the bottle from the kitchen. Then he speaks about "the decisive moment" of Henri Cartier Bresson, the photographer Mare likes, and Ansel Adams.

*This is such a coincidence,* she thinks. *Ansel Adams took the photo of the landscape on my fridge.*

They speak about Yeoville and books and music. She tells him she studied art. They discover they both loved portraiture. She also tells him about her thing for dead trees.

"Dead trees?"

"I know. It's mad. I love them. I brake for dead trees," she says. "They're the best thing to draw. The bark looks like charcoal shading – is charcoal, in fact – and like dried mud raked by a huge comb."

"You're nuts, you know that." He looks at her with smiling eyes.

"I know."

Then he makes her give him five Likes and Dislikes, off the top of her head.

"Okay, Likes?" she says, unable to resist. "That would be rock, folk, soul – especially Otis Redding – the colour black, and the sea … Dislikes? Cosmetics, high heels, pastel colours, bath candles."

"That's only four Dislikes," he says.

"Okay. Number five," deep breath. "Being alone."

"Me too," Will says.

*Letter, Mare to Mielie*
*Sunday 31 March*

Helvetia Court, bed

Mielie, it's happened! I'm in love! It's CRAZY!

Maybe I'll speak to you before you get this but I'm so vividly aware of every moment of my life right now – you know what's going to happen, don't you? Prepare for an avalanche of words.

Oh where is Toni Palmer when you need her? Toni! He Looks Like GEORGE MICHAEL!!!!

I swear. I fell off my bike in the rain – I actually skidded across the tar with it on top of my leg – and who should rescue me but a god. He even CARRIED me up to my flat because it was too sore to walk.

Sorry, Mielie, Toni's asking me if he was gentleman enough to tuck my dress under his legs-carrying arm … Toni, thank you for that. I wondered if he would, but didn't want to interrupt his chivalry to say: "Em, Sir. Would you mind not letting my dress hang like that. Just that my friend Toni Palmer's friend once got very drunk at an Orientation Week party and was carried past several university residences – past parties being held outside – by two gallant, and themselves drunk, young men who had not neatly tucked up her dress and who, therefore, most effectively flashed her g-string to the whole of first year."

His name is Will. Omigod. I can't believe this feeling, Mielie.

We were talking in my flat afterwards, having some whisky and cigarettes, and I couldn't keep still. I was on the couch with my leg up, and he was on one of the Louis what-what chairs. The way he licked a cigarette paper, or the way his lips left the glass, made my insides lurch like when the Big Wheel starts up again. The cogs grind, it rocks you up there in the night sky and you lift, slowly, higher.

Then I told him I hated being alone, and he said "Me too", and it was like having Space Dust in my veins. You know those sweet lumps you pour on your tongue and they pop against the roof of your mouth like mini fireworks? It felt alien and trippy and the noise was quite loud, in an airy way, inside my ears.

We finished all the whisky and the cigarettes. He said he'd pop out to Rockey Street and get me more. But I fell asleep on the couch. When I woke up hours later he wasn't there. I'd given him the keys but he must have decided not to disturb me.

He slipped a note under the door, though. Written on the back of an autobank slip:

"So long, Marigold ..."

And under that there was an X.

I haven't loved an X more since the '94 elections.

Naturally, the first thing I did was to hobble over to find my Leonard Cohen record. The words of "So Long Marianne" were on the sleeve, thank goodness.

He can't have meant goodbye. Do you think he was trying to say something else?

There's: "You left when I told you I was curious / I never said that I was brave ..."

Or maybe it's the big kicker: "I'm standing on a ledge / And your fine spider web / Is fastening my ankle to a stone."

I wish you were here and we could unpack it all together.

X Mare

PS: Another line is "Oh, you are really such a pretty one / I see you've gone and changed your name again."
I haven't changed my name, though. I feel different, but I'm still Marigold.

*

*Letter (continues), Mare to Mielie*
*Monday 1 April*

I'm back.

Today I left for work as usual. At lunchtime I pushed through the turnstiles at Independent Newspapers, security tag around my neck, sights set on a pepper-steak King Pie and a diet Coke (me and my habits, I'm like Mitchell's friend Walker).

I was in a dwaal. All morning long I'd been thinking about Will. More than thinking about him. My heart was thumping against my ribs, straining. It was like my body was being pulled by an invisible leash. I had to fight against it to stay in my seat in class, stay in the lounge at teatime, resist the urge to run at the canteen windows and peer down all the streets on the off-chance of seeing someone who looked like him, just for a fraction of the thrill.

When I looked up from the turnstiles I saw him.

He had one elbow on the security desk, a messenger bag across his chest. He was smiling at me. I was drawn across the lobby by a magnetic force. I have no memory of my feet moving, just his smile getting closer.

"Hello, Girl Reporter," he said.

"Hello, Mister," I beamed.

He said he knew a good place for noodles. It's called the Yung Chen Noodle Den, at the far end of Chinatown.

He poured us Chinese tea. He dropped berry-red chilli sauce into my noodle soup. He bought me a sweet dumpling for pudding. He gave me a mix tape, after he paid the bill.

"What's this for?"

"You were hurt. You need cheering up."

"I don't feel hurt. I feel happy."

"Well then, it's a present to celebrate."

"Thank you."

"It's a pleasure. And actually, I kind of did it for myself." He put his chin in his hand, leaned forward a fraction, looked down, picked up a mint. "I can't stop thinking about you. I needed something to do."

Mielie, sorry for the word-for-word but obviously I've memorised everything he's ever said to me. I feel like I'm in the middle of a miracle. That's all I can call it. It's a miracle because it's my whole life's dream, my dream forever, come true.

Anyway, I glanced at the tape. Seeing his handwriting was gift enough. Isn't that insane! If the whole thing had been in another language, it would still have been a treasure to me: his writing, on a page, for me.

I scanned the song list: Nothing Compares to U, My Baby Just Cares for Me, You Do Something to Me, So Long, Marianne … My face was burning up, so I blurted out something to break the tension, something like: "Oh, a Sinatra version!" As if that was remotely relevant to what was going on between us.

He seized the lifeline and announced that his job was writing CD reviews. "So we're both writers!"

After that I probably bellowed something about the time, because next thing I was clattering my chair and bumping into people on the way out. We walked back mostly in silence. When we got to the last block on Sauer Street, he took my hand. I stopped and faced him. I didn't want to be walking hand-in-hand outside work.

"That was lovely," I said.

"You're lovely."

"No, you."

"Hey, d'you wanna go for sushi after work?"

"I'd love to." Big grins. He makes me so loopy words just tumble out of my mouth. "I've nothing else on."

"Shall I come at five?"

"Perfect!" (Pause for more grinning.) "Thank you for the tape."

"Pleasure, ma'am." (Staring at each other, grins dropped now, heat building up again.) "You should go."

"I know."

"So, go."

"You go."

"I don't want to."

"Me neither."

"I'll see you later, Beautiful."

And that shut me up. I couldn't do anything but nod. I might have curtsied, who knows. I have no memory of anything except floating up into the air, limbs swaying, sun on my skin, love ballooning in my heart.

Part of me is nervous. It's not hard to see there's an imbalance. He is so extraordinary in every way. Your basic great-catch template. He's intelligent, well-read, private school-educated, suave, massively good-looking, rich, very sensitive, very funny. Home run, Marigold? Right? But I feel, uh, a bit intimidated maybe?

Dammit, I have to go. Again! He'll be here in 15 minutes!

I'll post this on the way. It might even reach you before we manage to speak to each other on the phone.

XXX Mare

Nick Wilkinson Junior is sitting on the couch in his Illovo flat. It's mid-morning and he's just made himself an espresso. Mare's at work. It's true that he can't stop thinking about her. It's like that song on the mix tape he made her: she really does "do something" to him.

Will stands up. He wants to go somewhere, but there's nowhere to go. Usually at this time of day he'd be shopping, or at a coffee shop. He'd be with one of his friends from school, or a girl.

He could go for a run. At school, Will won the 800 metres three years in a row. He loved it – not just the sound of his name being shouted from the stands, but the freedom of it. He always ran in an old white vest and worn rugby shorts, no socks. It annoyed his parents and puzzled his mates. Other boys had branded running shoes, breathable running kit. Will liked to demonstrate, year after year, that he could outrun all of them without Nike or Reebok. When the gun went off, he felt like an animal, a big wild cat or even a buck. Natural and alone.

Will always ran loosely for the first lap, air against his chest, a loping stride. The joy of it made him want to smile as he ran. He wants to smile now. The second lap was harder, but even more pleasurable. He'd pick up the pace, arms tighter. His face would get hotter, blood in his temples. His breath was hot, eyes fixed. In the end sprint, the anger kicked in. He would run past his rich, superior father and his style-obsessed mother. He would feel the old cotton of his vest and the rubbing of his canvas takkies and he'd hear, *I don't need you, I don't want you. I hate you! This is my life, my life. My life!* He liked to break the tape on "life!"

Will hasn't been for a run in the open air for years. It's dangerous, and dirty. He drives everywhere, everyone does.

If he went to the gym now, though, he might run into a connection, and he doesn't want to see anyone he knows. He only wants to see Mare.

She's like that running vest, the canvas takkies. Nothing expensive, nothing fancy, but plain and light – just what she is. She makes him feel the joy of the loping run, the heat of the second lap and the rebel rage of the sprint. There's something about her that's the crowd, too. She's cheering for him as he runs, in his unbranded kit, all alone.

Mare is the only person in his life who doesn't know his Joburg set – know him as part of that crowd, as his father's son, his mother's son, as old boy of his school.

It wasn't like that when he met her. He'd just thought she was hot – or hot enough – and he was curious to get up close to an arty, lefty chick. One thing Will can say for himself, he can spot a trend, and sticking to your cultural enclave is no longer fashionable. No, Will's always been ahead of the trend, and things are changing.

He didn't expect to really like her. Then again, you wouldn't expect the most popular guy in school to find his only joy in sweating around the track.

Now, on the couch, he's noticing he doesn't have that sense of peace he usually has after what he and his friends call "notching". Because he notched her nicely, last night. Shouldn't feel any need to go back, he did his work and got his reward.

It started with him wanting her, urgently. Having sushi with her on Monday night, smoothing a paper serviette over her lap, had been one of the biggest turn-ons of his life. But he knew he had to play the romantic game. He'd had to pace himself – more like a 1500 than an 800 metres.

Luckily, when he'd pulled into the circular drive, she'd bolted from the car. Tripped over the front steps.

He'd spent Tuesday in a state of pacing frustration. He knew he wouldn't be able to wait until the end of the week.

Wednesday, he'd waited for her at the bus stop outside Helvetia Court. Swept her off for a cocktail. He spoke to her about *The Great Gatsby* all the way down Jan Smuts Avenue. When they got to Rosebank he said, "Right, Long Island Teas. I know the place. Picasso's."

While they were waiting for their order at the bar – and because they couldn't talk above the noise – Will followed Mare's eye to a Cubist-y mural. She made him see his life differently, this girl.

"Sorry," he said when they'd found a table, "I suppose this isn't a place to impress a fine art graduate."

She smiled and his blood pumped. She'd made him wait in her flat while she'd put on a dress, and flip-flops. He got her talking about her painting. She told him about school in Cape Town, about her friends, her family.

When Mare went to the ladies', Will's eyes strayed to a man outside, holding a small dog. As the man fussed with the dog's ears and mumbled endearments, Will remembered Patty. He'd adored her. She wasn't allowed on the furniture, but Will would lie on the carpet with her, nuzzling. He cuddled her on the pool loungers, and told her all his primary-school secrets. When she died, all Will could think about was how he could feel his heart beating when he held her, and how he couldn't hear his heart anymore.

"I feel like celebrating," Will said, when they were back in her flat. He meant it. He felt happy.

"I know," she said.

"Shall we have some champagne?"

"Uh, it's not something I normally have lurking in the fridge," she said.

"Check the freezer, would you?"

Then she stood in the doorway holding up the cold bottle with a quizzical grin. He'd left it there earlier.

While he was peeling the foil off the bottle, he said: "Hey, shall we listen to the mix tape?"

She nodded.

She gave her assent to everything after that.

*

*Letter, Johnny to Mielie*
*Saturday 6 April*

Mielie,

My pet.

Greetings,

Apologies.

I know.

I KNOW.

I'm sorry.

It's been months. I am your sister's keeper and what have I submitted? Sweet Fanny Adams. Even now, I'm near paralysed with remorse.

The thing is, I'm spoilt. Mare reads me the letters she gets. Often while I'm driving. Suddenly she'll grab, from the bum pocket of her jeans, a fold of onionskin papers covered in your handwriting, or Toni's.

I'm sure, by the time you get this from me, that news of Wonderful Willy will already have shot down the grapevine like a charge down a lightning rod. He is a god, I don't deny it. He is the poster boy for poster boys. As Fouché says: "Jissie maar hy's fokken MOOI!"

From what he, Mitchell and I could make out, there's a six pack under the man's white T-shirt, and a pair of rock-hard spanspeks at the rear. He has a MAG-nificent arse. M tells me he doesn't own a swimming costume, he swims in his undies, or nothing. This quote travelled rather quickly around our house.

The winter in Joburg is long and difficult, I'm told. I suspect Mitchell and I will get through it by clinging to the hope that one day – in early spring, perhaps – Will shall be persuaded to take a dip in the pool, no costume required. He may opt for undies OR nothing. Either way. We'll endeavour to keep it down to a scream.

Last night, when we met him, was okay. What I mean is, he didn't blow me away.

After we'd met, and once Mitchell, Fouché and I had recovered our senses and offered him an orgy – I mean drink – one found oneself somewhat underwhelmed. The three of us are apt to forgive a great deal in the presence of a brass-hard bottom and enormous member. We're guessing – you may call it fantasising – but we feel there is evidence of extra-large bulginess in the fly area.

I digress. He's perfectly charming, well brought-up. His social manner has something of the chameleon. He tried to be a bit gay, early on. I didn't find it annoying, exactly, not tiresome either, just a little eager. I was happy to move on. After all, it was quite sweet – maybe – if he was trying to impress us because we are Mare's friends. Look, some may have found it condescending. All right, enough. Suffice to say: it's the lesser of two evils.

At dinner I found myself dumbstruck. He commandeered your sister, sitting close, whispering, giggling. He kept saying "you must try this" and giving her forkfuls of food. They were served the same food. How did she miss that? Mare is many things – impulsive, impatient, self-involved – but she is bright. And bold. In this home we call her The Bold and the Beautiful. With a fierce, huge heart. I couldn't stand seeing her opening her mouth to be fed like a baby bird.

I'm not a gossip but I am thorough. I've been doing my homework and having a think. Normally I wouldn't bother with other people's lives. Let them make their own mistakes, I say. I have a badly-behaved, veteran gay and his pack of unruly friends to deal with. To say nothing of my tin can car and a boss who treats me like a child.

Digressing, again! My research reveals that my and Mare's perspectives on Will differ in several key areas.

In NGO-speak, then – in no particular order – here are some of our points of divergence.

1. The keys for the flat
On the evening of the day they met, he goes to Rockey Street for emergency fags and liquor, and POCKETS THE KEYS. Does Mare understand that keys can be copied? Handing over your house keys is what we in Johannesburg call "a security breach".

2. Picasso's
He took her there soon after they met. A moment please, while I choose my words carefully in this regard. Fake. Pretentious. Plastic. Moneyed Joburg sucking at the teat of imported mall culture. If that's what Mare wants, she should move to Wyoming and vote Republican.

3. The show bed
Yes. There is a show bed involved in their early courtship. Will took Mare to the movies at Rosebank Mall. Adjacent to the movie house, located at the bottom of an escalator, there is a furniture shop. As your sister recounts the incident, her new boyfriend pulled her onto the abovementioned show bed and kissed her in front of the moviegoers.

Don't for a moment imagine a swift peck. Apparently they lay there, smooching and giggling, until A SECURITY GUARD advised them upright, She found this to be hilarious.

Fuck me. I don't think so. She's been doing well at work, starting to make a name. Would she have been rolling around in public if her Cadet School class was watching?

4. The wine-red velvet mini-dress

Will bought your sister a wine-red velvet mini-dress. She wore it last night. General vibe? Carnaby Street. It looks damn fine on her, I'll give him that. But he DRESSES her now? What is she, a handbag chihuahua?

Mitchell tells me I'm jealous. I am. This is my best friend. I've been trying to look after her. And now she's shaking me off like our friendship means nothing, like she was just hanging out with me waiting for something better.

It's like she's forgotten I exist. On this point I am not exaggerating. By her own admission: "Oh, Johnny! I forgot I could phone you, when I fell off my bike!" At the time, to make light of it, I told her she was "terrible, Muriel" – but she really is, and unrepentantly so.

I know that falling in love makes fools of us all. Of course. What worries me is how ready she is to be molded. I've known her for close to a decade. Is this really what she's always wanted? He has a proprietal air, Mielie. I don't like it.

Aargh! Listen to me! I sound like someone's mother! I'm going to do some gardening, work off a little steam, figure out what I'm trying to say.

I'm back.

My brinjals are coming along beautifully. I told them, "You guys …" – they like it when I say that nasally – "… You guys are as big as butternuts!" They glowed with pride.

I realised I don't need to figure out what I'm trying to say. I have actually said it.

We're going for an Easter Monday picnic at the place where Walker rents a cottage. Has Mare told you about our "ancient" friend Walker? She can be such a jock. A classic peak-of-powers ageist. Like, I'm a glorious specimen of youth, why is everyone else so hideous?

Walker is not hideous. He's rather beautiful. He has thoughtful eyes. He thinks before he speaks. I find his depth alluring. I think his depth is the very thing that Mare finds unnerving.

I'm not interested in match-making M and W, by the way. I think Walker might actually be a bit of a stretch for our Mare, even if she didn't find him physically repulsive. He's a serious guy. Personally, I'm interested in his principles – and his Struggle heroics, if I'm perfectly honest. Mitchell tells me he was a firebrand in his youth, proud and brave like the proverbial young lion.

What does one wear to a picnic? I'm not sure I can risk shorts.

Love and gils,
Your Dear Johnny

PS: Who said: "I am the horse that ought not to be flogged"?
Answer: Ray Phiri

# CHAPTER 11

*Letter, Mare to Mielie*
*Monday 8 April*

Helvetia Court, lounge

Darling Mielie,

You probably haven't got my last letter yet, what with Easter and all. But you will have got it by the time you get this one, so you already know about Will.

Because I know you will demand the details: it's hard to describe, what's happened to me since I met him. In every minute since we've been together, I've found him … how can I say this properly … er … the polite way might be "blindingly desirable".

He stares at me a lot. He strokes my cheek. He smiles at me with his hazel eyes and his beautiful lips. We have sex about a hundred times a day.

Confession: I gave him a poem. Yip, in week one. I did. Because I love him. And because I write poems. And because I have no money.

Mielie, you never write. Are you alright?

You'll notice I opted for alright instead of all right. Don't you hate how our English teachers acted so anti-American? You'd think they served in Her Majesty's Forces, the way they carried on. Who did they think they were? They weren't Brits, anyway. Just white South Africans who grew up in the sun, at a geographical remove of a million miles – er, kilometres – from the place they called "home".

I can hardly talk, I suppose. I like Jane Austen as much as the next girl.

But ARE you okay?

At least I didn't write OK. I suppose I should have some gratitude for our teachers – despite the fact that not one of them managed to teach me what a gerund is, nor how to not split an infinitive.

When you start splitting infinitives you can't stop. It's like split ends. You have to trim above the split or the hair will just keep splitting. I like the word splitting. I imagine a woman in a bar in the American South, chin in hand, saying "I don't know, honey, he just keeps splitting". Like, he keeps leaving and staying at the same time.

But today is a day I could learn what a gerund is. Why? Because we left the picnic early, so I have time. I'm sitting here at my flat. Will's gone to the shops to "relax". Pity the tills, I say.

Will made out like he had a headache, but in the car on the way back he told me the real reason why we had to go. He finds Walker boring – as do I – and he doesn't see why everyone rates him so highly – neither do I. We both find his famous silence and secrecy outdated. It's not like he's still being pursued by the security forces or anything.

But shame, Walker did look quite upset when we left. He rents the main house on some historic property. It's owned by the university. We all walked to see the chapel before lunch. It's a lovely chapel. He was showing me the big stained-glass window when – oh! Will just phoned. He's on his way home.

Love you.
XX Mare

PS: It's finally autumn here. Colder, bleaker, drier. There are no palettes of gold and red and russet down the avenues. It's not like Cape Town. Here there's no chilly afternoon shadow, no damp roads in the morning. It's still hot in the day, but the nights are dry-cold. Vaseline has been purchased from Checkers (for lips) and all remaining tights checked for ladders.
I like it. It suits my mood. I feel clear, sharp.
I feel like finally there's a bright light shining on my life.

Mitchell Palmer and Johnny Barton are lying in bed together in the evening light. Both men are smiling.

Mitchell breaks the silence: "Well, I wouldn't have gone to Walker's picnic at all if I'd known you'd had *that* up your sleeve."

"Hm, thank you." Johnny says. He raises his eyebrows suggestively. "I'm glad we went, though. Imagine if we hadn't been there, when Mare and Will left."

Mitchell puts his head on Johnny's bare chest. "Christ. So fucking rude."

Johnny puts his hand on Mitchell's head. "Outrageous. Did you see Will in the chapel? Just sitting in a pew adjusting the turn-up of his jeans. Ignored everything Walker said. Then taking Mare into the bushes on the way back to the house. And they turn up half an hour later, red in the face with scratched legs. 'We just went for a walk'. Ja, right. And then Will has a headache. Just as Walker brings the last salad to the table. And they must go, immediately. *I* almost punched Will's lights out. I don't know how Walker restrained himself."

"I know," Mitchell said. "But he looked more heartbroken than angry. Shame, sometimes it looks like it's taking all his energy just to hold the pieces together."

"Not like you, talking about hearts."

"Look what you've done to me." Mitchell raises his face. "Shall we have a beer? In bed."

Five minutes later, they clink bottle necks.

"It goes back to Jane." Mitchell takes a swig of his beer.

Johnny puts his bottle on the bedside table. "Walker's first girlfriend, the big love of his life?"

"Coaster please, and yes. How did you figure that out?"

"I might be a little nosy."

"Yes, well, she died. Did you know that?" Mitchell says. He holds his chin up, staring out from the headboard.

"God, that's terrible."

"It was. He felt responsible. He's been heartbroken for years." Mitchell turns to face Johnny in bed. "The thing is, I've known Walker since I was a teenager, literally. In all that time, I've never seen a sign of romantic inclination. No interest, no attraction to anyone."

"Right."

"He's been in mourning, basically. Then you introduce him to that maniac friend of yours, Marigold – sorry, darling – and he lights up like a Christmas tree. Relatively speaking, of course."

"Okay," Johnny says. He turns to face Mitchell. "But what's wrong with that?"

"Are you serious? Walker lost out. She's with Will. He got excited about someone for the first time in a decade and he lost out to a pretty boy."

"Of course. Yes. So what should we do?"

"Look, this picnic was a train wreck. Walker invited Mare before she got together with Will. It was part of his 'plan'. But I think that from now on we should keep them apart. I don't want to see that look on Walker's face again for a while."

"I agree. Until things calm down."

Mitchell swings his legs over the bed. "Yes. Although, personally, I couldn't be happier that Mare is with Will. If Walker had propositioned her she would have rejected him – because she can't see a good thing if it drops out of the sky onto the roof of her building – or she would've strung him along and crushed the life out of him entirely."

"Harsh," says Johnny, getting out of bed himself.

"But true." Mitchell knots his dressing gown decisively. "Your friend has the emotional maturity of a prepubescent."

*

*Letter, Mielie to Mare*
*Tuesday 9 April*

Mare! How is your poor leg? My blood literally ran cold, just reading about it. The rain, and the tar, and the root-canal rawness of it all. You had to be so brave.

And then Will.

"Well," as Mum would say, "who am I to have an opinion?" – swiftly followed by THE opinion – but the phrase "head-on collision" springs to mind. Because there you are, innocently riding along on your bike in the rain, then your life changes in a split second – and you, my darling, will never be the same, I fear.

I'm sorry, because I know this is probably not the response you'd like. But I can't pretend – and I never will, with you – so please trust me when I say that everything I think about this situation is only because I cherish you. Please try not to take offence.

When I think of how vulnerable you were, barely able to move, let alone walk, in the company of a total stranger, while no one else on earth even knew that you'd hurt yourself – badly – and then you go and let him in, straight through the front bloody door …

I mean, I get the whole meeting of minds and the mutual combustion of acknowledged loneliness … but Mare, here's another thing: You don't know the man from a bar of soap. Like, yes, cool, good manners and even better looks, but where's, you know, the letter of reference? How can you be sure he's not weird?

I know you're not one to shy away from quantum leaps into the unknown, even on an ordinary day, but I just wonder: Are you testing your limits? Or is it perhaps danger that you crave?

And how is work, dare I ask? You didn't move to fall in love, you know. You moved to grow your dreams. You owe that to yourself. Because you're gifted. But without the discipline part, well, that's all it is: a gift – unshaped, unhoned, undirected. Please do remember that.

Love
Mielie

PS: Is it possible to just not hurl yourself headlong into the deep end, please Mare? I can't look after you from so far away.

*Letter, Tess to Mare*
*Wednesday 10 April*

Balfour Road

Dear Mare,

Mielie's never here. Edward, Edward, blah blah.

She says you've got a boyfriend. Care to share?

I'm going away for the weekend with Mira's family. The condition is that I stop swearing. I'm sick to the back fuck teeth of not swearing. There's a swearing jar in the kitchen so I have to put in 50c if I swear and Mom hears. She's told Mira's parents to tell her if I swear. Fuck that for a ball of shit, ha ha! Just joking.

When are you coming home?

Check you,
T. Ashford (signed)

*

*Letter, Mare to Mielie*
*Wednesday 17 April*

Helvetia Court, bed

Hi Mielie

Thanks for your letter. Containing no details of your romance with Edward. Thanks though. Really. Now you think I'm being sarcastic. I'm not. If I was doing this on a computer I could delete all that. I mean it, though. In a letter from you, even a tirade would be a pleasure to read, gloomy rehashes a delight.

On the subject of Will, I understand I've been guilty of some risk-taking behaviour, but I don't think I crave danger, or test limits for the sake of it. Not particularly.

I honestly don't know, Mielie, what else I could have done. I literally have no idea how I would have got upstairs, after I fell off my bike, if it hadn't been for Will.

Do you know he put my bike in the garage for me, when it got dark? Was it reckless of me, to entrust him with all my keys and my one significant possession? Or should I have left it outside to get stolen? Okay, I should've phoned Johnny. Okay, I admit, I didn't think much at all. I liked falling in love with Will that evening of Saturday the 30th of March, date never to be forgotten. I wanted to. Is that so bad?

Want to know what I really think? I think that adventure, risk, passion – falling in love with a handsome stranger in this case – following your heart, basically, is what life is all about. I live for opportunities to follow my heart. Everything else is filling time, the straight and narrow. I live for the twists and bends, the turns in the road.

Thank you for advising caution, but there's no point pretending I don't love him. Do I trust him? I dunno, do I trust my heart? It's like asking if I trust my feet to walk. I suppose so, there's no separation. I love him, I trust him, there's no question of whether I should. I do.

And it doesn't stop me loving you. I hope you know that.

On that very clear and eloquent note,
XX Mare

*

*Friday 19 April*

On Friday evenings, Cape Town International Departures heaves with the SAA-to-London check-in.

In the weeks that have passed since she first mentioned London, Edward and Mielie had been over it all many times. Their future. Their careers. He's tried hard to explain that the strongest pull in his life, for as long as he can remember, has always been what other people want for him: to be a high-flying architect.

"But what about what you want, Edward?" Mielie asked him again, and again he didn't answer directly. He said he just wasn't ready to leave with her right then. But that the time would come, most likely.

On the drive to the airport, they were quiet in the car.

So, landside of Security now, there are things Edward still needs to say. Whatever else is going to happen to them from now on – and neither of them really know what that will be – there's one thing he does know: this evening, when he lets Amelia Ashford slip through his fingers and into the big wide world, it needs to be a proper goodbye.

He holds her close – one arm crooked around her neck – and breathes heavily into the side of her head.

"You okay, Edward?" she asks him.

He doesn't answer at first. He hasn't imagined it would be quite this difficult to speak, when the time came. "Mielie," he manages. "There's so much, really. But the main thing is …"

He doesn't say: *I really don't want you to go.*

Instead, he says: "The main thing. Is that I can't ask you to give up your dream."

"But you are my dream," Mielie says. "And I won't give you up."

He doesn't say: *For me there's only you, too.*

"Because I'm not enough," he continues, "and I never will be, to ever make up for what you'd miss out on, is why."

"But you'll come soon, like you said you would?" Mielie whispers into his ear.

Her temple feels him nodding. "Promise?" she says. "Please."

He steps back, both hands on her shoulders, looks into her eyes and says: "I will."

Over the tannoy system, they're calling. For the last time. And would passenger Amelia Ashford kindly make her way to exit C13 immediately, as she was now holding up the flight.

"Okay-last-touch," he pinches her lightly on the arm and smiles. "Better go now, then. Or never."

Through Security, she slings her daypack over one shoulder. He's watching intently from the other side. She smiles and waves one hand, then funnels with the crowd onto the travelator.

*"Thank you!"* Edward imagines shouting, as he watches her recede. *"Thank you, Amelia Ashford!"*

In his mind she turns, quizzical: *"For what?"*

*"The stuff!"* he'd shout. *"You know. Everything you helped me see."*

She'd shake her head. He'd need to explain.

*"Stuff that doesn't usually come out into the sunlight. Not in my life, anyway!"*

But she's gone, and Edward is surprised to find his hand over his face, and that he is crying.

*

*Postcard, Mare to Toni*
*Monday 22 April*

Hey Toni,
Look after my sister.
Mare

# PART THREE

# CHAPTER 12

*Friday 26 April*

In the mornings, from her upstairs bedroom window, Toni has a perfect close-up view of the upper decks of passing buses. She's getting to know the regular commuters. Some of them even wave. From the left-hand side in the middle section, they have ringside seats to her getting-dressed-for-work routine – towelling herself dry, applying body lotion, curling her eyelashes, mousse-ing her hair, adjusting her g-string, or putting on clothes.

Conveniently, South Wimbledon's Route 19 stops directly outside No. 227 Haydons Road. In order to maximise her time indoors, Toni has befriended the next-door children, who stand sentry every morning and yell "BUS!" through the letter slot when they see it approaching. This affords her just sufficient time to stub out her cigarette in the kitchen, grab her handbag, run down the passage, slam the front door and hurtle – with minimum exposure to the elements sure to ruin her hairdo – up the stairs of the double-decker that will take her to the station to catch the train that will take her to Waterloo, where she will catch a tube to Leicester Square, from where it is a short walk to her office in the heart of Soho.

Every morning, upon the children's dutiful yelling, Mielie awakes with a jolt, yanks on her dressing gown, throws open her bedroom door, charges down the passage to the kitchen – where she encounters Toni stubbing out her cigarette – presses her nose up to the digital clock in the geyser (because she hasn't yet put in her contact lenses), sees the time, shouts: "SHIT!" and hears the front door slam. Then she washes her face, sprays on deodorant, throws on her waitressing clothes, grabs her bag, and steps out into the morning air.

Every day, she walks three kilometres to work. Starting along South Wimbledon's fumey bus route, she winds her way past houses and shops, through the main business centre, up the hill that takes her to The Village, arriving, right at the edge of The Common, at Café Rouge.

Walking back through Wimbledon at night, she looks at the windows of the houses, their lamp-shaded lights glowing from behind the lined, softly draped curtains, and wonders about the lives being lived inside. She wonders if something as comfortable and established as that could ever be hers.

She imagines an attic room somewhere, with wooden floors and windows, and a cast-iron bath in the middle.

More than anything, she wonders about Edward.

Cape Town seems very far away.

*

*Letter, Mielie to Mare*
*Monday 29 April*

Dear Mare

It could be the cider – Scrumpy Jack, cloudy – or the unrealised potential of things and people, or the endless dislocation of each moment from the next, but suddenly I'm dizzy. And I have blisters from waitressing – Never Say Never Again. I'm in a pub somewhere in Covent Garden, because it's my day off and I need a change of scene.

Home of the blister, this time, is a suburban, pseudo-French health-hazard of a brasserie near Wimbledon Common. I traipsed the whole of The Village last Monday, dropping my CV at every pub and restaurant. Eventually, with only one copy left, I arrived at Café Rouge. "You can start tonight," they said, and I did.

The staff there comprise a fair cross-section of the United Nations – a circumstance of such linguistic and cultural complexity, it's miraculous any meals (usually accompanied by wild gesticulations and the shedding of tears) ever make it to the tables at all. We chat over fags on beer crates in the back alley. Vignette-vignette.

Most of them are younger than I am, which doesn't bother me really, except for when I caught sight of myself in a mirror, mopping urinals at oh-one-hundred hours, and had a vision: wrong side of 40, still waitressing nine-times-eight-hour shifts a week, with too much lipstick and ample cleavage, like that lady in Baghdad Café.

On Friday, I was ironing my shirt in the upstairs storeroom, standing in my bra in front of the window, and I looked up into the eyes of a dustman on the fire escape. It was raining, of course. SO romantic …

It is actually going to be quite romantic, the whole long-distance thing with Edward, I think – you know: the longing, the letters, the enduring belief.

Meanwhile, on the decidedly unromantic domestic front, Toni and I moved into Wimbledon South. The "South" part is not immaterial. Wimbledon itself constitutes the leafy suburbs, with glass gazebos, off-street parking and white wrought-iron front gates. Many of the houses have stained-glass windows and plants in pots on the porch.

South-side, meanwhile, things are somewhat less picturesque. Decidedly less leafy. Semi-industrial, almost. The streets are lined with drab buildings in dire need of a thorough scrub-down: oily car-repair workshops, tatty micro-loan offices, dingy pubs and greasy take-away joints with garish neon signs outside.

Our digs is one in a row of identical two-storey houses, not of the red-brick-and-climbing-rose variety. Banish all thoughts of bohemian squalor, too. At best, it's safe, legal and clean – although Toni begs to differ on this point, particularly. She's already made us "vacuum" the carpets with sticky-tape-wound-round-fingers, and not for the last time, I fear.

I wish I could also say it's aesthetically inoffensive, but the outside walls are as pitted and as flat as a sesame bar. The window frames are grey metal. The back garden is a small rectangle of dreary, unkempt grass. It was littered with lumps of concrete, until one morning we removed it all in a fit of efficiency – Toni with perfectly manicured fingernails, shouting: "Jesus wept, Mie-LEEE! What KIND?"

The bathroom upstairs is special. Really, it is. Salmon pink from ceiling to floor, with textured tiles and rancid carpet, tastefully installed – amongst other places – up the side of the bath, which leaks, no seriously LEAKS, to the extent that we've had to rig up the ironing board with all our pots lined up on top in what has become the primary catchment area: the dining room downstairs.

We're busy overcoming the initial obstacles of a Nigerian landlady of evangelical persuasion and a dawdling Mr Fix-It. We're trying to somehow make this place our own. A few draped kikois lessen the nauseating effect of the dark-brown furry sofas. I've Prestik-ed some precious pictures on the wall around my bed, and I'm hoping that, gradually, it will become a place to come back to after strenuous days, to read and write in, and reassemble a sense of self.

I'll probably drive Toni right off the edge, perilously close as she is to it already. You know how she is. Everything has to be just so. Her just so. Like, how she hangs washing on the line and how all other human beings on the planet hang washing on the line are simply not the same. She hangs her clothes in equidistant formation in her cupboard and can't for the life of herself fathom why anyone wouldn't.

Shortly after moving in, we were blessed with an unseasonal spell of sub-sub-zero conditions, coupled with a blown geyser and no electricity. Suffice to say Madam has seen fit to trek 2km each morning, armed with toiletry bag and hairdryer, to perform her grooming rituals at her friend's place down the road. We had to sleep in the same bed last night, just to keep warm. Very Cool Britannia, indeed.

We had our housewarming on Saturday, marked by a single orange balloon sticky-taped over the glass front door. People came in swarms and stayed. Everyone got horribly drunk – most notably Toni, who passed out around midnight, but not before coercing the one-and-only Damian to have sex with her on the carpet of her room, with enticements to the tune of: "If it's not you, it'll be somebody else".

Next morning, she said she reckoned she'd rather it had been.

I think of you often every day, Mare. You live in my heart. Mum phoned the other day. She said I should be more supportive of you and Will. I hope you know I support anything that makes you happy.

I will write more soon, I promise. But in the meanwhile: please take good care of yourself. And please do write, whenever you have the urge.

My love as always to you and darling Johnny,
Mielie

PS: Edward's a funny guy, you know. He doesn't write his name in books. Doesn't believe in possessions, even. This he did write, though, in a second-hand copy of Mario Vargas Llosa's "Aunt Julia and the Scriptwriter", which I found in my backpack on landing:
To Mielie
With all my love,
Edward

"With all my love."
Now there's a turn-up for the books.

*

*Sunday 5 May*

Marigold Ashford has joined a gym.

She said she never would, but circumstances prevailed. More specifically, Will presented the gym membership to her as a gift.

She told him the heated pool was heaven. He said running on a treadmill was a good thing, but running while watching her in the pool below was bliss.

If Mare were honest with herself, she'd admit she has more fun at the gym with Johnny, on Sundays, than she does with Will all the other times. No longer pounding up and down the huge, freezing-cold Ellis Park pool now that winter is approaching, Mare has discovered the joys of walking across the gym floor with Johnny to the water cooler and back, to – as he puts it – "keep our fluids up." En route, they observe people straddling machinery, and mutter scores out of ten under their breaths.

"Seven and a half. Two o'clock."

"Excellent ankles."

"Mn-hm … Oh! Straight ahead. Jackpot!"

"Argh! I wish I'd seen that first."

"Ab-so-LOO-tly. 'Nother lap?"

This banter makes them happy. It also helps to plaster over the crack that's developing between them over Will.

Johnny never mentions Mare's boyfriend, and this makes her wonder what he really thinks. So today, driving home through the tree-lined Oaklands avenues, she casually drops his name.

"It's nice that I get to go to gym with you and with Will," she says, slurping on her freshly squeezed orange-and-apple juice. Johnny always buys her one, after gym.

"Mn-hm," Johnny says.

"I mean, you love the gym – and he's always been a gym person."

"Look, I'm not a gym history specialist," Johnny doesn't smile, "but 'always' may be an exaggeration. Did he take his first steps in a gym, do you think?"

Mare makes a racket sucking up the last bits. "Goodness only knows, Johnny," she says. "Maybe he did."

"Probably," Johnny counters. "Born with a silver spoon in his mouth and a treadmill belt beneath his feet."

"Shame, be nice man, Johnny," she says. "I wouldn't even be here if it wasn't for him."

"Right, like on this earth?" Johnny says.

"Oh, stop!" she says. "You must be getting your period. No, I wouldn't be Driving Home From Gym unless he bought my membership. And you and I get to see each other more, thanks to that, actually."

"Jeez, Mare," Johnny says, changing gears crossly as they pass Joburg General Hospital. "Have you not even noticed?"

"What?" she asks, all innocence.

"That you and I only ever see each other on Sundays now, when Will's visiting his parents – notably, always without you." He changes gear and rounds another corner. "Why is that, I wonder."

Mare opens her mouth several times to reply, but finds she can't.

"And stop doing that with your mouth," Johnny says. "You look like a barbel."

"Johnny," she says. "Johnny. That's unfair." She's tempted to whine. She resists. "You have no idea what a feeding barbel looks like."

He hesitates for a millisecond. "Well," he says. "Very few people do."

They drive in silence for a bit.

"Anyway, stop doing that with the gearstick," she says, eventually. "You look like an uncertain chameleon."

"Oh, touché," he says.

"Yes. Touché," she says.

Mare and Johnny love saying "touché". They're not entirely sure what it means, but it makes them feel like characters in *Chariots of Fire*.

In her flat, waiting for Will to get back from his parents (the Sunday papers unread on the couch), Mare tells herself that Johnny doesn't understand how passionate she and Will are about each other.

Nonetheless, that night, to reassure herself, she raises the parent issue with Will.

"Will …" she says.

"Yo."

"Willo … Is there, uh, any particular reason I didn't come with you to your parents today?"

"You went to gym with Johnny."

"I know. But only because you were at their place."

Will puts down his book and sits up in bed. "Sweetie. I thought you wanted time with Johnny."

"Well, I do. But I thought maybe you didn't want your parents to meet me … and that was why …"

He sighs. "Darling," he says. "You are more than welcome to every part of me, everything you see here …" he draws an air circle below the elastic of his shorts "… and anything else you want. If you'd like to meet my parents, I'll take you next week."

"Oh!" she says. "Well. Thank you."

"So would you like to go?"

"I don't have anything to wear."

"Excellent! Don't wear anything, my dad and I would love that."

"No, man! You know what I mean."

"OK. Well how about this: Next weekend we go shopping for an outfit for you and you can meet my despised parents at Sunday lunch. Okay?"

"Okay."

"I would never …" He shakes his head at her. "I'm so proud of you, baby, you know that don't you?"

"I think so."

"I am. I am so, so, SO proud of you. It's just that I love what we have. I love just being us, you and me."

"I love it too."

"I love us."

"Me too."

Then he kisses her deeply.

And as Mare is going to sleep, with Will's beautiful, proud-of-her arm across her chest, she thinks: *My life will never, ever, get better than this.*

*

*Letter, Johnny to Mielie*
*Saturday 11 May*

Westminster Mansions

Darling

Your letter of 29 April to Mare refers.

While not oblivious to your flagrant disregard of my own to you, of oh-six April as I recall, I do acknowledge that you've been busy:

1. Moving country

2. Leaving your lover

and therefore:

3. With all matters irrevocably life-changing.

Forgiveness is in order.

Before I continue, 2. above especially refers.

Mare has of course previously shared all the necessary – and even the unnecessary – details pertaining to the nature of your attachment to Mr Edward Taylor. Extrapolating from such first-hand intel, I-for-one believe this separation to be only of a temporary nature, and live in hope – no, belief – that the two of you will soon be reunited.

Were I he himself, I'd already have "climbed, highest mountains" and "run, through the fields … Only To Be With You" (cross-ref: U2: The Joshua Tree; 1987).

Resuming with 1. Moving country.

I was particularly delighted to hear that you are co-habiting with the precious Toni Palmer. God bless her. Please tell her, from me: "God bless you, Madam. You're a class act, and the world is grateful."

Regarding the fiasco of the Arctic weather, coupled with a complete electrical power failure, please do also congratulate her on my behalf for braving the third-world discomforts of Europe, thousands of kilometres from her native land.

My further observation, which you are free to share, is that none of the above would've happened had it not been her worst nightmare to begin with. In life – in every situation – it is always our very worst nightmare that is bound to come true.

Your sister's relationship with Will is perhaps also proof of this axiom.

Here is a relationship that appears to the casual onlooker – i.e. not me – to be ever intensifying, to the exclusion of all else.

Your sister and I only see each other once a week these days, on Sundays, when her boyfriend visits his parents and we (are therefore free to) go to gym. That Mitchell is at the same time in bed reading the Sunday papers – and I mean ALL the Sunday papers – is not immaterial. He gets his exercise in the morning. Yes, he does a spinning class at six: fast cycling in a darkened room with club music and a head-setted instructor.

So, come Sunday afternoon, I'd rather be reading the papers in bed with him. But this is the time that Mare so generously affords me – and I take what I can get these days.

It's come to that. And I have a theory: the fact that your sister hasn't yet met her all-consuming boyfriend's parents, living on the other side of Rosebank as they do, would suggest that he has no desire to accompany her across the north-south divide. Ever.

Were I in her position, I'd be offended.

When I imply as much to her, she takes offence.

Be all that as it may, I ache to visit you and Toni in your new abode. It sounds gloriously tasteless. The kind of place we could sit and drink tea with slightly vrot milk and smoke incessantly between bouts of wheezing laughter. In short, and not unlike your salmon bathroom: a fright.

I can talk. My home is a fright in its own way. Too large, too full of things, always full of people. Mitchell lives large. He is irrepressibly social. The doorbell rings off the hook.

This morning some work colleagues of his arrived for brunch. We were asleep, with empty wine bottles and smeared plates from the night before still littering the table. Mitchell had forgotten he'd invited them., but such is the charm and energetic resourcefulness of my partner that within minutes our guests were seated on the front balcony, drinking Bucks Fizz.

Fouché, a regular dinner-and-overnight guest, emerged in his underpants and a cardigan, open to skin. I was tasked with clearing the table while Mitchell whipped up Eggs Benedict for five and Fouché drew out our guests on subjects as diverse as urban regeneration, free-range chickens and John Kani's acting genius.

Socially, my favourite type has always been the eccentric, and these are in no short supply here.

I miss you two eccentrics too.

Love,
Johnny

*

*Letter, Mare to Mielie*
*Monday 13 May*

Helvetia Court, table

Dear Mielie,

Thank you for your letter. Thank you for the camera-pan of Wimbledon and South Wimbledon. Thank you for the short film, "Housewarming". And all of it just rattled off with no crossings-out, you cow.

Seriously, I've been craving those images. I can just picture you tramping around, dishing out your CV. I know the tramp of those boots very well. I know what it feels like to be behind them on a path, with the smell of dust and sun up my nose … Careful, I'm about to become a Juluka song. Wouldn't want to bring on a bout of homesickness.

And I mustn't phone you! Even if I could afford it I don't have your number. (Don't tell it to me, ever.) You do know I'm there with you, though, don't you? You do know I'm next to you, squeezing your hand, all the time? And at the same time I'm here, in my own weird movie, feeling your hand squeezes, especially when I read your letters.

I miss you so much, Mielie. I haven't written you nearly enough proper letters. I can't believe it. I've had so many conversations with you in my head, I feel I've written to you every day. That's so like me: It happened in my mind, so it's happened. Anyway.

My news: Will gave me a pair of moss-green leather gloves. Mum's hand-knitted ones let in the wind. Will's are beautiful. They have a vintage vibe. I don't even know where he found them. They are the colour of fresh moss, and there is a subtle fan, three perfect lines of sewing, on the back of my hand. The thin, soft leather covers my wrist, slips under my sleeve – not like those cheap ones that end at the wrist bone and make you feel both cold and giant limbed.

In other news, we handed in the Knock n Drop community paper on Friday. Page 9 is my favourite. It's my Parktown Prawn story. On the front page there's actually an eye-catcher block about it: "Meet The Monster".

I saw my first one in the corner of the garage one evening when I was parking my bike. "This is brilliant," I thought, standing at a safe distance. "They say you should write about what's close to home." Hijackings? Hm. Vlakplaas death squads? Not so much. But Parktown Prawns? Now there's a story!

The title, I decided, would be "Parktown Prawns: Revenge on the Middle Class?" Because they migrate to Parktown, you know? According to my research, the Parktown Prawn will feast, with grossly enlarged, meat-tearing mandibles, on virtually anything, including rotting fruit. It has long, twitching antennae, also known as horns. It has scarlet-streaked hind legs. It lives in burrows and it likes water.

Quoting my own text: "Covered in an armour of cuticle, the Prawn is not afraid to enter homes." (Why does Fifi Ashford pop to mind?)

"It may seek out a dark burrow – like a cupboard, or a warm, empty shoe. If the Prawn is disturbed while eating or nesting, or even worse, cornered and threatened, the large wingless cricket may leap in a random direction or emit a nasty-smelling fluid." (Are you struggling to shake the Fifi image? I am.)

"The die-hard warrior of garden and home refuses to leave; according to urban legend, attempts at drowning and suffocation fail to kill the infamous Prawn."

On reflection, I see I didn't assert myself much in the area of hard news. My thinking was that it would be better to concentrate on strengths, and learn new skills at a reasonable pace. So basically all that means is that I'm going to have to put off calling myself Intrepid Girl Reporter for another few months. Wouldn't it be lovely, though, to be one? I'd be on the beat, notebook in hand, like one of the girls in Scooby Doo. Who says I lack ambition?

The big test is going to be the course newspaper. It's due mid-July. After that we find out whether we get the much-vaunted six-month contract in the newsroom upstairs. The salary is almost as terrible as it is for cadets – R3000 a month instead of R2000 – but if I don't get it I'll have to go home. Obviously, a fate worse than death. I couldn't leave Will.

Hm, as someone not naturally prone to brevity, I'm quite delighted to finish my letter here. I shall write again soon, but for now I shall bask in the achievement of having written to brief. I am aware that "to brief" doesn't necessarily mean writing short. But perhaps it should.

All my love – nothing curtailed about that,
Mare

PS: Do you remember the only poem I ever had published in the campus poetry journal? Picture it on its own clean, white page.

<u>Untitled</u>
By Marigold Ashford

You're reading this
Because it's short
Aren't you?

PPS: Is Edward there?
IS EDWARD THERE??

# CHAPTER 13

*Saturday 18 May*

Like most young Commonwealth hopefuls, Amelia Ashford soon discovers that the streets in London are not paved with gold. Despite her British passport, her accent is wrong and she knows no one.

But, although not quite living in the postcard, she's pulling through. Thanks to quite a lot of chatty effort on Mielie's part, plus a few heated exchanges with Mourad the Moroccan chef, the kitchen staff now treat her like one of the boys. She finds this helps to ground her in reality, because mostly, being apart from Edward, she has a sense of watching her life from the outside.

Three teenagers come in one Friday, calculatedly blasé, and request a seat in the smoking section. Mielie directs them to the corner furthest from the manager's suspicious eye. They order one plate of chips, one coke and one hot choc between them. Mielie has a rush of fondness, like she would smuggle them anything, but her best bit is when the one, all of 15 years old, leans forward with a twinkle in his eye and says: "Rainy old day out, innit?" Between them they smoke a box of cigarettes in 45 minutes.

And now today, during a particularly hectic shift, riddled with yelling brats, Mielie's manager (George Best, whom Toni refers to as George Not The Best), quite uninvited says: "Let's get married".

Mielie – on hands and knees at the time, picking peas from between the floorboards with her fingernails – says: "Okay, when."

"Tomorrow," he replies, punching numbers into the till like a zombie, omitting to blink.

"Oh good, I'll have time to phone my mother," she says. "She'll be so relieved."

*Letter, Toni to Mare and Johnny*
*Monday 20 May*

19h15
The Ball, South Wimbledon

Yes, peeps. Mielie and I are fine, not that you asked. We live for your news, though, see? It's top of the list.

The list goes:

Your news = 1.

Benson&Hedges = 2.

Tins cider = 3.

A rare evening when we have all three is joy unsurpassed by orgasm. For my part, anyway. Mielie's probs forgotten what that is.

Unsurprisingly, we never have any money. This is due to the fact that while Scrumpy Jack is cheap enough to support a nation of alcoholics, and B&H expensive but do-able, it's the buses and tubes that chew our cash. Ex-HOR-bi-tant! Not joking.

On the upside – and there is only one – Mielie and I get to go to The Ball. Quote-unquote. It's our Cinderella dream-come-true.

Full name: The Ball and Racquet, aka Boring Racket.

Upholstery: a greasy blend of dark green and maroon.

Chief attraction? Being a mere staggering distance from our front door.

I'm here right now. Just me and the usual loser lurkers, plus the juke box, plus someone's excessively stinking hound, slobbering on flea-infested rug, stage left.

On Friday and Saturday nights it's different. This is when a herd of young southern-hemisphere men invades the place. These are our brothers with jobs on construction sites, who daily fold their beefy bodies into the backs of vans and traverse Greater London, far from their big sky, bakkies and braais.

Brenda-The-Ball-Owner's-Wife keeps them all in check. She puts her head on one side as she listens to their stories, like the mums they're missing, though they'd never say.

She calls us all "love". This, despite the fact that everyone's both swined and stoned before they arrive – tinnies, see: cheaper. Just yesterday morning I awoke to discover our washing machine full of empties. Ever-so-thoughtfully packed to the lid. True story.

Mielie sometimes comes here after work on weekends. If I make her promise.

There's always a Craig or a Shane grabbing one of us off our barstools, suggesting we "have a shag". An offer – especially tempting phrased thus, you'll agree – we always politely decline. It would be like lying down naked in a rutted field and being run over by a tractor. Don't you think.

Instead, after last rounds we sometimes allow them plus their newly selected imminent shags to plough through our front door and spread themselves over what furniture we have.

Most people end up standing squeezed into the kitchen. Where I would pass out from the smell, the glass-rings and the ash spilt everywhere, were it not for being screaming-pissed by then myself.

Onwards
Ever
Toni

PS: Mielie is so-so. Acting-wise, she rates her chances low. She told me that on a bench. Plus no Edward. Poor chick.

PPS: I'm having sex with a bicycle courier. Most usually in the delivery room at work. Worth it.
And Marry! You're fornicating with a god.
Just please don't go batshit on us darl.
Your people need you, preferably intact.

*Letter, Mielie to Mare*
*Tuesday 21 May*

Hello Mare

I got your letter as I was tearing out of the house this morning – later than usual, so I had to take a cab. I tried to read it on the way, but the driver was a chatty soul and there were speed bumps.

So eventually, at work, having refilled all the sugar bowls, and wiped down the salt and pepper sets, and polished the cutlery, and lined up the coffee plungers, and written up the specials on the chalk board (with accents in all the right places, because "we're French, right?"), and ironed the aprons, and wiped down the bar, and bundled the linen off to the laundry, and blah blah boring-blah, I couldn't stand it any longer, so locked myself in the loo and proceeded to read.

Your letters are like fiction I can't put down, which is why I read them over and over again (and not only in lavatories at work).

Edward hasn't written yet. Every time I get back from work, I hope I'll find something – a postcard on the doormat that his hands have touched, a stamp he's licked and pressed. He did leave a message on the answering machine the other day, though. Toni burst into my room yelling: "Mielie! Mielie! Edward left a message and he's going completely mental!"

Of course I played it back right away. What he actually said was: "Hi Mielie. It's me, Edward. I just wanted to say that I hope things are going well for you that side. And that I miss you like mad …"

He also said: "If you're sad, you don't deserve to be." And: "Not a day goes by that I don't think of you."

I tried to call him back, but there was no answer. And he doesn't have an answering machine, so he won't know I even tried.

Hmmm. Long distance. Not nearly as romantic as I'd hoped.

I just hope he didn't fall in love with the idea of my acting success. It's a tough scene here. Tougher than I'd anticipated.

I know it's early days still, but in the absence of any career-enhancing lucky breaks, and in an effort to dig myself out of what feels like a bottomless pit of poverty and ineptitude, I've subscribed to a casting magazine and paid (a mere 98 pounds) to be featured in the Spotlight catalogue + CD Rom. I've also had photos printed and am sending them off to every agent and casting director beneath the never-present sun.

I didn't expect my distinctions to count for absolutely nothing. As one agent said on the phone: "But, your qualifications … what's UCT Drama School? Now if we were talking RADA, darling …"

So I've taken on a part-time, work-from-home job. Reading movie scripts. I'm quite enjoying it, actually. I have to pick them up in Oxford Street in Central London, take them home, and read them. Then they want a three-paragraph synopsis and a full character breakdown within five days.

I'd just picked up a new batch, and on the spur of the moment decided to go and see a movie, Secrets and Lies. So there I was at the ticket booth, battling to open my purse while carrying a whole pile of scripts. I held them out to this guy behind me in the queue and said – wait-for-it, you're going to die – I said: "Sorry. Would you just hold me for a minute please?"

He looked at me, smiled (and-one-and-two-and-three) then said: "I'd love to."

Blushing, I said: "No, sorry! Gosh! Sorry … I meant: Would you just hold These Scripts for me, for a minute, please?"

And he smiled again, and said: "No, I don't think you did."

I guess I could do with someone else's flesh being close to mine, for just a minute – and not in the sense of arms-aloft-in-tube-ride, either.

Afterwards, sopping wet at Waterloo – because I somehow always manage to forget my umbrella – and feeling forlorn, I murmured to the ticket seller: "Wimbledon, please."

"Coming back love?" he said.

I shook my head.

And then he said "Yeah," resignedly, to no-one in particular: "The nice ones never do …"

London. Gotta love it.

So, ja. It's one of those smoke-a-thousand-cigarettes-then-empty-the-ashtray-and-light-up-again kind of nights, again. I'm listening to Crowded House. The bit about freedom and a paper cup seems fitting.

On the up-side, my boss George gave me a fifty-pound bonus last week, which I promptly went out and spent on a skirt and jacket the colour of bitter chocolate, of the "Wallis" label, to which I had been referred by a Spanish waitress with a keen eye for style and quality. I think you would approve – borrow, even. I also worked at a private party – horsey set – for which I was paid 75 pounds in cash, which I promptly blew on some basic necessities at M&S: a black button-up lambswool jersey to replace the last (of more synthetic character, now diaphanous); a crepey shirt, woollen waistcoast (on sale, to match Wallis skirt) and a long-sleeved, goldy-black lycra top for party purposes.

Mare, I MUST finish this letter right now, and post it tomorrow, or I never will, and another one from you will arrive, and I'll never catch up. So I'm going to sleep now, thinking of you all the time.

Sinead O'Connor and "Nothing Compares".
And in the words of the memorably effusive Edward:
"Kind regards"
Mielie

PS: "But most of all I missed your neck."
Said who? In what?
Sam Shepard: Fool for Love.

PPS: Mind … the gap.

*

*Saturday 25 May*

One Saturday afternoon, walking back up the hill with her wet laundry, Mare spots Will lying outstretched, in full view of the street, on the hideous couch that he's moved onto her balcony. His ankles are crossed and he's wearing nothing but a pair of boxers, sunglasses and untied boots.

Walker, having just bought the paper on Rockey Street, is in his car on his way to visit Mitchell. Near the top of Cavendish, he sees Mare on the street ahead of him. Not wanting her to see him driving past and suspect him of spying, he pulls over and parks – with an unintentionally clear view of Helvetia Court, and Will on the balcony. He watches Mare enter the building, and lingers. A few minutes later he sees her on the balcony too, leaning against the French doors. Will is reading, with two cups of tea steaming beside him. Walker watches her lips move. He watches her smiling.

"What are you doing?" Mare asks Will.

"The sun's wonderful."

"It's nearly winter."

"All the more reason to enjoy these raa-ays."

"You're in your underwear."

"I know," Will says. "And you're fully dressed. It's all wrong."

"Are you actually insane?" she laughs.

"Sh-sh. Into your cozzie now, off you pop."

"I will not."

"Bikini at the dry cleaners? We don't mind on this beach. Look, that chap's wearing nothing at all."

"You are insane." She turns around and heads inside.

Will jumps up and stops Mare in the lounge. "I made you tea and everything."

"I'm not going out there undressed."

Then he kisses her and takes off all her clothes anyway.

Walker hears Mare's high-pitched laugh through the balcony doors and starts the car.

Afterwards, Mare puts on her Speedo with a big T-shirt over it. She and Will lie on the couch together, reading, and she tells him that the sun really is wonderful on her legs.

Nick Wilkinson Junior has come to a decision. It's the kind of decision that, in retrospect, you realise was one of the biggest choices of your life. Strangely, at the time, it felt more like an itch getting scratched. He might have decided while he was in a restaurant, waiting for his brunch. Or in the shower. But, sometime in the past few days, decide he did.

Will's never been in love before. He's had plenty of sex, and some of the girls might have loved him. But before Mare, there was no love from his side. She is like a current, sweeping him along.

Very soon after meeting her, Will left the sex room in his mind and went to another place – not a room, but outside. The sensation is more like floating. Her laugh, the look of her, the things she says, all of it makes him feel like he's riding thermals. He knows, with certainty, that he's addicted to her. He knows this too: he'll never feel the same again, not with anyone.

Of course Will enjoys this feeling. The world he lives in with Mare excludes all else. He's kept it this way, deliberately. She is separate from his world of boredom and resentment. But the secret he's made of her can't last forever. There will be consequences, sure, and he's not happy about that. Still, there is a bigger picture for Will that he can't ignore. A bigger picture for Mare, too. She needs protecting.

Therefore, tonight.

Will and Mare fetch up at The Lizard Lounge on Rockey Street. It's very late. They sip their whiskies.

Then Will lifts her hand from her leg. He stares at it with intent and tenderness in equal parts. Strokes and massages her fingers, then kisses her. For a long time.

Mare is the one to pull away.

"Will." She takes a breath. "We should go."

He doesn't have any chirp in him. He normally turns on the twinkle when Mare sounds serious. This time he just gazes at her. He feels like he's in a dream. It's that surreal, that intensely emotional.

"Baby," he says. "Aw, Marry." He turns over her hand and strokes her fingers again. "I've never felt like this before."

"I know," she says. "I really know."

"I want to explain …" he says. Then: "No. I must do this right."

Will pushes himself back from the bar with both hands, grinning with a fraction of effort. Most people wouldn't notice that hesitation. Most people don't notice how quickly he grins, usually. Mare has.

"I have a plan!" he says to her, chipper again.

"Oh?" she smiles.

"Yes, a plan!" he says. "Dinner tomorrow! To celebrate you, my darling. You are my darling, my darling forever. I've been watching you in wonder, you know. Please say you'll come to dinner with me."

"Okay, sweetie. Shall we go now, though? I'd love to take you home with me now."

"Please take me home with you."

Will is drunk – they're both drunk – but when the cold night air hits them they sober up. They turn the music up loud in the car and sing all the way up Cavendish.

When they get home, Will partially undresses Mare in the kitchen doorway, carries her to bed and makes love to her.

It's the first time he's properly made love to anyone.

*

*Letter, Will to Mielie*
*Saturday 1 June*

203 Rudd Court
Illovo

Amelia Ashford,

Sister of my beloved, I feel like I already know you, as if we were pen-pals or something. I've seen photos of you, seen your handwriting, read things you've written in letters (not everything!).

I've heard so much about you. I know the colour of your eyes is "not khaki, exactly, but sort of shaded jade, like the sea when the clouds are brownish-grey, can you see it?" I can't always see it, but I always nod and smile. I would kill myself if your sister stopped saying things like that to me. Now you and I have a secret. Keep it, please. You would have a suicide on your hands, honestly, if I stopped hearing phrases like "shaded jade" coming out of her mouth.

Back to you.

I know the tone of your skin is "the colour of peanut butter" – and that you have a particular fondness for peanut butter, particularly on buttered Provitas. And now I have heard the sound of your voice.

Mare played your message on her new answering machine the other day, when we'd just arrived back in her flat. She said you sounded serious – you did – so she dialled your number in London while I put on the kettle for tea.

It was about the car. What was that phrase you used: "inappropriate and irresponsible"? Did you say "lording it over" – or did I imagine that?

I don't have an older sister, but if I did, I hope she would lay the law down like you did. You had us quaking in our boots. It's amazing that we've lived here in Joburg this long, day to day, without you being here, in person, to manage the risks to our reputations.

I'm teasing you!

We're not getting the car. Mare was convinced not so much by your horror at the idea of her being "kept" – you fail to understand, Amelia, that in Joburg we all need as much help as we can get from each other, all the time – but by the expense of ownership.

In the end I caved. After the phone call I said I would pay insurance, maintenance costs, even petrol, but she wouldn't have it. I said I would set up an account, she'd never have to ask … but "no" it was.

I'm writing to you, dear Amelia, because I don't want you to think I'm … what would they say in London? … "some flash git"? You mean the world to Marry and she means the world to me. I haven't done very well, I don't think, at gaining Johnny's affection – though Lord knows I've tried – and the fact that there's no love lost between me and their friend Walker doesn't help.

I like you so much already from your letters, I was so looking forward to us becoming a threesome – just KIDDING! Seriously, don't frown at me like that.

If we meet in person, Ms Ashford, I shall buy you a drink, raise my glass to yours and say: "Cheers to you, for having the best sister in the world." It's amazing to think that you've known Mare since she was born. I spend a lot of time thinking: "Where has she been all my life?"

So this is my defence, on the car story, and I'll never bring it up again: The last thing I wanted to do was burden Marry with additional expenses. I had actually hoped to save her money and hassle. My thinking was – and I stick to this – I'd rather have her driving in and out of the basement parking at work than standing around at bus stops in Pritchard Street in the evening. When she moves upstairs to the newsroom – of course she will – her hours will be longer than they were at Cadet School. Plus there's the bike. I saw the mess she made of her leg and ankle just from slipping in the rain on a driveway at 20 kay an hour.

Finally – try not to roll your eyes – I wanted to get her a big, eff-off gift because flowers and cocktails aren't enough. This girl is special. This girl is a dream. She needs to remember that.

I've told her "I love us" and "I love this". It's true, and it will always be true.

Yours,
Will

*

*Saturday 1 June*

As any good waitress knows, there's a delicate balance to be achieved, serving couples. "When explaining the specials, make more eye contact with the lady than the man … in fact, *always* make more eye contact with the lady," Mielie explains to a gaunt trainee from Poland one afternoon.

"Approach the table from an angle best suited to not breaking up a clinch," she says, before demonstrating exactly that. "Retain a cool indifference to anything you overhear – squabbles, declarations of infidelity, soul-searching interrogations ..." she continues on her way to the lift with the dirty plates "… and have those dessert menus on hand for presentation in the split-second before a silence becomes an awkward one."

It's the beginning of June, the early evening of one of London's very first watery-sunny days. Mielie becomes aware of a tall person standing in front of her, speaking with an urgency that pulls him into sharp focus.

She ignores his words and points an arm at an empty window table. Once seated, Mielie asks if he'd like something to drink – whereupon he falls to pieces, can't string two syllables together, buries his face in his hands and asks for a few moments to pull himself together.

"Let's go through this one more time," she says, in a kind, mock-patronising way, with the first sense of sexual power she's had in a while. "You just nod where appropriate, okay? Would it be liquid refreshment you're after?" (Nod.) "Alcoholic? Non-alcoholic?" (Bewildered gaze.) "No look, you've got your teas, coffees, espressos, double espressos, regular or large cappuccinos, chamomile or mint infusions ... None of those?" (Entirely blank now.) "... Okay, then so… you've got your beers, your lagers, your draughts ... stop me when I'm getting close ..." she continues. "So how about a soft drink? Hey? There's citron presse, elderflower, or Coke/Fanta/Sprite/soda water, your freshly-squeezed orange juice, your ice/no-ice, lemon/no-lemon …"

And then he grips her wrist very tightly and manages to splutter: "Whisky. Just whisky."

# CHAPTER 14

*Saturday 1 June*

Marigold Ashford is standing in the hallway of her flat opposite the young man she adores. Will has just arrived. His jacket is zipped and the keys to his Merc are dangling from the fingers of his right hand. They are staring at each other but neither of them is speaking.

"Tell me again," Mare says.

"It's the Hermanus house. The building, the repairs, the improvements, whatever. My parents started a whole lot of work and everything's gone over schedule."

"And you have to go there now, and supervise it all until it's finished?"

Will says nothing. He's turned his head to look through the lounge to the balcony.

"I mean, right now?" Mare says, after he's turned back to face her. She is wearing the wine-red velvet mini-dress he asked her to wear to the restaurant. Her bag is on the telephone chair.

"It's not—" Will starts. "No. Not right now. Right now I have to go and pack and then I have to leave at four tomorrow morning."

"We could still—" Her hands are shaking.

"We can't though. I can't—"

"What?"

"Mare. It's my parents. I just had this whole conversation with them. I can't—"

He is staring at the parquet. She tilts her head so that she can see his eyes.

"Please just trust me," he says. "I have to go. It's my parents. They—"

"They what? I don't get it," she says.

"It's nothing! I just have to go, that's all." He takes a step towards her. "But I love you."

"I love you, Will." She is breathing fast.

"Look after yourself, okay," he says.

Mare starts to cry. He grabs her and holds her in the hallway, her tears running down the leather of his jacket, leaving no marks at all.

*

*Sunday 2 June*

The man returns to the brasserie where Mielie works the next day and sits at the same table. This time, he orders a pot of tea. He asks Mielie to bring him a second teacup and, assuming he's expecting company, she agrees. The second teacup is for her. Mielie agrees to sit down with the man, but only because George is out, and only because it's nearly the end of her shift anyway. The truth is, she likes the way he rakes his fingers through his hair, and she likes the way he looks at her – not longingly, exactly, but 'pleadingly' might be the word. He seems to require conversation with her like some people lost at sea require a flotation device.

The man, not surprisingly, is religious about film. Mielie thought he had a movie-lover look about him and it took her no time at all to draw him out. He speaks with great passion about Scarface, Orson Welles and people Mielie's never heard of.

When the tea is finished – when the man, whose name is Vincent, is literally shaking the last drops of tea from the pot into her cup – Mielie wonders if she should leave with him. He might take her to a London park, sweep her quite literally off her feet and, once he has her on the grass, amid the daffodils and bumblebees, kiss her with a sweetness she's forgotten.

He could be a madman. He might stand on lawns at twilight and shout with great passion at the gathering clouds about Chaplin and Tarantino. He might come back, turn up out of nowhere, a grinning face pressed up against the restaurant windows, making smoke clouds with his breath until she's finished cleaning inside, and afterwards they'd have a chance to walk into the middle of the pitch-black common and throw stones across a moonlit pond.

Might it be enough? A London man, a whirlwind of a man who's the opposite of Edward? Could this man – or some other man – replace Edward? Could anyone, ever?

"It's not disappointing," Mielie tells Toni that night. "It's just like blinking. You blink away the fantasy and get on with your life."

*

*Letter, Mare to Mielie*
*Sunday 2 June*

Helvetia Court
Night

Dear Mielie

Sorry, it's me again.

I've been phoning.

I left messages.

I wish you were here now.

It's awful.

It's 10pm, I've been crying all day.

Will has gone. Not forever, but he left suddenly last night.

I still don't properly understand why. Something about supervising building work for his parents in Hermanus. There's no phone there and he couldn't say how long it would take.

Anyway I'm not just crying because he went away. Not only that. It's because of last night. I don't know. I'd been building it up in my mind.

Okay.

Oh, bloody hell, not again.

Whisky.

FUCK!

I didn't know there was so much crying in me. I could be a tear donor.

There are no tissues left. I'm onto toilet paper now and my nose has gone red.

The thing is, on Friday night we went out. We ended up at a late-night place on Rockey Street. He said he'd been "watching me in wonder" and that he wanted to tell me something, but that he wanted to do it right so would I wear my velvet mini and he'd take me out for "proper Italian" on Saturday night.

He said he needed to see his parents in the afternoon. (They're just back from their holiday place.) He'd tell them when he saw them that we would be coming together for Sunday lunch today.

I didn't think terribly much about it on the Friday, or even yesterday morning, which we spent together at Fourno's eating pastries and drinking coffee. I think we were there for three hours. I really was quite worn out, so it was nice just to soak up the sun. We talked about family trees. He told me how it'd been for him growing up, how he'd longed for a sibling, especially a sister. He told me in detail about all the CDs he'd been reviewing while I had my head down at Cadet School. We talked and talked, there were times we were both reading, there were times we just sat and looked at each other.

I wasn't thinking about what he wanted to tell me. Far from it. I was just feeling warm and safe and so, so happy.

It was only when he'd dropped me at home and I was lying in the bath that the thought first snuck up on me. I thought, maybe he wants to move in together or something. Because then it would make sense for him to do it before his parents meet me on the Sunday. Then they won't have a chance to object, or negotiate.

Jeez, Mielie, it was momentarily thrilling – dizzying even – to imagine being suddenly in a couple, suddenly someone's partner, not the androgynous, culturally marginal, intellectually otherwise, Vs-upping journo-punk I like to imagine I am.

I've never had a desire to take things to the next level with Will. I've always thought we're already at the top level – on the top floor, in the penthouse, nudging the clouds … But the thought of this man, this individual, who I love more than I ever imagined I could love anyone, loving me back and wanting to live with me. That. The statement. The question. It made my heart bang against my chest.

But, then, no. He arrived with a closed face. It hurts to remember it, how he didn't explain anything properly, how he left in a hurry and how I stood on the balcony, in the rose light – our rose light, for our celebration night – and watched him leave. And then, as his Merc pulled out onto Cavendish, how I lost my spine and my breath and collapsed in tears in the stupid wine-red dress and how I haven't been able to stop, properly, since.

I'm not weepy because I feel like I lost out on the fancy dinner, and the big question, and the meet-the-parents.

I'm bewildered, yes, but all that's really happened is that my boyfriend's gone on a trip. I think the reason I can't stop crying is because of the shock.

Mielie, I think I've been alone this whole year, even when I've been with Will. Love is different to friends and family. It makes you soar in the sky, but it doesn't trudge companionably alongside.

It's all too much. I'm going to bed now. I could do with being put on a drip. I am a drip.

Please. Someone take this pen out of my hand and push me onto my bed.

X Mare

PS: I'm at work now. It's Monday. Here's a bit of news: Will left me the key to his flat. He dropped it in my postbox. I might have preferred one of his postcards with a love note. I found it this morning. It was just the key and a paper tag with the address. We never got around to going to see his flat together. I suppose he was feeling bad about that. It made me happy, anyway. It felt more like a promise than an apology. I hope he phones soon.

PPS: It feels like you haven't written to me lately – unless a letter from you got lost in the post. That would be tragic, like when Ernest Hemingway left a complete manuscript in a suitcase on a train. That actually happened. It was the only copy. It's never been found.

*Letter, Pauline to Mare*
*Tuesday 4 June*

Balfour Road

My darling Marigold

It's been almost four months since you left. The weather is cooler. The rains haven't come. We need them now. The mountain is parched.

I miss you, and your phone calls, but also perfectly understand how your time must be flying, what with your work demands and all those that come with having an especially close partner, too. I do hope your whirlwind lasts a long time. Will, like your father, is a prince among men. They don't blow through one's life every day, and when they do, you'd do well to make sure you hold onto them.

Edward has been here several times, since Amelia set off to conquer the world. I do hope she and Toni are enjoying the English summer! The royal parks are magnificent this time of year. I remember the displays of flowers in the beds … the dappled light is so romantic, and the girls in their summer dresses … The summer I was in London we used to go skinny-dipping in the Heath ponds at night! Memories …

Yesterday, Edward brought bags of irises from Eland. There's very little left of the garden there, I'm sorry to say. The earth moving has started. I saw the machines and the men in white overalls when I drove past to walk on the Pipe Track.

I encouraged him to stay for tea. He was very helpful on the subject of renovation. "Structurally, could we go up?" I asked him. He found the weight-bearing walls and pointed out the cross-beams. I've promised to seek out the plans.

I mentioned Amelia's name several times but he didn't open up on his plans to follow her, unfortunately. He has that look about him, more so now than ever. His face looks overcast, as if he's squinting through cloud.

What a wonderful young man he is, though. I've no doubt that he and Amelia will find a way to be together again soon.

Oh I almost forgot! I saw Fiona and the woman I suppose to be her mother – Geraldine, is it? She is our dear Edward's mother too. It doesn't seem possible.

I was in the art shop in Gardens Centre when I saw them pass. Both were carrying handbags over the crooks of their arms. Fiona looks well. She was wearing a baby-pink jersey. Geraldine was wearing a tightly knotted silk scarf, with a string of pearls. They seemed to be disagreeing about something – or perhaps they frown with their chins up and speak over each other when they're agreeing. Geraldine looked frightening – even at a distance!

Later, when I was coming out of the Pick n Pay, I saw them in the window of a beauty shop, having their feet soaked. I never thought of inviting my girls for pedicures. Should I have?

My dear Marigold, I ought to make a start on my dal now. I've become a vegetarian, you know. I feel so much lighter, cleaner. I buy spice mixes to add interest. I'm a regular now at Deli Masala, down the road!

I think of you and Amelia all the time. I miss Daddy but Janet and I have our mountain walks. It's so important to BREATHE.

Love,
Mummy

P.S. Tess is pestering me for a Great Dane. Perhaps not the worst idea? A dog would surely be good for security?

*

*Letter, Johnny to Mielie*
*Friday 7 June*

Darling, hello

No doubt Mare has told you that Will has gone.

It's been six days. The light on her answering machine is unblinking.

Nonetheless, she expects him to make contact any minute. She assures me he'll explain everything when he comes home – soon. She is an excuse-making genius.

Have you heard the one about the renovs going over schedule? Or about the house having no phone? What's his excuse for not using a tickey box?

This debacle causes me many raised eyebrows, head shakes and middle-distance stares, but the one that makes me purse my lips the most is this:

Why did he leave her the key to his flat?

I'm writing this to you from my bed. It's cold, and there's no ways I'd usually be doing anything involving pen and paper at this point on a Friday evening, but you need to hear this. We did it. We went to the flat. I didn't write to you last night because Mare needed a drink – needed several drinks – after our inspection of Mr Nick Wilkinson Jnr's abode.

When we arrived in Illovo every pizza place and cocktail bar was teeming. We found the block easily. His flat is on the second floor, light-filled. It was a little creepy, like in those movies when the detective discovers the crazy guy's wall covered in photographs, or a nasty, homemade altar to a victim. The difference is that Will's big secret is not an obsession with a person, but rather an obsession with stuff. He owns a lot of stuff, Mielie.

The first thing you see when you walk in? CDs. Hundreds, if not thousands of them, floor to ceiling against one wall. Next? The books. So many books, so many shelves, wall after wall, even around the front door. Everything is arranged in alphabetical order. He has collections and full oeuvres, all in the same edition. It must be worth a packet. It must have been a full-time job to assemble it all.

The furniture is expensive, modern. The hi-fi and TV are state-of-the-art. The kitchen is streamlined, with gleaming appliances. There are no pictures on the walls, not even a fridge magnet. There are many mirrors.

I stood in the entrance with my mouth open. Mare was wide-eyed and breathless. Oh, his wonderful taste and so on. How could she have missed the coldness of the space?

We went into the bedroom to see if he'd left something there for her – a note, anything. What did we see? A walk-in wardrobe. Like the books and CDs, everything is arranged neatly, by type. There's the family of leather jackets, the family of wool coats, the large family of vintage middle-blue jeans, the family of takkies and running shoes … and then there are the related families: the suits, the collar shirts and the blazers.

I'll give him this, the boy has taste.

Darling Mare, she couldn't help touching almost every garment. She breathed in deeply but stopped short of hugging jerseys or sniffing sleeves.

I said nothing about the extravagance of the wardrobe, and the obsessive repetition of styles. She said something about how he must have inherited all this 60s stuff from his dad … I managed to keep my mouth shut, but I'll open it here.

There is no ways Nick Wilkinson Jnr lives in hand-me-downs. He has a gift for presentation, and a weakness for shopping. Furthermore, he is a classic collector. It's all about the chase. Everything he owns has been hunted down. He is a man who would enjoy the pursuit of a sartorial impossibility – or an out-of-print book. I doubt he's worn half those clothes. I doubt he's read a fraction of those books. I wonder if he reviews CDs at all. It's quite possible he just buys them.

Take that famous leather jacket of his, the one he's always in. Was it his dad's, as Mare assumes? Or is it from a vintage shop? And if it is, let me tell you, Mielie, you don't get a vintage leather jacket like that at the charity shop opposite the old Olympia bioscope a block below Rockey Street. That's off a rack at a boutique in London or New York, a place called … I'm letting my mind wander now … Strawberry Fields … or Frock, Yeah. Soho, Manhattan, Brooklyn maybe. Can you picture it, Mielie? Don't get me started on the pure-wool vintage suits, the Chelsea boots … they probably belonged to John Lennon.

So why did Will leave her the key?

It makes perfect sense to me that he always wanted to keep her out of his Illovo flat. It reeks of soullessness.

Why change his mind now?

Did he think that maybe she'd be blinded by his possessions? In other words, she wouldn't be so hurt by his behaviour if she was bowled over by his wealth?

No.

Giving Mare the key was Will's way of taking off his mask.

In my view, it's possible he's not coming back. The thing he was going to tell her? Just that. He thought he could buy her a nice dinner and explain to her why she could never fit into his life. Thank God he didn't do that in public. He tried to buy her a car to soften the blow. Now, instead, he gives her a glimpse into his habitat. He hopes she'll see "how different they are" and why he had to "let her go".

If that's the case, she doesn't get it. She thinks he's inviting her deeper into his life … his life of second-hand goods, his literature- and music-loving life, his life that's so at odds with his upbringing … Mare persists in believing there are hidden depths to this weasel.

His life is not at odds with his upbringing. It's a perfect expression of it. He is greedy, selfish and a coward. But she is determined to delude herself.

I would prefer it if he just disappeared. If he never had appeared, in point of fact.

With much love to you and my Toni,
Johnny

PS: It's Sunday now and I confess I am fresh from the M-Net movie and perhaps mildly affected by whisky and not a little emotional. (It was a goodie: Awakenings with Robin Williams.)

I fear our girl's heart is cracking. She's like a balloon that's just been pricked. It has yet to shoot zig-zag through the air, spilling its contents. This is the calm before the storm. She is putting on a brave face. But she's pale. It was a week yesterday, you know.

My opinion is unchanged: Will has left Mare and he's not coming back. He left like a gay man leaves his lover when the lover threatens to tell the wife. At the speed of light, without forwarding address.

It breaks my heart to say it.

I would throw myself under a train for Mare, you know I would, and you would too. She's the kind of girl you don't love in half measure. It's only polite.

But if he loved her like we do – like she deserves – how could he leave the way he did? How could he be living and walking on this earth and NOT PICK UP THE PHONE? Every phone box he walks past, does he slow his pace, consider dialling her number? He walks on by. He looks the other way. He's made his break.

It makes me livid. He picked up Mare as if he was picking an item off a shelf – and now he's decided to leave her because she's not worth paying what it will cost him, socially.

Dammit, friends. I fear my cheeks have turned an unattractive shade of russet. Please God I'm not bursting capillaries.

Work tomorrow.

xxxxxxxxxxxxx

~~Jonnny~~

JOhnny

*

*Letter, Mielie to Mare*
*Saturday 15 June*

My dear Mare,

You'll want to know this first: Will sent me a letter.

It was dated 1 June, so I can only assume that he wrote and posted it in a brief interlude immediately before visiting his parents that same day. I'm not going to go into detail about it here. Sorry, because you probably want me to, more than anything else. I just can't remember it all, and I'm not at home, where the letters are. I'm Having a Ball. AT The Ball. And even though Will might be behaving rather strangely at present, no one ever deserves to be misquoted, hey?

Suffice to say it's clear he adores you. He did come across as incredibly vain, to be honest, but he does want you to be happy.

I swear these days, apart from the start of the next interminable waitressing shift, the sound of post is all there is to get up for in the morning, and the urge to wee. So imagine my astonishment at three envelopes plipping on the doormat, almost all at once: one from Will, one from Johnny and one from you. Did you forget to post yours immediately? The postmark on the envelope is dated later than your letter.

Johnny told me everything you're going through right now. It just seems so cruel and undeserved. I know your thing with Will has been about so much more than sex (plentiful as that has been, by all accounts – relished by Toni, if no-one else).

I don't suppose you've heard from him?

There is comma-however-comma always a place for hope, I know, and I don't blame you for clinging to it.

You think I don't understand, but I do. It's the same with me and Edward. I'm bewildered by the impact of our lives colliding. It was sudden and extreme and I had no idea that it would hurt this much, to be so far away from him.

So I know that hope is not always a choice, but more a necessity. But also, hope can be a cruel thing, I think. Perhaps best abandoned early on.

I say this because I was shortlisted for Lady M at the local Am-Dram society. There was a glimmer. And yes, you are correct. There is no need to skid around the parquet, screaming in your socks, because I didn't get the part. I just found out today. They phoned me at work, to tell me that another chick (of now-forgotten double-barrel surname) clinched it in a neck-in-neck race to the final choice. I haven't called to wish her well … am awaiting sincere congratulatory feelings.

The South African producer – with whom I wish it could be said I hadn't slept – once! in what must have been a deeply troubled patch at university – told me that the British director had found my energy to be more manic than my opponent's. And that faced with the fact that the Macbeth they'd already cast was pure manic energy, a combination of his M and my Lady would give way to unadulterated mania, and distort the balance of the play. And there I'd been thinking that I'd been the one who came across as too withheld and cerebral. But no! Hooray! Visceral me.

Enough on that. "What's done cannot be undone." I nevertheless await the day that M is cast alongside, not before, his Lady. When the latter is not just a counter-balance to the man, but the play's driving force, in her own heartbroken, manic, falling-to-pieces right.

I dropped an entire tray of drinks at work the other night. In the movie version, customers patted my arm and left huge sympathy tips. In reality, I had to mop up all the broken glass and fallen liquid, and pay for the whole thing out of my cash float. Then I smoked two cigarettes in a row, out in the alley. I might have been fired, but my sales figures are tops.

Oh yes! Just when I thought I'd run out of trivia: We went out for Toni's birthday to Planet Hollywood. It's one godawful edifice to vulgar capitalism and little more than an exercise in crowd control. Bouncers with headpieces, etc. Pic enclosed for fridge. You do get to get a squirt of your fave designer perfume in the Ladies, if you're prepared to queue for half an hour, but the lighting's still neon-tube variety, not unlike every retail fitting room I've ever had the misfortune of trying on clothes in.

Anyway, the evening came to an exuberant close back home – after a cab ride with several other people sandwiched against windows, during which Toni and I embarrassed ourselves by being far too chatty – with her on a chair atop the dining-room table in her outdoor coat and sheepskin slippers. She brandished a joint in one hand and a bottle of whisky in the other, and sang along – with gusto – to the latest Westlife album. Johnny would have wept – possibly even choked – had he been there.

I hope this story cheers you up a bit.

"Good night sweetheart, well it's time to go." (Yay for the free peanuts.)

Trudging companionably, and loving you, every step of the way.

Last touch,
Mielie

# CHAPTER 15

*Letter, Mare to Mielie*
*Monday 24 June*

Dear Mielie,

Thanks for taking the time to write. May I just repeat, though, because there seems to be some confusion around this issue: I HAVE NOT GIVEN UP ON WILL.

Please don't ever ask me to dust myself off and move on. You don't know what you're asking me to give up. A life without Will? That's not what I want! Anything but. Think about it, what has he really done wrong? Left in a rush and been a poor correspondent for a few weeks?

May I also repeat: Mielie, you have never met him. Toni has never met him. Johnny has not really given him the time of day. If you had met him I'm sure you wouldn't have said what you said in your letter, Mielie.

I'm going to play back some of the things you said to me about Will (the power of the direct quote: Journalism 101).

About the letter: "I just can't remember it all."

About Will: "He comes across as incredibly vain, to be honest."

Seriously, how would you like it if I said these things about Edward?

And about details of our physical relationship: "relished by Toni, if no-one else" (editor's emphasis).

I'm sorry if I sound shrill. It's hard. It makes me feel even more alone, not having you here to talk to about this.

Phone rang, sorry. Pavlovian.

Back to your letter. "Her own heartbroken, manic, falling-to-pieces right".

Says more about you than Lady M, methinks. It's a car smash. It's like the pedestrian being hit by the car in a car smash. Being able to understand this is your only saving grace right now.

But Hells Bells, Mels. I've been mulling this over. I have all the time in the world, you see, so pour yourself a mug of Scrumpy Jack. Myself, I'm going to make a cup of tea otherwise I might just stare out of the window until I get weepy.

Right, I'm back. With my cheeriest mug, too. The Jungle Book one from Tess. She associates me with the movie because I know all the words to The Bear Necessities.

I wish I was lying in a London park with you, soaking up the sun. If we were side by side we'd be able to figure out what's going on. I'll just pretend. Oak leaves overhead. Sun on toes. Eyes closed against the glare. Here goes:

When I think about Edward, The Catcher in the Rye comes to mind. Have you read it? If you have, you'll know the whole being-forced-into-a-box thing.

If I transpose my image of Holden Caulfield onto your young Edward, I imagine him at the edge of a sports field, or staring out of a multi-paned sash window. There he is, good at maths, popular enough, straight-down-the-line future architect or engineer. He's been on that course since he chose his matric subjects. It carries him all the way through Varsity and then – bam! – Amelia Ashford. Force of nature. His chair touches yours at The Ruby … a spark. And a chemical reaction that changes everything.

I think you opened his eyes. To art and expression, a bit of wildness, a bit of complexity. I think you showed him some of what he'd been straining to see in the Ego-scented sunshine of Fancy High.

I don't think he is mental, Mielie. I think he's perfectly sane. He's madly attracted to you, but he thought he could have the summer romance and then get back on the path to success, because that's been the strongest pull in his life for as long as he can remember. And it is, in a way, everything. It will impress his family, his friends. It will buy him security, a degree of professional fulfilment. He will become – and this may be the biggest compulsion of all – what everyone has always wanted him to be. The choice to defy them, as a therapist in an elbow-patched jumper might say, is one that only he himself can make.

By the way – therapist scribbles in notebook – when Ed says, "you do not deserve to be sad," I think he's talking to himself.

Keep on truckin'
X Mare

PS: African penguins mate for life.

*Letter, Mare to Edward*
*Tuesday 25 June*

Helvetia Court

Dear Edward

It's been so long! Like nearly five months, who would have thunk it? I'm worried about Mielie – and you. Why aren't you together? You should be, here or there or anywhere. I sound like Dr Seuss.

I have a boyfriend – keep your incredulity to yourself, if you don't mind – and I love him, and he's far away, and it's HORRIBLE. So I can say with authority that if there's no life-or-death reason for being apart, don't be.

Listen, no-one's ever going to hire me in the post of Wise One. I'm a flippen idiot, but I'm not wrong about you and Mielie. I've known her all my life. She's maddeningly effing perfect, but she's worth giving anything up for. So what's holding you back? If it's your mother tying you to Cape Town, telling you to be some high-profile man of substance and you don't want that, tell her to shove it. Anyway, she'll grow to love my sister. It's impossible not to. But then you already knew that. And we all love you, man. Yes, that's Mum, waving her arms in the background. She's saying it too. Tess doesn't need to say a word. You were assured of her lifelong commitment from the moment you showed her the way up the swing tree at Eland.

Eat a snoek for me.
XXXX Your sister Mare

PS: Obviously you can't tell Mielie I've written to you. She would skin me alive, like she's been threatening to do for decades … but this time she really would.

PPS: Write back to me if you want. You probably won't. Never mind.

*Letter, Mielie to Edward*
*Wednesday 26 June*

Dear Edward

I'm sorry I've not been returning your calls. These days, I find letter writing a more controlled form of communication. On the phone, your voice in my ear, combined with the distance of your body, makes things almost unbearable.

Writing, I only have to deal with my memory of you, and how you are to me these days. Because you're distant. I can't put my finger on it more precisely. You just are. So distant, in fact, I sometimes find it difficult to breathe.

And when I think of what I must sound like when I talk to you, I can only think of a tape recording, because of how impersonal our phone calls feel.

You suggested, in one of your messages, that I get a fax machine, so we can "stay in touch", and I agree it might be more immediate than posted letters, but really there's no substitute for the real thing. Because the thing is, Edward, life is fragile, and time is short.

It's devastating when you realise that things can only be the way they've become, and I know I can't ask you to promise me anything. But Edward, please. Please tell me that you still believe in what we have. I need to know.

My love as always,
Mielie

PS: I asked the sales lady at a department store here to spray some Calvin Klein One on my wrist a while ago. Because that's what you wore, I explained. They say scent is the closest sense link to memory. And I wanted to remember you in detail. She agreed it could make a good advert.

PPS: "I wasn't born to lose you."
(Sophie B Hawkins: I Want You.)
If you haven't heard it, you really should.

Mielie puts down the pen. It's early morning. She's been thinking about what to write the whole week: crossing the floor at Café Rouge, walking home after work, lying in bed – especially lying in bed.

She woke up thinking about Mare and Will, and what Johnny said: "She's not worth paying what it will cost him". She had a shocking sense of loss, that cold shock of something valuable – an heirloom, a diamond – being suddenly, irretrievably gone: stolen, forgotten, dropped down the sink by mistake. She overcame the jolt – that waking-moment jolt – first by breathing, and then by composing the letter in her mind.

She re-reads it now. "Please tell me that you still believe in what we have." She feels light-headed. Long distance is a machine she can't operate. Her breathing is quickening. She hates this. There's a clunking of gears, metal parts crashing and scraping. What's happened? Why won't he come? Why won't he say? She clenches her teeth. Her body is tingling, she needs to move. Her bare feet step one in front of the other to her bedroom door. She walks down the passage. Her pyjamas brush against her skin. That's better, Mielie, calm down. She finds herself mouthing the words.

"Morning, Mielie," says Toni.

"Any messages?"

"Who from?" Toni says. "Ed? Will?"

Mielie leans against the door jamb.

"Nada," Toni says. "Although that in itself might be a message from the universe … innit?" She knows Mielie loves an accent.

"What's the message from the universe?" Mielie says.

"'Men are pigs.' Coffee?"

*Letter, Edward to Mielie*
*Friday 5 July*

Hello Amelia

I am so sorry I am hurting you. It was never my intention and I would erase it if I could.

You are the most important person in my life and nothing can change that.

I would do anything for you, and there is nothing you are not worthy of.

Even with all the distance between us, I am not that far away if you need me.

It is painful being without you. I kiss you often, in my mind.

You have a beautiful, complicated spirit, and I have certainly never deserved you.

Please give me a little more time, Mielie. I think I can do better.

I also think we will somehow be together forever. On some plane. You'll see.

All my love,
Edward

*

*Letter, Edward to Mare*
*Monday 8 July*

Dear Mare

Thank you for writing to me. It means a lot and I have been thinking about it ever since.

Whereas I admire you and your ability to just go for it, I struggle to make decisions. But you have reminded me about what really matters.

As a result, I have taken leave and booked a plane ticket to see your sister in London this weekend. Please keep it a secret. I would like it to be a surprise. I know she is sad about us.

I did not expect to meet Mielie when I did. I am still not sure that I am ready for her. There are many things weighing on my mind.

My family may have created the impression that she is somehow not good enough. Ironically it is the opposite. I often wonder if I am good enough for her. I want to show her I take our future seriously.

Before I go to London I have some issues to take care of in Pietermaritzburg. I should have taken care of it all a while ago. I am hoping it will clear some of the clouds.

I hope you are having fun in Joburg. It is a really good place to experience, if you watch your back.

Edward

*

*Letter, Mielie to Mare*
*Thursday 11 July*

Dearest Mare

Greetings from the All England Lawn Tennis and Croquet Club, with lashings of strawberries and cream. Needless to say, the tennis is over, and neither I nor Toni made it to any of the games. It was crazy-busy at the restaurant, with people from all over, which at least made a change from the usual suspects, swanning around in their jodhpurs and tweed.

More recently, Wimbledon's been in a state of flag-flying, Castle-Lager-swilling apoplexy. Mandela's here, as you probably know. He threw a huge party for the Queen at the Royal Albert Hall, headlined by Hugh Masekela.

Toni and I declined to attend. Instead, we holed ourselves up at No. 227 and witnessed the whole spectacle on telly, courtesy of BBC. Each time our president filled the screen, Toni sat bolt upright on the couch, eyes closed, chin tipped towards ceiling, and said – in the lower vocal register, unusually – "Oh Captain, My Captain!", before slumping back to resume her manicure.

I'm sorry if my last letter came across as judgmental, as always. I was actually trying not to sound that way. I know I have no right to judge: not you, nor your choices, nor Will as a standalone human. But I think I can still reserve the right to an opinion on how he treated you (or how you let him). So I have to say this before it's too late and I spend the rest of my life wishing I'd just told you what I feel in the moment.

I really didn't like that he threw his money around, took you to places you couldn't afford, and insisted on feeding you and choosing your clothes. It's not generous or loving. It's commandeering. Toni agrees. So does Johnny. So I'm not alone on this point.

Whatever transpires, you and Will are going to have to get to the other side of this thing, you know. Separately or together.

Just please don't feel deserted. I adore you, for following your heart, for reaching the hairpin bend in the road, and for trying so hard to lean into it.

Love always,
Mielie

PS: You know, the more I think about it, the more I agree with you. Edward is a bit like Holden Caulfield in Catcher … and yes I've read it, you basket. You gave me a copy for my 18th birthday. Salvaged from somewhere, with sallow sticky-tape peeling off the spine.

*

*Friday 12 July*

He wakes up with a sour taste in his mouth: drink, and too much of it. The sun is bright. He feels sick from the wine, and sick with regret. His hands are trembling. He gets up, uses the bathroom. Near the phone he finds a scrap of paper and a pen.

*Whatever happened, I blame myself.*

# CHAPTER 16

*Sunday 14 July*

Mielie is upstairs at the brasserie, preparing her section for the Sunday evening shift. Someone's at a table, writing something in a book, with "Jessie, paint your pictures" on its third lap of the day.

She doesn't know how long Edward's been there, but suddenly he is. Framed in the doorway, looking at her.

She stands still, watching him coming across the room towards her. Dust particles suspended in the light.

He stops, puts one hand on the base of her back, the other on her upper arm, and kisses her – just beside her eye, above her cheekbone, very softly.

"I didn't know where to find you, Mielie," he says quietly, his forehead on her temple. "So I just came here."

She feels his breath on her skin, sees the pulse in his throat.

"Statistically, Edward," she says, "you stood a very good chance."

Then both her arms are around him, her fingers in his hair. And they stand like that for a moment, saying nothing. His warmth infuses her.

Then she pours him some coffee and they sit at a table, in the slanting light.

She has so many questions. When she'd read the part in his letter about being together "on some plane", it'd felt like being struck with an axe. Mute with confusion and a newfound lack of confidence, she asks none.

He asks how things are going, and she tells him she's working 72 hours a week – same-old, same-old – plus the part-time script reading, and that it's difficult to talk properly, at work.

"Mielie," Edward says very quietly, leaning back in his chair and looking into the sugar bowl all the while. "My distance. It's not been out of indifference, but out of respect … You've got so much to offer the world. So much to give."

*Problem is, Edward* – she nearly chokes, holding it in – *I only want to give it to you.*

Instead, they're both silent for a bit.

Then he says: "You know, when I saw you from the doorway just now, it was like seeing you again for the first time."

"Long time ago now."

"Yes," he says. "Feels like it."

Then more silence.

Then: "Well," he continues, "so long as you're okay …"

Mielie refolds a napkin on the table.

"I'm flying out again, tomorrow night," he announces. "I couldn't get much leave. But I would very much like to see you, if possible. When you're not working."

He tells her the number of the place where he's staying and she scribbles it down on her order pad.

"Will you be in touch, then, tomorrow?"

Yes, of course she would.

It's quite a tough shift for Mielie, after that. Silent weeping in the kitchen – eyes closed, hand over mouth, and Mourad, always, shaking his head.

*

*Monday 15 July*

Next morning – the morning that will forever be the morning of the day that Mielie and Edward part, again – they meet at Wimbledon station.

Edward has a small bunch of peonies, a book of monologues for women, and a set of second-hand picture frames, picked up at a market en route.

He says there's a movie they could catch, at the Odeon. So that's what they do. They have popcorn, Maltesers, the lot – sitting really close in their chairs, both feeling as if their bodies don't end where the other's begins.

It's not so much a sense of fusion as an utter lack of definition.

Afterwards, they walk down the hill to South Wimbledon. That's when he tells her more about his mum leaning on him, as has been the case ever since his father left and everything "went pear".

"She's not like your mother, Mielie," he explains. "She isn't kind. But she is my mother. And she is lonely. And I do feel obligated to her. It's different, you know. Being a son."

Mielie listens. He says he'll try to tell her about it properly one day, and she thinks: *One day? When does that kick in? On the other side of the life we don't get around to living together?*

By now they've arrived at No. 227, and he comes inside and meets Toni. Mid-manicure, she hugs him: "Mind The Tips, Edward! And about bloody time, wouldn't you say?"

He seems distracted. He wanders around. He fixes the bath leak upstairs.

Then they sit at the dining-room table with Toni – even fewer words, with even longer gaps between them, and lots and lots of stirring of tea.

When Toni goes off to The Ball, Mielie hopes they'll have some proper time alone at last, in bed, to break the awkwardness, repair their connection. But Edward says he has to get going.

It's better outside. They walk a while, and afterwards when Mielie plays it back in her mind, she sees the moving clouds.

Edward watches her sidelong as they walk. His life has felt empty, since she's been gone. She's been luminous, in his dreams. That twinkle. That spring. He thinks about the time she took him to a tiny cabaret theatre in Kalk Bay, with oxblood walls and chandeliers. He saw her face reflected in the mirrors – more alive than anything he'd ever touched or known.

She was sad, even then, he knew. And it terrified him. It still does. Because now she seems sadder than before. There's a darker note.

"Look, I'm sorry if it's anything I've said or done," he says at last, both hands deep in his pockets. But he knows he's culpable. He hasn't even told her the worst of it.

"Actually, Edward, it's what you haven't."

"But what about you, Mielie?" he deflects, the way he knows so well how to do. "What's happened to, you know, your dream?"

"I'm not sure what you mean," she stops, exasperated. "Do you mean the one where I'm standing in the ballroom? The ballroom with the ceiling-to-floor balcony windows and the extravagant vases of flowers, in a full-length drop-dead blood-red dress, champagne glass in hand? … Where I turn around, cameras flashing, agents and directors falling over themselves for my attention, and I thank you for letting me follow my dream?" she asks. "Because that's your fantasy, you know, Edward. Not mine. And I can't make it come true."

"It doesn't have to be like this, Mielie," is all he says.

"I know!" she says. "I know it doesn't. You think I want – no, *deserve* – what did you call it in your card? 'Acclaim'? Is that what you think? Because yes, if I have to be honest, I once did want it. But only because I was supposed to."

"Mielie …"

"And I do want to act, you know, Edward. But it's not for the applause. It doesn't really matter if I don't become the actress I wanted to be." She throws her head back and looks up at the sky. The clouds are moving in quickly, soaking up the daylight. "I just want you," she says, quietly. "And you won't give me that."

*Things can only be the way they've become*, her last letter said. Now Edward knows what she means.

She wipes her eyes and starts walking again. "So I guess that's that, then. Feelings aside."

By the time they get to the station, it's starting to rain.

Mielie is trying very hard to hold things together. To not be angry or tearful. They're standing there in the crowds, surrounded by brollies but without one between them, and they're running out of time.

She does cry. He does speak softly into her ear.

Then it's Mielie's turn to watch Edward recede into the crowd, and wish she could run after him, and make him stop.

*Letter, Mielie to Mare*
*Tuesday 16 July*

Dearest Mare

Here's my latest. To add to the pile I imagine you've tied with a ribbon. I hope you've fire-proofed the lot. I have yours all together, too, in a box I'd reach for before anything else, in the event of natural or unnatural disaster.

I'm guessing still nothing from Will? I'm apprehensive about that. You've given him the most precious thing you have in the world – your heart – and whichever way you look at things, whatever you overlook or make excuses for, he isn't taking care of it, Mare.

So, latest news from the British Home Office is that Edward materialised out of the blue. Wearing blue, even – forget-me-not, or cornflower. You'd know the shade.

I wish we'd had time to do something wonderful, like take a train down south and cycle along country lanes. We could've stayed anywhere. I wouldn't have cared, just as long as we'd had a chance to carry on being in love. And happy. They're not the same thing anymore though, are they?

He gave me flowers, some second-hand picture frames and a book of monologues for women – "Hello IRONY!", as Toni observed.

He met her at our house and fixed the bath leak. So the ironing board is now the ironing board and the pots are the pots – no catchment area required.

When we said goodbye in the rain at the station, he pulled me close, let me cry into his neck for a bit, and murmured something about wishing with all his heart that I could somehow – he knew there was a word for this – somehow TRANSCEND it all, and be okay. Like when he met me, even though Dad had just died.

Were we breaking up, Mare? I dunno. But it's an apt phrase, don't you think? Remember Mum, describing that funny thing that happens with bodies in "the break-up phase" … how a person tends to go all hunched and crumbly and unattractive? At work today, I kept catching myself in "the hunch", so am now concentrating on my posture. And trying very hard to transcend.

I went to the common after my shift, just to walk and be in nature for a while. Because there has to be something redeeming in that, and in routine. I walked for a long time. And it struck me, while walking, that it's so easy to forget what being a child feels like. You always see them running. But I don't run, ever, anymore.

Anyway, in and through all of it, you really are the brightest star in my night sky. Please know this to be true.

Love forever
Mielie

PS: I got home from the station to a note on my pillow:
"I love you, Mielie. I am so sorry I have to leave."

PPS: Screw the suffocating picture frames. I like my pictures the way they are: dog-eared, with the Prestik showing through.

PPPS: I think what happened is, I was the one who fell.

*

*Postcard, Edward to Mare*
*Tuesday 16 July*

Hi Mare
I am back in South Africa and have just landed in Durban.
I drive to Cape Town tomorrow.
I have only one thing to say and that is that you are right. Your sister is perfect.
You are a very special person, Mare.
Your family has always meant a great deal to me.
Thank you for everything.
Edward

*Postcard, Mare to Edward*
*Tuesday 23 July*

Edward!
Shot for the postcard. I've always wanted one of dolphins, jumping through hoops at the Durban Aquarium.
Why do you say "thank you for everything" in a way that sounds startlingly similar to "goodbye"? Why, Ed?
Mielie tells me she saw you. Empty picture frames, no promises? What?
You're being a chop. Your attempt to be more romantic failed.
Love anyway, Mare

*

*Letter, Mare to Mielie*
*Wednesday 24 July*

Helvetia Court, bed

Hi Mielie,

This year: this. The year Will and Ed breezed into our lives and then buzzed the fuck off.

It's been nearly two months since Will left. We were only together for nine weeks in total.

What are we, Tabard? How long have we been drenched in man repellant?

I don't know. Dad adored Mum, to the end. What's wrong with us? With you, I mean. Obviously, there was nothing about me that led to Will disappearing – oh, noooo … it was all because … er … why was it again? Oh, that's right. No-one has any flippen idea. But it couldn't have been me. Right?

Aw, Mielie. I'm so sorry about Ed. "Sorry to leave." I big yaws? God, this long-distance thing is not exactly a walk in the park, is it, despite your walking in the park? I do still believe he loves you. He'll be back in a flash. Same with Will. We can't rush these things.

Work is fine. It's challenging. It keeps my brain occupied. We handed in the course newspaper and now I'm waiting to hear if I'll get the job. I know I must keep working hard. I still need to learn so much, like how to keep myself out of the story, listen more, think harder, read more widely, chatter less.

But when I'm not actually taking notes or typing, I'm thinking about Will.

You know when you start to doubt your own voice because people are shouting you down? I can hear what this sounds like, in your ears and Johnny's, but there's a reason Will left in a hurry, and a reason he hasn't made contact. It's not what you think. He's never been terrible to me, why would he start now?

I have an alternative to the villain theory and it's this: Will is planning a big surprise, and he needs some time alone. I know it, I know in my heart he wants to make a real-life commitment to me – like moving in together. It's taken me a while to be sure, but only because I didn't feel the same. It's not that I don't want to commit to him, it's just that I already am, completely. There's nothing more I need to say or do. But I guess men take it in stages.

He gave me the key to his flat as a kind of clue. It's so like him. And why did he leave in such a rush? Of course I've thought about that too. He wrote to you and then went to his parents before he came to me, remember. He must have told them what he was planning to do, and they ended up getting into a fight. When I saw him he was completely rattled. They do hurt him, his parents. He is capable of being hurt, you know. Maybe he didn't trust himself to spend the evening with me. Maybe he felt in danger of ranting about the argument, and then ruining the surprise.

I honestly think he left to protect me, and right now, in Hermanus, I think he's feeling pulled in opposite directions by his parents and his feelings for me. He's taking some time to gather his strength.

I miss you. If only we were together, I could thoroughly convince you about Will – and the three of us could hash out WHAT THE HELL is going on with Ed.

Love XX Mare

PS: Guess-the-quote: "Jem was a born hero."
Answer: To Kill a Mockingbird.

For bonus points: Who is Jem?
Answer: You.

*

*Thursday 25 July*

Mitchell enters the Westminster Mansions flat at seven as usual, tog bag slung over one shoulder, suit jacket folded over an arm. His hair is combed back and his face is hot.

"I hope Mare isn't busy tomorrow evening," he says as he closes the door. "I can't imagine she would be …" He crosses the floor to where Johnny is washing lettuce – "Hello darling," – and kisses him. "I've invited Will for dinner."

"What?" Johnny turns off the tap.

"I just saw him at the gym."

"WHAT?!"

"It's not complicated," Mitchell says, taking a lid off a pot. "I saw him at the gym and I've invited him to dinner tomorrow. You shall invite Mare. We deserve to know what's going on."

Johnny gets Mare on the phone straight away. It's his beating-heart hope that Will's first port of call was not the treadmill, but her flat.

"Any contact from Will?" he asks, trying to sound tired.

After putting down the phone, Johnny finds Mitchell on the couch.

"What did she say?"

Johnny plops down beside him and picks up the remote. "Well, she's free tomorrow night. But she doesn't know he's back."

*Letter, Mare to Toni*
*Thursday 25 July*

Helvetia Court

Toni

I'm trying to be calm. Wishful thinking. I haven't felt calm or secure since Will left. He's still in Hermanus I think. It's been a while, but I haven't written him off. Never will. I've taken up drinking more than usual instead. Eating, too. Smoking, excessively. I see you tutting. Yes, I'm a cliché.

In my defence, there are factors here – factors other than my proclivity to "roll in shit", as Tess once so charmingly described my emotional declines – that are beyond my control.

Joburg, late July. So, so dry. The grass turns a nauseating yellow-beige. Flyaway sand shows through in patches, like mange on a street dog. The sun is piercing – unforgivingly bright, exhaustingly drying. Lips crack to the point of bleeding. The nights are cruelly, maniacally cold.

I spend my mornings at court. Did I mention I'm a full-time court reporter now? Mostly I'm up and down wide, draughty passages, on and off wooden press benches, recording the testimonies of child abusers, hijackers and forensic pathologists.

The court building smells of sweat and cigarettes. Everyone seems to have a gun to check in at security. The cops in their patchwork leather jackets look haunted. Case after case is postponed. Reason: "lost" docket. Prisoners escape – or are assisted to escape – even from the holding cells below the court. A gun battle has occurred on the steps.

I write at least a story a day. I've been on the front page a few times. I'm on top of it, my beat. Just that it's a subterranean world. Suits my mood.

Then at night-time I'm hyped, like now. Too much coffee after court, probably. It's free in the newsroom. So, before bed I get on my bike in the jeering cold, and I ride. Not down to Rockey Street – I can't, can't go into those places I went with Will.

From Helvetia Court I ride past the mad movie-set water towers. Over the ridge, down the dark pass. Through Bertrams, into the valley. Out the other side into Troyeville. Rockey Street is tame compared to this. Another subterranean world. Through a dark maze and then, the lights of Bob's Bar: my new home-from-home.

I play pool, drink whisky, smoke and leave before I start seeing double. Johnny disapproves. Mielie would too. No avoiding it, though. What else am I supposed to do?

Often Mitchell's friend Walker is there. We play pool, silently. If we do speak, it's about work. He's a news junkie, he follows everything. Sometimes – often – he drives home behind me. I think he's depressed. Usually we both stay on until they lock up.

Will is, as they say, everywhere and nowhere. His parents' names crop up: in the Business Report, on the Society page.

Online, I search "Hermanus" and "Wilkinson". I read the police press releases in the news editor's out-tray. I'm starting to really worry. It's not funny, Toni. If he'd been in an accident, who would tell me?

Yours,
Bonkers, Bellevue

*

*Thursday 25 July*

Nick Wilkinson Jnr is stopped at a busy intersection in Sandton. He's in the driver's seat of his Merc, waiting for the lights to change. Will hates Joburg, he realises. Hermanus was painful – the pain of being without Mare crashed against him day and night, like hard waves breaking. But the northern suburbs, his home for all his life – these flashes of light, the billboards and the rushing metal – fill him with rage. He's never felt it more. He feels like his eyes are flashing too, like that panther behind bars at the zoo.

He's made his decision. Not that he had any real choice. Hermanus was merely a period of torture he saw fit to inflict on himself. He lied to

Mare about the house, of course. There wasn't anything for him to do there. The real work was breaking his addiction to her.

So here he is, reporting for duty. Just because you don't have a job doesn't mean you don't have bosses.

Will hadn't even told his parents about Mare. He could've phoned them from Hermanus and spilt the whole story, but what was the point? Instead, from the evening he arrived, his routine was to pour himself a whisky and settle on the white couch facing the sea. When he picked up the lounge phone it was to call Astor, not Mare.

Will was good at keeping secrets. No one ever needed to know. On the phone to Astor, in Hermanus and on those Sunday afternoons while Mare was at gym with Johnny … he'd felt no impulse to mention Mare. He felt confident he'd be able to take the secret of Marigold Ashford with him to his grave.

The traffic lights change. Will accelerates. *It won't be that hard,* he thinks. *It won't be such a big change. Mare was the big change. This is best for both of us. All I'm doing is going back to how things were.*

*

*Thursday 25 July*

Around nine, Tom Walker is standing at the bar at Bob's, eyes trained on the door. He knows Will's home, because Mitchell told him earlier when he phoned to invite him to Friday supper. He isn't looking out for Will. He is hoping to see Mare.

Now this: The back of Nick Wilkinson Jnr's head, disappearing through the doorway.

Walker jumps up. He calls "Will!" He pushes through the crowd to the door. But it's too late. He's gone.

Walker darts down the road, scanning the side streets. He's missed him.

Later, Mare arrives.

She appears at a pool table next to Walker and yawns. She was waiting at home for Will to call, then lay down for a minute, fell asleep, and woke up at ten. So now here she is.

Walker gets her a drink and then tells her what he saw, finishing with: "I'm not even sure it was him."

Mare's eyes are gleaming and the questions come thick and fast. But Walker is unable to say what the man was wearing, whether he was carrying car keys with a vintage leather tag, if he seemed to be looking for somebody, if he'd ordered a drink and what it was, or how long he'd spent in the bar.

"I told you, I can't even be sure it was him."

"God, Walker, you're so UNhelpful," Mare says. She grabs her jacket. "I have to go now. He might have gone to my flat. If he comes here, for God's sake tell him where I am. Can you manage that, at least?"

*

*Telephone answering machine message, Mare to Mielie and Toni*
*Thursday 25 July*

"Mielie! Toni! Will's back, he's here. Walker saw him tonight at Bob's … I'm so happy!

I haven't seen him yet but I'm like, I swear, I'm like Muhammed Ali, hopping from foot to foot in my corner, start of the tenth round, bruised, bleeding from the lip …"

*Telephone answering machine message, Mare to Mielie and Toni*
*Thursday 25 July, seconds later*

"Yes, I was saying, I'm hope personified … In the other corner? Oh, that's big George Foreman, the Knockout King: bigger, stronger, tipped to win … But I never despaired! That's why I'm Ali, charged with optimism.

Gettit?

My Will is back. I have the will to live! Where there's a will there's a way!!

… GOOD NEWS!!! Finally! Okay, I—"

Mare arrives at Mitchell's Friday-night dinner party alone. Will fails to arrive at all. This fact is not mentioned by those who knew he was invited.

Afterwards, Walker follows Marigold out onto the balcony.

They'd sat together at supper. Walker wasn't sure if he was imagining it, but he sensed her leaning into him occasionally, and he thought he felt himself leaning into her – just a fraction of a tilt, the most timid dance of solidarity.

On the balcony, after lighting her cigarette, he asks her if she's seen Will yet.

She says yes, then no. She hasn't seen him, but he's probably been to see her.

"Probably?"

"Almost certainly."

"Has he phoned?"

"He might have. I've been busy."

"What about your answering machine?"

"I know. But I forget to put it on." She flicks ash off her cigarette "Plus. It's more his style to surprise me. Why do you care?" she asks.

"I do. I don't. Whatever."

"You do, you don't?"

"I do," he says eventually.

Mare puts out her cigarette.

"I do care."

There's another pause. Mare crosses her arms. They both stare fixedly into the sky above the valley, lights twinkling.

Then: "Listen," he says. "Forget I said anything."

"Oh, I doubt that's going to happen."

"No, I'm serious. I was just … being protective."

"There's no need."

"I know," he says.

He offers her another cigarette. She takes it. He lights it for her, lights his own. She exhales.

"Will and I," she says, "we are in love, you know."

"Oh."

"We might not have been able to contact each other for two months, but we are in love."

"Right."

Mare looks at Walker's eyes. She takes a breath and looks away again. "He just had to get some things sorted out."

"But now he's back."

"Now he's back."

They stand and smoke in silence for a while. If they hadn't been smoking, they would have drifted away from each other then, to be alone.

To think.

# CHAPTER 17

*Letter, Mare to Mielie*
*Saturday 27 July*

Westminster Mansions
Bed

Hello Mielie

I'm lying in Mitchell and Johnny's spare bed. They believe in a high thread count in this house. I believe in that too, but am unable to run to Egyptian. The linen here rustles. My duvet cover is so thin it barely sighs.

Fouché is in the kitchen. Earlier I heard him fussing about the eggs not being room temperature – and how could Mitchell be expected to work with eggs that will never poach, straight from the fridge?

Johnny went out earlier to buy ground coffee. An emergency run. When he got back, he said he had to tell me something.

This is the something: Will was invited to the dinner party here last night.

Johnny doesn't know why he didn't come.

I told him it's because he knew I'd want to talk to him alone first, that's all. And that I was fine. I said I honestly didn't know what Will was dealing with – and yes, it was really, seriously hard waiting for him to make contact. But fine.

Johnny didn't look convinced. But he's never trusted Will. Then he fixed me with his eyes and said: "Have you spoken to Mielie about this?"

I'm telling you about it now.

Will's story, when I finally get to talk to him, will be way more interesting, I assure you. For that, I suspect I shall pick up the phone to London.

Meanwhile, today holds: too-cold eggs, perfectly poached, followed by a gym session, followed by ablutions and stabs-at-beautification.

Next Saturday: The Rolling Stones concert.

I hope by then my rolling stone will have rolled into me with the express intention of making magic and staying together forever. Song after song.

XXX Mare

*

*Letter, Mare to Will*
*Sunday 28 July*

Dear Will,

Hello darling.

It's been days. If you've phoned you didn't leave a message. I'm desperate. What's going on? All the weeks you were away, and now this. I can't think why, but you must be punishing me for something. Are you?

Is it because you think I don't love you enough? I know I love you enough, but I have to allow for your perspective, your interpretation.

Have I eroded your trust in some way? Do you feel like I've kept things from you? I'm not sure what. But if I have, I didn't mean to.

Was I too Cape Town art-studenty and snooty and dismissive? I am a bit like that, I've been told. Do you think I act superior to YOU, in some way? I don't feel superior to you, not in any way. Surely it wasn't my work? I understand that you may have felt abandoned when I was so busy at Cadet School … I'm sorry if you did.

Is it the money thing? You know I don't have any money, but when you paid for things, did you feel like I wasn't taking any initiative? You know, like the pressure was always on you to decide what to do?

And socially, you know it hasn't been perfect. It's fair to say that Johnny has held you at arm's length. And I'm hardly integrated with your family and friends. I made such a fuss about not meeting your parents, and of course you've never met my mum or either of my sisters. I just always assumed that you would, eventually.

Finally, to swing the pendulum in the other direction, was I not "bossy" enough? God, Will, I feel certain I know you, but I don't know men. I'm not one. I have no brothers. My father was an unusual man (honorary woman, really). Maybe I could never be strong enough to match you in the way you might want to be matched. I guess it's possible that deep down you want the ruler-swishing schoolmarm … or the tight-lipped, tight-tits Power Mom.

Really? Well, you backed a loser with me. They say prospective grooms should meet their future mothers-in-law because daughters turn into their mothers. If you'd met my mum, you'd have seen that the chances of me becoming increasingly pouchy-faced, soft-chested and teary-eyed are, if not 100%, then very high.

I'm not saying you're a prospective groom.

I love you. I don't care what you are.

But come now.

XXXXXXXXXXXXXXXXXXXXXXXXXXXXXXXXXXX

*

*Sunday 28 July*

After soccer, Tom Walker drives up Cavendish, on his way to Mitchell's.

When he looks up at Helvetia Court, he sees that the windows of Mare's flat are dark. This concerns him. If Mare isn't upstairs on a Sunday night, studying the papers, where is she? He doesn't like the thought that she's especially, miserably swined and is now weaving her way to Illovo, to stake out Will. Of course, she could be with Will.

Walker continues driving, scanning the traffic lanes for a red Honda 50cc and a pair of moss-green leather gloves.

Around eight, the phone in Mitchell's flat rings. The M-Net movie is a Steven Seagal, so the TV's off. Mitchell's in the shower.

"Would you get that, Walker?" Johnny calls from the kitchen, where he's stirring a gravy.

It's Mielie, returning Johnny's call. "Don't disturb him if he's dishing up," she says. "He told Toni he was phoning to see if I'd heard from Mare, and I haven't."

"Oh," he says. "This is Tom Walker, by the way. I'm an old friend of Mitchell's."

"Yes, I know. Mare's told us about you," Mielie says, carefully. "You haven't seen her, have you?"

Walker says he hasn't – he doesn't say how much he wishes he had. The fact that Mare has told her sister about him is both surprising and encouraging.

"Sorry to alarm you, if—"

"No, no, it's fine," he replies.

"Well maybe she's with Will," Mielie says. "He's back, apparently …"

"Yes, he is."

"Mare said. And now Johnny's worried that she's driving around drunk looking for him."

"I just drove past her flat and the lights weren't on." Walker feels obliged to create some context for what he's about to say. "Yes, so we've spent quite a bit of time together recently," he continues. "Not at my instigation, but we have. And I've, uh, I've needed to see her safely home sometimes … actually most times, Amelia."

Mielie takes a deep breath. "Walker," she says. "I hope you know. I hope you know how much that means to me, and how grateful I am. I hope it's not a problem …"

"Not at all," he replies, surprised at her ease and openness. "It's my pleasure, not a duty."

"Yes," says Mielie. "I know what you mean."

"And it must seem to you – I mean … how can it not seem to you …?" he falters.

"That what?" she says. "That you're too old … to be hanging out with her?"

"Well, I was refusing to be conscripted around the same time Mare was … refusing to attend a single-sex primary school. Uh–"

"That's right, you're ancient!" Mielie laughs. "Don't worry," she says. "Really."

Then follows an almost awkward hiatus, which he breaks as follows: "Look, it's Sunday night and I haven't seen her since Friday, and really, I know I have no right to interfere, it's just that I do care about her, you know."

Mielie is quiet again for a bit, while Walker's statement hangs in the air. His hand is at his mouth.

"But you're probably right," Walker says, breaking the silence. "They'll be together. And I realise that she loves him. Absolutely. And I hope he'll endeavour to, uh, to deserve her. I do. I … I do want her to be happy. And thank you for your time. Goodbye, Mielie."

Walker puts down the phone.

Then she puts down the phone.

Both stand alone in their empty spaces, wondering what's happened.

*

*Telephone answering machine message, Mielie to Mare*
*Sunday 28 July*

"Mare! God. Where are you? I just spoke to Walker, at Johnny's. They're all worried about you. Your lights are off. You're not answering your phone. I'm guessing you're with Will … Mare? Stern face now. Just phone Johnny when you get home, please."

*

*Telephone answering machine message, Mare to Nick Wilkinson (Snr)*
*Monday 29 July*

8.43am

"This is a message for Nick Wilkinson Senior. It's Marigold Ashford here, calling from The Star newspaper. I'd like to speak to Mr Wilkinson about his son. My number is 011 688-4221 or 011 678-6923 at home. My email address is m d a at the star dot com."

*Telephone answering machine message, Mare to Nick Wilkinson (Snr)*
*Wednesday 31 July*

8.43am

"This is another message for Mr Wilkinson Senior. Mr Wilkinson, it's Marigold Ashford again. I know you're very busy but I'd love it if you'd return my call so I can find out if Will's okay and stop bothering you at work. Thanks. It's Marigold. Sorry, my number is 011 688-4221. My home number is oh—"

*

*Telephone answering machine message, Mare to Nick Wilkinson (Snr)*
*Thursday 1 August*

8.43am

"This is a message from Marigold Ashford for Nick Wilkinson Senior. Mr Wilkinson, I won't phone you again. I'm sorry if I've annoyed you. Will is very important to me. I just wanted to know he was okay, that's all. I won't send you any more emails either. Okay. Sorry again."

*

*Postcard, Will to Mare*
*Friday 2 August*

So long, Marigold
It's been so long

*Telephone answering machine message, Johnny to Mielie and Toni*
*Saturday 3 August*

"Hi, 's Johnny. Sorry for late … Mare's 'sleep. We saw Nick Fucking Wilkinson at the concert. Some trophy blonde. Sorry, bit pissed …"

*Telephone answering machine message, Johnny to Mielie and Toni*
*Saturday 3 August*

"Jus' unbelievable, like, oh, we've all moved on now, by mutual fucking agreement? Like me and Mare over here and you on the other side, you and some princess in a silk cammie. He—"

*Telephone answering machine message, Johnny to Mielie and Toni*
*Saturday 3 August*

"Ag, man … Mare's sleeping now. But like Will and this girl and all their stupid friends jus' gonna live out their lives together now, in their perfect fucking jeans, round their parents' twelve-seater tables on Sundays, clinking glasses and being offered jobs by family frie—"

*

*Sunday 4 August*

Mare awakes to the sound of rustling. She's in Mitchell and Johnny's spare bed again. It's Sunday morning.

She remembers immediately. Last night. The concert. God, here's the first stab of pain.

When Mare spots Will in the beer queue, she doesn't notice at first that he's with someone. The second she sees his head, the curve of his neck, she stops dead. The rest of the crowd disappear, and it's as if he's advancing towards her.

It's weird, like the near-death experiences she's read about. In that moment, Will is bathed in light. He looks like a religious icon, haloed, levitating, the centre of a beautiful Italian fresco – not just a body among other bodies in denim and leather at a rock concert.

Will doesn't notice Mare and Johnny. She throws her arm up and shouts "Will! Will!" She shakes Johnny's arm: "He's there! Look! There he is!"

"He can't hear you, M." Johnny looks sad.

And then Mare sees the girl. Yes, sees him put his arm around her, languidly, bored.

She's smaller than Mare, slim-shouldered. She makes him look taller than he is. They're in matching leather jackets. Even from a distance, Mare can tell hers cost a bomb. Butter-soft leather, subtly fitted at the waist, then subtly flared. *Calfskin*, she thinks as she watches her lean into him, snug under his arm, tilted against his trunk.

She has wavy blonde hair. Her 501s swell at her hips. Curves. And biker boots. Brown. Buckled. Camden Market, maybe.

They aren't talking to each other, just standing there like they've been together their whole lives, and will be forever. Mare has never felt so excluded from anything in her life.

Johnny takes her hand as they're swept further in. No going back.

It's a blur now. She's lost sight of him.

"Try not to panic," Johnny says. "It might not be as bad as it looks. Come on. Maybe she's his cousin or something. Try and relax, just keep walking."

Then she has to sit down and Johnny says: "Shall we find them? It might be better than hiding. Honestly, there might be a simple explanation."

And Mare says: "I don't know, Johnny. I'm scared. It's weird, I'm really scared."

She's shaking and struggling to hear anything, even though Johnny has sat down next to her and is holding her hand on her leg, talking so close his head is touching hers.

Then he does what Johnny does. He puts his arm around her and loudly declares: "Look at us! From a distance we could be a couple too! All these Joburg men, dreaming about your ample breasts and smooth thighs, they're all looking at us now thinking: Ah! Oh God! Oh, no!" Here he makes stabbing gestures at his heart. "Oh Lord, strike me down now! She is taken! Here's the proof! That's what they're saying, you see."

Johnny makes Mare lift her head.

She's looking around the stands, thinking how surreal it is to be in this dream with all of Joburg present, when she hears Will say: "Howzit."

How had he found them? And where was the strange girl?

(Now, under the duvet, staring unblinking at the ceiling, it occurs to Mare that Will merely chanced upon them sitting on the railings by the public loos. Perhaps Blonde needed to reapply her Body Shop berry-scented lip-gloss, or dab some Angel on her tender throat.)

"Will!" Mare says. She jumps up and throws her arms around him, because that's what her body does when it sees him.

His body is stiff, unyielding. He seems embarrassed, eager to release.

Johnny stands up slowly.

"So, guys," Will says, including them both in a there-you-are, open-arm gesture. "Howzit going?"

To Mare, this is not a dagger to the heart. It feels like a sword. Cold as ice. A blade weighing down on her so heavily, it's hard to lift.

Johnny grips Mare's elbow.

"Will," Mare says again. He glances towards the Ladies. "Will! Didn't you get my letters? My messages to your Dad?" Or something like that.

"Sure, thanks, of course," he says. "Actually I haven't been here long." This he addresses, inexplicably, to Johnny. "Ja, I didn't expect to be back so soon."

"Wha—" Mare starts, but Will cuts her off.

He produces a fake smile: "So how are you guys?"

*You guys.* The phrase swirls in Mare's head. She can't see or hear very well. She might faint. She drops back down to sit on the railing, hands gripping metal, clenching her jaw and trying not to fall on the path. She starts weeping buckets, unable to stop.

Through her hair, Mare sees Will's hand on the railing. He's on his haunches next to her. It reminds her of when she fell off her bike. It makes her hope. She imagines him moving the hair from her face and whispering to her it's all going to be fine, that he loves her and this is just some part he has to play because someone has a gun to the US president's head, and only if he pretends not to love her and to be with some other girl at a rock concert, the world's not going to be blown up.

"Marry," he says.

*Why did he have to say that?* It still makes her face hot, her heart yearn.

Mare lifts her head and looks at his face looking up at her.

"Marry, listen. We'll talk. Just not now. I have to go now. You'll be cool with Johnny, hey? Look after yourself, okay?"

*People say look after yourself when they don't want to look after you themselves,* Mare thinks.

When Mick Jagger comes onto the stage, he looks like a cock, crowing.

They leave the concert early. Johnny is only too happy to drive Mare to his flat, and put her to bed.

Sunday morning, in the Helvetia Court lobby, she plunges her key into her postbox door. Johnny watches in the speckled mirror as she does a little dance, hugging a postcard and a thick envelope.

"Ha!" she trills. "Johnny! It's from Will! … He must've come here today!' She is frowning and smiling at the same time.

In the lift, she turns a shining face to him.

"This is going to explain everything."

Johnny is peering into a bottom cupboard in Mare's kitchen, looking for long-life milk, when he hears a wail – almost a shout – of agony.

She's standing in the hallway. Her face is white and contorted, her pupils dilated, her mouth open. And now there's not even any sound.

She has her arms out, supporting herself in the kitchen doorway.

Johnny stands up. "Sweetie." He holds his arms out to her. Mare is glazed and breathless.

Before he can catch her, she crumples and drops, in a heap, on the kitchen lino.

Johnny gets Mare onto the couch. The contents of the envelope have exploded all over the cushions and the floor. He clears a space for her and she lies there, in a pattern of sunlight, like an invalid.

"I'm making tea," Johnny says.

When he comes back with the mugs, Mare gathers up the papers and hands him the messy pile.

"You should read the one from Will first," she says, sniffing.

Johnny pads off to the bathroom for toilet roll, then scooches up beside Mare, and proceeds to read.

*

*Letter, Will to Mare*
*Sunday 4 August*

To: Marigold

I was glad to see you looking so well at the concert last night. It was unfortunate that my greeting upset you to the extent that it did. I am extremely fond of you – as I am of all my friends.

If I gave you the impression that we were anything more than friends, I apologise. It was not my intention to lead you on. I would not have deliberately created such an impression.

I hope this helps to explain why I did not make contact from Hermanus, and why I have not replied to your messages since my return.

You will see that I have returned the letter you left for me at my flat last Sunday. Enclosed you will also find dated transcripts of your telephone messages, recorded on my father's answering machine at work in the same period, as provided by his secretary.

It is possible – though not certain – that my father will decide to pursue legal action against you. What has been discussed is a restraining order at least, a harassment suit at worst.

Should he take this decision – it would be an action to protect the integrity of his work environment, not an attack on you personally – he wishes to do you the courtesy of providing copies of the evidence he would be forced to advance.

I hope you will continue to think of me as a friend, as I do you.

Yours sincerely,
Nick Wilkinson (Jnr)

When Johnny finishes reading, he puts down Mare's handwritten pages, and the Wilkinsons' typed pages. He takes Mare's hand. She's still crying.

"Okay," he says. "Okay. God. Sweetheart. You need to get a grip."

She does an enormous nose-blow and jerks her shoulders back: "It's fine, Johnny. Don't worry about it. No. Honestly. Please. Don't ask me to pull myself together. I can't. I'd rather you just left. It's not—" Tears stream out again.

"I know it's hard," Johnny says after some time.

"You don't!" She flicks her hair off her face. "You have no idea! How can you expect me to pretend that this – any of this – is remotely okay!"

Johnny is quiet for a bit. "Want me to stay here tonight?"

"No. But thanks. I just can't be with anyone."

"Can I take the papers? I'll check the legal stuff with Mitchell. And Mielie needs to know."

"I want them back."

"I know."

When Johnny gets to his car he stares up at the glass doors of Mare's flat. He thinks of her lying on the couch. That was how he left her.

# CHAPTER 18

*Letter, Toni to Mare and Johnny*
*Monday 5 August*

Dean Street Post-production
Soho, London

Hi guys

Again, the office notepaper is not intended to impress.

I dare not venture out to purchase alternative stationery, due to the unfortunate yet inescapable fact that summer here is blistering hell.

Not because of anything you could identify as actual sunshine, you understand. It's the bodies, see: UN-deo-dorised. Roll-on or aerosol, the concept appears not to have caught on much outside the colonies.

Autumn can't come soon enough.

I ride on the bus, on the tube, and I queue and I shuffle in a crowd with the best of them, and I think: How much more can a person take?

I ask you this with tears in my eyes.

Because she's here, my friends. She is actually right here, in South Wimbledon.

We endure against all odds, only to be blessed with a godforsaken house guest. Joy!

My cousin Kristal Smith.

Not a random person answering to the name of Joy.

(This, merely to clarify.)

My luck, as fate has determined, is that my mother adores her cousin, Kristal's mother, but I tell you for the record: the apple fell faaaaar from that tree.

And she has changed not a jot since her youth.

By this I mean her grey-green eyes.

Her dark hair falling naturally into a perfect Rachel.

Her skin unravaged by African sun.

Has she lived in a cave her whole life? A castle turret?

One has to wonder, one really does.

Also: she has rosebud nipples. I swear on my life.

Why do I know this? We're sharing a room. (Read: bed.)

Yep, like I need a hole in my head.

Like no long-lost cousin the world over ever *didn't*, she rocked up on our doorstep one ill-fated afternoon just recently, all familiar charm.

And in dire need of a place to stay.

She'd phoned Mitchell, hadn't she.

And bright spark that he is, he'd GIVEN her our address.

When I opened the door, she breathed "Oh-my-God!", like I'd surprised HER, then threw her arms out stiffly for a hug.

"Ah-muh-Gahd!" again. "To-neee!"

She looked past my shoulder.

"Oh my WORD, it's perfect!"

Yes I hear you, Johnny. I see you nodding sagely.

Not only is she someone who decides what she wants, she acts like it's hers already.

I like to be kind, friends. You know this to be true.

I extend a hand, when faced with no alternative.

But here's the thing:

She's a freeloader of note. Cash-strapped, pretending not to be.

E.G.

She's been here for over a week, and is yet to enter a grocery store.

Oh wait, she buys us drinks. That's her contribution to housekeeping.

She helps herself to whatever she finds in the fridge or bathroom, and in return we get free Scrumpy on tap.

And she's vacuous, I tell you.

Likes aquariums. Goes to them "just to stare …"

As if this highly original gesture somehow adds to her non-existent mystery.

It's too much, especially at The Ball: the baby backpack, the dainty jewellery, the spaghetti straps.

What is she the queen of? Fairies?

Oh no.

She's the queen of masculine fantasy:

A bit of damsel-in-distress, a bit of oops-you-caught-me-standing-here-in-my-Wonderbra, a bit of I-like-showering-naked-in-water-falls.

Get it?

She's only ever been interested in men, and how she can use them.

Never had a female friend in her life.

Told me once that when she goes to North Beach, where the surfers are, she makes sure to:

A.) wear a white bikini

B.) cover herself in Factor 50

and

C.) Only ever swim alone.

ALONE, people.

I share this with you quite for free.

So I'm hoping it's going to be a brief encounter.

I'm not at my best, when compromised.

Even less so when required to share ablutions.

And a bed.

And my hairdryer.

Pause to imagine:

I have short hair. Hers is lustrous.

So my hairdryer WILL burn out.

If not tomorrow, then soon.

How is this fair? How sustainable?

Is it just me, or is catastrophe imminent.

Choice, as you always say I always say.
Love to you, Lunatics
Tones

PS: Mielie seems oblivious to Kristal's not-very-nice party trick, the one I call Price-Tagging:

"Mielie! Where did that come from?" she'll exclaim, pointing at cardie.

(Mielie removes cardigan.)

"That T-shirt! How much did it cost?"

(Mielie does a lips-only smile, says Jeez Kristal, I can't remember, pushes past her. Kristal trots behind.)

"Have I seen those Mary Janes before? Where from?"

Apart from the repellent superficiality of this repeated performance, it's just plain weird.

Like she's trying to get inside Mielie's skin.

Something's up.

Can't put my finger on it, but mark my words.

PPS: Mare, you are riding your bike on dark roads and through cold valleys late at night, sloshed.
So I pose to you merely this:
Is love worth actually dying for?
Is that what you believe?

*

*Monday 5 August*

On the Monday evening, Mielie travels to the agency in central London to collect some scripts – only to be told they're at the casting agent's house, all the way in Morden.

The whole way down the Northern Line, she thinks about Edward and cries – eyes down, so no one will see. Not that they'd notice anyway.

She gets off at Morden Station, only to realise it's one stop outside her travel zone. At the Tickets and Assistance booth, she tells the man behind the glass that she needs an 80p extension because she's overshot her zone, and he tells her this will cost ten pounds.

"Come on now, you're joking," she says.

"No madam, I am not," he says. "If you come through here, I'm going to fine you ten pounds. Or, you can go back into your zone, purchase your 80p extension there, and come back."

Mielie is stunned. "What the hell's a Tickets and Assistance booth DOING on the platform side of the turnstiles if you can't get tickets or assistance here?" she asks, wishing she had ten pounds to throw at him in scorn.

He doesn't reply.

In that moment, she imagines being arrested – dragged off kicking, screaming and biting through uniforms, anything rather than having to hear another "take care, luv".

Fortunately, however, the good sense their father tried to imbue in his daughters from a very young age – and with staggeringly different outcomes – prevails. So Mielie tears off down the escalator, stands sobbing alone on the empty platform for ten minutes, catches the tube back to South Wimbledon, buys the abovementioned ticket, tubes back to Morden, storms up the escalator, shoves the ticket through the slot at the turnstile and shouts: "HAPPY?" to the man behind the glass.

She's so upset, she has to stop at Victoria Wine for a packet of Marlboro Plain and smoke three in a row on the pavement.

*

*Letter, Mielie to Mare*
*Monday 5 August*

Dearest Mare

When I got home just now, Toni was out and the phone was ringing. It was Johnny. He told me about the concert in detail and then he read me everything.

Oh Mare. The horror.

There's no ways Will wrote That Letter. Text analysis 101 applies: passive voice, zero use of the common contraction. And as for "Yours sincerely" … And the bit about continuing to think of each other as friends!! How does one begin to address everything that's so appallingly wrong with that statement? You NEVER thought of him as a friend. So continuance is not a consideration, it's a fucking whitewash. You were LOVERS. Fact. Obliterated in a single sentence. How dare they.

And then: "This is not an attack on you personally." Well then, Napoleon, what the fuck exactly do you call the threatened action? A RANDOM attack, just to make a general point, to no one in particular?

It's a full-on attack. The clan flexing its collective muscle. Deflecting you by putting you down. Intimidating you with threats and accusations.

And please, go on, tell me. Tell me exactly about being FORCED to advance evidence … Classic case of aggressor-plays-victim. While you were the one who felt inadequate, like you had to prove that you were worth Will's love.

It makes me so mad. Them squashing you like a bug beneath a heel. They are total heels. They should be ashamed.

Oh Mare. You were always the romantic – a condition for which, I know, there is no cure. But you phoned his father to say you wouldn't phone anymore, spelling out your email address when he already had it … that's probably not ideal. I love you for being irrepressible, Mare. But it's probably not ideal.

I think something's happened – we don't know what – but something HAS happened, and Will can't tell you. He definitely wrote the "so long" postcard, though. God, it's sad. The double meaning. He sounds like he's staring down the prospect of a life that excludes you. You, the love of it.

Losing you isn't something anyone could recover from, ever. Not really. You do know that, don't you?

Whatever transpires, I don't doubt that this is a defining moment in your life.

All that matters now is you not losing track of how precious you are, and how you move on. Because your life will go on. And you have to let him go.

I love you,
Mielie

PS: "Stand tall, Rose Red. Stand straight and tall."
No prizes for guessing.
You know it was Dad.

*Monday 5 August*

For a change, Mitchell, Johnny and Fouché are at Walker's place. Mitchell and Johnny popped in on the way back from gym and Fouché was already there, lying full length on the stoep in the last of the sun.

Soup and bread were provided, Johnny called Mielie, and now the four men are still on the stoep, in the cold. Walker has poured them all another glass of red, and they listen as Johnny reads them the Mare and Wilkinson letters.

It's a moonlit night, and a somber affair – though not devoid of gossip. There are regular eruptions of expletives – mainly from Fouché, still prone on the couch, but now under a dusty blanket.

"I can't believe that *poes*," he says, carefully placing his wineglass on the concrete floor once Johnny has tucked all the pages in the envelope. "This is the last thing she needs."

"A harassment suit," Walker sneers. "Morons."

"Harassment suit," Mitchell repeats. He zips his windbreaker up to his chin. "They have no fucking idea who they're dealing with."

"They were smoorverlief. Soos katjies in 'n kombers," Fouché continues. "Then: Kwa!"

"True," Walker says, his eyes travelling over the grasses to the highway at the bottom of the property. "He'll live to regret it."

*

*Letter, Mielie to Mare*
*Friday 9 August*

Mare,

I was about to go to sleep but I turned the light back on to chat to you. Even if it is only on paper. You've been so much on my mind.

How are you this evening, Miss Marigold? I hope you're letting Johnny care for you. If Toni and I were there we'd be doing the same. We're thinking of you all the time, though not chatting as much about you and Will as we would be if Kristal wasn't here.

Has Toni told you about our houseguest, cousin Kristal? She's such a clot.

The other evening when I was cooking, in she breezed, asking what was for supper and declaring herself to be starved. So I said it was just a kind of veggie stew, nothing special really, and in she moved on me, like: "Oh there's millions of exciting things you can do with veggies … Do we have any honey?" (Nope. You live here and you know there's no honey. Honey.)

"If only we had a bottle of red wine …" And then she started with the herbs, as if casting a spell. Tossing flakes of dried oreganum into the pot, lighting candles, changing the music to something mesmeric … basically just surrounding herself with all things exquisitely feminine – none more so than she.

Mostly I try to ignore her – as if she's ever got anything interesting to say anyway – but still, she's got this way of permeating everything … wafting around in her slip dresses and butterfly clips, waiting to be netted by some lucky man.

I asked Toni why we've never met her, if they're cousins. She threw her head back and said: "God, I wish I'd never met her. She used to come to the hotel with her mum in the holidays, i.e. Ruin My Summer."

It was my turn to clean the carpets yesterday, and I found quite a sad thing under her and Toni's bed: a fake diamond tiara in a see-through plastic box. And next to it – resting on a dark-blue faux-velvet plinth – a small, handwritten card, dated December 1984. "Happy Christmas, little princess," it said. "Love you like crazy, Dad."

I asked Toni about it. Kristal's dad got it for her specially from Charisma, the ballet shop in Durban, and it was the last thing he gave her before he died. "Shot stone dead in his restaurant," Toni said. "Kristal was eating strawberry ice-cream."

So I've been trying to be nice to her, while hoping she buggers off soon.

Oh Mare, I'm afraid I'm dropping off now.

So much love to you,
Xxxxx

*Letter, Mielie to Mare*
*Saturday 10 August*

My darling Mare

Listen, I'm at work – just the evening shift today, and it starts in an hour, but I wanted to tell you what happened this morning. It's left me feeling odd.

Kristal came into my room with two mugs of tea – all sleepy eyes and tousled hair and rose-print flannel pyjamas.

Next thing, she settles in at the end of my bed, crosses her legs beneath the duvet, and fixes her shallow eyes on me.

She hoped I didn't mind her asking – sorry for crossing the line, if she was crossing any line – but: what was it LIKE, having Peter as a brother and especially, you know, Fiona as a sister-in-law?

Sunlight streamed through the window. I yawned.

She said that must seem weird but Fiona has always been her idol. Coz-like … when she was growing up in Durban, she seriously worshipped the ground Fiona walked on. She wanted to be just like her. She wanted to BE her, basically …

I was still waking up, Mare.

Of course I knew that Edward's family came from Durban, originally, and that he stayed on at his boarding school in Maritzburg when Geraldine and Fifi moved to Cape Town after the divorce. But how did Kristal Smith know Fifi? I had no points of connection.

Turns out their fathers were best friends – from-like-WAY back, on the border … Her dad was the best man when David Taylor married Geraldine, really young – Shotgun (giggle) if I MUST know.

I heard a floorboard creak in the passage. Toni, probably, listening in.

"So … that's quite something," I said, eventually. "You've known the Taylor family for your entire life?"

A wide-eyed nod. Oh yes, she, Fiona and Edward basically grew up together. Their dads even took them camping, sometimes, while their moms stayed home. But shame, all that ended when her father was murdered, and she and her mum moved to Maritzburg, to be closer to family.

So my best friend's cousin grew up hero-worshipping the person who half-became our sister-in-law. And spent her childhood holidays with Edward.

"Wow," I said. "Small world."

"It is, isn't it?" she said. Then: "Actually," (pious smile now, eyes down) "Edward took his parents' divorce really hard … he's SUCH a softie! …" and his dad remarried quite soon. So sometimes, instead of being uncomfortable round his step-mother or going to Cape Town for the mid-term breaks, "Eddy stayed with me and Mum instead."

I kept quiet. Where was she going with this?

Transpires Edward took Kristal to his matric dance, and they were each other's first real loves. As in: Losing their virginity together, if I got what she meant.

Outside, the wind-chimes tinkled. Toni coughed in the passage.

The words came out before I could stop them. There must be some mistake …

He never even mentioned her name to me, Mare. But clearly he mentioned mine to her, because: No, she absolutely did mean that very one-and-only blonde-haired, blue-eyed Edward Taylor. And she was totally sure he wouldn't mind her telling ME, of all people, about their past, because basically he thinks of me as a sister, and basically that's what I am, really, aren't I? A sister. In-law.

You can't argue with that line of thought, now can you?

And oh, how it broke his heart to leave her, when he went to Varsity in Joburg. She knew it did because he wrote her the saddest letters … One of which emerged now, from floral pyjama pocket. His handwriting: neat, slanting, unmistakeable.

I hate cold tea, but I drank it.

And they never actually broke up, exactly, she continued. But you could say they drifted apart … Anyway, she was trying her best to come to terms with how things had sort-of – but not really, like, really-really – ended between them. And at least she had a picture of him to treasure …

Suddenly, there he was. My Edward. Smiling through a plastic sleeve in his ex-girlfriend's purse.

A tear slid down her cheek. She said she knew she should just look after herself and not still be there for him. She knew she was being stupid.

I resisted contradiction and stared at her instead.

She hoped, she said, she really-really hoped that she could trust me not to breathe a word about her real-true feelings to anyone … but she had no one else to turn to. Seriously, did I have ANY IDEA how lonely she was? How hard it was? To be her?

More cold tea. You wouldn't have deigned to drink it, Mare.

Time stretches, and my heart aches when I think of you.

# CHAPTER 19

*Letter, Toni to Johnny*
*Sunday 11 August*

BURN WHILE READING

Johnny.

This morning's hangover? Category: Savage.

I have nevertheless summoned the stamina to write to you, and only you, for a single and most specific reason:

What I am about to tell you no one else can ever know.

You must burn this Johnny, I mean it.

Yes, line by line.

Light up right now please my friend.

These words should already be ash.

Don't believe me? Oh why must I beg.

I'm suffering severe dehydration as it is.

And possible actual alcohol poisoning.

But please, give no thought to my personal wellbeing.

We must focus on the crisis at hand.

Jump with me, then, direct to punchline:

Kristal screwed Edward.

Recently. In Maritzburg. Before he came here to see Mielie.

I may be guilty of slight exaggeration, when occasion merits.

But this is not one such.

It is instead a plain and simple fact.

I.E.

It either happened, or it didn't.

It did.

Couldn't make it up if I tried.

Right. I smell sulphur. Good.

But WHY are you always fumbling with matches?

Get a lighter, you cheapskate knob.

Full catastrophe herewith:

Last night, circa 6.30pm.

I'm in the bath, as per usual – pores, nostrils, fingernails, eardrums, all completely vile.

Enter Kristal in fog of liquor.

This mingles with the steam – window's painted closed, why not – to create an especially aromatic ambience for my temporarily sober self.

She has an idea. The idea is that we go to Mielie's brasserie for supper.

Special treat. She's paying.

I carefully remove a slice of cucumber from my left eye socket to check I am not imagining this.

Nope, there she is.

Perched atop the lavatory seat, all smeared mascara and nonchalant limbs.

"Kristal," I say. "Should we perhaps consider this:

A.) When you're sober

B.) When Mielie's not working, and

C.) In a location where Mielie's not employed?"

The minx concocts some bullshit story about wanting to pay us back for letting her stay with us, and also to tell us a secret: "I heard you in the passage this morning, Toni, when I was talking to Mielie. But there's more. I happen to be closer to Edward right now than you think …"

I'm sitting forward in the bath, looking straight at her. Not blinking.

"Really, Kristal, how so?"

Johnny, Mielie made me swear not to talk about their relationship with anyone while she's still trying to figure things out in her head. So Kristal doesn't know about it. Not from me, anyway.

This is when I think to myself, Johnny, I think:

I'm not the one who's blinded by pain.

That person, right now, is smiling while she's dying inside and clearing plates and serving drinks to assholes.

That person is someone worth actually fighting for.

Therefore, I require facts.

So: "Go on, Kristal," I say in extra-carefully modulated tone.

"Please go ahead and tell me what you mean."

"I MEAN, To-NEEE …" (fake-heartfelt sigh)

"Oh what do I mean? The thing is, see …" (pseudo-dramatic deep-intake of breath) …

THEN she pipes up – this is The Moment:

"Eddy and I, we slept together in Maritzburg last month."

One night, Johnny. That's all it took.

For Edward to step left of centre and screw the girl he DIDN'T love.

Facts:

He contacted Kristal beforehand.

To tell her he was on his way to London and had something he needed to say before he left.

Then he drove to Maritzburg and met her in town.

At Stuttafords, where she worked as an Oaktree salesgirl for longer than anyone cares to remember.

And they went out to supper somewhere nearby.

The way she tells it, she was over-excited to see him again, was jealous when he told her about loving Mielie, and consequently got slaughtered.

She says she insisted she was fine to drive, but he insisted on following her in his own car, to be safe.

Which he then did. Perhaps not entirely sober himself.

And then he saw her upstairs, to the door of her flat.

And God only knows what happened then.

But they did end up having sex.

I for one am not going to speculate about how someone is capable of such an action.

But it was good, according to her.

(In case you're wondering. Not saying you're the type.)

I lay back in the bath, Johnny, eyes closed, to hear all of this.

So.

Kristal knew about Mielie and Edward all along, since before she got here, Yet Omitted To Say So (YOTSS).

I rose to face her, starkers.

"Get out."

"Toni! What …?"

"Get the fuck out. Right now, I mean it. Get out of my house, and while you're at it, out of my life."

She put a hand out, clutching my arm.

"But … but, I'm telling you this because I need your advice," she said.

"Advice?" I said. "Oh shoot me while I'm standing up."

I'd have taken a common bread-knife to her right then, honestly I would, had I only been certain of defying arrest.

Instead, in seething silence, I packed her stuff while she sat crying on the bed.

"Toni," she was saying in a fluster. "You and Mielie are like big sisters to me."

(Some women just can't resist calling other women "big". Ever noticed? I have.)

"Except we're not sisters, are we Kristal? Whatever, hey," I think I said. "It's over now. It's done."

I called a cab and escorted her, in it, to the Balham squat.

(When dealing with sociopath, leave nothing to chance.)

Damian the Australian can have her for free.

Then I went to the restaurant to find Mielie.

To NOT tell her about Kristal and Edward's latest encounter.

Because no meds would suffice.

My heart was in pieces for her.

But also you know what Johnny, I was feeling quite bad for my own self too:

Homesick, furious, sick to death of propping people up.

And the non-stop coping.

Also, not fitting in.

*

*Saturday 10 August*

When Toni found Mielie, she was sitting – cider in hand, head against window, looking out.

"Right, bitch, we're going dancing," Toni said. "Oy, George, lend us a fifty."

"Never," George said, not looking up.

"Fuck off, George, I'll pay it back," Toni said.

Dead silence.

"Cheesegrater: you. Fingertip: me," she continued.

"Go home won't you?" – his endearing reply.

"Georgie," Toni said. "Mielie could walk out on you right now. Isn't a restaurant in Wimbledon wouldn't take her in a flash."

"Not listening."

"We all know you're in love with her. Just open the till, there's a pet."

Then Mielie piped up: "Hey Toni, Bren at The Ball offered me a job, did I tell you? Been thinking …"

(Till pings.)

"Never again," said George. "And it's coming off your salary, Mielie, a tenner a week."

She took the money and shoved it in the back pocket of her jeans.

They rushed for the door.

Then Mielie stopped, turned: "Hey George, you're The Best!" she said.

*

*Letter (continues), Toni to Johnny*
*Sunday 11 August*

We ran into the street like children on the last day of school, yelling all the way to the bus stop.

Found an 80s club in Central London.

Two shots down the hatch, first-up, then the dancefloor.

We slammed our feet, we swung our arms, we shouted lyrics, we claimed our space.

All camaraderie and sadness, like soldiers on leave.

Outside, afterwards, we collapsed on the pavement, stripped to our vests. No make-up.

Sweaty upper-arm to sweaty upper-arm.

"God, I needed that," I said.

Mielie stuck her legs out in the gutter, slumped like a marionette when someone's cut the strings.

I was digging around for cigs when I heard her gasp.

The gasp cracked and turned into a sob.

"Babe!" I said.

I gripped her round the shoulders.

There was already mucus everywhere, and tears.

"Ag, Toni …" she said. "I am so, so sad ..."

"Oh, babe!" I said. "I know."

She was making me cry, you must know, Johnny.

"I want to go home," she sobbed. "I can't do this anymore."

"I know," I said, sniffing. "It's the worst."

"Why can't everything just be like it was?" She was cry-laughing now.

"Exactly! Fuck!" I smacked the tar.

"I HATE this place. I HATE IT!"

Think I might have thrown up in the cab. Poor bloke.

Wouldn't be the first such occasion. For either of us.

But still.

And that, my friend, is that state we're in.

Edward and Kristal are psychopathic liars.

Mielie and I now-confirmed bergie-tramps.

Exiting in blaze of glory,
Toni Palmer
(Madam to you)

*

*Sunday 11 August*

Kristal Smith has never been in a squat before. When she wakes up on the couch of Toni's former home, it is amongst ashtrays and take-away boxes.

The night before, after Toni kicked her out of the meter taxi, the busted front door had been answered by Damian the Australian himself. Kristal had followed him into the lounge, which was full of people and Midnight Oil playing loud. The room was dark. People were smoking joints and drinking tins of lager and cider. Kristal heard someone say "Who's that?", and someone reply: "Some chick who knows Toni, you know, Damian's ex." After that Kristal was handed a drink and after that she helped herself.

When she fell asleep on the couch the party was still going with the Crash Test Dummies. At some point Damian covered her up and slipped a pillow under her head.

The first thing Kristal does, in the early morning light, is wash her face, brush her hair and change her clothes. She also applies "natural" make-up. When she enters the kitchen Damian is already there, dressed only in his underpants.

A few hours later, after Kristal has dressed herself for the second time that day, she drops a notebook into her handbag and, mouthing the words that she'll write to Mielie as she walks, takes herself out for lunch at McDonalds.

*

*Letter, Kristal to Mielie*
*Sunday 11 August*

Dear Mielie.

When I woke up just now I didn't have a clue where I was. I thought maybe I'm dreaming but I pinched myself and nothing changed. Then I remembered!! Toni chucked me out last night when you were working and then she bought me to this terrible squat.

I think I'm in Balham. It was dark when we drove here and I was crying so much I didn't hear what she said to the taxi driver. I just heard him say he was from Ganah and I wondered if I will ever get in a taxi that isn't driven by someone from Ganah. I said to Toni is there anyone even LEFT in Ganah and she told me to shut the F-up.

Anyway, wherever the squat is, I don't plan to stay there one second more than I need. It's really gross.

I had to sleep on a filthy couch with no sheets or anything, just a thin sleeping bag with a broken zip. They gave me a pillow but it was so totally disgusting I put some undies in a Tshirt rather. You would die. Also!! Their is no toilet paper in the toilet!!! You have to bring your own in and out with you. I didn't pack any toilet paper from your place, so now I'm truely screwed.

There's not much furniture there actually. Its mostly like just a whole lot of shit on the floor. And when I say shit I mean SHIT.

I can't believe this time yesterday we were drinking tea in your bed and I was opening my heart to you about Edward and everything. You must of been a bit suprised. All that time I stayed with you and Toni I was looking for the right time to tell you about him and me but you always just like shut me out. Sometimes I felt like you were trying to pretend like I wasn't right their in front of your eyes. Its not a nice feeling when a person does that to you but anyway I just wanted to be your friend. And now Toni's really really mad at me…… I know she can sometimes be quite hard on people but I never thought she could do something this bad to ME, like hello! I'm your cousin!!

Did she tell you why she chucked me out? I told her Edward and me slept together when he came to visit in Maritzburg last month. She didn't even give me a chance to tell her the whole story. She literally just threw me down the stairs and out of the door.

Or maybe she didn't tell you?? (How would I know. I'm not a mindreader.) Anyhow if she didn't tell you then now you know.

Eddy and I couldn't help it, Mielie. It was hard for us to be so far away from each other when he was at university, especially for me because I wasn't the one studying and meeting other people but I stayed faithful to him anyway because I knew in my heart that he loved me and he just needed to get a qualification. He is really clever and I didn't want to be selfish and hold him back. And then he moved to Cape Town and I wrote to him but he never answered. I felt so scared he was forgetting about me, but I never stopped loving him. Then he came all that way just to see me so I knew that he wanted me the same way he always did.

You know he doesn't talk a whole lot hey Mielie but that night it felt like he was trying to explain something important so I shut up and listened. He told me about you. Yes I know you slept together but I didn't want to make you embarassed yesterday so that's why I didn't say anything about that.

We got a bit trashed and I wanted to get a taxi but he said he would follow me home in his car rather so I let him and then we ended up in bed together...... HOT-capital-H is all I can say!!!

I promise you I wouldn't hurt you and tell you the sex part if there wasn't something else....... this is SO hard for me...... really-really hard. I'm not a person who can open up to easily but I badly need advise. Because I missed my period last week!!! I KNOW!! Oh My WORD!!! And we used a condom and everything!!

I can't tell my mother she will literally freak!!! So what do YOU think Mielie? What would you do in my situation? Don't say you would make sure you didn't fall pregnant to start with. I can hear you saying that and also I saw you take the pill. If you aren't with Edward anymore then why are you still taking the pill?? You don't seem like a person who sleeps around. I'm not saying Toni sleeps around but actually she does sleep around. I'm just asking..... If you were in love with someone and you had their baby inside you and no-one else knew, not even him, would you tell him or not? 'Coz if I tell him about the baby he will marry me for sure but I know the time is not right for that yet. I need to get his mother on my side first otherwise she might cut him out of her money and I just can't do that to him. He deserves the best of everything and he shouldn't give all that up just to be with me.

So should I just keep quiet and get an abortion? If that's what you think I must do then I will. What do you think???

Please write back to me soon and don't breath a word of a lie..... not to anyone not even Toni.

I don't know what I would do to myself if anyone found out.

Yours respectively xxxxxxxxxxxxx Kristal Smith

*

*Tuesday 13 August*

Mielie Ashford is walking.

She is on her way, not to an audition but to an interview for an office job in one of London's biggest talent agencies. She's prepared, and properly dressed – Toni saw to that. Several times she'd said to Mielie: *This could be your big break.*

Mielie understands the importance of this morning, but she can't get her head straight.

She walks and thinks about Edward. About his being trapped. She feels trapped too.

She's always had freedom – full access to all the facts, all the options. Now she only has the facts. She feels straightjacketed.

*It's back-to-front,* she thinks. *The straightjacket is making me mad. I'm not mad-hence-the-straightjacket.*

At Piccadilly Circus – at the statue of Eros, of course – a loved-up couple stops her and asks her to take their photograph. As she clicks the shutter – "SMILE" – she feels a sudden, ripping pain. *It's over.*

Shaking, she hands back the camera and then suddenly her hands are on her knees. *This is what they must mean when they say "pull yourself together".*

She walks on.

*Edward. Kristal. Edward.*

What can she do? She can't do anything.

What does she feel? Not angry. Not with Edward. She aches for him – too kind to shrug Kristal off, as he should have properly, years ago. He didn't want to leave a hole in her life, not after her father's murder. So he kept up their correspondence, and she manipulated him. Like she always will. Poor Edward.

Mielie is counting down the numbers. The Oxford Street address is coming up. She glances into a shop window. Fails to recognise herself. Sees an older girl, bent in the crowd.

She signs in at security and takes the lift to the correct floor. She checks her watch and slips into the Ladies.

In the mirror, her skin is flushed, her eyelids thick like slugs or blisters.

*This can't be me,* she thinks. *But I know this person. Is she me? Am I her? It can't be. I'm not here. I've run off somewhere, down the hill in the garden at Eland with Mare. We're going to fetch the doll she forgot. We'll be late for bath-time, and I don't care.*

Her ears ring, her heart throbs in her throat. The shaking hands must stop. She runs cool streams of water over her wrists. She nods. She smiles. She tilts her head and widens her eyes.

"Hi!" she says brightly, to the mirror.

*And I am WHO, again?*

They're going to ask her that, any minute, and now she's panicking a bit.

Mielie Ashford is alone in a bathroom in a building in a strange city, and she can't for the life of her remember her own name.

# PART FOUR

# CHAPTER 20

*Tuesday 13 August*

There is a fire escape linking the alley to the roof of the double-storey building that is Café Rouge, Wimbledon. On ground level, the rubbish bins hunker in a stench that mingles with the smell of chips and pastries, piped through the extractor fan. The steps are especially slippery when it rains – grey slabs of metal awash with water from an even greyer summer sky. The gutters erupt in see-through curtains falling past the windows, themselves aslide with rain.

If Mielie stands on the step, her back against the dark-green door with the sign that says EMERGENCY, she can just about press back far enough behind the fall of water from the gutter edge to smoke her cigarette and breathe.

*Maybe it's not over,* she thinks. *Maybe there is more. It's okay. There is something you can do. You can write to Kristal. Okay, okay.*

There's never an ashtray, not even where you ARE allowed to smoke, but Mielie doesn't like just to chuck the butt after grinding it out between bricks.

That's why she goes to the bins. She knows the smell will be worse when she opens one – just a chink, just enough to stuff another stupid now-drenched stompie under the plastic lid.

At the bin she hears a sound – just the smallest, most fragile of sounds.

She hesitates. Mielie wants to leave the sound and the smell inside, walk away from the rubbish and the stompies and the zig-zag staircase against the sky. But that sound belongs to something, and it's crying.

She lifts the lid. Then: two little eyes, peeping through the darkness, about half-way down. Mielie holds her breath, reaches into the sodden darkness, and finds its body. Just a handful – shuddering. She can feel its heartbeat, its wet little nose right beneath her earlobe, tiny claws at her collar.

The rain keeps streaming down on both of them – hair plastered to skin. She's out of time. Tables will be waiting, glasses empty, meals ready to be served. So she puts the kitten in her apron pocket – instantly soaking her order pad – and opens the dark green door.

Inside, it's hot and noisy. The lights are bright. Mielie needs to move fast between the tables, past hands reaching to grab her arm, eyes making contact for service.

She spreads her hand across the top of her apron pocket, gets to the top of the stairs, then down to the kitchen and into the cupboard-room where all the dirty laundry goes.

Mourad is irate. Where the hell's she been? Food's getting cold in the lift to the service station. People could get fired.

Mielie crouches, trying to make a nest for the sweet, blinking bundle – balancing on mounds of linen piled up in the dark.

She can't let Mourad see. He'll go mental. But the pots and pans are still bashing around, so she reckons it's safe. To grab a saucer and saunter, casually, to the fridge. For just a tongue-lap, a dropperful, a fingertip of milk. Something to let it know that everything will be okay, even when she's gone.

At the end of the night, once Mielie has mopped the floors and cleaned the bathrooms, she sits at a window table, waiting for George to cash up. She hopes the kitten's found a spot to curl up in. She pictures it: a puddle, purring. She knows, any moment now, it will affix itself like a brooch to her shoulder, underneath her raincoat, and together they'll walk home.

*

*Letter, Mielie to Kristal*
*Tuesday 13 August*

Dear Kristal

Thank you for your letter, and for trusting me with its contents.

It arrived as I was leaving the house for a job interview in London this morning. It went okay, I think. I'm hopeful I will clinch it. If I do, I'll be an assistant to an agent's assistant at that company in Oxford Street that I've been reading scripts for.

In the meanwhile, I've read your letter several times. I've also been wondering how you've been feeling, since you popped it in the post.

You say you're worried that you might have hurt me by telling me what you did. But please don't be. There's no need. I believe that I lost Edward – and by Edward, I mean his heart and soul – long before he slept with you, again. I imagine you're also feeling a sense of relief after getting it all off your chest, though. It's not a nice secret to have to keep all to yourself.

For myself, I'm very glad not to be in your situation. It is hectic. But another way of thinking about it is that it could be so much worse. Imagine if Edward didn't love you anymore? These things happen, all the time, and to most people, actually.

Then where would you be, Kristal? Pregnant with the child of someone who has little interest in the person you are, let alone in the idea of spending the rest of his life with you?

If that were the case, there'd be only one word to describe what I would feel for you – and that, I'm afraid, is pity.

You asked my advice about whether to tell him you're pregnant or not.

Thank you for valuing my opinion, but I can hardly see what difference it could make.

Equally, on the topic of abortion, it is really only you who can make that choice. You give me too much power, really. I have no say in this, and honestly no feelings either way.

But if you really do need someone to talk to, perhaps you'd like to meet at The Ball on Thursday, for old times' sake? And maybe you and Toni could patch things up?

No need to reply – we'll be there at the usual time, for happy hour, and you can let me buy you a soft drink or two.

Hope you're getting used to life in the squat. It sounds dire!

Maybe see you soon?

Mielie

PS: Don't worry about anyone else finding out.
If you decide to keep the baby, they'll all know soon enough.

*Wednesday 14 August*

Next morning, seeing the kitten-brooch clinging to Mielie's pyjamas, Toni says: "What's THAT?"

Mielie explains how she found him.

"And Edward loves cats," Mielie says. "He was separated from his mother too soon."

"The kitten, you mean? Not Edward."

They call him Borg, after the famous tennis player.

They want him to believe he has the will to triumph.

*

*Letter, Toni to Johnny*
*Thursday 15 August*

21h09
The Ball & Racquet

You always think things can't get worse, Johnny.

Yet. They always do.

Last time I wrote I was hungover.

This time I'm sober.

Basically.

Okay, almost.

Anyway: Mielie KNOWS.

So much for trying to keep it a secret.

She doesn't know you know, though.

Do keep it that way, friend.

On the Tues following the Sat fiasco, she received a letter from Cousin Kristal.

Presumably divulging details.

Of her and Edward's Secret Life Between The Sheets.

I say "presumably" because Mielie won't let me read it.

Though God knows I've tried.

It wasn't in the rubbish bin, her handbag, or any of her drawers.

She just told me Edward had been unfaithful to her, and that she guessed that must be why I'd chucked Kristal out.

I answered in the affirmative.

Then tonight we came to The Ball.

Only post-arrival did Mielie announce she'd also invited Kristal.

My eyes might actually have popped out of my head.

She said something about a white flag in times of war.

Exiting with dignity. Bowing out with grace.

I was like: No! Unleash full wrath.

And then I spotted Kristal.

By which I mean I spotted her hair.

Have I mentioned it's ALL ABOUT THE EFF-ING HAIR with this chick?

Oh-my-God, the brushing, the tossing, the shedding, the clogging.

As per when she stayed with us.

Cousin Kristal – hair aside – was carrying a wrapped bunch of flowers.

Almost certainly from a garage shop.

"Hello, ange," she beamed at Mielie. "These are for you."

You know how Mielie loves a yellow chrysanthemum. Not.

They kissed cheek to cheek.

"Yellow's the colour of friendship," said Kristal. "But I'm not the superstitious type, you know."

(Uh, symbolic, you mean? Dearie me.)

Mielie bought a round of drinks.

A tequila and a cider, each, for her and me.

Kristal asked for Lemonade.

I'm thinking: Out of character?

Oh yes, she was nervous.

Giggling and looking round the room.

She looked at me oddly too, I thought.

Like she was worried I might know something important.

Is it possible she'd forgotten that I already did?

(Not The Sharpest Pencil, Johnny, have I mentioned?)

She's going on and on about how little of an idea we can possibly have about how bad things are in Balham.

I'm battling to commiserate.

Then she stops. Hand flies to mouth.

How rude of herself!

She hasn't even ASKed if Mielie has any news about The Job.

(Mielie's applied for a job in Central London, Johnny. We're living in hope, this side.)

Mielie says not yet.

"I don't understand though, Mielie," Kristal says. "If the acting thing's not working out, why don't you just give up?"

"The point, see, Kristal," I think I said, "is that that's exactly when you don't."

I only said that to disagree with her on principle.

In fact for myself I couldn't agree more.

Staying here is giving up.

BUT – novelty factor – once again this isn't about me.

Oh, Kristal knows all about not giving up, she assures us.

The whole thing with Eddy, for example…

(Deft swerve in conversation, back to the topic she craves.)

She, believe her, could never give up on him.

And has never had even the slightest reason to be jealous.

They're just going through a rough patch.

But he's devoted to her, according to her.

Totally. (Hopelessly?)

Yesss, I broke out into song.

Kristal's clutching her glass now. White knuckles. Both hands.

"You guys had any contact?" Mielie asks.

Kristal acts like she doesn't hear her.

Which might have been the case.

Because jeez it was loud in there, by then.

Then Kristal says something about moving back to Cape Town.

And needing somewhere to stay.

And could Mielie maybe put in a good word with Peter?

In case there's anything, maybe babysitting, going at Eland?

Mielie has to remind my cousin that Edward's own sister Fiona, Peter's wife, is the reason they all had to move out of Eland in the first place.

And that she should approach Fiona directly, if Eland is where she wants to be.

Then Mielie knocked back an Aftershock, just for fun.

It was just on the table.

Maybe someone sent it over "for the ladies".

I honestly couldn't say.

Hell's teeth, Johnny.

"Chow for now" – as they don't say in the classics.
Tones
(signed with flourish)

*

*Letter, Johnny to Toni*
*Wednesday 21 August*

Westminster Mansions

Toni,

I thank you for your letters, both reduced to ashes. It surprises me that I am – yet again – the one deserted at the puzzle table, completing the jigsaw.

Allow me to fit the pieces together.

1) There is no absolute proof that Kristal slept with Edward. She could be lying.

2) In contrast, the veracity of Kristal's claims to be "on terms" with Edward is proven by the following:

* Kristal produces a note addressed to herself, in Edward's masculine, repressed handwriting.

* She has procured a photographic likeness of Mr Taylor for her wallet – sorry, purse.

* She has knowledge of the Taylor family names.

* Edward's recent melancholy-slash-hangdog attitude, which could be the result of his secret goings-on with Kristal.

Moving swiftly along – minus whiteboard, mind you – to where this leaves us now.

Mielie must be bereft. She has been deceived. Certainly by Kristal, and Edward has withheld information. I would be angry, in her shoes. Withholding is cowardly, indecisive and insulting. It suggests that the withholdee (??) can't handle the truth.

But does it mean that Edward didn't fall in love with Mielie, and that he's not in love with her now? A firm "no".

So, how to feel? Let's return to the facts.

Edward fell in love with Mielie knowing he'd have to cut things off properly with Kristal at some point. Easy to fall in love with Mielie, not so easy to live with the looming severance of Kristal, and what it might imply when the severee – look at me go! – is as unstable as a wine glass on a wicker table, and manipulative to boot.

Kristal knew Mielie was a threat. She knew she might be thrown over. That's why she headed off to London to snoop and destabilise our friend. What else is she capable of? Consider this: Is she capable of getting Edward drunk and luring him into bed? She might be. If so, how complicit was Ed? (Unfortunately, ladies, the groin sometimes leads a chap into places his heart and mind later regret. This is well known, but often not understood – and rarely forgiven – by womenfolk. Gays are no less hurt by infidelity, but perhaps more understanding. An aside.)

Now, before we start weeping and rending our clothes, mull this over in your pretty heads: why did Ed involve himself with Kristal in the first place? And what's changed, if anything?

By your own account, Madam, she's pretty and she presses male buttons. That's all very charming when you're 16, the flirtiest girl at Pietermaritzburg Girls High. But what then? After school she fails to educate herself, she fails to form friendships, her only interest is in keeping Edward. Why? She wants to be Fiona. And she needs money for that. Edward would not only place her in Fiona's orbit, he's a good bet for high earnings and inheritance. Kristal has long ago projected herself into Mama's Camps Bay penthouse, trust me.

Kristal has twin challenges ahead of her.

She is, clearly, devoid of class. Being also without money or social status, she will have to go on a charm offensive to win over Fiona and

Mama – a not impossible task, neither being positioned to judge classiness themselves.

Her second challenge is to win back Edward, to the extent that he's prepared to renounce Mielie. This too is possible. Edward has tended to do what he's told by the women in his life.

Mourn we might, yes, for the loss of what we thought things were, but which they are not. I admit to mind-bending frustration at the fact that what's right won't fit. Very bad, this, for Mielie. But despair? Ah ha! Noooooo.

It could be over, it could very well be over, but the full-stop has yet to be written.

xx Johnny

PS: In happier news (so said the master of understatement): please "see enclosed".

*

Together with their parents, Mitchell Palmer and Johnny Barton
request the pleasure of your company
at the celebration of their union
on the 14th of September, 1996
at half past three in the afternoon
Bayside Hotel, Sea Point
Dinner and dancing to follow
Dress: smart casual
Regret no children

Soon after the arrival – through the metal slot in the glass front door – of Mitchell and Johnny's invitation, and the subsequent telephone conversation in which her brother, to her delight, asks her to be his Best Woman, Toni decides she's had enough.

Two full days are spent see-sawing between the venting of spleen against all things English – loudly, abrasively, and to Mielie's embarrassment – and fantasising about the ceremony.

Toni complicates the morning kitchen-bathroom scramble by speculating about the main course on the day: "Mitchell loves seafood. Perfect in the dining hall, With View Of Sea … excuse me …" She squeezes toothpaste onto her brush. "But not everybody likes it." She considers this as she brushes her teeth.

Mielie moisturises without access to the mirror.

Toni spits and rinses, but fails to vacate the spot between the loo and the carpeted bath. "My guess is … a choice of starters – seafood but one of them," she continues. "And oysters with the champagne. Mitchell won't be able to resist. Being who he is, i.e. himself."

Mielie reaches around her friend to replace her cream and finger-tweezer her toothbrush from the shelf.

Toni plonks herself on the lid of the loo. "That aside, what do best-dressed Best Women wear to gay 'commitment ceremonies', anyway?"

"The same, surely," Mielie says, elbowing her way to the basin.

"As what?"

"As to any wedding," Mielie replies. "What's required, as we both well know, is everything well-cut: the hair, the toenails, the fingernails. And, not least, the jacket."

They debate whether Toni should in fact wear a suit – an Yves Saint Laurent-type woman's suit, with a deep V … something sheer and blousey underneath, and killer heels.

"Oh no. Lesbians," Toni's eyes widen. "I'd be lezzy-bait in that."

Now, at Happy Hour at The Ball, she's ranting again. This time it's about their blocked toilet and the landlady refusing to pay the plumber. Toni chooses to see this as a destiny-confirming sign.

"Oh for crying in a bucket of blood, MieLEE!" She signals "the usual" to the barman. "Everyone thinks we're on a 'gap year'" – air quotes – "and yet." Just the index finger now. "Pause to consider: ARE we travelling Europe, seeing the sights?" Eyebrows raised, as if asking for real. "Are we SAVING? No, we are not. We spend everything we earn, merely to survive. We can't even afford to visit a friend on the other side of London. If we had any friends, that is."

Mielie understands Toni's point of view. They might have British passports, but it's still an us-and-them situation. And Mielie and Toni are not "us". Only sometimes, if they remember to stand on the correct side of the endless, endless escalators, do they feel they have a chance of blending in.

"So when the airline asked if I wanted single or return, today, I knew," Toni's telling her. "I'm sorry, Mielie. I've bought one-way."

Mielie smiles and shakes her head. Perhaps not the best time for her best friend to have a life-changing epiphany, but that's epiphanies for you.

"It's okay, Toni," she says. "I understand. And you don't need to worry, you know. Your deposit will cover next month's rent, and I'll be able to find another housemate by October, surely."

Toni has no idea how much Mielie wants to follow her back to where you dry your washing in the sunshine. But she has no intention of getting on a plane to anywhere close to Edward.

She knows that if you can't imagine something, it generally doesn't happen. And she can't imagine herself getting off the plane, walking across the tarmac, entering arrivals, trying to look indifferent.

She doesn't tell Toni this because then she'll demand the one thing she can't give: a thorough explanation – one that goes beyond "he screwed Kristal" to "and now she's pregnant".

So instead, Mielie just says she can't afford a ticket, plus what about Borg, plus she's just heard she got the office job, starting on Monday. This prompts Toni to buy a round of double Springbok shooters, which they down simultaneously. Then they sit quietly side by side on their barstools for a bit.

For Mielie, the recent sequence of events could best be classified as farce, in which (as in life) timing is everything:

Exit Ed, stage right.
Enter Kristal, stage left.
Exit Kristal, not insignificantly also stage right.
And now, exit Toni – stage dive.

# CHAPTER 21

*Telephone answering machine message, Mitchell to Mielie*
*Saturday 31 August*

"Mielie, Mitchell here. It's come to my attention, through my Best Woman, that you're prevaricating over attending my union with Johnny. This is sad news indeed. It has always been my intention to keep my lover happy, you see. And my lover would be unhappy if you were unable to be at our nuptials. I have therefore purchased you a return ticket to Cape Town. It will be delivered via courier. Tell your new employers it's a prior commitment. Your neighbours must look after Borg. See you on the 14th. No arguments."

*

*Wednesday 4 September*

On her third day as an assistant to an agent's assistant at ICM in Oxford Street, Mielie has to get a stack of CVs and photos to a casting director in Covent Garden.

The absolutely-bloody-final deadline is 6pm, and when it becomes apparent to her that not a single courier in all of Greater London is available, she decides to run the stuff down there herself.

When she gets there, the street door is ajar, so she charges up the narrow wooden staircase to the studio at the top. The office is buzzing with faxes and printers and several ringing phones, but the people working there go quiet as she bursts in. There's an awkward moment as they stare at her, standing there trying to catch her breath.

Eventually, one of them – older, in a kaftan, with scarlet hair – asks if she can help, and Mielie explains that she's from ICM, dropping off CVs for the auditions. She holds out all the envelopes.

"Oh right! You're a legend," the woman laughs, then peers at Mielie through the top half of her bifocals. "For a moment there I thought you were an actress."

*Email, Mielie to Mare*
*Thursday 5 September*

Hello my darling

You're so quiet. I know we'll be together next week, but still I live for your news.

Mine is that I've left the brasserie and started a full-time office job at the talent agency I've been reading scripts for. I'm hoping to progress from one-day-at-a-time to a slightly more expansive view. But anyway, a major perk of this career trajectory is that I'm now connected to email. Wouldn't-it-be-luvverly not to queue at the post office anymore?

I work in a corridor. The assistant I'm assisting tosses applications on the floor between our desks – "That's a yes, that's a no, that's a fuck-off-im-ME-jitly" – for me to peel off the not-red, worn-out carpet tiles and reply to. Fundamental to my job description is to never, EVER, put Hugh Grant on hold. I have so far caught a glimpse of Gary Oldman, and made tea for a big-shot director called Shekhar Kapur.

I wanted to call you from work on Tuesday evening, but I had to dash off to see a play – not before (literally!) brushing past Alan Rickman ("No-no, after YOU") in the what-felt-very-narrow-at-the-time office hallway.

I went to see a musical – Sondheim's A Little Night Music – at the National Theatre. Judi Dench knocked the breath out of my body the moment she emerged on stage. I had a front-row seat, and the orchestra was right there, steeply tiered like angels.

One memorable line: "I should never have flirted with the possibility of rescue, when I had no intention of being saved."

The guy across the corridor represents composers. After he's left for the evening, his assistant plays music really loudly. Tonight it's Vivaldi … "Gloria! Gloria!" It's going to be the soundtrack for a new movie called

Shine. It's beautiful. It reaches into some distant part of my brain and makes me feel suspended, somehow, millimetres above reality.

Oh Mare. It's been such a sad time, losing Dad, and that sadness isn't going to go away. Not really. Not ever. We'll be in our 40s before we know it, and maybe then we'll look back at it all, and see it through a different lens.

Meanwhile, I think we're becoming the adults we're going to be. The things that are happening now will never leave us. They may eventually have to be buried somehow; they might make our daughters one day think we're cows.

In all your brave endeavours – with, I know, such sometimes flailing spirits – please remember that nothing is lost. Nothing, ever. And there's nothing humiliating in defeat. It just means you tried harder and cared more.

Love, always
Mielie

PS: Please tell Johnny, when next you see him, that he is now the only male being on the planet whose company I desire (including Ralph Fiennes, although I have taken the liberty of installing him as my screensaver).

PPS: Sometimes I think there are invisible strands criss-crossing the earth … not like the ones we learned about in geography. They cut and shock us on our way through.

You and I are strong, though, Mare. We will pull through. But I'd be lying if I didn't admit to the odd stress attack, when my temperature rockets and I can't breathe. If you experience similar, please take it from me, the only thing to do is to gulp gallons of water. And remember, always: waterproof mascara.

*Email, Mare to Mielie*
*Thursday 5 September*

JOHANNESBURG
By Marigold Ashford

Did that to make it look like I'm working on a Johannesburg Regional Court hearing. Must stretch this paragraph out to required three lines – standard intro length, keep going, thank you.

So aren't we the Thoroughly Modern Millies? Letters speeding through the air faster than light. Airmail on steroids. It's like written conversation. I can have a thought about you, write it down and send it. I can't believe how easy it is. It allows for tight editing. Briskness. Keeping to the point. I imagine you're enjoying the delete key very much. I shan't use it. I welcome improved legibility but abhor the pressure to self-censor.

Thought: Hugh Grant?! Have you met Hugh Grant????!!!!!! Have you spoken to him? His voice is a big part of it …

Are you IN the picture with Ralph Fiennes on the screensaver? What the hell?!

You got a job on the red carpet. You're IN the casting room. In London.

You are ready and you deserve this.

You are that wiry Kenyan man, breaking the tape with your chest.

Please can I be your date for the Oscars. Pllllleeeeeezzzzz ...

Love
Mare

PS: Mielie, to be honest I'm just trying to get through the days and stay upright. I get these Counting Crows August and Everything After moments. It's bad. The weather is appalling. At night, a butcher's coldroom. The morning air has needles in it. Even if you remember to keep your lips slavered with Vaseline – I don't – your fingertips crack. Your calves and forearms itch. Your scalp sheds dry skin. The inside of your nostrils dry out. Some people get nosebleeds. Colds travel like electricity. Static shocks happen when you least expect them, for instance when shaking hands. If you don't condition your hair, it stands up around your head like a madwoman halo.

So what happens next? There must be hope, because as of 1 September we officially entered spring.

PPS: Before I heard you were coming to Cape Town, I posted you Lyndall Gordon's Shared Lives. I like it because it's South African. It's about ordinary women and their ordinary lives. Not men's adventures On the Road or Into the Heart of Darkness.

*

*Email, Mielie to Peter*
*Monday 9 September*

Dear Peter,

How are you?
Mare and I are going to be in Cape Town this weekend for the unofficial marriage of our dear friends, Johnny and Mitchell.
I arrive on Thursday morning.
It would be lovely to meet somewhere and catch up.

My best wishes to Fiona and Booboo,
Mielie

*Email, Peter to Mielie*
*Tuesday 10 September*

Hello old thing!

What an excellent surprise to hear from you.

Fee and I are very well, despite being exhausted. The renovation goes on and on. We are past the earthworks stage, at last. A nightmare.

Of course we must touch base. I'm consulting for Rooff these days. I could pop out for a coffee on Thursday at 11. Wait for me downstairs – yes?

Wonderful news about the wedding, by the way. Venue? Wine farm? Delighted you're flying back for it, too. Who paid?

Mielie, it almost goes without saying that you and Mare need to make this occasion work to your advantage. You might both presently be "ripe for the picking", but this, need I emphasise, is sadly not a permanent state. You'll be surprised how quickly it transitions to being – there's no polite way to put this – "on the shelf". There are bound to be numerous Johannesburg-based mover-shakers among the guests, any one of whom could help to secure your futures.

You and your sister might think it's old-fashioned for women to pin their futures on rich men – Mare probably goes so far as to consider herself a Feminist, capital F – but please do hear me out on this.

An independent mind is all very well, Fee agrees. But how's that going to pay the bills? Acting (viz. waitressing) and writing are not Medicine/Law.

Our advice to you both is to wear something nice, and (in Mare's case) BE nice.

Peter

PS: Question from Fee: Is Mitchell a woman's name?

*

*Email, Mielie to Peter*
*Tuesday 10 September*

Hello again, Peter,

Thanks for getting back to me. I can meet you for coffee on Thursday at 11. I'll catch the train in from Woodstock.

Peter, Mitchell is not a woman's name. Johnny is our school friend and Mitchell is his partner. They've been living together this year in Joburg. They've been very good to Mare, actually. They live in the same suburb. The venue is Mitchell's family's hotel in Sea Point.

If you must know, Mitchell sent me a return ticket without asking. I wasn't intending to come, but now I'm glad I am, as it will give me a chance to be with Mare. She's been having a tough time these past few months.

Oh, and we both have proper jobs now.

See you soon,
Mielie

So here Toni is on the family hotel terrace, in a bikini and sarong, ice cubes tinkling in her pre-sundowner drink.

Who passes into view? Edward. Trotting down Main Road, Sea Point, in front-pleated chinos, frowning.

"Oi!" she shouts. "Edward!"

He looks around in that cartoon way you do, when you don't know who's calling you, or from where.

"Edwaaaaard! Over here!"

He screws up his face and makes a visor with his hand on his forehead.

"It's Toni, idiot!" she shouts, beckoning. "God Ed, get in here for a cocktail, now!"

Edward, Toni's pointed questions allow her to discover, is still living in the communal house in Observatory. He's still working at the architecture firm in town and, armed with flowers and a magazine, is at this minute on his way to visit his mother. Meanwhile, ensconced at Eland, Peter and Fiona have performed all manner of atrocities in the name of home improvement. Edward visits often at the weekend to help his sister achieve "perfect finish". Booboo has a live-in au pair now.

"A live-in au pair?" Toni asks politely. "Fancy."

"Ja."

*Sometimes,* Toni thinks, *you feel like you'll never get a word in.*

"So … hmm," she says. "So she – I'm assuming it's a she – is living in the house? How's that for Fiona and Peter?"

"Oh," he says, shifting in his seat uncomfortably. "Look, I should probably go."

"Well, no one's tying you down, Edward," she says. "I'm just trying to catch up."

"No, I know. It's good to see you. And I hope you'll pass on my regards to Mielie, I–"

"Your regards? You mean your KIND regards?" Toni asks. "Why? Aren't you in touch?"

"No."

"No?"

"I mean, I've tried, but …"

"She's gone silent."

"Ja. Yes. She has. Completely. And–"

"Maybe it's better that way?" Toni probes. On Mielie's behalf, naturally. Then drops bomb: "We know about you and my cousin Kristal, you know."

Edward pales. Now his elbows are on his knees, his head in his hands. "Kristal's your cousin?" he says in disbelief.

"Yes. She came to stay with me and Mielie soon after your – er – fleeting visit."

Edward is quiet for a good few minutes, during which Toni replenishes the ice in their drinks.

"I just want to explain," he says. "I want to tell Mielie what happened. I wanted to tell her in London." He shakes his head again. "I couldn't."

Toni watches him intently and waits.

"But I suppose that doesn't change that it did happen," he continues. "Mielie has every right to cut me dead."

Bare feet on the table, Toni leans her head against the back of her chair and closes her eyes. "You're a fucking asshole, Edward. You really are. What on God's green earth is going on with you?" She shakes her head in wonderment, then sits forward again: "What is going on In Your Mind? Seriously." The head-tilt-to-hear-higher-wisdom, followed by: "No! Don't answer!"

She returns to the recline position: "I have more to say. A lot more, Edward. Believe you me. But in summary, for my sake alone: if I was Mielie, you'd already be dead. But luck's on your side. I'm not. So just listen up. She's coming here. To this very terrace. This weekend. For my brother's unofficial wedding. You need to see her, Edward. Cheers."

*

*Thursday 12 September*

It's a trek from South Wimbledon to London Heathrow. You have to give yourself enough time. Last week, Toni had reportedly squeaked through check-in with less than a minute to spare.

Mielie doesn't mind the twelve-hour flight. It takes longer to drive from Joburg to Cape Town than to fly from London to either. Watching the yellow line on the screen that shows how far you've come and how far you have left to go, Mielie reckons they must be close now.

She peers down at the folded mountains, the scattered dams and patchwork vineyards – False Bay a sweeping arc against one side of the peninsula, the Atlantic carving past the other. Table Mountain, Devil's Peak, Lion's Head – the familiar three-part silhouette. Sea, mountain, sky. Blue on blue on blue.

A bumpy landing. A scramble of blankets and babies, human debris and stale air. And then they're out.

Mielie stands on the tarmac, blinking.

She walks to the terminal, gets her backpack, and walks out into Arrivals.

Edward's not there.

At the counter in the coffee shop, having kept Mielie waiting a full fifteen minutes outside the Rooff building on the Foreshore, Peter Ashford makes a big deal of patting down his pockets, as if trying to locate a wallet that's – bemusingly – not at hand.

Mielie pays. They sit down. He gets right to it.

He and Fee feel it would be a good idea to have a get-together at Eland the following evening, "for family and friends" – the whole of the wedding top table must come. If Mielie could extend the invite?

He'd called Pauline and she'd told him about Mitchell, Walker and Fouché: lawmaker, ministerial adviser and surgeon, respectively.

"You can't imagine how relieved we are that Johnny and co have taken Mare under their wing," he declares. "Her best bet, we've realised, is to stay close to the gays. At least that way – even if she is a perpetual accident-waiting-to-happen – she'll never want for much."

Peter glances about him. Mielie wonders if he has enough sensitivity to be ashamed. But no, Peter is not ashamed. Indeed, he may feel that what he is about to say will benefit the entire coffee shop.

"They're a bright bunch, it would seem," he says through a mouthful of chocolate muffin, "*and* well connected ..." He swallows. "They're all doing very well for themselves, thank you very much," – he laughs a resigned-to-it-all, yeah-we're-the-ones-now-suffering laugh – "in the new SA."

Now he makes a double stop-sign with his hands: "I will not say 'gravy train'! The term will not be heard to pass my lips! But just think about it," – wiping his mouth with a napkin now: "they are literally walking the corridors of power – and they have no descendants!"

A pause.

Then: "They wouldn't … surely … they don't have *dogs*, do they? They surely wouldn't give it *all* to the dogs?"

Mielie sips her coffee. "Johnny and Mitchell don't have dogs."

"Wonderful." Now he peers through the coffee-shop glass at the pedestrian traffic outside. "Look, the time's not exactly ideal for entertaining," he points out, in a you-gotta-do-what-you-gotta-do way. "Fee's mother is the soul of generosity, don't get me wrong. But we're feeling the pinch, to be honest … You've seriously no idea … Look, we get by … I'd be lying if I said we weren't comfortable," he concedes. "There's just so much that needs doing, you know."

Mielie braces herself for the latest instalment in the ongoing saga of Eland's entirely unavoidable basement-to-attic overhaul.

"And doing it properly, as I'm sure you can appreciate, costs an arm and a leg … At one stage we even considered selling the Land Rover … the blue one we use for Namibia? So you can just imagine."

"Yes, Peter," Mielie says. "I really can only imagine."

The irony, she fears, is lost.

"And with a London trip coming up, too …"

"Why are you going to London, Peter?"

"London! Why, to shop."

Turns out not even the chi-chi-est of Constantia decorators are able to sate Fiona's heart's most precious desires.

"It's all very well to say that you stock St Leger & Viney, but if it's last season's, well, what's the point? As Fee says, you can't be too careful, when you're talking this kind of investment … Killing us, as it is."

"Will Booboo travel with you?" Mielie allows herself a montage of scenes in which a sticky-fingered Booboo runs wild in fabric shops.

"Thank God, no," Peter says. "We were going to leave him with Sweetness – we couldn't exactly take her with us, now could we? I mean, apart from the cost of the ticket, it just wouldn't work, having the staff tag along … But then we appointed an au pair." His face crumples in a rueful, this-if-nothing-else-will-ruin-me grin.

"But apart from all that," he says, "it's a great relief to Fee that you and Edward both appear to have moved on."

Mielie listens, frowning – the fingernails of one hand pressing into the other.

"But nevertheless we've taken the precaution of not inviting him to tomorrow's 'do'."

*

*Friday 13 September*

Mare spends a total of five minutes readying herself for the grand evening event at Eland. Three of those minutes are spent finding her takkies and tying them, the other two searching for cigarettes.

"Why can't you make an effort?" Pauline fusses, following her middle daughter down the passage as Mare looks for shoes. "Why not wear a dress? … Honestly, darling, Peter and Fiona will have gone to so much trouble. The least—"

"So much trouble?" Mare interrupts. "Mum, Peter is trying to make business connections and marry us off."

"Well, I doubt he's that calculating," Pauline says. "And even if he were, perhaps Fiona's extending an olive branch."

"An olive branch!" Mare scoffs. "Ah," holding up her fake All-Stars, "there you are. Fifi is not extending an olive branch. She only wants to gloat. She wants to rub our noses in our denuded garden, our bulldozed kitchen and the fact that Edward hasn't moved to London."

Mielie, with Mare in the passenger seat, steers the car into their childhood street. Mare stares.

It's like cutting to a new scene in a dream. As familiar as the girls' own blood in their veins, Eland is also surreally altered. Gone are the unkempt hedges and chicken-wire fences sagging behind. In their place are smart, high, beige walls, with ivy forced into a strict diamond pattern.

Mielie stops in front of the new gate – an automated, swirly metal affair. In the centre, Peter and Fiona have had "P&F" welded, in curly script.

"It's a bloody country club," Mare says. "Do you think everything is monogrammed, or just the gate?"

Mielie unrolls her window and presses the button on the intercom. The sisters hear the sound of far-off church bells ringing. Then the gate opens.

At the top of the driveway, where there was once an expanse of mossy brick, there is now a central water feature – complete with naked cupid – tightly encircled by gravel. Gone, too, are the white walls and stripped-pine window frames. Through a neat inversion, the outside walls are now deep beige, with white window frames and sills.

And where the hydrangeas once spread their laden branches under the windows, there is now tar, with painted lines for parking.

The girls have barely made it out of the car when down the front steps shoots Kristal Smith, with Booboo on her hip.

Mielie gets it in an instant: Kristal is the new au pair. She is momentarily dumbstruck.

"Mielie!" Kristal gushes. "I thought you weren't coming!"

Mielie and Mare's nephew wriggles to escape as Kristal bounces him on her hip. She's wearing a chiffon top and push-up bra.

"And you must be the famous Mare!" she squeals.

Mielie's sister declines to respond. She has frozen, mid-step, and is peering, through twilight and tears, into what is left of her childhood garden – more specifically, at a cleared spot where the oak tree used to be.

"Well, here we are!" Kristal gestures to the front door as if she is the hostess and the Ashford sisters are visiting Eland for the first time: "Welcome, both!"

"Mielie!" Kristal stage-whispers on their way up the steps. "I'm *so* nervous! Between you and me …" On the doorstep, Kristal leans in so close her lips brush Mielie's ear: "Edward's mother is here!" she whispers. "I have-to-have-to-have-to get her to like me. So we can speed up the announcement of you-know-what."

"I think you'll find that biology will do that for you," Mielie says, under her breath.

Kristal gives her a friendly slap on the forearm, a little too hard. "Careful!" she giggles. "No-one knows!!"

"No?" Mielie looks squarely into Kristal's face. "Not even Edward, yet?" She cocks her head.

Kristal cocks hers, too.

Inside, Eland's front hall, once a dim but colourful collection place for coats, scarves, hats, hockey sticks and rolled-up drawings, is now a cold grey box – everything in perfect proportion, assigned to its appropriate place. Dominant in the space are an oversized chandelier, the portrait of Geraldine Taylor and a trio of giant, identical mirrors. The Victorian tiles are covered with a white shagpile rug. To Mielie, this single item seems to guarantee for her still-innocent nephew a lifetime of apprehension and shame.

She looks around in polite appreciation, and for somewhere to put her bag – somewhere that won't disturb the elegance, disrupt the balanced lines.

Kristal shouts for Peter, then makes off with Booboo "for din-dins", leaving Mielie alone in a cave of silence. Mare's still outside. There's a small set of photographs, neatly framed on a wall behind a lamp – one of Edward in his graduation gown, and one of Fiona on a horse.

Mielie's standing there, looking at the pictures, listening to a clock ticking in its hollow glass jar, when a door at the end of the passage opens and a Maltese poodle bursts out. It scuttles down the passage, yapping and snapping at her feet.

Then Geraldine Taylor walks slowly towards her, scoops up the poodle, and extends a hand. "You must be Mielie," she says.

Geraldine's flesh is cold.

"Hello!" Mielie says. "Yes, I am. It's a pleasure to meet you at last, Mrs Taylor."

The poodle barks loudly in Mielie's face – a high-pitched volley of rasping sound.

"Oh shame!" Mielie laughs. "Have I frightened it?"

"It's a she, isn't she, my Sweetie?" Geraldine says, nuzzling the dog in her arms. As she walks away across the hallway, the barking continues, directed over her shoulder.

*It's a silent war,* Mielie thinks, *between the woman whose body a son exits and the lover whose he inhabits.*

Mare enters the hallway, smoking.

"Come in, girls!" Peter beckons from the top of the stairs, securing his cufflinks as he trots down towards them. "Walker's here, in the lounge! … Walker!" he shouts into the echoey ground floor. "The ladies are here!"

By the time the Ashford girls enter the room behind Geraldine – Mielie half a step ahead, as though leading her younger sister by magnetic force – Fiona has positioned herself at the drinks console on the opposite side of the room, her back to them and her hand on the neck of an ice-cold bottle of Pongracz.

Walker stands. Seeing the two girls together makes a fist of his heart. They aren't as different as they think they are, and their similarities are emphasised by the bright hallway light behind them: a pair of vulnerable shapes, hands almost touching, merged like grey paper dolls.

"Walker, I'm Mielie," the taller paper doll rips away from the other and hugs him spontaneously. "It's so lovely to meet you."

"It's lovely to meet you too. How was your trip?" He guides Mielie to the drinks table, making easy small-talk along the way.

Peter turns to Mare, her hair lank, her skin yellowish. "You've been ill?" he enquires, unable to mask his dismay at his half-sister's loss of bloom.

Mare doesn't answer. Her eyes say: "Back off, prick."

Once everyone has a drink, Peter toasts his guests loudly, before itemising the disappointments that he and his wife – pooped from a four-hour forage at The Waterfront earlier – have suffered. Much as Peter and Fee had hoped to bring good friends and family together, he explains, Mitchell and Johnny had begged off, citing family commitments. "The other one … the doctor?" was on call all week, had negotiated cover for Saturday only and was therefore flying in the next day.

"Very jet-set," Peter observes, casting a meaningful glance in the direction of Mare. She stares right through him.

In the dining room, the dinner table is set between four large pots containing ornamental braided ficus trees. There's an embroidered linen cloth, with matching napkins – sage, the edges scalloped. There are long-stemmed glasses and the cutlery is heavy.

Through the windows, Mare can see it's a balmy evening. She wants to be outside, in it, alone. But she's trapped at this table, where, it would seem, there's absolutely nothing for anyone to say.

Peter proceeds to quiz Walker on his job title, his address. Walker answers politely, keeping things brief and trying to change the course of conversation to include the sisters, but to no avail.

In the succession of silences that ensue, Mielie also tries, repeatedly, to make conversation, but Geraldine – plucked, sculpted, disdainful – when not ignoring her completely, succeeds in closing each opening down.

When Booboo is asleep, Kristal joins the table for dessert. She could not agree more with anything Geraldine can think of to say. If the weather had been awful, it had indeed been "absolutely terrible". If a certain shade of lipstick was salmon, it was "exactly that: like sushi!". If London taxi drivers were impressively knowledgeable, they were "encyclopedias".

And Fiona, she herself is quick to assure Mielie, couldn't be happier with Kristal. She's been giving her gifts. They've exactly the same taste! Imagine!

"You're like part of the family!" Fiona tells her au pair.

"Oh!" Kristal exclaims, her hand on her heart. "I couldn't be happier here!" Turning to Mielie: "And my room's just stunning."

"Your room?" Geraldine enquires. This is news to her.

"Oh, yes," Kristal gushes. "Fiona and Peter need their rest. I said to them, you must let me live in. I can handle it."

"Kristal sleeps upstairs, next door to Booboo," Fiona says. "In Mielie's old room, I think?"

Mielie nods numbly.

Her only comfort lies in the fact that Geraldine and Fiona are soon to discover that Kristal is pregnant with Edward's child. And she can guess how well that will go down. Au pair material is one thing. Snaring the family's only son is something else entirely.

"It's quite hard to tell you're being ignored by someone who's virtually expressionless," Mielie says to Mare in the car on the way home.

They don't talk much, otherwise. They just drive quietly, retracing the route they followed all those months ago, the day they left Eland and the lives they knew.

# CHAPTER 22

*Saturday 14 September*

It's six minutes to three at the Bayside Hotel. Johnny Barton is standing alongside Mitchell Palmer, in his wedding suit. The two men are poised just inside the doors onto the terrace, waiting for them to open.

Johnny and Mitchell are a sight that will, in a matter of moments, bring tears to their guests' eyes.

First, the clothes.

Did the couple wear pastel shirts and matching white cotton suits, like a pair of Miami pensioners? They did not.

Did they go for black suits, *Reservoir Dogs*-style, with skinny black ties and greased-back hair? They did not.

There was some speculation that linen suits would be worn, recalling Robert Redford in *Out of Africa*.

But no. The suits are grey.

Their cotton shirts complement their eyes and skin tones: Johnny's is royal blue, Mitchell's icy pink. Both are wearing irises. Mitchell's buttonhole is deep pink with white streaks. Johnny's is white and gold.

Outside, on the side lawn between the hotel terrace and the Palmers' home, the sun is strong, but golden. It's one of those windless spring afternoons: remarkably clean, crisp and un-busy. On a day like this in Cape Town, the Ashford sisters couldn't feel more at home. There's a focus to the light, the sky is white and grey-blue, but the trees are all citrusy, zesty light between the branches. Leaf shadows are dotted on the street like confetti.

The guests are standing on the side lawn, with the sun on their arms and the backs of their necks, greeting in whispers, waiting. The music plays softly. All eyes are on the stoep doors.

Mare Ashford shifts in her heels on the grass. She is Johnny's Maid of Honour, but she is standing alone. She and Toni were not asked to be part of any aisle procession, nor were they given flowers to carry. Mare wonders if she feels excluded, at her first groom-groom wedding. She decides that if she does feel like Mitchell is stealing her best friend, or that Johnny is stealing the happily-ever-after that should've been hers, she mustn't.

She's distracted by the sight of Mielie, moving off the shaded stoep. Her sister is a shimmering candle, with her hair catching the afternoon sunlight as its flame.

Toni had done well. She bought Mielie a flowing cream dress – not buttery, but the actual colour of pouring cream: soft, rich, smooth. So creamy you want to put your finger in it. The silk swishes around her upper arms like collapsed petals, the soft diagonal seams and crushed silk blurring her outline.

Mare has never seen Mielie's hair straightened. She's also never seen her thinner, so insubstantial. She's almost unrecognisable without her tan and mop of curls, her features prettified for the day by professional make-up. Even her lips are pale, not the big, mobile, colour-of-watermelon mouth Mare grew up opposite.

Mielie stops by a flowerbed, with her hands clasped together in front. Mare squints to see her nails. They are sculpted in a pearly shade, hands and feet. They are like the insides of seashells, smooth and perfect.

She looks like somebody's well-behaved wife, and Mare hates it. She tries to catch Mielie's eye, make a face, stick out her tongue – anything to turn the light back on behind her sister's eyes.

The music changes. The first "dah!" of Here! Comes! The Bride! rings out. The wooden doors open. And now here they are, in the doorway: the couple, already a couple, holding hands.

They stop for a moment, beaming at everyone. Then they descend into the garden, the guests parting to create an aisle.

The wedding ceremony takes place under a very large tree. Johnny and Mitchell's vows are identical. Fouché does a reading – and Walker, who is officiating, gives a sort-of sermon.

Afterwards, everyone gets rose petals to throw: cream, white and hot pink. Guests hug the couple and then it's champagne-and-photographs.

The sun is setting over the sea. The sky is a riot: fuchsia, sea blue, lilac, gold, ink, with white streaks across it like ribbons. It mirrors the ceremony: the swirling of gowns and coloured shirts, the forming and splitting of chatting groups. Beneath the changing sky, the sea is serenely grey-blue.

At the centre of it all, Johnny and Mitchell are united, shaded and still under the tree, like the untroubled sea.

Dinner is called. Mare has yet to speak to her sister, Toni or the married couple. Now, her attention is taken by Walker as he crosses to where Mielie is standing. He draws alongside her and all-but puts his hand in the small of her back. He leans towards her to whisper something. Her made-up cheek lifts in a demure smile.

As they move together across the grass, there's something familiar, clichéd almost, about the look of the two of them.

It comes to her then. The realisation bites like a horse-fly. They are the bridal couple on top of the cake come to life. He: tall, handsome, black-suited. She: elegant, self-contained, in her flowing cream silk gown.

After dinner, on the candlelit terrace facing the sea, Toni is the first to take the mic.

From the opposite end of the top table, Mare watches her rise. Toni is wearing pink – as is Toni's mom, The-Mother-of-Mitchell. Even Johnny's dad has on a pink shirt. Mare wonders if there'd been a special request, one that hadn't been communicated to her. She's in her aubergine satin, the one she found in a Long Street vintage shop, and black shoes. She hopes she didn't spoil the one photo she was asked to join.

"Yes," Toni grins across the tables. "I am here to talk about my brother Mitchell."

She begins:

> What I know about love I know from him.
> Mitchell's love is uncompromising.

He loves. And he'll fight for love.

He would fight for me, for anyone in our family.

That's why he became a lawyer.

He goes into battle for love. For him, there's no contradiction there.

For him, love is not peaceful, it's not something you sink back into.

It's a victory, a cause, a call to arms.

It's thrilling, it brings out the warrior in him.

Loving freely, loving large, is his idea of justice.

Love starts in the spring of his heart and gathers momentum as it courses through him.

With my brother, love is not a stream, it's a river.

He rains knowledge and purpose on his river and it rages.

You go ahead and ask him about how he loves Johnny.

Look in his eyes. He will drown you.

His love is a torrent. It will sweep you up.

That's how he will win this battle.

That's how he will consign all those homophobes to the caves where they belong.

That's why not just marriage but adoption will be legalised for all gay couples before my brother draws his last breath.

Cheers to my brother. The magnificent Mitchell Palmer.

The terrace erupts. Deep breaths are taken, hands rise to chests, napkins are applied to eyes and cheeks. Toni will relive this moment often over the years, standing alone on the sea-facing terrace.

Mare's speech doesn't go down quite as well. It's not well prepared. People clap, but there's no cheering. She reads from her pages, without looking up:

Hello. Thank you for giving me this opportunity to speak, Johnny and Mitchell. And congratulations. You are beautiful.

It's an honour to be Johnny's Maid of Honour. I am honoured to be one of his oldest friends. He is my dearest friend. I hope this doesn't change that. I hope I haven't done anything to change that.

I'm afraid I didn't write and rehearse a speech beforehand. I'm feeling bad about that now. I see that so much planning and prep has gone into this evening. I didn't expect this to be so grown-up. But I guess that's what marriage is. That's how it should be.

So, some of you will know that I make a rule of saying what I think. Well here goes: When I found out Johnny didn't shop on my side of the street, I was sad for two reasons. One was that he wouldn't come into my shop …

She pauses for laughter that does not come.

And I'd kind of been keeping an Open sign on the door for him. But also, I was sad because he wouldn't have children, and because he would be the object of prejudice. That's three sadnesses. Let's say my disappointment doesn't count.

Mitchell, I don't know you very well, despite all the meals you've cooked for me and all the furniture you've sent my way. I'm a little intimidated by you – not jealous! But I hope we'll get to know each other better over the years and our relationship will go from strength to strength.

It wasn't until this year that I realised how hard you have to fight to be in love. To defend your choice of who you love. But that love is everything. It's EVERYTHING. I still believe that.

Love is nothing to be ashamed of.

If love is allowed to rise to the surface, if love is shared, it ripples outwards.

Johnny, we've been on different wavelengths this year. But that doesn't change the fact that I've known you since we were both thirteen, and I intend to be your queer dear forever.

When we met, we were buds of people really – more children than teenagers. I think we've always loved each other. I hope that's true. I love everything about you, like the way you're obsessed with birds. You memorise the markings and the individual birdsongs. You're like that with people too. You search for every mark of difference. You're not put off by the enormity of the task.

Most people don't see birds. You, Johnny, you see all the different types, and clearly. They're such frail little things, and so unnecessary to us – sorry, maybe unnecessary is the wrong word, maybe "incidental to our lives" would be a better way of putting it – but you don't mind that they have nothing to offer you. You love them for what they are. I wish I could be more like that.

When I think of you, Johnny, I think of you growing a pumpkin the size of a football on a balcony in Yeoville. Who does that? You take a plastic bucket and a patch of sunshine the size of a cushion and you create a magnificent object, an armoured object, with fruit the colour and intensity of the sun setting over a tropical ocean. The seeds are as big as fingernails, packed with growing power. The stalk alone is the width of a ski-lift cable. You did that from a dried seed. You tended it, gently and regularly, with tap water and a rectangle of sun. That's what you do. You shine your warmth on us, you sprinkle us with your love and you make something huge, glowing, magnificent, something full of seeds that can keep on and on growing.

I love you so much. I'm so sorry this time of your greatest happiness coincides with such a bummer of a time in my life.

Thank you and have a wonderful evening.

This is a very special occasion and I wouldn't have missed it for the world.

Thank you.

*

*Letter (unsent), Mare to Tess*
*Sunday 15 September*

Balfour Road bedroom

Dear Tess,

It seems I don't have anyone to write to anymore. The wedding was bad. I couldn't focus on it and now I'm in disgrace with everyone. No one wants to hear it anymore. No one wants to hear "Will".

When you exhaust people's patience you have to start talking to yourself.

So now there's a real me and an outer one – the clothes-wearing, words-speaking one.

The only happy moment the real me had yesterday was standing by the fishpond at the side of Toni's house. I related to the pond. It's all I am, inside. Insects buzz around above my head. They light on the surface. They barely make a ripple. My work, my body, everyone I encounter – including the people I used to love – they are as light as gnats. The buzzing is meaningless.

Inside, in the pond, all the weight, the heaviness – even my hair and clothes – are lifted from my body. Memories of Will dart through me, like fish. I love their rainbow scales, their angel fins. Bliss, the idea of having them swirl around me, through me, forever. When I'm in the pond, I don't want to emerge.

At Toni's pond I kicked off my shoes. I stood in my dress in the water. In the dark my dress was deep purply-brown, slinky, cool. It was the colour of pond weed in shadow. It made sense.

Mielie called me while I was standing there. When I heard her voice, I realised that all I want is to be with the memory fish, in the quiet.

Love
Mare

PS: Guess the song:
"Nobody knows where my Johnny has gone / But Judy left the same time."
Answer: It's My Party and I'll Cry If I Want To.

# CHAPTER 23

*Sunday 15 September*

Edward Taylor walks down the lavender-flanked path to the front door of the Ashford's Woodstock home. He's walked this path many times, when he lived here, and even a few times since Mielie left for England almost five months ago, when the weather shifted and the wind and sunshine disappeared.

He's been keeping himself busy. His job takes care of his weekdays, and the weekends he spends at Eland. He tells himself that planning and supervising Fiona's renovation is good experience. The truth is, he struggles to say no to her, or to his mother, who also demands that he eat dinner with her on Wednesday evenings in Camps Bay.

Edward tells himself that any evening arrangement is good. At least he is spared the darkness, alone, when his emotions inevitably shift from misery to guilt and back again. He is bloated with regret.

He's here to see Mielie. To ask her forgiveness and try to explain. He's tried to calm down, driving around the block several times before parking, then sitting behind his steering wheel for several minutes before getting out.

Beneath his skin, his longing is like a pulse, like the anguished beat of an unhealthy heart: too fast, too intent.

Now he's on the verandah. The door – its stained-glass panels so familiar – is ajar. The south-easter jangles his nerves. Something is different about the place, today.

He hears voices inside.

Mielie's – he'd know it anywhere. Mielie, his sunshine. Mielie, the wind who blows through him. For a while, in the summer, all the nagging in his head had been swept out to sea.

But there's another voice, too – different, higher-pitched, just as familiar.

Kristal. What the hell is she doing here?

For crying out loud, he thinks – and wishes he could.

In the sitting room, Kristal Smith – having arrived unannounced – is telling Mielie all about how she'd "just felt this instant connection" with Edward's mother on the Friday evening at Eland.

Mielie is still tired from the shocks of that particular evening; tired, too, from the wedding itself (especially the end part when Mare had needed rescuing, for a change). And she's tired from forcing things into bags – she and Mare are both due at the airport soon, Mare heading to Joburg, she to Heathrow.

She just listens. Sometimes her eyes narrow slightly as she ponders Kristal's lack of regard for any feelings she might have. She wonders how many weeks now, before Kristal starts to show. And how long before she tells Edward, who will do the right thing and marry her, with or without his family's blessing.

Kristal gasps. Smacks her own wrist! How selfish and insensitive she is, as a person, while Mielie – her trusted friend – sits right there, having had to endure the very same Geraldine's unbearable indifference.

Mielie assures her that she is totally fine.

That's when Edward knocks on the door.

At the sight of him, her heart catches in her throat and her ears thrum. She grips the front door.

"Hello," she smiles.

Edward. Even after everything, it's the same.

She wants to tell him how it's been.

Edward says nothing. He stares at Mielie, then nods. His eyes fill with tears. "I know," he mouths.

Mielie understands. It's not that Kristal has told him anything. What he knows is that their feelings are the same. It feels like the first time they met, here in this same doorway, him standing here and her standing there.

"Come in," she says. Funny to say it aloud. It's what she always thinks, when she sees him.

"Come *on*, Mielie!" Mare is shouting, as she struggles down the passage with a bulging suitcase. Pauline and Tess are behind her. "Oh, there you are." Mare stops at the front door. When she sees Edward, on the stoep, she shrieks and hugs him.

A car hoots. It's Toni, double parked.

"Mielie we MUST go! We'll miss our flights!"

As Mielie runs inside for her bags, she passes Kristal in the passage, en route to the front door. Mielie stops. Listens. She hears Kristal ask Edward for a lift to Eland.

"Wait!" Mielie shouts, almost involuntarily, from mid-way down the passage.

She can see Kristal and Edward on the stoep, just on the other side of the doorway.

"Bye, Mielie," Edward says. "You must go."

She is frozen as she watches them walk together, down the garden path.

It's the bunch of roses. That's what starts it.

Mielie and Mare are trying to squeeze all their luggage into Toni's rather small car. There are suitcases for the planes, and boxes – destined for the storeroom at Toni's – marked MIELIE: STUFF and MARE: DO NOT OPEN. Pauline has persuaded the girls to remove their possessions – including old schoolbooks and photo albums – from the Woodstock house, because there really isn't space for all of it there.

But if Woodstock isn't home, Mielie's wondering, where is?

"I suppose you're taking the front?" Mare asks, arms folded as she watches Mielie wedge her home-decorated trunk into the boot.

*Decoupage*, Mielie remembers her sister observing once. *How original.* Of course. On all things fine-art related, Mare's always left Mielie in the dust. Like the time when Mielie went to see her sister's final-year exhibition, upstairs in her studio at Art School, and battled to say anything meaningful. *I just want to know what it makes you feel, Mielie,* Mare had said. *If anything, that is.*

"Okay so I'll just be here in the back then, with the files and pillowcases," Mare continues.

"Ah thanks, Mare," Mielie says, handing her a bunch of roses, tied with gold ribbon, from the night before.

"Sorry?" says Mare.

"Would you mind having these on your lap?"

Mielie's about to close the door when Mare puts her foot in the gap. "No," she says. "No I won't have your fading roses on my lap. They're a total cliché, by the way. A bit like some people I know."

"Fine." Mielie grabs back the roses, and squashes her body over Mare's –protestations thus muffled – to balance the bouquet on the luggage in the boot.

Once Mielie is in the front seat, Toni slams her door, toots, and the three girls wave at Pauline and Tess on the kerb.

Mare holds her tongue until they're in the correct lane on the N2 highway. "So, what? Did Walker give them to you?" she asks.

Mielie and Toni exchange a glance, but neither say a word. Mielie sighs. She's watching the houses and the cooling towers, passing like a silent movie. "Mare, what is that supposed to mean?"

"Or was I not supposed to notice you wafting around with him, like it was your own private engagement party?"

Mielie swings round to face her: "Hey. You have eyes in your head, and you know very well how Walker feels about you, Mare."

"Do I though?"

"Sometimes, Toni," Mielie says, turning back to face the windscreen, "I think Mare's eyes actually face inward."

"Oh my God!" Mare retorts. "All I ever do is watch other people! From the sidelines, as it turns out …"

"Please Mare," Mielie says quietly. "Stop. I can't take this today, okay."

But Mare doesn't stop. "Why weren't you there for me last night, Mielie? Huh? I just lost my best friend. And my boyfriend. But no, it was all about you and Toni, for a change."

"God strewth, Mare, stop it now!" Toni yells, eyes fixed on the road.

"I thought we could at least talk at the wedding," Mare goes on. "I waited, you know, Mielie. All those hours while you were in the bath – alone – when we could have been talking … Then I waited until the speeches were done, and the toasts, and everything – all your official duties that were actually my official duties, as if you didn't know – and I hung around you for, like, half an hour, and you know what you did? You spent the whole time ignoring me, locked in conversation with Walker. Walker! The only person I have *left*." Her voice breaks.

"I wasn't ignoring you, Mare," Mielie says, still staring ahead. "I was just being polite."

"Polite? Is that what that was, today, too? Edward comes over and you act like you don't know him. You call that polite? You're not! You're cold, that's what you are. Cold, cold, cold!" She kicks the back of Mielie's seat.

"And then it hits me. You and Walker are a thing. It makes perfect sense. You're pissed off with Edward because he didn't come to London when you called. So now he's demoted to 'friend'. And you get Walker. Just your type. Tall and boring. Well, good luck to you both."

They drive on in stony silence for a bit.

"Mare, you are literally delusional," Toni says, eventually. "You can't see past your own nose – sorry, err, pain. Or maybe it's just that you won't."

"Really Toni?" Mare shouts, sitting forward in her seat now. "Really? Well forgive me for being heartbroken!" She slumps back. "Neither of you have any idea!"

Toni flicks her indicator angrily and changes lanes for the parking lot. Then she swings the wheel hard, into a space.

Mare gets her bags out of the boot, avoiding Mielie's body and eyes. She kisses Toni on the cheek while Mielie fetches trolleys. "Thanks, Toni," Mare says. "See you."

Before Mielie has a chance to say goodbye, she starts walking, fast, across the parking lot.

Mielie hugs Toni hard.

Mare sits on a bench outside Domestic Departures, smoking. That's where Mielie finds her, once they've both checked in.

"Move over, cow."

Mielie sits down next to her sister and stares at the soft white threads on the knees of her jeans. "You can't leave like this," she says.

Mare says nothing.

"We can't leave each other like this."

Mare glares at her: "Why not?"

"Look, I know you're sensitive …"

"Yes, we all know I'm sensitive," Mare tells a crack in the pavement.

"… but you're not the only one whose heart is broken."

"I never said I was! You always do that. Always."

"Always what?"

"Put words in my mouth."

"Mare," Mielie manages. "Can you just calm do—"

"Calm down! God, Mielie. Have you even asked me about Will?" She grinds out her stompie. "Do you have *any* idea how I'm feeling?" She throws her cigarettes and matches into her bag. "He's involved, Mielie. He's involved with someone else. He dropped me, okay. Like I didn't matter, like I was never even part of his life. Like I'm invisible. Like I'm nothing … He was all I had, and I lost him." Mare brushes a tear off her cheek and swallows.

"You went there for a job, Mare, and you have that," Mielie says.

"I don't care about my job." Mare kicks her heels on the pavement. "And you have no idea how depressing it is. It's not creative. It's just horror. And I've never got any money."

They're both looking at the cars, the drop-offs and collections, the passengers and their suitcases, the drivers edging back into the traffic.

"Can I get you a coffee, then?" Mielie asks.

They sit opposite each other at a wonky table in News Café. Mare slops coffee into her saucer. Mielie stabilises the table with a wodge of Autobank receipts, and speaks before her sister has a chance to start.

"I know he broke your heart. I really do."

Mare stares at her.

Mielie doesn't say: *And I know what it feels like to be losing someone.*

She does say: "But you don't have to act like you're the only one it's ever happened to, Mare. You aren't."

"I just feel what I feel," Mare says. "Can't you get that? And why is that so wrong?"

"It just happens," Mielie goes on. "People break people's hearts. And some people manage to recover, and others don't." She looks at her watch. "Could you maybe just try harder? If not for yourself, then for Mum?"

"What? Why? Jeez Mielie," Mare pleads. "Do you see what you're doing. You're telling me to lie, to make other people happy. Mum hasn't taught me anything about how to cope. Now I'm in a crisis, but she needs to be protected?"

Mielie ducks under the table to adjust the Autobank slips. When she comes up her face is hard. "Jeez, Mare," she says. "You take narcissism to a whole new level." She motions for the bill.

"Thanks," Mare stands up, shaking her head. "Has it crossed your mind that this is not a choice for me. That some of us can only play ourselves." She starts across the airport lobby. The squeak of takkies and the slap of flip-flops on the polished airport floor are all she can hear.

Mielie rushes after her. "Stop it!' she grabs her arm. "Don't do this again! I'm just asking you, please Mare … You need to think of other people too!"

Mare looks around her. Her hands form fists. "You know," she says through her teeth, "You get really close, Mielie. Sometimes I think you really see how much it hurts. But then you fuck it up, you really do."

She walks away again, and this time Mielie doesn't follow.

In the Ladies, Mare weeps. Her heart is as heavy as a towel dropped in the sea.

She'd wanted Mielie – or Johnny, or someone – to wring her out.

She'd wanted her heart to be wrung and for there to be sheets of water, puddles all over the floor.

She knows now that even if someone had wrung her heart out for her, the towel would still be wet, still hold sand.

There's nowhere to lay her heart flat, to let it dry in the sunshine.

It keeps getting sodden with tears.

Soon enough, the sisters are in separate metal tubes, repelled like opposite magnets, shooting through the sky.

# CHAPTER 24

*Sunday Times social pages*
*15 September 1996*

**WILKINSON-DELPORT MERGER**
**Perfect spring evening kicks off the Joburg social season.**

Local millionaires Nick Wilkinson and Ronald Delport threw a lavish party at the weekend to celebrate the merging of their two companies into Wilkin-Del Projects (see *Business Report*, p3).

The glittering celebration took the form of a three-course dinner, poolside at Summer Place. Guests included leading lights in the financial world, as well as Houghton socialites and members of the city's young glamour set.

Nick Wilkinson Jnr and Delport's daughter, Astor, were photographed together. The couple met while still at school; they attended Delport's Matric Ball together.

During his speech, Wilkinson Snr laughingly remarked that it would "only be a question of time before we're all back here for another merger".

Wendy Wilkinson, asked if her son might marry the Delport's only child, gushed: "Astor is a darling. We'd be thrilled for both of them."

*

*Email, Mare to Mielie*
*Monday 16 September*

Dear Mielie

It's happened. In-print confirmation: Will and I never happened. According to my own newspaper, Will and the girl from the concert have been together since school.

There is no hospital for this.

Her name is Astor Delport. It was in the social pages yesterday.
It feels like I've eaten rotten chicken. Like the nausea's kicking in and soon I'll be vomiting faeces.
Not ladylike, I know.
But no regrets from my side. It was real. It wasn't a mistake.
I loved him. Still do.

Have to go now
XX Mare

PS: "He brought us joy / We loved him well / He was not ours / He was not mine."
It's from the funeral scene in Out of Africa.

*

*Monday 16 September*

In the morning, Johnny phones Mare at work. She is crying at her desk. The phone rings several times before she answers.

"So …" Johnny says, and falters. "You okay today?"

"No, Johnny. Still not okay."

He asks her if she'd like him to fetch her and take her to Westminster Mansions. "You're welcome to stay," he says.

"Why?"

"Why come and stay? Because I'm worried about you. Because you've just been run over by a 16-wheeler of an arsehole shithouse called Nick Wilkinson Junior."

"He's not an arsehole!" she says. "It's not his fault! It's not him. I know Will. I trust him. It's not hi—"

"Okay, sshh!"

"Why?"

"Be-cause … it's an open-plan office."

Then he tells her it's okay, she must just wipe her eyes, blow her nose, tell her boss she's leaving, and meet him downstairs. "Okay?"

"Okay, Johnny."

Then he shoots into town in his Laser.

When Mare emerges into the glare on the corner of Pritchard and Sauer Streets, it takes Johnny a moment to spot her. She's not the same girl he met on the platform at Park Station that February. There are deep shadows under her eyes.

When he hugs her, she smells of stale smoke.

At Westminster Mansions, Fouché is at the stove, draining a fresh batch of pumpkin fritters. There are Woolworths bags on the counter, packed with strawberries, patés and cheeses. When Johnny leaves to go back to work, Mare is seated in a large wingback with Fouché behind her, brushing her hair.

Later, Walker comes round. Mare barely talks to him. Fouché makes her a toasted sandwich – triangles pointing up – and Johnny puts her to bed.

After dinner, with Mare safely under the influence of a strong sleeping pill, the gents – Johnny, Fouché, Walker and Mitchell – sit in the lounge with whiskies. Three matching tumblers sweat onto coasters on the coffee table. Only Johnny's balances on the arm of the couch.

It's a moonlit night, and the weather is warm. Summer's on its way. What could have been a tingly, twinkly evening punctuated by the joy of wedding anecdotes has turned heated.

Johnny rants.

He can't believe people can still justify being such cowards. Sure, Mare is probably as acceptable to the Wilkinsons as the idea of their son preferring boys. He can see that Mr and Mrs W have probably always exerted considerable pressure on Will – to keep the bloodlines clean, to keep everyone in polo shirts, to keep everyone on the same page with schoolboy rugby derbies and diamond mining. Indeed, Johnny can understand that they would push hard, and that these people, being wealthy and entitled, are accustomed to getting their own way.

"Lord knows it's not easy to come out. Or to be in a mixed-race couple. Or even for one of you to be much older, or younger. But you don't just give up, not before you've even started. Maybe you did once, but not now." Johnny pauses to gulp some whisky.

Mitchell watches him intently. "Good for you," he says. "I agree." He swallows a large amount of his beverage. "But Will has chosen the life of privilege, simple as that. It's an old South African story. Do what you must to stay in the old-boy network, make sure you don't get disinherited."

"But he has a huge trust fund," Fouché says.

"No trust fund is big enough."

"Exactly, Walker." Mitchell reaches for his glass. "And even if it were, his life would change. He'd have to stand up for something – or in this case, someone."

"So?" Johnny says. "Will is a manipulator. It's what he does best. He could persuade everyone around him that he and Mare are an edgy couple, ahead of the game, right on trend."

Mitchell pours himself more whisky and tilts it to the light. "Oh, darling. I'm afraid the tragedy is that deep down Will probably gave up before '94, I'm guessing around the time he left school and decided to never work for a living. He was never going to defend Mare to his parents, his set – and certainly not for the rest of his life. Letting himself love her was a last-gasp rebellion."

"A rebellion conducted in private? Does it count?" Fouché wonders.

"He had to drop her," Mitchell says. "In some ways it's the most mature move I've seen him make."

"Fok my," Fouché says.

"Mn," Mitchell says, nodding meaningfully.

"But if he's a liar, and a coward, why would Astor want him?" Walker asks.

"He's charming, popular. Good looking. She doesn't need money."

"Are they in love?" Johnny wants to know.

"She might be. I haven't the foggiest. But you may recall that earlier this year Astor's famous grandfather died, doubling her inheritance." Mitchell leans back and looks through the balcony doors. "I'm guessing that particular windfall was helpful in hardening Will's resolve."

"And there's no chance Mare is right?" Johnny says. "What if his family is bankrupt and they're forcing him, I don't know, blackmailing him, to marry Astor or something? So that Will gets the merged company when the dads die?"

"Dare to dream," Mitchell smiles.

*Letter, Mare to Will (unsent)*
*Tuesday 17 September*

Dear Will,

Johnny says you might have chosen your old life above me. I don't believe that. I believe you're being forced into something and there's nothing I can do for you – or for myself, for us.

So I should try not to think. Like I should eat, I should sleep, I shouldn't cry, shouldn't drink. It's impossible, Will.

Remember when you were waiting for me outside work and I persuaded you to take me to Kapitans, that old restaurant up some stairs? We had to go into one of the little side streets between Sauer Street and the Stock Exchange. It was above a crammed shop that sold fireworks. There were fake flowers on the table and the curry was delicious.

I had a sense of being old, of looking back at the two of us – young, giggly – among the plastic doilies. We would tell the story of how we ate in the restaurant that Mandela and Tambo ate at in the 50s. Before the Treason Trial, before everything. I thought we'd be together forever.

Remember when you took me to the Italian deli in Houghton? There were giant tins of tomatoes, wheels of cheese, blocks of cold meat as big as my thigh. We sat outside, eating salad and dipping our bread in green olive oil. We spoke about travel and all the things we wanted to see and eat. We were going to do it all together.

At the mall in Sandton we had our photo taken and printed on a plate. I imagined it hanging in our kitchen. We lay in bed, listening to music, holding hands. We woke up kissing.

Remember when we used to go swimming in the middle of the night? We'd drive to the Ellis Park pool, after beer and pool, in your black Merc. The road was dark, shadowy. Too close to the Harrow Road bridge. Too close to the Ponte Tower. There was danger everywhere, but I was never scared with you. I would have followed you anywhere.

We'd climb through a fence and jump into a public pool in the cold, at 2am.

You were exuberant when you ran into the water. I remember your whoop, as you leapt. There was something heartbreaking about it, even then … like you were someone who was conscious of their youth and freedom while still young and free.

It filled me with regret for you. It sounded like the music that was trapped in school uniforms, the poetry that was tamped down at the family table, the longing for skin and sex that grew in us long before we met. I recognised that. I was in that whoop, somewhere. We were the answer to each other's calls.

I wasn't wrong to love you. How could I regret you, Will? "The Wilkinson days." They act like you were like a drug-filled syringe, the Helvetia-honey light a menacing trick. Like you were some mind-altering drug. Like I was an addict. Like I need to get back to my life now.

It's not like that. I feel like I've lost myself. I'm not sure where to start to piece things together. There's no meaning, no sense of interwoven significance. There are just these floating memories, these disconnected planes.

I had a dream that we were married. But I'd been cheating on you and you'd found out. It was very detailed. Even while I was having the dream I was thinking, Oh! this makes so much sense. It's completely my own fault.

Oh Will. We loved each other. I thought the meaning of life was to love. Is the opposite true?

I can't get any emotion out anymore. I feel like that about truly beautiful things and about truly ugly things, too – unmoved and isolated. I feel guilty that they don't affect me. I could carry on writing all night, or I could stop.

I will always love you. Always: so long.
Mare

*

*Wednesday 18 September*

Walker slows down on the driveway outside Helvetia Court. He and Mare have been swimming. They're stopping here so she can get more clothes. He watches her enter Helvetia Court.

Walker's hands are shaking on the wheel of his car. He hasn't been able to speak since he saw her getting out of the pool. She did a little hop-dash to her towel. He caught himself looking at her drop-covered thighs. He was taken aback by the intensity of what he felt then.

Now he thinks of Will, and how carelessly he's discarded her. Mare, the one human being Walker craves. The one person he literally cannot bear to see in so much pain.

He wants to punch something. Instead, he revs the engine loudly, forgetting that it's been idling.

When Mare gets back in the car she slumps over, her wet hair hanging over her face.

"You're not alone, you know," Walker says as he pulls off.

They drive past the water towers in silence.

After stopping the car in front of Westminster Mansions, Walker turns to Mare.

"Alone is *exactly* what I am," she spits.

# CHAPTER 25

*Email, Walker to Mielie*
*Thursday 19 September*

Dear Mielie,

It was truly wonderful to meet you in Cape Town.

I have a favour to ask. Would you mind relaying some information to your sister on my behalf? It has to do with me. I feel awkward about sharing it, and am only doing so because I'm genuinely worried about her.

Mare is clearly heartbroken. Will misled her terribly. But I don't want her to be judged. I don't want her to feel ashamed of having loved Will wholeheartedly. She is not wrong to feel things as strongly as she does.

It is very dangerous to add judgment and shame to heartbreak. I know this because I was deeply in love once, before.

Her name was Jane.

We lived down the road from each other, in Parktown. We were everything to each other. She was beautiful, like your sister. Warm, wild, sensitive, artistic. I wanted to study sociology. My first choice would have been Wits but I didn't get in there so I decided on UCT.

Jane said she would follow me the next year, when she had her matric. I travelled home whenever I could – trains, buses, I even hitchhiked once – but she was … I suppose disconsolate is the word. She started drinking, clubbing, taking drugs. She blew her matric. Her marks weren't good enough for UCT. Eventually she was accepted at Pretoria Tech for a graphic-design course, and moved into a digs.

In my July vac that year, I went to see her parents. They didn't have the address of her digs. Every Sunday of that vac I spent with her parents. She never came for lunch, as they kept hoping she would. And then she vanished from my life. Her parents begged her for contact details, on my behalf. She refused. She never phoned me.

And then, finally, when I was doing my Honours, I got a call from her. She was at a friend's house in Pretoria. She asked me to come and see her. I got a flight as soon as I could. She was dying. She was a heroin addict.

She apologised for everything. She said her heart was broken when I left, and she was ashamed of what she'd become. She still loved me. I still loved her, of course. I told her that. I told her how hard I'd tried to find her.

I stayed with her until she died, and I think, after that, I lost my nerve.

But this is not about me. She reminds me of your sister.

And when I think of what Will has done to her… Does he have any idea what he's done? How much damage it's possible to *do* to someone's heart? When they love you and you leave them?

I hold myself more than partly accountable for what happened with Jane. If I could rewind, and just have another chance to make it all end differently, I would. But you can't rewind, and that's the point.

Simply, I cannot bear to see Mare go to a place there's no coming back from. She needs to believe in herself, regardless of who loves or leaves her.

Her vulnerability is part of her beauty. But the way she's wired is what gives me cause to fear on her behalf.

I trust you will pass this information on to her – if you decide to – whenever and however you judge best.

Yours,
Tom Walker

PS: Mielie, about that night at Eland House, before the wedding. I wanted to assure you that you are so much more than what Geraldine Taylor sees. At the wedding I had a sense of how hard you work to look after everyone else. But perhaps you could do with some looking after, too.

I have some very good, very old friends in London. They're all mad old Socialists but they have nice houses these days. Some of them have good jobs and some of them can cook. Nice thing about grumpy old lefties is that most of us are helpers at heart.

*

*Email, Mielie to Mare via Johnny*
*Thursday 19 September*

Hello Mare (and Johnny) … I tried to call you at work, Mare, but they said you were "off sick".

JOHNNY: Please can you print this mail, and give it to Mare when you get home from work? Please don't read any of it. You probably already know everything. But please don't anyway, just because.

Love,
Mielie

PS, Mare: Everybody Hurts.
(REM)

*Email, Johnny to Mielie*
*Friday 20 September*

Good morning Mielie,

I did not read it, I swear. Mare showed me the contents. She re-reads and re-reads the printout in bed.

How insane that he sees himself as a Will, in a way. God. With a hard G.

Unfortunately, Walker's intervention doesn't seem to have helped much. It's Mare's fifth day off work. Not only is she emotionally broken, she is physically unwell too. And distracted. She's lost the key to Will's flat – another blow. She's also talking about moving back to Cape Town. We take her to Helvetia Court daily to check the answering machine. She's all over the place. She acts as if she's the only one who's ever been desperate with pain. As if none of us have ever been reduced to attacking the dashboard at times, to wailing in the shower or hitting ourselves in the face, in the course of a bust-up. Am I right? Mielie, don't all of us sensitive types understand the temptation to end heartbreak by dropping serpents down our blouses? We've all imagined taking a nice, sightless swim with the lily-pads, or downing a vial of poison at dusk. Not so?

I'll take her for a walk tomorrow. We'll go to the botanical gardens south of the city. We can talk or she can walk beside me in silence. Either way, the fresh air will do her good.

Much love to you,
Johnny

*

*Saturday 21 September*

Tom Walker and Mare Ashford are back in the driveway of Helvetia Court. She's been upstairs, checking her answering machine. He's standing at the car, with the driver's door open. He puts out his cigarette.

"Well," he says.

"Thanks for that," she says.

Instead of going round to the passenger door, Mare walks to where he's standing. They both look at the sky. It's spring, nearly summer. It shouldn't be this cold in the late afternoon. The light is soft, watery, gentle. Mare is wearing a berry-coloured coat over a T-shirt and shorts. Her hair is pulled back into an elastic – too long to be loose, too short to be tied up. A strand has escaped. Her neck is exposed.

Walker lifts his arms. His gesture is an appeal for conversation. An appeal for connection. He tries – and fails – to find something to hook his thumbs into.

Mare's body is still, her arms crossed tightly across her chest. She is not speaking, but she's not moving either.

Walker is struggling to express himself. What does he want to say?

"I did read it," she says. "Your email to my sister."

Walker looks down at the stones on the driveway. He puts his hand in his pocket and finds his car keys there. "I don't expect you to understand," he says.

Someone in the flats is playing "It's Not Unusual" by Tom Jones. Mare glances up. There's the sound of cars on Cavendish. A taxi hooting. There are children playing ball at the back of the flats, against the garages.

It's not unusual for Walker to be exposed. He has revealed himself before. He's taken risks before, plenty. He just hasn't done it for a while.

It is unusual for Mare to avoid connection.

He is bent ever-so-slightly over her. Her body is curved towards him too. They're both conscious of their hands. He's moved his away from her. She is gripping hers together.

"I'm sorry," Mare says.

Why did she say that? Normally she'd be furious if someone told her she wouldn't understand.

*Because.* It's the first time she's noticed his eyes, when he was saying she wouldn't understand. *They are green, flecked. There's light in there, warm and rich. It's like the silver behind a mirror. It's everything. It's who he is, that deep light. It's what Johnny and all the rest of them like about him. It's his quality,* she thinks.

"I don't like remembering," he says.

"About …?" She doesn't want to say her name. She doesn't want to hurt him.

Walker turns his head towards the building. "I couldn't … No." He turns back to her. "I didn't. I didn't help her."

Mare pulls her coat sleeves over her hands. "Of course you did," she says.

He looks at her, square in the face. She experiences an involuntary tingle.

"Did you write to her?" she asks. "Letters?"

"Yes. I sent them to her parents' house because we didn't know where she was."

Mare watches him. "What did she say?"

"She didn't reply."

She tries to push the strand of hair behind her ear. "She might not have wanted help, Walker."

Using his name feels like touching him.

He shakes his head briefly. "I should have found her." He moves his hand to the car door, whether to get in or close it she can't tell. "I should have tried harder. Maybe I was angry with her. For not coming to Cape Town. For cutting me out." His hand stays on the door.

Mare has a flash of Walker as a younger man, at a rally. She feels his memories and sadness, heated in a mix. "God, Walker, I don't know."

There are hadedas on the grass. Mare watches them for a moment. She realises she disagrees with him, about trying harder. It takes her a moment to find the words. "Listen," she says, as one of the birds jerks a worm from the soil. "You were hurt. But you loved her. That's a gift."

He stares at her.

"That's a gift," she repeats. "Always."

Walker keeps staring at her. His brain is working but there is some giant boulder to shift in there.

"The sad thing is," Mare says, "she never stopped loving you either."

He parts his lips. He looks at Mare, then away again. "Then why she didn't reply?"

"Because …" Mare pauses. "Because she didn't want to drag you down."

Now he stares at the hadedas too. "I want to go back," Walker says.

"To that time?"

"No," he said. "I just want to go back to Mitchell's, I want a drink." He shakes his head, half-smiling. "I think we need a drink, don't you?"

They look into each other's eyes. They're conscious of their hands again.

"Shall we?" he says.

"We could."

"But …?"

"I'm sorry," Mare blurts.

"For what?"

Sorry for misjudging him. Sorry to have missed out on months of talking with him like this. Sorry he's suggested going to Mitchell's, too. "For being … for being a loudmouth and thoughtless. And. Uh. For not seeing. Not understanding. You know, what happened to you."

Walker looks at her hard. He jangles his keys in his coat pocket. Her cheeks get hot. "It's not—" he says.

"It is important," she says, panicking.

"Mare, what I mean is—"

"It's okay," she interrupts. "We should – shall we go? Shall we go back to Johnny's?"

He half-lowers his eyes. "Sure," he nods, without looking up.

*

*Email, Mare to Mielie*
*Sunday 29 September*

Dear Mielie

I hate weekends when you're far from your screen.

I'm at work. Someone has to be, on Sundays. There has to be something in the Monday papers.

I've been back at work a week. I'm honing my research skills. I'm starting to understand why people like hard news so much. You get to be a dog with a rat. It's an appealing persona when you're powerless.

Today's story is about a corrupt policeman who sold three gallstones and a human heart from the state mortuary. He was found guilty on three out of four charges. He ACTUALLY cut out a human heart, put it in a bottle and sold it for R2000.

You probably need me to reassure you I'm okay. That's the only reason I'm writing. I don't feel like it. There's nothing to say.

Okay, truth? It looks like I have professional ability and I'll be able to work and support myself, but on the emotional side … As Johnny Cash says of Belshazzar: "My friend you're weighed in the balance and found wanting."

I'm tired. I cry a lot. I want to be at home and alone all the time. My appetite for humanity has been completely wiped out, just like one evening of vomiting Tassies can eradicate your desire for the stuff for life.

Twice recently, at the movies, I've had to swap places with Johnny to avoid lashing out at: first, a man who ate one piece of popcorn every second without moving a muscle except those in his right arm, and second, a man with a runny nose who sniffed every two seconds – both THROUGHOUT the movie.

If I am okay, it's probably thanks to Walker. I've seen him a lot lately. He arrives most evenings around five, in time for a swim before it gets too dark, and then he takes me back to Westminster Mansions.

I acknowledge that early-evening exercise and eating (could've been four Es in a row if it wasn't for the "and") is better than going out late and getting pissed. It's a bit like being on parole.

We also listen to music in his bakkie. I'm not sure if I like it. Stuff I've never heard of. It's not like Will's. Mine, I mean. I get the sense he loves reggae too. Thank goodness he doesn't play it.

I was wrong about him, Mielie. (I can be so wrong sometimes, I think it might be an actual talent.) He's not boring. He's not unattractive. He sometimes says hilarious things when you least expect them, like "always take the high road", and "cruel and unusual", and "a proper degree of terror".

Generally, though, he's silent. I've never been more grateful for a silent friend. But if we have a friendship – if it's more than the relationship you'd have with your parole officer – it's not simple. Need I remind you, we are both single.

I think he hides a great deal from the world. (We could not be more different in that regard.) This alone is not interesting. What's interesting is mystery.

Okay so … Headline: I got turned on by him in the pool.

WHAT????!!!!

It was just for a fraction of a second – obviously – and then I was back to being indifferent. I suspect it's just Will aftershocks.

I probably shouldn't write about this on my work computer. People can hear me typing – the sound of the keys is bouncing off the walls. In a minute someone might come over and ask me What's the Story?

But here goes: He took me swimming this morning because I was coming here to work and he has soccer on Sunday evenings.

He always gets in after me. I never thought about it before. I just swim, with my head under the water, or my goggles fogged, until it's time to get out, then I do, and go to the changing rooms, and when I get back he's dressed and reading the paper, waiting for me.

He's always reading the paper. That's something you notice about him. I suspect this is why he's good at phrases. He says things like "revisionist tendencies", believing I know what he means.

Initially I was shy to ask him. Now I don't care. "What's 'realpolitik'?" He tells me. "Who's Anton Lubowski again?" Short bio.

So this morning. I get to the end of my length. I stand up in the shallow end, take off my goggles, and Bloody Tom Walker is pulling his T-shirt off right above me.

I'm not saying a flippen word about his torso. I needed to turn back to the water and give the pool an "OOWERhhh" face. AAaarghh!! It's 1996 and I am being PUNISHED for something. I lose the love of my life and my boring, big-brother parole officer turns out to be a god with a six-pack.

He hopped into the next lane and said: "Everything okay?" Poker face.

There's no point thinking about it. I'm starting to see the massive scale of my mistake. Not that I consider Will a mistake. It's just that he's ruined my life, the life I knew.

I went to Exclusive Books on my own yesterday. There was Will, on every page of the James Dean coffee-table book. Maybe it's just good fashion, but, like, garment after garment … and Steve McQueen, Paul Newman, Brando. Did he copy everything? Or is this just how handsome men present themselves?

Maybe I shouldn't be too hard on him. It looks like Brad Pitt learnt his pout from Jimmy D. George Clooney keeps his neck straight like Paul Newman. Frankly, all men should learn to scowl like Steve McQueen.

Oh well. I went out with a movie star once. What a dream.

I should probably approach the newsdesk now. The editor and I are the only people in sight. The way I've been typing he might think he has the Watergate scoop on the way.

Love,
Mare

PS: Write soon, please, but please don't tell me what I already know: that I need to focus on my future. Whatever it looks like, good or bad, I don't want it. There's really nothing more to say.

# CHAPTER 26

*Monday 30 September*

Mielie Ashford turns the key in the lock in the front door of 227 Haydons Road. The house is dark and quiet.

She steps over the post. She doesn't close the curtains or turn on the lights. Instead, she goes into the kitchen, opens the bottle of Jim Beam she got at Duty Free, and takes a slug. Then she sits on the furry brown sofa in the lounge, lights a ciggie, and draws on it hard. She's glad no one can see her.

It's been a tough day. Nothing out of the ordinary – just answering phones, couriering show-reels, copying and filing and sending out scripts. But there was something about the angular metal of the filing cabinets, and the sharp little plastic tags, and the way the papers kept catching on a torn piece of skin on her fingertip, that registered as being quite brutal, today.

And so that was how Mare Ashford's infinitely capable elder sister found herself weeping at 6pm in a photocopy room – that dreadful kind of weeping, when your contact lenses come adrift and hover, and you absolutely cannot make a single sound.

It struck Mielie, then, amid the whirring machinery and flashing lights, and with Lou Reed's "Perfect Day" piping down the corridor, that – in not coming to live with her in London when she'd believed he would; in sleeping with Kristal Smith when she'd had no inkling of that possibility; in then exposing her to the humiliation of finding out for herself; and (perhaps most of all) in not wearing a condom and thereby conceiving a child – Edward Taylor had not only taken the wind out of her sails, he'd broken the fucking mast.

On the pavement outside 227 Haydons Road, a streetlight shines through the fog. A bus shudders past, its windows alight, its tired people homeward bound.

Mielie is surprised how sad this makes her feel. Where is Edward this second? Maybe on his way home? She has such a clear picture of him in her head. His hands on the steering wheel. How he moves through air.

She gulps more bourbon.

For nearly two months she's done well at keeping Kristal's secret, as promised. Now, in a fraction of time between two arbitrary moments, she lets go. Walks to the landline, dials Edward's number and hears his voice.

"Hello," is all she says.

"Mielie," he says, sounding half apprehensive, half relieved. "It's good to hear your voice."

"Yours too."

"Thank you for calling," he says. "Are you home?"

She can barely hear him. It's a bad line. And again, the real distance, the dislocation, the walled-in avalanche of pain.

"It's not home, Edward," she says, sitting on the floor now with her spine against the wall – knees up, socked feet flat on the carpet. "I mean, I know I chose to come here and all that … I'm the one who left. But now I think I might need to leave again. I need to move out – and on."

"Will you tell me where you go?" he asks.

"Uh … I don't think so, no. I think … I think it's better not to, this time. Because you know if I do, well, then I'll always still be hoping you'll come, you see …" she says, hot tears sheeting down her face.

On the other end of the line, Edward listens.

"I mean, there's not even Toni now," Mielie continues. "She kind of filled up the whole space, when she was here. I'd get back and she'd be in the sitting room, watching *Friends* … Said it made living life worthwhile …" She tries to laugh.

"I saw Toni," Edward seizes his moment. "It's how I knew you were going to be in Cape Town. It's why I came to the house … I wanted—"

"Edward, I know," Mielie says.

"I know," Edward says – and pauses. "I mean, I know you know what happened with Kristal, because Toni told me. I've been having these long conversations with you in my head. Asking you to forgive me, and …"

"No!" Mielie says. "I mean, I've forgiven you already, Edward. It's not that."

"Because what I really don't want is to lose you … for you to move on, as you say …"

"You don't KNOW," she says. "I—"

"What?"

"You and Toni *don't* know everything I know, Edward … and what's worse is, I can't tell you!"

Edward's heart pounds in his chest. "Mielie, what are you talking about?" he says quietly.

The gap between his question and her answer gets too long. It sounds like something's muffling the mouthpiece. Her hand, maybe? Her chest?

"I promised I wouldn't tell anyone. And I haven't. And I won't."

"Who?"

"What?"

"Who did you promise?"

"Shit, Edward! Kristal! Who else could I mean?"

"Oh God." His worst fear come true. "Oh God," he says. "Tell me she's not …"

Edward hears the wind chimes outside her kitchen door. She's hearing them too, of course. Right there but also impossibly far away.

"It's okay," she says. "It will be okay. Really, Edward, it's—. I've been watching it all disappearing – everything we could've had together – like water down a plug hole, and I wanted to stop it somehow, but I can't."

"Listen, Mielie," he says. "In summer, when I met you, it was like … like colours changed, you know?"

"For me too," Mielie says. "And I was thinking on the way home just now … I was thinking that just because you love someone, it doesn't mean that they belong to you. It's actually the other way around."

Edward is quiet. Mielie Ashford. He cannot lose her now.

"So," she continues, "whatever happens in the rest of your life, please believe me when I tell you I will always be yours, Edward. I mean it."

He glimpses lunacy, like a shadow crossing a doorway in the corner of his eye.

"And by the very end, whenever that is, not a single day will have passed that I won't have thought of you."

Edward cannot speak.

"It's the colours," she says. "They won't change back."

"Mielie, are you okay?" Edward says after a bit.

"I'm fine. I mean, I will be. Of course I will be, again. I think I just need some time to … uh … to come to terms with things, you know. It's hard, though, because it's things I'd never personally have chosen. I'd really never have chosen this for you, Edward. I need you to know that I wouldn't."

This, Edward thinks, is what *he* has chosen, even if unconsciously.

"I just really needed to hear your voice," she's saying. "And to tell you I love you anyway. And to say goodbye."

"Mielie, please. Don't hang up," Edward says. "Come back! Come back to me. We can—"

"I can't come back!" she screams. "And we can't do anything! We could have … but now we really can't!"

"Mielie," Edward's pleading. "Please don't go—"

But in a single heartbeat, he finds that she has.

Mielie lies on the sofa, drinking more Jim Beam. She gets through several more ciggies too. When she's smoking, she isn't also crying. It's one or the other, she discovers. This will continue for as long as needed. Probably the rest of her life.

She remembers taking turns to blow the dandelion, in Edward's courtyard, under the stars. She forgot to make a wish.

*If I could just see the sky,* she thinks, *there'd be somewhere for all of this sadness to go. Right now it feels like it's just sliding down the walls.*

"'Then in the spring something happened to me,'" she whispers.

"*Yes, I remember,*" she imagines Mare whispering back.

"'I fell in love with James Tyrone and was so happy for a time.'"

*For a time, for a time, we were all so happy for a time,* Mielie thinks as her breathing slows.

"Eugene O'Neill, of course," she says out loud. "Long Day's Journey into Night."

# PART FIVE

# CHAPTER 27

*Tuesday 1 October*

"Kristal!" Edward calls loudly up the stairs at Eland. "Could you come down here for a minute, please?"

Kristal stops at the top. Edward is standing very straight.

"Why not come up here?" she smiles, lifting a shoulder coyly. "Booboo's not here, for once ..."

"No, please just come into the lounge." Edward leaves the bannister and briskly crosses the hall.

Outside, it's a beautiful day. Edward is standing at the window, looking at the garden, when Kristal enters the room.

"I thought I'd made myself clear," he says quietly.

Edward hears Kristal stop, then close the door behind her.

"About what?" she asks.

Edward turns to face her. "When I came to see you in Pietermaritzburg. I knew you still had feelings for me. I told you it was over between us. That I was in love."

"I know that, Eddy," Kristal moves across the room towards him. "It's why I've been waiting ..."

"For what?" Edward asks. "I told you it was over."

Kristal shakes her head – her face a blink and a smile. "But?"

He looks her in the eyes, a hard stare. "But," he says. "Yes. Then we slept together. Drunk." He takes three strides away from her and turns again. "Do you think I'm proud of that?"

Kristal raises a hand to her throat.

"And then I went to London," he continues. "And I saw Mielie. And you know what? I should've just told her the truth. She might even have forgiven me, right then. I should have just told her, but I didn't. I was so ashamed. I couldn't find the words."

Kristal keeps very still and quiet at this point.

"But you made sure she found out, didn't you." Edward's voice is bitter now.

He can feel his temper. He must be careful now. The one thing Edward must not do, whatever happens, is throw Mielie under the bus. After everything she's been through because of him, some protection now is the least she deserves.

"Toni told me you told Mielie. About that night. She told me," he says, after taking a breath.

Kristal sinks – head bowed – to the edge of an ottoman, one finger loosening a button on her blouse.

Edward moves to sit on a sofa across from her. "Listen. We go back a long way, Kristal. I know you very well. And those memories will always mean something. But at some point you have to realise … that even though I've lost Mielie now … I'm not coming back to you."

When Kristal looks up, she has tears in her eyes. "Too late," she smiles. "I'm pregnant."

This is the exact result Edward has been hoping for, of course. He had to get the truth out of her directly, and now it's done. Now they can start dealing with the fallout. Elbows on knees, he runs both hands through his hair.

"Right," is all he says, eventually. "And this you were planning to tell me …?"

"I was waiting for the right time!"

"Oh right," he says. "The right time."

Kristal pushes her upper arms together to squeeze her cleavage and leans forward, chin in hands. "Come on, Eddy," she says, beaming her warmest smile. "You'll get over Mielie, eventually … She knows about our baby, by the way. And you're going to be a dad!"

At that moment, Kristal and Edward hear the front door click. They hear Booboo bound up the staircase and Fiona clack across the tiles.

She pops her head around the lounge door.

"Oh hello, Fiona," Edward says, standing. "Come in, we have news!"

*Email, Toni to Johnny*
*Tuesday 1 October*

NEWSFLASH!!!

Am hesitant to write anything at all.
Deadly calm and devoid of almost all feeling.
Obliterated by mere primal fact.
As are you about to be, my friend.
Yes, come over here to the hole in the fence:
Kristal Smith is pregnant.
Despite the near-total absence of medium-term memory my side, she's 12 weeks in, by my count.
Seeing as Edward – as you, Mielie and I know only too well – had sex with her in mid-July.
UNbeknownst to either of us – however – it transpires she also told Mielie she'd missed her period.
And swore her to silence on that front too.
None of us – not even Edward – knew about The Bebe.
Because our friend kept her word.
How do I know this?
My cousin Kristal is here at the hotel.
Yip. Run, maybe. Hide, not.
She arrived at lunchtime in a taxi.
Shaking and in tears. Apparently she and Edward were at Eland "just chatting" when Fiona arrived home to be told the news, by Edward, of the baby poor Kristal was carrying – sorry, "growing".
Imagine theatrical use of tissues.
Imagine bewildered voice saying Fiona "went ballistic".
As in:
- Framed photos smashed.
- All bottles swept off drinks console and smashed.
(Contents thus wastefully leaked. One must raise one's eyebrows here.)
- And glasses – The Family Crystal – thrown straight at humans, not walls.
Kristal got ejected from Eland on the spot.

And neither Fiona nor Geraldine Taylor will have anything to do with "that gold-digger" ever again.
Geraldine went so far as to say – on the phone to Edward – that if Kristal keeps the baby and he marries her, she'll have nothing to do with him, either.
As in: All Ties Cut (ATC).

OF COURSE he's going to marry Kristal.
He'll honour his responsibilities.
He's That Guy, is he not.
This time you have to tell Mare.
Everything, please. From scratch.
Mielie also needs to know what's happened.
So I leave you now.

X
Toni

*

*Wednesday 2 October*

It's Wednesday evening. Johnny has taken Mare out for a pizza at his beloved San Maria, and told her the story, blow by blow.

"And then, Kristal wears her down further by moving into her bedroom at Eland, to dangle herself under Edward's nose. And then, dear Mare, your sister has to deal with being humiliated by every member of Edward's family – all of them: Fiona, Geraldine, not to mention your idiot half-brother – the night before the wedding. That's if Walker's take on things is to be trusted, which I believe it is."

Mare – pizza untouched – sits very still and stares at Johnny. She remembers all the times she's accused Mielie of being cold and unfeeling.

"And then, around the same time," Johnny goes on, "her little sister – her beloved little sister – is reeling around at night, alone, thumbing her nose at the beast that is Joburg crime. Looking like she's going to get herself killed on the streets … or simply, deliberately, expire from grief."

Mare stares at the "To Die For" sign.

"Through all of this," Johnny continues, "Mielie's trying to help you, and protect you, by remote control. And your mum, and Tess. She doesn't ask for help, even though she needs it so badly. Instead she keeps trying to be the sensible one, as usual … Oh for God's sake—"

Mare has started to cry.

"Pass the Tabasco," Johnny says. "Honestly, what now?"

Mare is remembering Mielie begging her – literally begging her – to think of other people too.

The waiter is watching them. He takes a step forward, and then back. Johnny does not reach out to Mare. Instead, he beckons the young man. "Yes, hello," he says. "May I have a jug of tap water and two glasses please? Thank you so much."

Johnny waits for her to look up. "Mare, I've known you and Mielie for a very long time," Johnny says, holding eye contact. "And I will love you until the day I die." He pauses to take a bite of pizza, and continues through a mouthful: "If you die before me I will throw myself on your coffin as it's lowered into the ground."

He makes her laugh.

"Oh, yes," he swallows. "And if you're cremated, they'll have to pull me back, bodily, from the furnace."

"Ew." Mare blows her nose on a used napkin.

"I know. I love you that much."

"I—"

"No. Now listen. This is the thing I am actually trying to say. Mielie's been keeping Kristal's secret – and suffering – for going on two months now. Without either of us being there for her. We've known she was suffering. It's all there in her letters, conveniently in print. If we'd actually read what she's been writing to us, it would've been obvious that she was not okay. Is not okay. There's enough proof of feeling there for anyone – even you."

The waiter arrives with the water, puts the jug and glasses on the table. Johnny waits, but Mare can see he hasn't finished. The waiter leaves. Johnny starts up again before the man is out of earshot.

"But what did we do? Zilch. Because, simply, it was far more convenient for us both to hold on to what we wanted to believe. That she's strong. And that no matter how bad things might get for her, we could count on her to make sure everything worked out in the end." He takes an angry drink of water. "It's fucking unspeakable."

Of course Mare cries again then, actually splashing her Napoletana. She'd even told her sister there was no way that Mielie could ever, possibly, truly understand.

A tear rolls down Johnny's cheek too. He wipes it off with his hand.

He doesn't hug Mare or make her laugh.

He lets her cry.

*

*Letter, Mare to Mielie*
*Wednesday 2 October*

Helvetia Court
Floor

Dear Mielie

It's late now and I'm crying. Again. Not for Will this time, or for me. I'm crying for you. You're in so much pain, I can't bear it.

Johnny took me for a pizza earlier. Toni told him to tell me everything I didn't know … about all you've been through since Kristal dropped the bomb.

I was a mess. I still am. I can't believe it, Mielie.

You broke up with Edward so he could marry Kristal?

How can it BE? It's not possible! It's not right! Kristal's never loved Edward. Not the way you do. All she wants is Fifi's life. The mansion and the four-by-four. She's vain, deceitful, scheming. Edward hates her type. His mother, his sister … He can't want one of those for a wife? How could he? How could he love her AND you?

There's three slugs of Three Ships left in the bottle. I'm going to finish it now.

Okay, back. Phwoo-aah! It's better if I don't drink, but now would not be the time.

When I got home tonight, I re-read all your letters. Johnny's right, we sidestepped the truth.

I think it's because I always thought you were unsinkable. I see now that you are that duck with the legs going like pistons underwater, to make it look like you're floating. You're very convincing. But it's no excuse. I wasn't there for you.

I've been so selfish, so blinkered. I will hate myself forever for this you know, Mielie.

You never met Will, yet you held my hand through all of it. And I haven't even been grateful.

I only heard criticism. I imagined you firing off words like a soldier lying in a field, using up rounds of bullets.

But now when I think back to our arguments, I only hear tired frustration in your voice.

I hope I can change. I hope you will forgive me.

I want to help you. If you come home, I'll try. You could come and stay with me, and maybe you could let me look after you, for once.

I'll type this up and mail it in the morning.

I wish I could be with you right now.

With all my love,
Mare

*

*Email, Mielie to Mare*
*Thursday 3 October*

My darling Mare

Thank you so much for writing to me. It helps me so much to know where you're at, and to know that you're here with me. Really.

You say you're wrong about stuff, often, but about me, lately, you're right. I have to stay buoyant. It's how I get through the days. I just about get it together to bath and eat too, but it's difficult with zero appetite.

Mare, I'm sorry I couldn't tell you about Edward and Kristal before. I didn't want to keep any secrets from you. You were already going through so much in your own life, anyway. But I'm really relieved that you know now.

Don't, please, whatever you do, tell Mum. I don't want her to worry. And there's nothing she could do to change anything anyway, or to make it better.

I also asked Peter not to tell her. He called me last night, can you believe. Actually to ask if I've "made any progress with Walker" – what's with everyone, about that? (Your swimming pool encounter had me fascinated, Mare. Will you kiss him soon, do you think?)

He said things that side are really bad; Fifi's still in bed. He also confirmed that Edward is standing by Kristal, as he should of course, while Geraldine's urging her to abort.

Oh! Why is it that every time I start writing to you, all ten phone lines start ringing, and I'm the only one not lunching or at gym?

Hang about, please Mare. I'll come back.

Okay so now it's 6pm here and my colleague's just thrown a pile of scripts on the floor between our desks. "Those can be filed," she said.

I hate the passive voice, Mare! I hate it so much. I hate it even more when the subject does not even then become the agent. It just gets ripped out of the sentence and disappears. Which is unfortunate, because it reduces the sentence to a statement of what is already obvious. Yes, scripts are certainly file-able. But they can't file themselves. "Those can be filed BY YOU," is what she should say, if she doesn't have the manners to say "Could you please file these scripts?" to start with. But she doesn't say "by you", does she, because it's implied. There's no one else to do it, from what I can tell, round here. Nor to pick the scripts up off the floor.

Right. Scripts have now proven their file-ability.

Sorry, I sound like a martyr.

It's really not too bad, working here. This evening's soundtrack is The Piano. It makes me feel like life is a movie, and I for once am in it. There isn't a script and I don't know the plot, but I'm sure there is one. There must be. It might only be revealed in retrospect, but there surely must be a plot.

Meanwhile, there's only circumstance: what happens when, where, and to whom. The why remains a mystery.

From my desk in the corridor, I can see through the glass walls of my boss's offices out onto the roof of the building next door, and the snow-cloud sky behind it.

There's always a peculiar sadness, in the dying autumn light. Somehow, it feels sadder this year. Like we'll never again be who we are right now. Like there's only just this once.

Oh Mare. I could scream till I'm blue in the face – and I often do – that it doesn't matter that I personally don't understand why Edward did what he did with his body, but it does. It does.

And then Peter goes and says, on the phone last night: "There's plenty more fish in the sea." And I just wanted to yell: "But I wanted that fish, Peter! It's the only one I wanted! Don't you see?"

Please survive Will. I need you to.

My love forever,
Mielie

PS: It's snowing now. It really is.

PPS: Yesterday, I was smoking on the pavement in Oxford Street. In the shop windows, the new Clinique skincare display has got this massive, pale-green clock. I was thinking it's a cruel thing, to remind people their clock is ticking. Like they're running out of time. I was kind of chatting to you about it, in my head, and missing you with all my heart. I was thinking I could do with something – anything – from you, badly.

Then there it was – your email in my inbox this morning, when I got in to work.

And there's the thing, see, Mare. You really never know what could happen, from one moment to the next.

*

*Friday 4 October*

Tom Walker has persuaded Mare to use his car. They've been swimming. Both are having dinner at the Radium Beer Hall with Johnny and Mitchell later, but Walker has to meet a colleague first and Mare wants to bath. They've agreed that she'll drop him at the Radium and bring the car back later.

He parks the car in a side road lined with jacaranda trees, and they're in that moment: mid-conversation, knowing that one of them has to make the first move. Either he has to get out or she has to ask for the keys. They're both avoiding it.

It's a warm spring twilight – their hair still wet, the car windows open, the last streams of sun on their arms.

"Okay, I should go," Walker says.

"What's your rush?" Mare says.

"My colleague's coming, and we're meeting the others at eight."

"I suppose. But also, in general."

"In general?"

"Ja. You're always in a rush to get away from me," Mare says.

"What?" Walker is dumbfounded, annoyed, even. "Are you joking?"

"You're always the perfect gentleman," she says. "Big brother. Not as in *Big Brother* … but we'll be having a nice time and then you'll kind of … pull rank …"

"Pull *rank*?"

"I don't know how else to say it. You get all officious … or brisk."

She pauses. Walker looks through the windscreen at a bakkie slowing down alongside them. He feels vulnerable, suddenly. "You think I'm old. Of course I am, to you."

"It's not that!"

"It used to be," Walker says, after a pause.

"It's not that. I swear. Anyway, age isn't everything."

"Age is experience."

"You didn't just say that!" Mare squeals. "You said youth was passion."

"Nope. Experience is everything. So what's the issue?"

Mare puts her feet up on the dashboard. She has bare feet, chipped nail polish, no jewellery.

*This girl,* Walker thinks. *Just skin and hair and bones and life.*

"I wish you'd stop feeling you have to look after me," Mare says.

"I would if you didn't need looking after."

"That's a cheap shot."

"Good point."

In the side mirror, Walker watches a man approach the car. He bends to put his face right in the window space, close to Walker's.

"Next time, okay?" Walker says.

"Please, I need—"

"Just give me five minutes. Okay?"

The man looks at Walker, then at Mare. She's staring out of the other window, at a hedge. *This man could draw a knife on me without her noticing,* Walker thinks.

Then Mare swings round. "Hello," she says to the man. "Would you mind? Please? We just need five minutes."

"Okay," he says. "I'll be that side."

"Okay," Walker says.

There's a silence. Mare's legs need shaving. She tries to pull a hair out of her shin. Walker wonders if she's lost her impetus. She hasn't.

"Listen," she turns to him. "I'm not interested in you babysitting me. I thought we were … getting on."

"We are."

Mare takes a deep breath. "I like you, Walker, seriously. Do you think you can stop playing bodyguard? I don't mean to sound ungrateful, it's just that I'd really quite like to be friends."

"Friends."

"Ja." She smiles.

The air is dense with possibility.

She does a tiny fart. "Oh, God, sorry!" she laughs.

Walker laughs. He tries to get serious again, but too soon. There's another laugh in both of them. Then he rushes in, still smiling: "We weren't made to be friends, Mare."

Her profile hardens. She stares through the windscreen.

"You know what I mean?" Walker says.

The man is back at the window. "Oh, right." Walker gives him R2.

Mare gets out of the car and walks around to the driver's side.

Walker gets out and hands her the keys.

"I don't know why you have to suddenly meet with a mystery colleague, anyway," she says. "Why can't you just come with me to my flat?"

"Mare – you'll be in the bath. And … I—"

"What?" she says. "What's there to worry about? It's not like you're gonna do something you'll regret."

Back home, Mare pulls off her swimming costume and tosses it on the bed. Not knowing why, she walks past her dressing gown and to the bathroom naked. She's not used to walking around naked. She doesn't sleep naked and she usually only takes her clothes off when the bath is run.

She stands in front of the bathroom mirror, then backs away to see as much of her body as possible. She can't see much, so she steps into the empty bath and stands on her tiptoes.

"So what?" she says. "It's just a body."

Mare reaches over and turns on the taps. "It's not who I am," she mutters, as the water starts to run.

# CHAPTER 28

*8pm*

Fear, to Mare, smells like the sweaty fur of a cornered animal.

It's in her mouth: sour, meaty, like the blood-soaked paper at the bottom of a polystyrene tray.

It's in her sweat: salt and dirt, the sharp smell of adrenaline.

*9.30pm*

*It's illogical, extravagant.*

She thinks this in the moments after he shoots her.

Why lead her over to a tree, her back turned, the gun between her shoulder blades?

She thought he might tell her to kneel down. That he was going to execute her. The darkness, the tree, the firelight from the squatter camp. A nightmare. A Goya painting.

She thought: Is this *it*? She was terrified, but disbelieving. The danger was significant. Death was knocking. But was this really the last minute of her life? Was she not even going to try to save herself?

Mare waited for her life to flash before her eyes. It didn't. She wondered, if she were to die now, if the montage would come. She doubted it. The threads of her life remained tangled, in a clump.

She felt like that, at the tree.

You idiot, she thought. All you've ever done is wallow. You need clarity now, strength, purpose, but all you've ever done is accumulate – experience, language, emotion, compacted together. You were supposed to separate the threads, weave something, make something of yourself.

She must have shifted, or maybe he slipped on an exposed root. He didn't mean to shoot her, she knows that, but the gun went off and the bullet went into her. It burnt.

He shouted. He ran. She was wet. The pain arrived.

It was like biting on metal, on shards of ice. It was the taste of panic, powerlessness.

The metal won't yield, the ice won't melt, it won't stop. Hot oil, poison, thorns. Raw flesh, the smell of an animal brought down.

*9.45pm*

Manuel Fernandes is checking stock in his Engen garage on the highway near Vosloorus, south-east of Joburg.

A movement on the security TV catches his eye: a girl walking onto the forecourt from the direction of the highway. She is carrying nothing.

*9.47pm*

The front glass doors open and a petrol attendant comes in, helping the girl to walk. Her blood is on his uniform.

There's red on her T-shirt, jeans and shoes. Blood in her hair and bloody marks on her face.

She's bleeding from her left shoulder. Her nails are clean.

She says she needs help – she's been hijacked and shot.

*9.48pm*

Fernandes guides her onto the couch in his office and calls an ambulance.

He's had hijack victims in the shop before. They get dropped on the other side of the squatter camp – far enough to give the hijackers time to drive away – and they run to the highway, towards the lights of his garage.

*9.49pm*

The girl lies on the couch. It's hard for her to talk.

She asks Fernandes to call Johnny Barton, and gives him a phone number.

She tells him her name, too.

He writes it all down and makes the call.

Then he asks her if she wants water, but her eyes are already closed.

*10.18pm*

Fernandes takes the man to the couch. The man kneels down beside the girl. He touches her hand and face.

On a black dustbin bag beneath her shoulder, blood is pooling. Her lips are colourless, but she's breathing.

The man tries to talk to her. She doesn't reply.

*10.23pm*

The ambulance arrives.

The paramedics place the girl on a stretcher and rush her into the ambulance.

The man shakes Fernandes' hand. He hands him a business card. The name is Tom Walker.

*10.46pm*

Walker and Johnny arrive separately at Joburg General Hospital's accident and emergency unit, Walker just ahead of the ambulance, Johnny from the direction of Yeoville.

The paramedics wheel the girl on the stretcher through the glass doors. She's on a drip, with a blanket over her, and her eyes remain closed.

One of the paramedics asks Johnny if he is family.

"Practically," is his reply.

The paramedics confirm that Mare is alive, but that it's not looking good.

She's lost a lot of blood.

*What time is it?*

The lights overhead are bright – too bright, like a spotlight.

There are voices, mumbling voices.

It gives Mare joy to feel her fingers against the sheet, to feel her naked body against the cotton of the hospital gown.

Dr Marius Fouché appears. He tells Walker and Johnny that Mare is in the trauma ward and there is no immediate need for surgery.

She was shot from the back, he explains. No one was aiming to kill her. Certainly, no one was aiming for her heart. The doctors' best guess is that she was shot in error, and at very close range.

The bullet has significantly damaged her bone, tissue and nerves. There is internal bleeding and a danger of infection. She may require surgery later.

Meanwhile, she's been given blood and placed on a new drip.

She has not regained consciousness. She was extremely lucky.

At 2am, Walker is standing at the trauma ward payphone. He phones Pauline first. It's Tess who answers. When Pauline comes on the line her voice is choked, half by sleep and half by panic. After breaking the news, Walker offers to fly Pauline and Tess to Joburg.

"Yes, we must come. I'll pay. It's all right, we must come now," Pauline says.

Walker offers to make the arrangements.

He phones Mielie next. She clears her throat briskly on hearing his voice, then doesn't interrupt once. He wonders if she's taking notes. *No,* he thinks. *This is her famous brain at work. She's memorising everything.* Mielie says she will notify her work, her neighbours and her landlady. She will stay by the phone and wait for Walker's call with details of her flight. He will pay.

Johnny will phone Toni. But not now; when it's light.

They'd all been at Johnny and Mitchell's flat when Fernandes called.

Initially, there'd been mild concern at her lateness. This had worsened as the night progressed. Truth be told, Walker's concern was at no point mild. He was distraught.

Before supper, he called her flat, only to get her answering machine. Johnny said this was a good sign, that she was probably on her way. When everyone had eaten and she still hadn't arrived, they'd gone first to her flat – in case she'd just fallen asleep there after her shower – then back to Westminster Mansions to wait.

She might have gone looking for Will.

After filling in some forms, there's nothing else for Walker and Johnny to do but wait.

# CHAPTER 29

Johnny and Mitchell return at the start of Saturday's mid-morning visiting hour. Walker leaves his post and returns to the payphone. Again, it's Mare's mother he phones first.

Pauline answers in tears. She can't come, they can't come now, she's saying. It's Tess, and school, and work. There's no-one that can stand in for her, she's so sorry. She feels terrible, it's breaking her heart, but Tess is the little one, she has to stay and look after her. Please will Walker phone every day, and if there's any change. They need to know everything. Walker says of course, of course he will.

Mielie answers his call on the second ring. He tells her he's booked her flight for the following day. She's ready to leave. Mielie will stay with Walker. He won't go to work this week; they'll use his car.

When Walker returns to Mare's bed, Mitchell is holding Johnny's hand. Johnny's been crying. He sniffs loudly and says Toni sends her love. Maybe she could pop in on Pauline, Mitchell suggests. And tell Edward, Johnny says.

Fouché arrives then, with another medical update.

*

*Sunday 6 October*

It's still, out there on the streets. Windless. Walker is hardly ever awake at this time. The stillness is like a spell. Headlights search the darkness. What are they looking for? Victims? Love?

He turns from the trauma-ward window to look at Mare. Her eyes are closed, her body motionless. There are needles in her veins.

He hasn't slept. Fouché told him to go home with the others and get some rest. He couldn't.

Now he sits down on the grey plastic chair beside Mare's bed. Amid the sterility, the stainless steel, the boiled cotton and mopped floors. The air itself seems cleaned by chemicals. He watches her heartbeat on the monitor and wonders when she'll wake up. He needs her to wake up.

Was it always going to end like this? With tubes up her nose, in a threadbare hospital nightie, only just breathing, to a soundtrack of sirens and medical machines?

Tiredness comes over him in waves. Emotion comes in waves.

*Waves,* he thinks. She waves to him. *A girl on a roof, hanging washing. The salty mist of memory, desire made flesh.*

*She waves at the city. I'm here! So innocent. She waves in the face of danger.*

*She makes waves. Her influence ripples out. Her image settles in the minds of others.*

*She doesn't know how beautiful she is to him.*

*Unwittingly, she becomes a character in other people's dramas.*

*Unwittingly, she becomes prey.*

*A nightmare and a dream.*

When Walker closes his eyes, he time-travels.

He sees himself as a child, standing in a stream. It's a rushing stream, swollen with rain, on a farm somewhere. It's a real memory. He's too afraid to take a step. He thinks he'll be swept away.

All these years, he hasn't moved. He's just been trying to stay upright.

Now Mare is wading into the river. Will she be washed away, or will she pull him out?

He dreams of being rescued. He wants to be loved.

Together they could take each other to shore.

The sun rises. Still, she doesn't stir. She seems further away from him now than ever. It scares him.

All he wants to do is help her. It's the one thing he can't do.

She's showing him, he thinks, that he can't keep trying to be the world's great helper forever.

He's known since before Will arrived. He's known since he saw her for the first time, when he first heard her talking. He's known it's time to stop mopping up puddles in other people's lives. To start living his own, and to be primary in it. To love and be loved.

"Mare," he says. "Please open your eyes. There are things I need to tell you. Please wake up, please wake up. Please wake up so I can tell you."

He could tell her how conscious he was, initially, of their age gap. How she surprised him by knowing all his music anyway. How he heard her sing, saw her sway to the chorus, watched her mouthing the words in the car. Felt her movement through the seat, felt the shift of her thighs in his own. How, when the tape played, the beat was a swing with both of them on it.

How he'd fallen in love with everything about her. The way she messed with her hair when she wrote, how she held her head when she was reading and threw it back when she laughed.

He couldn't imagine getting bored, or seeing her as a problem that needed fixing. She was too full of life, and its twists and turns. She took the zig-zag in everything.

He wants to tell her all of this, but she wouldn't hear.

Her toes peep put from under the sheets. He sees the chipped polish on her nails. He pictures the same toes on his dashboard, Friday evening, before the hijack. He thinks of this and weeps.

*

*Email, Johnny to Toni*
*Monday 7 October*

Toni,

It's so weird to be at work. It's all wrong.

I'm trying not to be dramatic, but I know her like the back of my hand. I've seen her in pyjamas, school uniform, paint-spattered overalls and wet raincoats. I've seen her in her swimming costume, even naked, once (by accident). But I wasn't prepared for the smallness. She's like a lolly stick – like those Orange Maid lolly sticks – so thin, so flat, so unmoving.

Mitchell stopped yesterday to get an armful of roses. I thought he was being absentminded: we gave her flowers yesterday. But he said: "She's still in hospital today, isn't she?"

As the magnificent Des'ree reminds us: "You gotta be hard / You gotta be tough / You gotta be stronger."

Oh shit, I was supposed to make you guess.

# CHAPTER 30

*Monday 7 October*

Mielie Ashford sits in a plastic chair beside her sister's bed in ICU.

A few hours ago – thanks to Walker – she was in an aeroplane over central Africa. Then – thanks to Johnny – she caught a meter taxi from the airport to Johannesburg General Hospital.

It is general. There are ten beds, all occupied, with identical sheets and blankets, lining the walls on either side.

It is also specific. One woman is propped up, staring. Others are asleep. Some have the curtains pulled around their beds. Sometimes, there are shouts.

Mare's status has deteriorated to critical, as Fouché has explained. The wound could be infected. The inflammation is not going down. The pus, too, is a bad sign.

Hour after hour Mielie sits there, barely moving. All she does is stroke a soft part of her little sister's hand with her thumb.

Mare's hand is like the meat of a mussel or clam – a soft, salty animal that can't move, except for the odd twitch – and Mielie's is the shell.

Nurses come, check machines, fill drips, and leave again.

Sometimes Walker is there too. He leans his head and shoulder against the wall, arms folded, eyes on the patient.

It's strange for Mare to be lying there, too weak to move or speak. It doesn't stop her thinking. She wishes she could write it all down.

What isn't strange, is knowing Mielie's there.

She's been calling for her, all the way across to London, so it doesn't surprise her she's made her material.

"Mare," she hears Mielie say her name quietly. "Hey Mare, it's me. It's Mielie."

*Mielie, angel.*

Mare smells like pencil wood and Breeze soap (the orange one).

"I brought some pictures for you, by the way," Mielie says aloud. "I thought you'd like to have them with you here."

She holds one up above Mare's eyelids. "The first one's of Dad, when he was young. It's the one you really like, Mare. The black and white …"

A flutter, a twitch, anything?

Mare's eyes, beneath the lids, are still.

Mielie holds the picture in both hands and looks at it. "He's on that really cool motorbike, one leg bent with a foot on the footrest and one foot on the ground. No helmet, just his high forehead and windswept hair."

*Dad and Mielie walked on the mountain.*

"And he's putting on gloves, and looking over his shoulder at the camera, smiling … Did you know there's writing on the back? It says: 'Open road ahead' …"

She holds up a different pic for Mare to look at.

*If I could only open my eyes.*

"This is the one of Mum," Mielie says. "When she's very young. About our age. In Penzance, I think. I can just imagine it, Mare … the grassy clifftops, the crashing sea."

*Before Mum and Dad met.*

"It must have been windy – her hair's all over the place, despite her pale silk scarf …" Mielie holds the picture in her lap now. "She's not looking at the camera, though. She's looking up and out, maybe following a sea bird, flying."

Mielie looks at her sister's eyelids. "Mum looks at things the way you do."

*This was all before we happened. Or they did.*

*Email, Johnny to Toni*
*Tuesday 8 October*

Last night's visiting hour was dire. We all needed Des'ree – in a drip.

Walker doesn't appear to have had a proper sleep since it happened. Outside, it could be summer or winter. He doesn't know or care. When he inhales and exhales his whole face seems to breathe – drawn in with dread, then swollen with love.

You'd imagine Mielie would be soldiering on with Walker, shoulder to shoulder. The old Mielie would have understood her duties, assumed them instantly and performed them tirelessly. That's not what's happening.

Mielie sits in the plastic chair, hour after hour, barely moving, looking smaller and paler than I've ever seen her. She holds Mare's hand. They look as beaten as each other. They looked like children walking into the wind.

*

*Email, Toni to Johnny*
*Tuesday 8 October*

Johnny,

I can't be there so you have to do it for me. Clean Mare's face with a hot, clean cloth. Wipe her hands, even between the fingers. Comb her hair. I don't care if there's still blood in it, comb it.
Empty the water jug. Clean it. Refill.
Take the chair out from under Mielie. She needs to stand. She needs to move.
These are our girls, Johnny. They need to remember that.
Tell Mare I love her so much I let her beat me at backstroke that time. I bet she was grinning on her back the whole of the second length. I turned my head and watched her legs kicking.

Mielie is my sister.
And you, Johnny, arriving at the Woodstock house with the clink of cider bottles.
My life is you three, at a table, and the fourth chair for me.

Tell them.
T.

PS: Kristal is still here. I hardly see her. Mum has put her in a single room in the hotel, on condition that she leaves before high season.

PPS: Cape Town is the same. The weather in October makes me feel like exams are starting soon. If I was in London now it would be the beginning of another long, dark, filthy winter. Lucky fucking escape.

PPPS: Phone me, prat.

*

*Wednesday 9 October*

In the very early hours of the following morning, Mielie watches the curtains move. Drowning in sleep, resurfacing.

She dreams that she writes a story that is published, and Edward comes across it, years from now. He's in a bookshop, some nondescript afternoon in a small town near the sea. Her book – lying on a table – catches his eye.

It's raining, of course, and he starts reading, without knowing it's from her.

But he does read it.

Fouché comes, checks on Mare, and writes some stuff down, shaking his head.

He puts his hand on Mielie's shoulder.

Then, perhaps because she says nothing, he leaves.

For a while, since everything with Kristal and Edward, Mielie has been speechless. Now, words – in her letters, in the past – and the faint pulse in her sister's wrist are all she has.

So: "Do you remember, Mare?" she grabs at a straw. "Do you remember, when we were small? All those cartwheels and handstands we did on the grass? Running and running, till we had blotches in front of our eyes? And then we'd fall down, waiting for them to go away? … We did that lots, on weekends, hey."

*The lawn at Eland. An idyll.*

"Mum never called 'Bathtime!' or anything, out of the window," Mielie goes on. "I just knew it was, from the colour of the sky and all the birds flying, suddenly … I told you it was bathtime, but you always wanted to play for longer, Mare. And I always said we must stop."

*Where were Mum and Dad? What were they doing in that huge house, so far up the garden? Why was Mielie the one who always had to tell me it was bathtime?*

"Your hand would fly to your mouth, and your eyes would go all big and surprised, and you'd say you'd forgotten something – a pencil, a notebook, a doll … And then you'd start running back down the hill, to get whatever it was."

Air comes in through the window crack. It's warm and floral. The smell of night. "But halfway you'd stop, turn towards me, stretch your hand out, and call my name."

On the plane from London, Mielie had heard her: *Come on, Mielie! Come on, please, Mielie!*

"I could barely see you. I was scared you'd get lost, Mare, and it would all be my fault. But I knew if I followed, we'd both be in trouble …"

*Losing you isn't something a person could recover from, ever.*

"It would get dark, Mare. The birds would be quiet, and Dad would tell us we really needed to learn to take better care of ourselves, and to just please think of Mum …"

*I hope there's someone with her now.*

"So," Mielie says, "instead of grabbing your hand and running back down the hill with you … which is what I wanted to do, really …"

*I wanted to get to the bottom, you know.*

"… I'd sit and wait at the top. And I'd call your name, Mare. I'd call and call until you came back."

*She's waiting again. She's calling.*

Time is in free-fall. There's no safety net.

"Come back now, Mare," Mielie pleads, quietly. "Wake up, please. You know it's time. You don't need me to tell you that."

Mare hears car tyres on the wet road. She opens her eyes.

Everything is very clear, very stripped down, very clean.

Mielie's eyes. More familiar to Mare than her own, lying there, coming into consciousness, the blurry edges sharpening into chairs, machines and a dark window – slightly open.

Mielie's gaze is sad and steady, not searching for answers or demanding an explanation.

Mare looks back at her directly. "Your eyes are bruised," she says.

"I know," Mielie replies.

Once, on their way back up the garden to the house, Mare had asked Mielie what being grown-up would feel like.

"How should I know?"

"Because you already are," said Mare.

"Why do you ask, anyway?" Mielie had given her sister a quizzical look.

"Oh I don't know. I just want to be sure. Of how things will feel, when I grow up."

Sunlight poured across grass.

"Well," Mielie had said. "The only think I know for sure is that we'll have bigger shadows."

Now: "I don't want to be your naughty little sister anymore," Mare says.

"I know," Mielie says. "It's enough."

She doesn't offer Mare water, doesn't make her drink, doesn't ask her anything. She's not telling her sister to say something, to come inside, to thank the lady. She does keep hold of her hand, though, without gripping.

Mare's throat is very, very dry. "Could I … water, please?"

Mielie slides her hand behind the back of her sister's neck, tilts it, brings her lips to the glass, and she drinks.

"I'm so glad you're here," Mare says.

"I always was, you know."

"I know. But not like this."

For both of them, it's the night they call it a day.

*

*Friday 11 October*

If you don't like hospital smell, you wouldn't like this bathroom. It's like standing in an empty antiseptic bottle.

Mare stands panting in the doorway. The walls are tiled to the ceiling. White. Pink? She isn't sure. No window.

She'd had no idea how weak she was. The bathroom was just down the corridor. Now she's feeling faint, seeing spots. She's not sure she'll make it across the gleaming floor to the cubicle.

Starting to fall, she reaches for a handrail on the wall, draws herself into the room and then, because there's no one here and why not, she drops.

The light green, state-issue hospital gown keeps its airy distance like a bell and her bare bottom hits the cold tiles.

Once she's settled – back against tiles, palms down, legs out straight – she has time to consider the situation.

It's morning. It's summer outside. She shouldn't be so cold. But everything is different in hospital. No night or day, no days of the week. Pain is shocking, like an assault, and then anaesthetised. Her whole experience here has been like an alien abduction. Passed from bed to bed, person to person, cleaned, cut, injected.

She's going to the toilet, she decides. She can make it now. She needs to stand up carefully – if she pulls too hard on the rail she might rip her stitches – and she needs to take six or seven steps to the toilet, with a brief stop to open the cubicle door.

Mare is halfway up the wall, her forehead clammy, her shoulder throbbing, when the door opens.

"God, Mare," says Mielie, getting her hands under Mare's arms. "Slowly now," she says. "Okay. Hand on the rail – that's it – and now we're going to the toilet. All right. Lean on me. Step. Good. Step. Okay, let go of the rail now, Mare. We're going to this loo. Well done. Okay. Turn. And sit. There."

Mare is sweating and out of breath. Mielie sits down on the cubicle floor.

"You're completely white."

Mare smiles. She has no idea why.

"Head between your knees, please," Mielie says.

Mare is upside down now, looking at the brushed-steel toilet bowl.

"Do you need a nurse?"

"No. Just need a minute."

Mare thinks about being upside-down, in the darkness when you should be in the light, in the light when it should be dark.

"Mielie," she says, still upside-down, "I nearly died."

Mielie says nothing.

"It was like they say," she continues conversationally. "There was heavenly light and everything."

"God, Mare."

Mare lifts her head and rests her back against the cistern.

"The funny thing was, I didn't rise up."

Mielie waits.

"I thought it might be like that. Like jumping on a trampoline and then just rising, not being pulled back down."

"What was it like?" Mielie looks tired.

"Well, it was more like caving."

"When have you ever been caving?"

"Okay. Just what I imagine. I came out at this pool. It was in this beautiful kind of domed cave, and there was blue light on the walls. Then I was in the pool, deep down. It was beautiful. Clear. I had no weight and no pain. I thought: 'Where's Will?' Because, you know, I'd imagined so many times, kind of going into this dark pond and being with him there, you know just kind of swimming in the memories and the feeling."

"Jeez, Mare."

"I know. It's gross. I thought if I killed myself I could just be with him eternally and relive it all, you know, over and over, like that would be my idea of heaven."

"But he wasn't there."

"He wasn't there. And nobody was. It was just nothingness. Just nice, warm water. Maybe forever."

"By the way, do you need to wee?" Mielie says.

"Oh, I'd forgotten about that," Mare says. "Just now. But let me tell you this."

"Okay."

"Okay, so I started swimming."

"You're a good swimmer, Mare."

"I am. I thought, Will's not here. Nobody's here, so I'm going back. Then the lights kind of went out. I know that sounds weird, but suddenly I didn't know which way was up. It was scary, but I thought, dammit, I need my people. I want my life. This is so stupid, of course it's not over. Then I started running out of breath and all I could think of was you, Mielie. I had to get to you. It was just so stupid, the idea of leaving you. It was just a mistake."

*

*Saturday 12 October*

The appearance of a young man in the doorway of the ward after midnight is shocking.

Mielie looks up to see a staring, red-eyed creature, clearly quite drunk. He is leaning against the doorframe, wearing Levi's and a black leather jacket. He looks a bit like George Michael.

She remembers Mare's description: Will.

With as little noise as possible, Mielie pushes herself out of the chair and crosses the room to face him – well aware that any second, Mare could open her eyes.

"Mielie Ashford? Nick Wilkinson Junior," he bows with a sweep of his arm.

"Will, for God's sake, stop it! What do you want?" Mielie demands.

"Oh, I just came to see the love of my life."

Mielie glares at him: "You are unwelcome."

Will doesn't move. He's looking over her shoulder at Mare.

"I mean it – out!" Mielie shoves him in the chest.

Will staggers slightly, sideways, his eyes still trained on Mare. "I need to talk." He's raising his voice now.

"Clearly," says Mielie. "Okay, parking lot ..."

He smiles and shakes his head. "For real?"

"Just GO!"

Without another word, Will sets off, soldier-marching to the lift.

"You have no right to be here!" Mielie hisses at Will, waiting for the lift.

"You don't think I miss her?" Will slurs.

"Too little, too late."

"Oh God, so pious."

"It's not just what you did," Mielie says. "It's how you did it, Will."

"Such a Cape-Town-liberal, UCT-graduate thing to say," he says. "Try harder, Miz Ashford. Senior."

Mielie puts her hands on her hips, tilts her head quizzically.

"I didn't write the letter, the one with the telephone transcripts. Okay? My father dictated … they told me what to write. They told me—"

"I'll listen to you for the time it takes us to smoke one cigarette, then I'm coming back up here. Clear?"

In the lift, as the lights count down the floors, all the way to G-for-ground, Mielie and Will say nothing.

"You never believed I loved her," Will says when he's lit their cigarettes and taken a long drag. "Of course I fucking loved her." He exhales skyward. "She knows."

"That doesn't explain—"

"Oh shut up for just one second won't you, Mielie." He flicks his ash towards the bushes. "Don't you know your sister? Do you think she's stupid? That you're the only one who can judge a situation, or – even better – control it? Because she can't be trusted?"

He takes another drag. "Fucksakes, she's right about all of it. We lived in each other's bodies … In each other's heads." This time he exhales in the direction of the hospital windows. "That's where we both lived. It wasn't just her. It was both of us."

He inhales again. "You lot have probably made her doubt that by now … Well, well done for being so wrong."

Mielie says nothing.

"She's the only one who wasn't wrong, as things turn out," Will continues. "Ja, even you. Mare definitely knew. How did she know? Please. *How did she know*? Of course she knew."

"So you left? Funny way to show it."

"Know what, you're right. I didn't mean to fall in love with her. Want to know the truth? I saw her on her bike. I parked my car so I could see where she lived and maybe see her get off her bike, that wet dress clinging to her, check out the face under the helmet. Ja, Mielie, I'm a pig. I'm a guy, I check out girls and I imagine getting them into bed. Big thrill for me, imagining bagging a Yeoville chick. My parents and friends would be so horrified – part of the thrill."

Mielie just smokes and looks at the sky.

"But I was just looking. Then I saw her pull into the driveway and she fell … I went to help her. But it doesn't matter how it started. What matters, Mielie, is … I did fall in love with your sister."

"Maybe," Mielie says, left hand cupping her right elbow, looking at the burning end of the cigarette between her middle and index fingers. "She's not going to die, by the way. If you're interested."

Will pushes his fingers across his forehead.

"Because you haven't asked," she says. "But I assume you came 'cause you heard she might."

"That's not why I came." He crushes his butt.

They stand together in the dark, on the tarmac, looking at the square of light – the double doors to the hospital.

"So. Why are you here?" she eventually asks.

"Couldn't stay away, Mielie." Will raises his face to the night. "Can't shake her. I didn't know it could be like that. Every girl I've ever met is vain, stupid, fucking icy …" He shakes his head. "You have no idea …"

*Oh, I have some kind of idea, Will,* Mielie thinks, but doesn't say. She doesn't need to say anything because he's still talking.

"… No idea, at all, what it feels like to be forced into a corner. To be forced to know my place. And throw her away."

*Yes, you did,* Mielie thinks. *You threw her away, Will, just like that.*

"And look at me now!" Will says, turning a slow circle in the car park, arms outstretched. "Back where I started!" He stops and faces Mielie: "I'm a fucking prince. Everybody loves me. Oh, so long as I stick to the rules. Can't mix oil and water, Mielie. Mare would have hated everyone in my life and they would have hated her back." Arms limp at his sides. "Had to wake up, shake it off, get back to my life. Oh, my perfect life."

"It's your life, Will," is all Mielie says, crushing her own cigarette on the tar. "I'm going back inside now. Do you want me to tell her what you said?"

"Tell her."

"Okay, I will. Because I believe you. And she probably needs to know." She takes a step closer and speaks straight to his face: "But Will, I mean it. If you love my sister as you say you do, don't ever try to see her again."

"I'll do whatever you want," he says, "if you promise me something."

"I don't think you're really in a position to be making deals."

"God, you're hard to like!" he laughs. "Sorry. I'm sure you're very nice, Mielie. Perfect, like they say."

"So," Mielie says, ignoring this. "What?"

"Just don't let her end up with Thomas Fucking Walker."

Mielie crosses her arms.

"God, you think I don't know he's got the hots for her? You can practically smell it. The picnic at his place – pathetic! And glued to her bedside. Yes, I've been in the car park, watching. What I do, remember? Stalking. Where do you think I've been since I saw the story in The Star?"

She raises one eyebrow. "How romantic."

"I swear, Mielie. Don't let her do it. He'll just … *smother* her. Or mother her. Or something. She will literally *die* of boredom."

Mielie gives Will a last look. "You're ridiculous," she says, and heads back to the hospital doors.

She doesn't look back. In the light of the foyer, Will sees her check her watch.

# CHAPTER 31

*Letter, Tess to Mare*
*Sunday 13 October*

Hi Mare,

I hope you're feeling better. I'm okay but Mom was all over the freaking (I didn't say it) SHOP. She went all pathetic again. I told her, how am I supposed to get my homework done in a cloud of scented candle smoke?

How am I supposed to concentrate with scratched Abdullah Ibrahim records playing?

So anyway we got a Great Dane. She is AWESOME, a full-grown grey and charcoal Harlequin (that means patchy). I call her Merle. Her name at the rescue centre was Shirley …

Say
No
More.

It's cold and I've been wearing Dad's clothes and even Grandpa's old hats and jackets.

Mom is now making a disgusting curry with no meat. Some art school friend of hers is coming over.

Say
No
More.

Mom has been helping me with my oral History project Where I Live. Did you know there was once a Woodstock Beach? Mind frek.

We're taking Merle for a walk now.

When are you getting out of hospital?

Love
Tess Ashford (signed)

*Thursday 17 October*

Mare stays in hospital a full two weeks. Mitchell and Johnny continue to bring new flowers every day. The ward fills up with them.

*Friday 18 October*

On the day Mare is discharged, Walker brings twenty-four muffins for the nurses.

Sister says the nurses will enjoy the treat, but that there's no reason to feel indebted. "We're just doing our jobs."

Of all the things the nurses did and said to help him and Mare, that statement is the thing that will always move Walker most, afterwards.

Here she is again, in this flat.

Mare walks into the dim hall. The cut-off phone, the chair next to it where she sat and cried to her mother, where she asked: why, why?

The bathroom, where Will towelled his beautiful hair.

The kitchen where he must have spotted her postcards on the fridge, before tricking her into believing they were soulmates.

The ghosts swarm. Mare sees herself slumped in the hall. She sees herself from a distance, as Walker has done.

She walks past the phone, through the doorway.

Here is her bedroom where she and Will slept, the sheets they shared – *and did what we did,* she thinks. This is where they woke up together, where they laughed and read. The sheets are still rumpled by the girl who twisted and cried in her sleep, longing for her lover, dreaming of dark water.

Mare stands on the patch of floor between the bed and the wardrobe where she got undressed, that evening. Her swimming costume is on top of a small pile of clothes – shorts, T-shirt and a towel. The wardrobe door is open.

Mare sits on the corner of the unmade bed. The sadness still takes her out at the knees.

She's surprised by how slovenly her bedroom looks. There's grit on the parquet floor. It comes in under the balcony doors. The window panes are black-edged with grime from the cars, the taxis, the buses. She can hear them on Cavendish, Bezuidenhout and Jolly.

She is conscious of Walker in the bedroom doorway. She puts her hands on her knees and pushes herself up.

As she moves towards him, she realises there's already a physical sense of him against her. It's been there, she realises, since she walked into the flat. He is against her and around her. It's erotic. She wants to explore him. One day he will be close enough to do that. He won't run off.

"You okay?" he asks.

"I'm fine," she says. "Thank you, for everything."

The Yale lock clicks. Standing at the door, Mare can't hear Walker walking to the stairwell. But she can see his legs in her mind.

He'll be in the lift lobby now, wrestling with the security gate from the inside.

Mare moves slowly to the balcony doors, so that she can watch him cross the driveway in the rose light.

Walker passes the postboxes. He doesn't pause to berate himself, as he did before, for waiting too long to give the girl a note, invite her for a meal, get her on the phone. He doesn't pause to look at himself and hate his reflection.

He knows he is leaving her alone. He doesn't blame himself. Mare knows how he feels. It's up to her now.

*

*Saturday 19 October*

In Mare's dream, the intercom is buzzing. It's insistent. *Walker.*

"Can I say something?' she says, after throwing open the door.

He doesn't move. She steps towards him and hugs him lightly.

"You're not saying anything," he says, smiling.

"I was going to say I owe you everything, and how can I ever make it up to you," she says into his shoulder.

"Oh, good. Say that."

"No."

"Oh."

She pulls away. "You know I told you about how, when I lived here, I used to wish I was somebody's daughter, somebody's sweetheart?"

"When you lived here?"

The ghosts are memories: smoky, see-through. "Yes. Well. I don't want to be somebody's daughter or somebody's sweetheart, or even somebody's sister, anymore. I want to be myself. And yours. All this time, I've been falling in love with you."

Walker's face is still. He swallows hard.

"Can I come and stay with you? It's not that I need looking after. Please, I just want to be with you. All the time."

He looks like he might burst into tears. "Of course," he says. "Yes. Of course."

The intercom keeps buzzing. This time, Mare wakes up.

"Walker!" she shouts into the intercom, breathless.

"Mare! It's me! Open the bloody door!"

"I thought you were Walker."

"I'm not. Buzz me in," Mielie says. "God, finally."

Mielie has brought a bucket and mop. She's also brought Handy Andy, Windolene, Domestos and a cloth.

"Where's Walker?" Mare asks.

"He dropped me on the way to work. He has loads to catch up on. Plus he has to sort out the car-insurance situation. They'll take the courtesy car if he doesn't finish the paperwork."

"Oh."

"So you get me, instead. Do you have a broom?"

"Of course. All witches have one," Mare sighs, and slumps onto the telephone chair.

Mielie leaves Mare to pant, and goes into the kitchen. She puts on the kettle and runs a sink of hot water. Mare hears the fart noises of her nearly empty dishwashing-liquid bottle.

"It's nice," Mielie says, when she comes back into the hallway with two cups of tea.

"Of course, you've never been here."

"It's nicer than my place in London. I like your parquet floors."

"Come in the lounge."

Mielie puts the mugs on the coffee table while Mare lowers herself onto the hideous couch.

"It's weird being back here," Mare says.

Mielie tuts. "Where did you think you'd go after hospital?"

"I don't know. Home. Or maybe Walker's place. I didn't think about it."

Mielie takes her tea to the balcony doors. "It's a cool view from up here." She turns around, the morning sun shining through her hair. "It's a really nice flat, Mare."

"It doesn't feel like home."

"I should hope not," Mielie says. "It's fucking filthy."

*

*Fridge Letter, Mielie to Mare*
*Saturday 19 October*

Mare,

It's lunchtime and I've called a meter taxi to take me back to Walker's. I'll get my stuff and come and stay on your couch, if you like. I'm also happy to stay at Walker's. It won't be for long, I'm going back to London soon. Your flat is clean and tidy now, and you're sleeping like a baby. Two good things!

About "home" … as soon as you're back to work, and back in the swing of things with your friends, you'll realise how much you've achieved this year. You were brave to come here, Mare, and you've done so well at work – it's a really big deal.

The Will stuff hurts, I know. Dear God, I know. And getting hijacked and shot isn't ideal.

I want to tell you something Dad said to me once, when we were walking on the mountain. I can't remember what we were talking about.

I just remember it was raining. He said: "At the risk of being the club bore, Mielie, I think it's worth reiterating that dignity truly is priceless."

I will always thank him for saying that. I've held onto it as tightly as I could, especially these last few months. The idea of dignity. I guess you have to have lost a bit of it, to know how precious it is, and then work very hard to reassemble it, and learn to love yourself again.

Hold onto this, please Mare. It's what defines us.

Love,
Mielie

*

*Letter, Mare to Tess*
*Sunday 20 October*

Look Tess, by the way, do you know how amazing you are? Do you know how unusual it is for a girl to be tough, and clever, and fast, AND dress like a punk? And still love dogs to distraction? You do know. Don't forget to remind yourself. You may feel out of place sometimes – I always did – but amazing things can happen if you stay true to yourself. Keep your fists balled, keep your mind clenched, keep frowning. You don't have to open yourself up like a flower to be loved.

Just a little sisterly advice there.

# CHAPTER 32

*Friday 25 October*

The pharmacy is on the corner of an intersection on Sea Point Main Road. It is the most ordinary of chemists. Its glass window is painted with plain black lettering – "Jonker's Pharmacy", it says – and there's a tinkly bell over the half-glass-half-wooden door.

The till is at the front. There's a woman standing there, wearing too much make-up. Edward smells her as soon as the door closes behind him. She's wearing a sweet scent, like strawberry milkshakes or candy floss. It is unpleasantly synthetic. It makes him think of children being tricked. There are condoms displayed behind the counter in fruity colours: watermelon, orange, lemon – like sweets.

Edward heads down the centre aisle toward the dispensary at the back. He sees hair dye, ear plugs, tweezers, nail varnish. Everything his eye falls upon makes him think of deceit and disguise.

Edward fingers the half-empty strip of pills in his jeans pocket. It crackles slightly. That's the sound of the pills still in their pods. The L of squashed plastic and popped foil is silent. These broken sections mark where Kristal has selected a pill – a mustard one, a red one, or a white one – according to the day of the month.

Here the chemist is now: grey-haired, white-jacketed, nametagged – husband of the till lady, probably. He doesn't look like the type of man to be interested in the possibility that Kristal has been lying to him.

"Can I help you?" the pharmacist asks. His silver nametag reads: Braam Jonker. He has thick spectacles and a silver pen in his pocket.

"Yes, please." Edward smiles. He draws the sheet of Triphasil from his pocket and places it on the counter.

"I can't fill a prescription without a script," says Braam.

"I know."

"And you can't get pills for your wife or girlfriend, even if you have her prescription."

"I know," Edward says again. He gets the feeling Braam deals with prescriptionless young men all the time. "I don't want any pills," Edward says. "I just want to know if these are contraceptives."

"They are." Braam Jonker takes a yellow handkerchief out of his top pocket and polishes his glasses with it.

Edward can feel the cashier's eyes on his back as Mr Jonker lifts the crackly pack off the counter and holds it some distance from his glasses. "Yes. Are these pills current?"

"Yes," says Edward.

"Well, your partner is ovulating right now."

"Does that mean—" Ed begins, cursing himself for blushing. "I know it's a stupid question, but just double checking … she couldn't be pregnant and … there would be no reason for her …?"

Mr Braam Jonker stares at Edward. "No."

"Ah," Ed says, and replaces the half-sheet of pills in his pocket.

"Your partner is not pregnant if she's been taking these pills," Mr Jonker reiterates. He notices a customer behind Edward, a woman with a sleeping baby on her back.

"Next," Mr Jonker calls.

"Thanks," Edward says, and turns.

In the aisle leading to the door Edward notices now, for the first time, the baby section. He sees nappies, dummies, formula, bottles. Alongside the bottles of Johnson's Baby Shampoo and baby lotions there are aids and ointments for new mothers.

Edward is buoyed by a wave of triumph. Unusually for him, he feels brave. Like he's just found a secret door. Like he's popped his head up in a patch of grass outside the prison fence.

This will not be his life. These smells and textures will not pervade his senses these next few months. He will not hold his own baby, he will not be woken in the middle of the night by his child. Edward is not belted into that roller coaster.

He quickens his step and sets the bell rattling as he leaves.

*Saturday 26 October*

In the first week back in her flat, Mare sleeps full nights and at least once during the day. A rough routine emerges. Mielie comes round in the mornings. She makes tea, checks Mare's dressing, and the sisters chat in the lounge. They talk about work, about creativity, Joburg, London, Johnny, Mitchell, Toni … They avoid Will, Edward and Walker as conversation topics. Sometimes Mielie makes scrambled egg and toast. One memorable morning, Mielie washes her sister's hair in the bath and the feeling of warm water on Mare's scalp is exquisite.

Pauline often phones at the end of her day, before she starts supper for herself and Tess. Walker brings supper, or Johnny does. There's some chatting, no alcohol, and more often than not, there's TV. Walker brings the papers when he comes and they talk about the news. He's still following court stories she covered, and is delighted to point out how bad the Magistrate's Court reporting is in every newspaper in the city since her "accident".

Mare still dreams of Will, vividly. In her dreams she runs into him. He takes her into a room and begs her to wait for him. His proximity, her attraction to him, his promise, is thrilling. It alters her breathing, her heart rate. In the dream, he never comes back. She waits and she longs for him but she is humiliated. All the feelings are still there when she wakes up. She lies as still as she can to hold onto them.

*

*Sunday 27 October*

Finally, here is the picnic at Walker's place. It's the picnic he wanted to have six months before, the one he wanted Mare to attend. Before Will. Johnny, Mitchell, Fouché, Mielie and Mare are gathered on rugs at the bottom of the property.

Mare is freshly bandaged and propped up with pillows. Her right arm is touching Walker's left, and her head is bent towards him.

She's been making toasts. She has just thanked Mielie – properly – Fouché – properly – and Walker – properly – for looking after her, not just after the hijack, but before as well. Her glass still raised, she has said the words to Mitchell and Johnny that she should have said on their wedding day.

Mielie is thinking how beautiful her sister is – so happy – when she's startled by Fouché's voice.

"Walker! Who's that?"

Fouché is pointing to the brow of the hill. Mielie whips her head around. Her first thought is that it's an attacker, and that they're trapped here, between the hill and the high fence along the highway.

But the figure does not appear to be set on violence. He's stopped now, peering down the hill at the group. Mielie can barely make out his form – a silhouette in the harsh Highveld sun.

"I see him, Fouché," says Mitchell. "A friend of yours, Walker?"

"I can't tell," Walker says, squinting.

The figure puts up an arm. "Hello!" it shouts.

Mielie feels her brain drop out of her skull into her neck. It's crushing her windpipe. It's Edward.

"It's Edward, isn't it?" Mare says. "Mielie, is it?"

It is. He's striding through the blackjacks now, ignoring the narrow path. Walker gets to his feet. Mare stands up beside him.

"Edward!" she shouts. Mare looks at her sister.

Mielie stays seated on the blanket. She turns away to face the distant traffic, audible through the trees: car-whoosh-car-whoosh. She puts both hands out flat beside her. Edward's shadow falls across her body.

There are greetings and introductions: "Hello … Walker …"; "Yes, Fouché, pleased to—"

"I'm sorry for interrupting," Edward says. I wanted—"

"Edward, dear," Fouché interrupts. "Please sit down and join us."

"Uh, thank you. Yes." Edward drops slowly to his haunches. "But—"

"Has something happened?" Mare asks. She puts her hand over Mielie's hand.

"Yes. No. I—"

Walker hands Edward a plastic cup of water.

"Why are you here, though? Everything okay in Cape Town?" Mare closes her fingers around Mielie's hand.

"Oh, fine, thank you." The water remains in his hand, undrunk. "And you?"

"Fine, thank you." Mare frowns. "How is your sister? And Peter? How's Booboo?" Mielie pulls her hand away.

"All well, thanks very much."

"And Kristal?" Mare smiles with her lips.

Mielie breathes in sharply. Edward glances anxiously at her.

"Kristal is … Kristal is trying on wedding dresses as we speak!" he blurts.

Mielie throws her shoulders back involuntarily. Her body rises to full height. She hadn't intended to stand, but now that she's standing, she might as well turn – that's what her body wants to do – and what the hell, she might as well run.

She's wanted to run for a long time, and now she does – the soles of her boots punching the stony path. She hears the shouts from the rugs, but she keeps on. Run, run. Run!

She's running as if to escape her shadow. She wants to be invisible. She wants to fly off the top of the hill into the sun, like a plane at the end of a runway. Her throat is burning, the sun is blinding her eyes, but her body is running away with her. Away. Away, away!

She trips on a root, picks herself up, wants to run, has to unhook her skirt from a bush, runs again.

Edward is catching up with her as she approaches the brow of the hill.

"Mielie!" He's right behind her.

"Mielie!" He doesn't touch her. Instead, he crashes through the tall grass so that he's running next to her. "Please stop!" he pants.

"No!"

Mielie speeds up, then lurches. She has to stop to regain her balance.

"Are you okay?" Edward stops beside her.

"No."

"Miel—"

"No. I'm not okay, Edward!"

Mielie's eyes do a trick then. They push Edward's body into the distance. They shrink him to the size of a thumbnail.

The other members of the party are watching the hillside in silence. Mare is leaning forward.

Edward lifts his right arm but it stays mid-air. Both bodies are braced. Mielie looks like she'd give him an electric shock if he tried to touch her now. Her back is almost arched.

"So, when is the wedding?" she asks.

"I've no idea."

Mielie frowns. "What?"

"I didn't ask."

Mare keeps watching them. Edward is not moving. Neither is Mielie. He's talking.

He tells her how he found the pills in Kristal's handbag. She'd carelessly left it open on the hotel terrace in Sea Point, where he'd gone to find Toni, to ask how Mielie was doing.

He tells her how, pills in pocket, he'd gone to the pharmacy, then returned to the hotel to confront Kristal – only to find her sitting on the same terrace, on another guy's lap.

"Some guy called Damian," he says.

"Damian?"

"Yes. One of Toni's exes, apparently …"

"Damian the *Australian*? From the squat?" Mielie asks in disbelief.

"I think so," Edward says. "Kristal stayed with him after Toni chucked her out …"

Mielie shakes her head. Was she dreaming?

Edward goes on to explain how Kristal had casually introduced him as a friend from London who'd been writing to her these past months, and had come to find her. Because he loved her, and wanted to take her back with him. To marry him, if she'd agree.

"And she said yes, just like that?"

"She did." Edward smiles. "It's all she's wanted, all along."

It's starting to rain. The picnickers hurriedly gather their belongings while fat, pre-thunderstorm drops bounce off the grass and soil.

Mielie's on the march now, towards the house. Her clothes swing as she walks. Edward is in step.

"How can I trust you?" she swings round to face him. "Why should I believe you?!"

The sun shines on Mielie's hair, through the uneven rain.

"Only because it's true," Edward says. "It's all true."

"It doesn't matter what's true now, or what was true then!" Mielie shouts. She takes a breath and turns away from Edward. "It only matters—" she starts, then turns to him. "It only matters that you didn't come to London. I waited – I waited and you didn't come. And then – Kristal – it was just an excuse. Because you weren't sure if you wanted me. You weren't ready, Edward!"

Mielie takes a long, deep breath. The oxygen doesn't steady her breathing. Instead, it brings on a sob, followed by another. She tries to talk through it, but soon she's crying hard. Her face is red and wet.

"You didn't care enough. You didn't! And you don't now!"

It's his slowness that calms her, eventually.

"I love you, Mielie," he says, slowly. "I'm an idiot," he adds.

Mielie laughs one snotty snort.

"I am," he says. "I'm an absolute idiot. And you're right. I've been avoiding commitment. I've been making excuses … London, Kristal, you're right. I should have stopped what I was doing, the day you said you were going to London. I should have gone with you."

Finally, Mielie can breathe.

"I won't let you down again, I promise," Edward says. "Please, can we—"

"Can we what?'

"Can we be together? Please?"

Mielie sniffs. "Where?"

"Where?" Edward laughs.

"Yes," Mielie says. "Are you coming back to London with me?"

"If that's what you want."

"If that's what I want?"

Edward pauses. "Or you could come home. I thought …"

Mielie's eyes widen.

"I thought we could get our own house. It could take a while bu—"

"In Cape Town?"

"Yes."

"Not too far from your sister, and your mother, your job? And I would be doing what?"

"Acting, of course," Edward says. "Your dream."

Mielie stares at Edward. Her eyes are glazed, as if she's just woken from a long sleep.

"Jesus, Edward," she says, and walks into the house.

He walks behind her but stops when he hears a bedroom door close and the key turn in a lock.

Johnny has his keys out. The rain is warm but heavy. He's almost at his car door when he jumps with fright. There's an unfamiliar car in the driveway and someone is sitting in the driver's seat.

"Jeepers, Ed!" Johnny shouts as he knocks on the passenger window of the hire car. "What you doing?"

Edward's long arm reaches over the passenger seat and unlocks the door.

He doesn't say anything, even after Johnny has tumbled into the seat, re-locked the door and settled himself.

"This is a bit like being at a drive-in," Johnny says over the rain. "I feel like we should get the speaker in."

Edward continues to stare through the windscreen. Johnny waits, then sighs, then pats him on the knee.

They are well into the meat of the conversation and Edward has yet to say very much. Johnny is explaining things to him.

"The thing about a big romantic gesture," he says, "is that it has to be an offer, not a request. It has to be an enormous, unconditional gift – of your heart, preferably – with no conditions attached." He pauses.

"I came to tell her I wanted to be with her," Edward says into the silence.

"Bullshit," Johnny replies. "You came to tell her you're off the hook and so would she please leave London and come live with you in Cape Town."

Edward is frowning. He seems confused.

"Your being together," Johnny says, "was conditional on her leaving London."

"But I said I love her. And I'm sorry."

"That's great, Ed," Johnny says. "That's a good start."

"What else am I supposed to do?"

Johnny puts his feet up on the dashboard. He leans his head back and looks at the roof. "You tell me." He closes his eyes and waits.

"I honestly don't know," Edward says.

Johnny sits upright again. He looks at Edward now, making full eye contact. "Listen, you need to know what you want. Do you know what you want?"

"I want to be with Mielie."

"I believe that. And workwise?"

"I hate my job."

"Sure, but what work do you want to do? Just say the first thing that comes into your head."

"I like making things. I like building stuff."

"Great. And where do you want to live?"

"I honestly don't care. Where Mielie is."

"Right," Johnny says. "So what you could have done was resign from your job and offer to join Mielie in London and get a job on a construction site."

"Well—"

"Listen, Ed," Johnny says, looking for the door handle with his hand. "Until you're ready to make Mielie a priority, you don't deserve her. Especially not after what you've put her through. Think about it."

# CHAPTER 33

*Letter, Mare to Tess*
*Monday 28 October*

Bedroom
Night

Tess,

It's dark outside. I can see the lights twinkling all across Joburg. I hope you're sleeping now. I thought I'd write down the whole story of how Dad died – as best as I can remember it, anyway. Because you weren't there (and that was no one's fault).

It took us by surprise. It wasn't supposed to be so soon. It certainly wasn't supposed to be the day after Christmas.

After you left for your sleepover at Mira's, Mum and Mielie and I had leftovers for lunch. Daddy wasn't up to eating. He'd spent the morning in bed. That wasn't unusual, obviously. Even before he got sick, he was always reading and writing in bed. He liked the sea view from the window.

Plus, he believed that his brain woke him up with good ideas, and he needed to stay put or he'd lose them.

I used to tease him about it. I'd say, "Know what wakes me up, Dad? Light. Hunger. Bladder. Noise."

"I can only speak for myself," he said once. "But if I neglect to heed the unconscious mind and its early-morning solutions …"

"Really?" Sarcastic.

"Yes … and if I turn my attention to pulling open curtains and turning on lights and taps … the inspirations that were there for the taking simply disappear, like smoke. That's why I stay in bed sometimes. To be with them."

"Nice one, Dad," I think I replied. "Remind me to try that excuse next time I miss first lecture."

To children their fathers always seem ancient, but even as a middle-aged man Dad was sedentary. Even in rude health, you could see him as a geriatric. He was always going to be one of those very old guys you see on paths next to the beach, or in shopping centres, being escorted by patient young people in uniforms. Except he didn't make it to the doddery stage.

Sorry. We were having lunch. Outside the kitchen window the wind might have been howling, bending the tree trunks, sending leaves skittering across the lawn, flapping the awning over the stoep. I don't remember. It seems so long ago now. I only know it was overcast.

After lunch – God, it might have been teatime, Tess – so let's fast forward to the bit I know is true. I heard a shout at the top of the stairs. It was Mielie. She'd popped her head round the door to check on Dad. He was awake, but his breathing was terrible. Her voice was choked.

Mum and I clattered up the stairs, me taking them two at a time, Mum a blur of scarves and handkerchief hems. Then we were standing around our parents' bed, looking at Daddy, like a scene in a made-for-TV movie. All our chests were heaving – even Mielie's. Mum put her hand on Dad's forehead. That gesture was also like something out of a movie. It all felt very unreal, comic almost. I forced myself to look, properly.

Dad's arms were long and limp on the duvet, his mouth was blue-ish, his eyes were pale, like cold opals, and his breathing – it sounded like he had things rattling in his throat. He was so suddenly sick. But the bed was not a sick bed. For months it had been a bed for sore heads and rests, not dying. He and Mum slept there together the night before, nothing unusual.

Dad said he had a terrible headache, terrible. He said it wasn't good. He said he needed to talk about money, needed to speak to us "before I go". Mum was all over the place: "Oh, no! What are you saying, Philip?!"

I can't remember what I did. Looked out of the window, probably. It was Mielie, of course, who lifted one of Daddy's marble-cool hands off the duvet and said: "You go ahead, Dad. I'm listening."

He looked into her eyes then. I could almost feel myself becoming a haze outside his line of vision. Mum wasn't in his line of sight either.

"Amelia," he said. He swallowed. "I didn't ..."

She waited for him to finish. He couldn't.

Then: "It's okay." She stroked his hand, held his gaze. "Don't worry."

I was terrified he would go and I would never look in his eyes again. I was about to shoulder my way into his sight. Of course Mielie made such vulgarity unnecessary.

"We're here, Dad," she said. "Mum's here, and Mare. And Tess isn't far."

He looked at us, long and lovingly. Then he looked over to the window.

Mum broke the silence. She was trying to lighten the mood but she sounded terrified when she said we all needed a nice cup of tea and we'd be right back to hear the rest of it in just a minute when she was sure Dad would be feeling stronger.

When we came back he was dead. He had his eyes open, facing the view, the view of the harbour where our boat had docked, twenty years before.

Brain tumour or no brain tumour, I wanted you to know, in case no one's told you, that it's quite common for people to wait until the room is empty before drifting off into their final sleep. The idea that the nearest and dearest should be there, at the bedside, for the moment of "lights out" is Hollywood nonsense. Dad very sensibly waited until the room was quiet and still before going to sleep. I wouldn't be surprised if he'd waited out Christmas, too. That's not uncommon, to decide to be there for a big event, and check out afterwards.

Please don't ever feel bad that you weren't there. We weren't either. He didn't want any of us there.

We all have choices, all the time, even in the moment of death. Mostly we choose our own outcomes. Emotions are powerful, and you shouldn't run from them. But when it comes to being a slave to your fate, or what you think your fate is, as Rizzo says in Grease, "There ain't no such thing."

See you soon, little sis.
X Mare

Pauline and Tess are on their way up Roodebloem Road. They're taking Merle for a walk.

For the people in the vehicles travelling up and down this arterial road of one of Cape Town's oldest suburbs, the matriarch and the youngest of the Ashford family make an odd sight.

Pauline's body is bent as she struggles against the incline.

Tess is walking up the hill bolt upright. She is gangly, with swimmer's shoulders. Tess's hair is unwashed, scraped back into a short ponytail. Her neck is long and straight – remarkably so. Her men's jeans and check shirt, fashionably oversized at the start of the year, no longer pool at her wrists and ankles. She is – for all her scornful attitude and filthy vocabulary – a coltish beauty.

Neither of them are speaking, at present.

An hour before, Pauline and Tess had closed the door behind Fiona, who'd come round with a cake for Pauline's birthday the next day.

Fiona had rushed in and out, head down, saying something about how she couldn't resist, she always made a vanilla cake the moment strawberries came into season. This gesture – and that the cake was home-made – had taken mother and daughter by surprise. It had been a fairly awkward encounter, but amicable at least.

Now Pauline breaks the silence, saying that Eland was always in the shadow of the mountain, anyway, and Balfour Road is much sunnier.

When Tess fails to respond, Pauline says she thinks Mielie and Mare had cast a bit of a shadow over their little sister too.

"One of the very many wonderful things about Balfour Cottage – I think we should call it that, don't you? – is that I always know where you are, darling," she goes on. "I see so much more of you now than when we lived in town."

Then she tells Tess about the big, English house Philip grew up in, and how it had surprised her when he'd told her how much he hated it. It was cold, and silent. Just like my parents, he'd said.

"We bought Eland because it was an investment. It was supposed to be our pension." Pauline takes a deep breath and looks up to see how much hill she still needs to climb. "I never loved it," she pants.

"Me neither," Tess says.

Pauline stops. "Really? I thought you girls loved it!"

"God, Mom. Mielie and Mare loved it. It was big and grand, like their ideas."

Pauline chuckles, hands clutching her knees. "You are funny, Tess," she says.

"You too, Mom."

Mother and daughter continue in companionable silence up the hill.

"I never want to go round to Eland, by the way, even if Fiona invites us," Tess says, pulling Merle from the gutter to the pavement as a truck rumbles past. "Tree gone, etcetera …"

"Fair enough," Pauline says. "But that doesn't mean we don't have to see them ever. We could invite them to our house, sometime ... Booboo needs to get to know his aunties, you know …"

Tess says nothing.

"I know what you're thinking, Tess," says her mum.

Tess looks at her sideways, suspicious.

"They never bothered to visit us before – Lord knows we gave up inviting them – so why make an effort with them now … Am I right?"

"Yes," Tess answers reluctantly.

"And that's fair enough, too, Tess," Pauline says, stopping again to regain her breath, looking up – hands on hips – at the mountain's lower slopes. In one hand she holds a pair of garden clippers, and a geranium cutting acquired from someone's verge along the way. "But perhaps one day you'll see it differently," Pauline continues. "It's hard having young children, or even just one. It was hard for me and your father. We became – how were we? – self-absorbed, I think, is the word …"

Tess looks straight at her mother, now.

"But you'd be surprised, darling, how things can change … As time passes, and if you give people a chance ..."

"If you *want* to, that is."

"And I think I *do*, now," says Pauline. "I think it's time. It's taken me a while, and I know we've all made mistakes along the way… we've all been emotional – yes, even Peter. He also lost his dad, don't forget ..."

Merle sniffs a lamppost. Tess bites her lip.

"But anyway, the funny thing with families, I think you'll find, is that if everyone just *relaxes* a bit ..."

"Like, gets over themselves, starting with—"

"Let's just start, Tess," says Pauline. "Let's just take things one step at a time."

Back in the Balfour Road kitchen, Tess flicks on the kettle and Pauline sits down at the table.

"Right! Back to Geography," the mother says.

"In a minute."

Tess leaves the kitchen and returns with several sheets of graph paper.

"Hey, Mom," she says as she sits down. "I was thinking, let's redesign the house the way we'd like it. We don't have to do any of it, but you have such good ideas."

"Why, thank you, my darling," says Pauline. "And you are very strong and very practical and very creative yourself."

"Pfft. So we could move the furniture around at least."

"Oh, we could do more than that," Pauline says, sweeping a textbook aside and reaching for a pencil. "I do own this house. We could take out a loan."

*

*Email, Tess to Edward*
*Wednesday 30 October*

Sup Ed?

Mom / Pauline says can you come over after work? She is going to take a loan and redo the house. Peter and Fifi are destroying Eland and environs. (TALK TO THE HAND, PETER.) "Signed-sealed-delivered". WHATEVER. We've got Balfour Road. So Mom / Pauline wants to open plan or "open up a courtyard" or something. Can you come? We're having a roast. NOT. Rice and yellow cauliflower. Ever heard about the health benefits of turmeric, Ed?

When Edward Taylor opens his email at work on Wednesday morning and sees Tess's message, he immediately flushes red. It's not the coffee. It's the appearance of "Ashford" in his Inbox.

Edward and Mielie didn't say goodbye in Joburg. He spent the night at Johnny and Mitchell's place. He phoned Walker's place several times but Mielie refused to speak to him. The next day he drove to the airport and boarded his flight back to Cape Town.

Edward reads Tess's email again. "Peter and Fifi are destroying Eland … We get Balfour." It makes him very angry.

Edward pushes back on his chair, arms tensed at full stretch. He locks his elbows behind his head, crosses his right ankle over his left knee. He's all angles now.

The information is no surprise. It's the sound in his head of Tess saying it. It's her lack of anger, her matter-of-fact tone, her willingness to take it on the chin.

It's also the thought of Pauline taking a loan, while his own sister lives in a house that she and her husband promised to sell in order to provide for a widow and a schoolgirl. *When are they going to sell Eland and hand over the money, anyway? Not until they've doubled its market value,* Edward thinks. *Fiona and Peter will give Pauline original market value and keep the profit. No doubt they've already made her agree to that.*

It's how unselfish the Ashfords are, and how selfish his own family is.

He can see Fiona, at this moment, shopping for pricey items to redecorate the room vacated by Kristal. His mother standing right beside her, thin-lipped, appraising, guiltless.

"Fuck you, thieves," he mutters. "How dare you? All you do is take, and take, and take."

He grabs the edges of his desk and pulls. His coffee slops dangerously close to the edges of the mug. This desk. This office. They've stolen from him too.

Edward stares hard through the window at the sun glinting off roofs, the haze over the City Bowl. It's only 7.50am. It's going to be a scorcher.

“What do you want, Edward?” Mielie had asked him, that afternoon they made love on the mountain. She’d asked again on their way to their Wimbledon station goodbye.

Johnny asked him the same thing in Joburg.

His mother and sister had never asked. They didn’t care enough. They didn’t want him to be happy. They wanted him to be rich.

He stands, rocking his coffee cup. “Oh, for fucks sake!” he almost shouts.

Then he marches across the office carpet, startling a colleague on her way to her desk. She says his name. He can’t hear.

Edward shoves open the door to the Gents. He enters the most distant cubicle and sits down.

“Fuck them, fuck them.” Edward wants to kick something. He wants to punch a hole through the cubicle door.

He closes his eyes and immediately sees Mielie. It’s all he ever sees. Mielie and her hair. Mielie with the sun on her skin. Mielie’s mouth moving. Her shoulders, her collarbones. Her hands next to his.

“You didn’t care enough,” he hears her saying.

Oh, for FUCK’S SAKE! Edward shakes his head hard. He is going to lose her. He is going to trade Mielie for what his sister and mother want. He’s going to stay on The Path. Because he’s a coward, and he knows it. He cheated and he lied and he continues to hide behind his suck-fest of a job, instead of doing something real. He’s not brave, not like Walker and Mitchell. He’s never dodged the cops or risked detention without trial. He wouldn’t have refused to go to the army. He’s never going to stand up to anyone.

He is never going to have what he wants. Dammit. Dammit! Edward smacks the toilet roll and tries to pull the holder off the wall.

He’s on the street now. He’s walking into a crowd of commuters coming the other way. He weaves through them, head down, unable to think.

He finds himself in the railway station. There’s a bench with a space on it. He sits. Crowds of people are heading past him towards the exit, about to be hit by the sun in the city. In the other direction: the long-distance trains. The platforms for the TransKaroo to Joburg, the Durban train, the Bloem train.

But Edward isn't going anywhere. He drove to Pietermaritzburg. He flew to London for Mielie. Then he flew to Joburg. What good did that do? It only made things worse. Idiot, idiot. Schoolboy. Idiot. He slumps on the bench.

*Mielie is going somewhere, though.* She was always too mature for him, he thinks. *More principled, too. And braver. She has a dream. She'll meet someone worthy of her.*

Edward makes himself imagine her with someone like Walker: the tall, moral power couple.

Fuck! There's nothing he can do. Because of his own stupidity, he is stuck and everyone is free to condescend to him to their hearts' content. It's already open season in his own family, now they know about him cheating, and being duped.

As he sees it, there's only one thing he can change.

When he gets back to the office, Edward pulls his chair in tight, downs his cold coffee and writes: "I resign".

*

*Thursday 31 October*

Mare has a bright, clear dream about Walker. They're driving down Cavendish. It's months before. Mare places her hand on Walker's thigh. Blood rushes to his face, his ears.

"I can hardly wait," she says.

In a parking lot at the start of a hiking trail in Cape Town she leans over and kisses him until someone behind them hoots.

They're on a fast road. It's after the hijacking now. Walker pulls off, suddenly, into a side street. He's barely stopped before their seatbelts are unclipped and Mare is in his lap. She can't keep still. She's impatient, vocal. It's exquisite, airless agony.

He stops kissing her, holds her off him.

"No more until you break up with Will," he smiles.

There was another dream, less clear. They're sitting in the dark, on a stoep, sharing a blanket. They've been having sex. Mare is blissed out.

Walker is drinking a glass of red wine now, at a table.

"I wouldn't have been open with you before," he says.

Fouché, who's appeared at the table, says too true, the sex would have been terrible, all that "child protection".

Mare reaches her arm out from the blanket towards Walker. She wants him to pull her up so she can sit at the table.

It's morning and she's in a kitchen with Mitchell. Walker has gone.

"It's not his job to help you out of things," Mitchell says.

Mare finds Walker in his car, reading the newspaper. The morning sun is shining hard on their faces.

"Do you … *desire* me?" she says.

She's squinting and worrying that the squinting makes her unattractive. Walker turns to her, shielding his face with his hand.

"Blindly. Blindingly," he says.

*

*Friday 1 November*

The two sisters are in the lounge at the Helvetia Court flat, going through copies of *The Star* and sticking Mare's news reports into scrapbooks. She's going back to work on Monday.

Mielie's clothes are on the line at Walker's place. All her things will be clean and dry in time for her flight the next evening.

"Have you decided what to do with your bike?" Mielie asks.

"I'm selling it. I forgot to tell you! Mum said it's booked, she's sending your Beetle up on the train."

"Oh, brilliant. So just set up a stop order and the money will go straight into my account."

There's an uncomfortable silence.

"*Joking*, Mare! But pay me when you can, okay."

"Oh, thank God! Yes. Course."

Mielie has finished all her sticking. "What about these?" she says, reaching for a pile of shorthand notebooks.

"Oh no, leave those," Mare says, scissors midair.

"They're all used."

"Ja, but—"

"Can't they go?"

"No."

Mielie tries to reach for them again.

"No! Mielie! It's not just notes …"

"Oh. Other writing?"

"Ja."

Mare takes the notebooks and puts them on the bookcase behind her. She stands, then sits. She picks up the scissors again.

"You know, I could have asked to buy the Beetle ages ago. Imagine, I would never have fallen in the rain and met Will. I would never have been hijacked." Mare is looking out, beyond the balcony. "I've been such an idiot," she says. "So much of what happened to me this year was my own fault."

"Don't be hard on yourself."

"True, though."

"Mare—"

"I mean it. I'm not being hard on myself. But I don't judge Will. The one I judge is me. I was so much myself in the way I loved him – I was so open, so trusting, Mielie – and I was proud of that. But I made myself too vulnerable. I made a fool of myself. Seriously."

Mare puts down the scissors and looks at her sister's face. "Will came to see you when you were in hospital."

"When?! You didn't—"

"I know. But I'm telling you now. He came in the middle of the night. You were fast asleep, full of painkillers."

"When?"

"Early on. First week? When it was bad, when things weren't improving fast enough. He was drunk, and good and rude to me. But what he said actually made sense. He said you didn't imagine it. He fell in love with you for real. It took him by surprise. He was very, very happy with you. But in the end he chose money – his lifestyle, I suppose – over love."

"Fuck."

"I know."

"What else?"

"He said he'll never love anyone like he loved you. And anyone who ever tried to make you doubt that was wrong."

"Wow."

"Ja."

"He is tormented about the love he's given up. But he did choose the life, Mare. He had love once, but he's always had money. He would have resented you, over time, for not fitting in."

"So I had no chance from the beginning?"

"Not for permanence, no. But you got love, and that's what you wanted, really."

"It's true. I don't regret that part."

"Good. No regrets then."

"No. One big one. I didn't handle myself well. You did. You had love, and it got messed up, but you've been – what's Dad's word? – you've been *dignified.* I wish I'd been more like you. You – how can I say this? – you never ran out of breath."

"I came close, Mare. Maybe I should've been more like you, in actual fact."

"Er-herm!"

"Really, things probably wouldn't have got so messed up if I'd followed my heart. I could have stayed with Edward in Cape Town, then none of it would have happened. I should never have made promises to bloody Kristal, that's for sure."

"Fucking Kristal. But you know, it was never going to be an easy year. Not after Dad."

# CHAPTER 34

*Saturday 2 November*

Walker is driving his new car back from dropping Mielie at the airport, with Mare in the passenger seat. They are silent. Walker doesn't know it, but Mare is blushing. She's thinking about that dream.

Mare watches the vehicles going in the other direction on the highway and tries to get her mind off Walker, her body off him in her mind.

She's remembering last night's dream, too. In it, Walker was napping next to her. He was lying so close she could feel his heartbeat against her back. When she turned over she couldn't see anything. She heard the rustle of a black rubbish bag under her, sensed warmth over her face and heard Walker's heartbeat again as he leaned over to check her shoulder wound. In her dream she thought, *That's weird, so unconscious means you can't see but you can hear and feel.*

Mare has no memory of ever being "at peace". She'd always thought that her life – because of the mind and heart that were at the centre of it – was the very opposite of peaceful. If she'd had to imagine the look of peace, it would have been a blurry picture dominated by lilac, her least-favourite colour. Mare hated lilac and all its relatives too: lavender, purple cloud, rosemary flower … soft, ineffectual colours. They didn't generate energy. They sat there, blandly, inoffensively, soothingly pastel.

What would peace sound like? Oh, a murmur in a church, the wings of a butterfly, the hum of a contented needleworker? God help us. Mare had never wanted that shut-down of sensation.

But peace with Walker wouldn't be like that. It would be the opposite of violence. It would be doors unlatching, a thrum of joy. She imagines the unclipping, whispered gratitudes and gasping relief.

Mare notices that Walker is pulling into the driveway at Helvetia Court. Barely a word having passed between them on the journey from the airport, she lingers in the passenger seat.

"I haven't seen you much since the hospital."

"You didn't see me much *in* the hospital, to be fair."

"You know what I mean," Mare says.

"What? What is it?" Walker turns to face her. His knees are very close to hers. His thighs are right there. His hand is on the gearstick, so close she'd barely have to move to touch it.

"Walker!" she says. "Are you ever going to make a move on me?"

He turns to face the front again. "No," he says, his profile hardly moving. "Now go home."

"Really?"

"Really."

"Yes, honestly. Just go inside. Check out your phone. Notice your kitchen. Invite me round for supper some time."

"Supper?"

"Yes. And make your bed."

"Oh, my bed now?"

"Maybe. I have this notion of being somebody's sweetheart."

Then Walker gets out of the car and opens Mare's door for her.

"You have my number," he says.

*

*Saturday 9 November*

Mielie Ashford has caught the bus up to Wimbledon Village. It's her first Saturday morning back home, and she's here to do grocery shopping.

She walks briskly. She's not cheerful but she's not fragile either. She's starting to feel more herself. When she left the house she remembered to wrap a scarf around her neck. On the way up here, she noticed the shapes of shadows under trees in the watery light.

On the high street, Mielie notices the display in a bookshop window. She hears the music playing in a clothes shop. She thinks about what she'd like to have in the fridge at home: a big wedge of cheese, fat tomatoes and a bag of peppery watercress.

She hopes Edward doesn't phone while she's out. He normally phones in the evenings, but it's Saturday today. He might phone when he wakes up.

Edward Taylor is alone. His body is tired. He's tried to phone, but no answer.

He decides to get a coffee. He's been spending a lot of time in coffee shops this past while. He likes the smell, and the feeling of freedom that he gets from sitting in a place where he's not required to be. People come and go. He can come and go. He can go where he likes. He has no job, no guilt shackling him to Fiona and Geraldine. He can think his own thoughts and make his own plans.

A girl walks past the window. Her profile catches his eye. That's another thing. Edward is free to fantasise about loving, and being loved. He does.

Edward finishes his coffee and stands up. He pays and leaves, to follow the girl.

Mielie is sitting on a park bench at the edge of Wimbledon Common with her shopping. She chose the driest bench she could find, with the most expansive view. She's smoking a cigarette, amused by the mingling of smoke and the clouds of her warm breath in the November air.

Edward spots the girl. She has her back to him but he knows it's her. In spite of his lack of sleep and in spite of his heavy backpack he feels a fizz rushing up from his feet.

Edward gasps and the cold air hits his lungs, sending another shot of bubbles into his body. His feet are moving faster under him now, he's running. The backpack bounces on his shoulders but his hiking boots make no sound on the grass.

When Mielie turns her head, alerted only by a sense of approach, Edward is running full-tilt, grinning. She has never seen him move so fast.

## Acknowledgements

Co-authoring a book with a treasured friend is a risk. Our friendship was the thing to protect, always more important than a paragraph cut or a deadline. Somehow we won a kind of jackpot from the universe. From start to finish, writing together was a joy – as much fun as writing to and receiving letters from each other was in the '90s. Our friendship deepened, we inspired each other, and together we learnt how to write a novel. (We were our own little class of two, passing notes, no teacher up front.)

Readers' feedback helped immeasurably.

Maire Fisher, Jenny Wade, Vanessa Hilton-Barber, Trudy Mofutsanyana, Anna Hug, David Savage, Jeremy Daniel, Xoli Qwenga and Bieke van Aggelen were kind enough to read early drafts and provide incisive feedback, along with encouragement. Emma van der Vliet and Henrietta Rose-Innes were an enormous help when we got stuck later on.

The Grail writing group, as well as Maire Fisher and Chantal Stewart's writing workshops, gave us the method to creatively explore our characters and their worlds. The writers in these groups are unfailingly supportive and we owe you an enormous debt of gratitude.

Anna Hug and Vanessa Hilton-Barber have been intensely interested and caring from the beginning. Thank you both for your kindness and insights throughout.

Henrietta Rose-Innes did the final edit. What an honour, and how valuable, to be on the receiving end of that extraordinarily tuned literary mind.

Angela Tuck, the one and only, is responsible for the cover and the book's design in general. You knocked it out the park.

At home, our families became louder cheerleaders as time went on.

David Savage has never wavered in his support – emotional and logistical. He invented the "dodgy investment" and, one Sunday afternoon, the phrase "my wife's wife". Ella Savage not only agreed to listen to her mother talk about the book, but asked questions too. Thank you, Ella, for urging us to "make a few copies". It was exactly what we wanted. Sam Savage has been loving, loyal and accepting throughout.

Fritz Kerkhoff endured the out-loud reading of several chapters, and his genuinely positive reaction, on each of several occasions, was regarded as being an encouraging sign. Thank you, Fritz, for never once complaining about your partner's near-total absence over many weekends, and with such calm resolve.

Close friends and extended family have been similarly loving. Thank you to the relatives and all the friends who've stood by us through the delights and disappointments of writing this book – even when we haven't shared a word of it.

Mignon Hardie, also a dear friend, several times offered expert advice, from a publisher's perspective, that guided us on our path. We hope you feel your presence in this book.

Kate Savage – on a Zoom call, during a lockdown – helped us understand legal processes pertaining to wills, debt and properties. Thank you, Kate.

Our eternal gratitude to the friends who inspired the characters of Johnny, Toni, Mitchell and Fouché. Family, really. And legends, all.

Thanks to Jane Austen, we were able to draw on the experiences of our early twenties without telling our own stories. Austen's first novel, *Sense and Sensibility*, informed the plot of *Love You Madly*. Her narrative structure freed us from writing about the people and events we had written about in our own letters. We are forever grateful to Austen for her writing gift – and her compassion for the girls who yearn.

## About the authors

Daisy Jones is a journalist, author, poet and illustrator. She covered the Truth and Reconciliation Commission for *The Star*, was a senior Education writer for *Business Day*, and her first cookbook, *Star Fish*, won the *Sunday Times* and *Radio 702* awards. She lives in Cape Town with her family.

Lucinda Hooley is a creative writer and content editor, working mostly in corporate marketing and communication. She's also a *Vita*-award-winning theatre and television actress. She lives with her partner on a farm in the Free State.